KRISTEN B. COLE

The Scientist

Contents

Chapter 1

*I*mmediately *crossing out long haul truck driver as a career option.*
After four and a half grueling days on the road with minimal stops, my ass was now completely numb and might never recover. I parked along the street and shut off the engine of my old Ford Cosworth, Marge, and I swear I heard her groan. She was in decent shape for being over thirty years old, but I knew I'd pushed her to the limit with this long journey. I couldn't just leave her behind. Although admittedly, the cross-country trek would have been much easier without my senile companion. I was pretty sure even she forgot where I parked her sometimes.

As I made my way up the sidewalk, the reality of the situation slowly started to sink in. The urge to let myself fall to pieces as I stood on the front porch of my new home was overwhelming. But I fought the temptation, telling myself I would get through this. *We* would get through this. I took a deep breath and walked through the front door of my new home and my new life.

My best friend called not even two seconds after I walked through the door.

I picked up after the first ring. "Hey."

"Did you finally make it?" she asked.

"You must be psychic," I said, setting my things down. "I literally just walked through the door."

"Actually, my psychic hotline rates are quite reasonable if you're looking for a reading."

"I think I'll pass. I've already got a magic eight ball giving me some bad advice."

She chuckled. "So how does it look?"

I glanced around at all the spacious room. 'Open floor plan' back in New York meant the hallway doubled as your bedroom.

"It's much nicer than I expected," I answered honestly. Not having to play a high stakes game of Tetris with my furniture where winning meant I had the ability to cram my life into a glorified shoebox would take some getting used to. Who knew basic living standards could feel so luxurious?

I was staying in the faculty housing units of Stanford University. They were a nice set of townhomes, all uniform in appearance. Each unit had its own bricked porch with some beautiful plants hanging from the rafters or sitting atop the walled-off sections.

The two blocks of homes were adjacent to one another, each configured in a U formation with only a walkway running up the center as a way of accessing each unit. The home came fully furnished in a tasteful design and was better than I could have hoped for, especially given the short time frame I'd had to look for anything.

All this room, though. I half expected to find Narnia in the walk-in closet.

"Oh, I'm so glad!" she gushed. "Isn't the weather here absolutely beautiful?! I swear that's one thing I won't miss about New York."

My best friend had already moved to California a week before I had and thankfully, managed to find a place that was close to her doctor.

"Yeah, it's okay," I said, not wanting to give California too many compliments just yet. But honestly, she was right. Not having to worry about choosing which rain or snow boots I'd be wearing for the day was definitely at the top of the pros column for Cali.

"Well, I'll let you get some rest. I'm sure you're exhausted. I just wanted to check to see that you made it. Do you want me to come over tomorrow and help you unpack?"

It dawned on me that her surgery was only a few days away, and I felt the nerves settle into the pit of my stomach. It was the whole reason we were here.

"No, you need to rest up before your procedure. Let's have dinner Sunday night, and I can sleep at your place after. That way we can head to the hospital first thing in the morning."

"Okay... See you then." She lingered on the phone for a few seconds longer as if she wanted to say something more, but eventually, the line clicked off.

I put the phone down and sighed. I could tell at this very moment she was doing the most useless thing possible—worrying about me.

It had been a month since she was diagnosed with cancer. One month of endless doctor's appointments, running tests, drawing blood, worrying, and searching. Searching for a doctor to treat stage three triple negative sarcoma, a rare and deadly form of breast cancer. So rare that only a handful of doctors in the US even treat this type of cancer. But we found one, the best one. The only problem was the drive from New York to California was one hell of a commute, which is why I quit my job and said my goodbyes to the people I cared about.

Together, we decided to move to the San Jose area so that we could be close to her doctor, who was supposed to be the leading expert in this type of cancer. So even though she should have been focused on what lay ahead of her—surgery, chemo, and just generally kicking cancer's ass—I knew she was sitting at home, worrying about me. I wished I wouldn't have let her convince me to get a separate place. I thought it would be best and easiest if we just lived together. But she insisted that I needed to have my own space that way, my life, as she put it, "Wouldn't revolve around her tits."

I went upstairs and claimed the bedroom that got the most sunlight. I figured I should get better acquainted with Mr. Golden Sun since he'd be around a lot more on this side of the country. Afterward, I checked out the rest of my new home with an enthusiasm on par with Mr. Squidward Tentacles.

As I walked slowly from room to room, the silence seemed deafening. A pang of longing shot through me to hear the hum of idiosyncratic noises that defined New York City life... my life. I was born and raised in the city and still couldn't imagine living anywhere else. I wouldn't dwell on it too much though, because while I loved the city, it was nothing compared to the love I had for my best friend. After all, I'm the only person who has ever heard her heartbeat from the inside.

Ever since my mom's diagnosis, I found myself in a toxic relationship with a temperamental jackass named sleep. Our biggest problem was that he was all over me during the day when he knew I was busy, but when nighttime came, he loved playing hard to get. That was when he wasn't ghosting me completely. Maybe he was finally changing his fickle ways, because when I woke the next morning, I glanced over at the clock to find I had slept for fourteen hours straight. I wasn't in the mood to analyze his motivations just yet.

My phone dinged with a notification that the moving van with the rest of my things was still a few days away. I guess the driver valued having feeling in his ass cheeks. *Selfish bastard.*

I was about to call to check in on my mom when the phone started to ring. It was my now *ex*-boyfriend, Garrett. We'd broken up a little over a week ago when I sat him down and told him that I was moving to California. He wasn't a bad guy, I just wasn't in love with him. We'd only dated for about six months and there was something missing— what Carrie Bradshaw would call the "zsa zsa zsu." I knew we would never make long distance work, and I took it as a "here's your sign" moment that I didn't even want to try. I meant it when I said that I hoped we could still be friends, so I decided not to ignore him like my instincts were telling me to do.

"Hello?" I answered.

"Hey, baby." I cringed a little at his use of the pet name, but maybe old habits die hard.

"What are you up to?" he asked.

"Just getting settled in at my new place in the land of perpetual sunshine," I answered sleepily.

"You really did it then?" Disbelief colored his tone. "You actually left New York?"

Well, that kind of pissed me off.

"Yes. What part of 'I'm moving to California with my mom' didn't you believe?"

"I guess I didn't think you'd actually go through with it. You love New York."

"I do, but you know my mom is my world."

Nothing but silence was coming through the other end of the line, so much so that I pulled my phone from my ear to check that we hadn't gotten disconnected.

"So, that's it? You're giving up your whole life here? Your career? Me? It's all just over because your mom needs you?" he asked sharply. "What if I need you?"

I really had to rein in my temper before I responded. I knew I shouldn't have answered the phone. Always go with your gut, people.

"What did you think would happen, Garrett? I couldn't stay for you. We weren't even in love."

"I was in love with you... I still am."

Well, that felt like a knuckle sandwich to the belly button. I didn't know what to say. He had never told me that he loved me. I had assumed we were on the same page. He didn't even seem that upset when I broke things off.

"Garrett, I'm sorry. I know this all happened really fast, but this wasn't something I planned. My mom is sick, and I'm going to be there for her... no matter what."

"Okay, I get it. I'm sorry." He sounded genuine, but I couldn't shake the annoyance I felt from his lack of empathy for what my mom was going through.

"It's fine," I said, unable to hide my irritation.

There was a long pause where neither of us said anything, and I wondered if this would be the last time we would speak. We'd met through his sister, Sophie, who was a production assistant on one of the plays I'd been hired to compose music for. I'd been taking jobs on Broadway as a composer and lyricist over the past few years, while also juggling some other minor writing gigs here and there. But I left it all behind. That type of work requires all of your focus and attention, which was something I was unwilling to give to anyone or anything besides my mom at the moment.

"You're going to hate California... Rumor has it they say 'excuse me' as an actual apology there and not a bark of annoyance," he teased, and I automatically smiled. This was the side of him I liked.

Garrett was easygoing, good looking by anyone's standards, and always managed to make me laugh when I was having a bad day. He was a forensic accountant at a big law firm and absolutely loved his job. I'd never ask him to leave his job or New York, and he didn't offer when I told him that I was moving, so here we were.

"I know. It's going to be the worst," I agreed, and we both laughed, easing the tension between us. "Although, I can't talk like that now. I've moved to the land where seldom is heard a discouraging word."

"I doubt there are any buffalo roaming in downtown San Jose."

"No deer or antelope playing either?"

"Nope."

"There goes my dream of the great American West."

We both chuckled lightly, reveling in our easy banter until the silence set in again.

"I'm going to miss you," he said after a beat.

"I'll miss you too," I admitted, and it was the truth. I'd spent the last six months of my life speaking to this man each and every day, sharing our lives together. It wasn't an easy thing to give up, but I knew in my heart that we weren't meant to be. I wished more than anything I could keep him as a friend, but I knew all too well that time and distance will kill even the greatest of relationships.

"Would you think about moving back if your mom gets better?"

"*When* she gets better," I corrected because I refused to think any other way. "I'll be on the first flight home."

"Meet you at Dim Sum Palace."

We both worked late hours at our jobs and that was our favorite place to get takeout since they stayed open late.

"No need to threaten me with a good time, sir," I said, playing along.

"Seriously, Hadley. I'll wait for you as long as I have to. I know you said you weren't in love with me, but it's only been six months. We were good together. You have to admit that."

"I don't know how long I'm going to be here. I don't expect you to wait for me."

"I know you don't, but I also know I've never felt this way about anyone. It took me by surprise when you told me you were moving and that we needed to break things off, but I've been thinking a lot about it since then. When I can get some time off work, I'll come and visit you. We can make this work."

"Garrett—" I started to say, trying to let him down easy.

"Don't say anything right now," he cut in. "Just think about it. We can talk more after your mom has her surgery and you get settled in there."

"I don't need to think about it. We both need a fresh start."

"You're saying that now, but things can change. Your mom could have a quick recovery, and then you'll be back in New York in no time."

"I told you what the doctors said. She's going to be in treatment for a long time."

"Doctors are wrong all the time. Your mom's tough. If anyone can beat this, she can."

"That's nice of you to say but—"

"I've got to get back to work. We'll talk more about it later."

He hung up before I even got a chance to respond. I put my phone down and pinched the bridge of my nose. This was turning out to be more complicated than folding a fitted sheet. I would just have to be more direct the next time we spoke. Would hiring a skywriter to etch it into the clouds be considered going overboard?

Okay, fine. Flock of carrier pigeons it is.

<h1 style="text-align:center">Chapter 2</h1>

"Are you nervous?" I asked as we tore through some of the best sushi I'd ever tasted.

Damn you, California. Sunday night had rolled around, and my mom and I decided to venture out for a nice dinner before her surgery in the morning.

"Not really," she said through a mouthful of the house California roll. "You did a number on my breasts when you were a baby, and they never regained the same pizazz they once had. Not too bummed to see em go."

"Sorry about that."

"Forgiven," she said with a swish of her chopsticks. I looked over at her, thinking of how besides our coloring, there was no denying we were mother and daughter. My dark brown hair and green eyes were my father's, but my bone structure was all my mom. She had beautiful, wavy auburn hair that she styled the same way for as long as I could remember—shoulder-length cut with her signature fringe bangs. "Besides, Dr. Gremillion said this surgeon, Dr. Fridman, was the best on the West Coast."

"Yeah, but it's still scary to go under anesthesia."

She shrugged her petite shoulders, and I wondered if she was putting on a brave face for me so I wouldn't worry.

"It'll be worth it to get a new pair of knockers. Did I tell you insurance is paying a hundred percent of the reconstruction? They'll be perkier than Elle Woods on her first day at Harvard."

"I think I'm finally starting to see the upside to breast cancer," I joked.

She raised her glass, and I lifted mine to meet hers. "To the upside of breast cancer."

"To a great pair of knockers," I added. We cheered our lemonades and spent the rest of the night laughing and catching up, trying to forget all about breast cancer and its many, many downsides.

The next morning, we got up around 5 a.m. and drove the fifteen minutes to the hospital. Marge was really sounding terrible, wheezing and groaning loudly every time I accelerated. The coast-to-coast drive did quite a number on her, and I was afraid I'd have to call in hospice soon. She was my dad's car, which is why I was having trouble letting go. He died when I was eight, and I didn't have much in the way of memorabilia, except for a few pictures my mom had saved and his beloved car, Marge.

When we reached the pre-op area, the nurse showed my mom the bathroom to change in. She emerged with a look of worry on her face.

"What is it?" I asked.

Her eyes were wide. "I don't know. I can't explain it. I'm just feeling like my end is in sight."

"What do you mean?" I asked, a bit panicked. "Everything's going to be fine, Mom."

She turned around in her hospital gown and burst into laughter. I finally got the joke with her rear end showing through the split in the back of the gown. Tears were rolling down her face from laughing so hard. I smiled but refused to laugh at such a corny joke.

"I thought dads only made terrible jokes like that."

"Well, that just goes to show you, your mom can do it all," she said, dabbing at the corners of her eyes.

"Except for getting off an escalator without tripping and falling when it gets to the bottom."

"That was one time."

"Twice!"

Dr. Fridman walked in, interrupting our argument. We'd flown out to meet him a few weeks ago and had our consultation for the mastectomy.

"Ms. Olivier, you're going to be first up on the schedule this morning. Are you ready?"

The atmosphere in the room suddenly changed, and we both sobered up quickly.

She nodded. "Yes, I think so."

I took her hand in mine and held it more to comfort myself rather than her.

"It's a fairly straightforward procedure on my end. As we discussed before, I'm going to be removing all the breast tissue and possibly some lymph nodes. Dr. Hildenbom will take over after to perform the reconstruction. You can expect to be in surgery for around four to six hours total." He said the last part while looking at me. I'm sure it was to let me know it would take a while.

"Any questions?" he asked, and we both shook our heads. "Alright, I'll see you in there."

He exited the room, and we both looked at each other, no longer able to put on our brave faces.

I hugged her tightly and whispered, "It's going to be fine, Mom. You've got this."

She pulled away, reaching out to wipe the tears from *my* eyes.

"I know that," she said with a gentle smile. "You can't kill bad grass." She winked at me, and I forced a smile on my face.

Twenty minutes later, we waved goodbye as they rolled her to the back, and I spent the next seven hours pacing back and forth in the lobby, unable to stomach even a bite of food.

I hadn't felt my father's absence so profoundly since his passing as I did in this moment. He and my mom had the same morbid sense of humor, and I knew he would have known the exact thing to say to ease the tension and make me feel like everything was going to be okay.

My father and I were different in so many ways, but what we did have in common was our unwavering love and devotion to the same three things in life: New York, music, and my mom.

His very first love was New York—the city that swept him off his feet in a whirlwind romance of uncharted dreams and endless possibilities. He would often say there was no other place in the world that you could go out at any hour, day or night, and never have to be alone.

I remember him telling me once that music was his best friend. It was a concept I didn't understand until much later in life, but now I understood perfectly what he meant. Music's the friend who knows your history, your dreams, and your fears—it never judges and is always ready to meet you wherever you are in life. Music knows all your soul's secrets and somehow, reflects them back to you in perfect harmony.

His love for my mom was an all-consuming type. Even as a young child, I could see their connection was deep and the love was unconditional. He once told me their souls would find each other in every lifetime, and I grew to appreciate its rarity. I knew I would settle for nothing less.

I was getting lost in the memories of my father when Dr. Fridman and Dr. Hildenbom finally emerged together from the OR area, and I practically tripped running over to them.

"Everything went great. Your mom is in recovery and will probably be there for a few hours. You'll be able to see her once they get her up to the room."

I breathed out a huge sigh of relief. "Thank you both so much."

"Good luck to you. I hope the rest of her treatment goes well."

I felt like I was finally able to breathe again. I went up to the room she'd be staying in for the night and waited until they rolled her in.

She came in looking pretty drowsy but smiled when she saw me. Her hair was tucked into a surgery cap, and the smattering of freckles across her nose stood out more against her now paler complexion.

"Hey kiddo." Her voice sounded gravelly.

"Hey, how do you feel?"

"Great. Linda here gave me the good stuff."

The nurse named Linda smiled. "I gave Ms. Gail some strong pain medication that should hold her over for the next few hours, but call if she starts to feel any discomfort."

"Thank you so much," I said sincerely.

Mom fell asleep not long after she got to the room, so I got my makeshift bed in order and proceeded to stare at her for the rest of the night, looking for any signs that something was amiss. She mostly slept, waking only a few times in the night to ask for water or pain medication. The next morning, she seemed more rested and alert.

"You look like shit," she told me first thing after waking up. I laughed because I knew it must have been true. I'd been awake for almost thirty-six hours, but I didn't care.

"Thanks, you too."

"Now, I know that's a lie. I'm rocking a brand-new set of C-cups. I can't wait to check them out." She started pulling back the dressings on her bandaged chest, trying to get a peek.

"Easy there, tiger." I pushed her hands away. "Why don't you heal up first and then we'll go bra shopping."

"You're no fun."

"Yeah, yeah. Are you hurting? Do you want me to call the nurse for more pain meds?"

"No, I'm actually pretty hungry though."

"Alright, I'll go grab you something," I said, making my way towards the door. I turned back to give her a stern look. "But you better leave those dressings alone while I'm gone, or I'll have Nurse Linda come in with the restraints," I warned. She stuck her tongue out at me as I walked out the door.

I didn't think mold spores would be brave enough to touch the food options from the cafeteria, so I walked right past it and got in my car to pick her up a smoothie and some quesadillas.

When I got back, I made her try the smoothie first to make sure she could hold food down. I wanted to wait a little longer but eventually gave in after she begged me for twenty minutes straight to give her the damn quesadillas.

The rest of her stay was thankfully uneventful. With her pain under control, and all her bloodwork coming back normal, she was able to be discharged a day earlier than we expected. While I'd miss sleeping next to the tranquil sounds of the overenthusiastic smoke detector disguised as my mom's heart monitor, it was time to bid farewell to Casa de Jell-O. I started to gather up our things while my mom watched with a huge smile plastered on her face.

"What?" I asked when she was starting to creep me out.

"Can't a mother smile at her beautiful daughter?"

"Not when you look like you're about to say, '*Whyyy sooo seriousss?*'"

"Oh Hadley, I just had a successful operation without any major complications. I'm feeling high on life."

"You're high on Vicodin."

"Beep! Paging Dr. Buzzkill. Dr. Buzzkill, come in please. Beep! Oh look, they're calling for you, dear."

"The pain medication has deluded you into thinking you're a laugh riot."

The nurse came in to give us our discharge paperwork and helped my mom into a wheelchair, and we headed home.

I drove us back to her house where I'd spend the next four weeks helping her recuperate. She was an absolute trooper, as I knew she would be. The first week was a little rough trying to keep her pain under control, even though she tried to hide it. After that initial bumpy week though, she seemed to get stronger with each passing day. When she started making Dolly Parton jokes, I knew the worst was behind us.

We spent the rest of our time together lying in bed, watching movies, and just vegging out. I'd essentially hit the 'out of the office' button on life. I just needed to figure out an automatic reply for those pesky life responsibility queries that adulting admin kept sending me.

We'd made it through the first leg on the road to remission with this surgery behind us. Next step was a few months of chemo, possibly longer depending on how her body responded to it. She was healing nicely though, and both surgeons gave her the all clear to resume her normal activities at the four-week mark. It was definitely a relief, because I was set to begin my new job next week and wouldn't be available to her 24/7 as I had been.

I wasn't expecting to find a job so quickly. California would seem like the land of opportunity for someone in the music biz, but San Jose wasn't exactly a music mecca. Los Angeles was really the place with the most job prospects, but it was over six hours away and would defeat the whole purpose of me moving here. So I settled for a job doing something I had absolutely no experience in and would probably fall flat on my face trying—teaching.

I had gotten a job as an adjunct musical composition professor at Stanford University. I knew my old friend and roommate from college, Sarah Samaha, worked there, so I called her up, and she graciously helped me get an interview.

I had my interview over a Zoom call with the director of the department, William Abel. He was in his late sixties, completely bald on top, but going for that classic look that ladies loved—leaving the hair to grow on either side of his head. He was overly friendly and managed to make me uncomfortable even three thousand miles away. He would stare at you with his eyes set just a fraction too wide to be considered normal after attempting to make a joke and smiling with his mouth slightly open, waiting for your response. I gave him the laugh he wanted, however fake it was, and he offered me the job at the end of the interview.

On the surface, the job seemed perfect. There weren't a lot of hours required, so I'd be able to make most of my mom's appointments. It was close to her doctor, and the pay was much better than I expected. The only problem was my teaching experience lacked a certain... existence. I had, however, seen *Dead Poets Society*, so if I had to resort to standing on Stanford's furniture to get it right, I would.

"I have that welcome banquet for the faculty on Friday night. You think you'll be okay to be on your own?" I asked my mom as we drove home from her follow-up visit.

"Looking forward to it, actually."

"Thanks a lot," I replied, brimming with sarcasm.

"You really should get a life, Hadley. Spending every waking moment with your mother for a month straight is not a good look."

"Stop getting cancer, and I'll think about it."

"Deal," she affirmed with a nod.

"So, you're really going to be okay?" I asked, feeling the need to double check.

"You heard the doctors. They both cleared me to go back to my normal daily activities."

"What are you going to do without me?"

"I might go cruise the town looking to pick up a handsome gentleman to spend Friday night with."

"Oh yeah? What kind of guy are you looking for?" I asked, playing along.

"I guess someone who's not intimidated by a woman with perfect breasts, maybe loves to cook, or at least enjoys eating late night snacks in bed together."

"Oh, I just thought of the perfect caption for your dating profile: *Single and Ready to Pringle.*"

"Outstanding. Sign me up!"

When we arrived back at her house, I watched her get out of the car, grab her purse, and close the door with perfect ease. I relented that she might be ready to be on her own... but was I?

Chapter 3

I t occurred to me that after a little over a month of living in California, last night was only the third night I'd actually slept in my new home. It was time for life to resume some type of normalcy, which included work and maybe even an attempt to make friends with someone other than my chromosome collaborator.

I arrived at the Stanford Faculty Club and texted Sarah to let her know I'd made it. I had those first day of school jitters, except the butterflies felt more like ostriches performing barrel rolls inside my stomach. Luckily, I knew I'd have at least one friendly face in Sarah. I checked my hair and makeup in the mirror one last time before I got out the car and smoothed down my burgundy wrap dress.

My phone dinged with a text from Sarah saying to meet her inside. I made my way inside the hall and started searching through the packed crowd for her. The hall was lined with floor to ceiling windows on each side with beautiful wooden beams running along the pitched ceiling and farmhouse-style chandeliers throughout. I finally spotted my old friend pushing her way through the crowd with that huge megawatt smile on her face. She looked almost exactly the same as when I had met her ten years ago with the exception of her raven hair cut a lot shorter, hitting her at the shoulder instead of the waist.

"You made it!" she squealed, and we laughed, embracing in a tight hug.

"It's so good to see you," I said as a few people bumped into us standing in the middle of the walkway.

"I know! I'm beyond excited that you're here," she said, walking us out of the foot traffic. "I'm so sorry to hear about your mom though. How is she? Did the surgery go well?"

I had filled her in on why we were moving to California, and she had periodically checked in on us throughout the process.

"She's great. The surgery went well, so she'll be starting chemo next week actually."

"Wow. I'm sure it must be overwhelming having to deal with all of that on top of moving to a whole new state."

"She's strong. We'll get through it together."

She smiled at me sympathetically. Sarah and I were roommates in college for a brief period when she was a senior, and I was just starting out at Northwestern. She graduated the semester after we started living together, but we had really hit it off during our short stint as roomies. She was a classically trained pianist, who looked like a cross between Jackie O. and Snow White. She'd practice Mozart by day and blare German industrial rock by night. I remember loving the dichotomy of how she looked and dressed in comparison to how she acted. She looked like a housewife from the fifties but could make Tupac blush with the obscenities that would spew from her mouth, especially if she'd been drinking. I couldn't wait to reconnect with her.

"Well, even though it's not under the best circumstances, I'm glad to have you here." She looped her arm through mine as we made our way through the hall.

"Thanks again for helping me get the interview."

"Please! With your resume, they were thanking me for bringing you to them," she said. "Speaking of interviews though, you'll definitely have to interact with Captain Creeper tonight. But hopefully, he'll be trying to kiss ass with the big wigs for most of the night."

"Hopefully," I agreed. I'd hate to get fired before I even started for a knee to the groin type interaction with the boss.

"Come on, let me introduce you to some of your new coworkers. I have one in particular that is dying to meet you."

"Why? What did you tell them about me?" I asked skeptically.

She just laughed as we walked up to a table that sat roughly ten people, but there were only five people presently seated.

"Hadley, I'd like you to meet Anna Huong, Instrumental Composition; Stanley Applebaum, Music History; Sally Jones, Sound Engineering; Talya Kenashiro, Ethnomusicology; and my dear friend Lionel Vaughn, Music Technology. Everyone, this is Hadley Olivier, our new adjunct Music Composition professor."

"Nice to meet you all," I said, taking a seat next to Lionel, who was practically bouncing up and down on the edge of his seat. He looked to be in his early thirties with an ethnicity I couldn't quite place. He had both Asian and Hispanic features with a neatly trimmed mustache and sporting a pair of really cool retro green glasses.

"You're Hadley Olivier," he said with barely contained enthusiasm. "You have no idea how freaking excited I am to meet you! My sister and I saw you perform a few years ago as Perón's Mistress in the Broadway production of *Evita*. You were incredible! I cannot believe you're here at Stanford."

"Thank you so much," I said, a little surprised someone here knew who I was. I had done a lot of work on Broadway over the past five years, so most of the die-hard musical theatre fans in New York were familiar with my work, but I wasn't expecting that here. I loved to sing, so I'd done a few acting/singing roles in plays over the years, but my heart was definitely in composition.

"You're a singer then?" the woman named Talya asked.

"Yes, I've performed in a few plays and sang backup on different soundtracks. But composition is my first love."

"Don't let her fool you. She's worked with some of the biggest stars in the biz," Lionel announced. "I heard you wrote music for Phoebe Bridgers and Frank Ocean."

"Calm down, Lionel. You're drooling all over her," Sarah told him.

"Sorry! If you can't tell, I'm a huge fan. It's not fair you're that talented and also that gorgeous. I both love you and hate you in equal parts."

"This is a very prestigious university with a well-respected music program," Stanley interrupted. He looked to be in his late forties with a mild resemblance to Jacques Cousteau. "I hope you didn't come here thinking your minor celebrity would allow you to skate by without putting in some real effort."

What the fuck was his problem?

"Fuck off, Stanley," Sarah snapped at him from across the table. "The only reason you got a job here is because your dad plays golf with the president of the university."

"Yeah, and didn't you almost get dropped last semester because enrollment for your class was so low?" Lionel added.

"Kids these days just aren't as interested in the history of music as they once were," he said, turning a deep shade of red.

"Isn't music history a required course for all undergrads?" Sarah asked pointedly.

"It is indeed, my friend," Lionel chimed in. "That's why you see Professor Graham's history classes packed to the gills. None of the students want to listen to Rumpleforeskin over here for an entire semester."

There were a few snickers from the rest of the table while Stanley stood up scoffing, and walked away from the table.

"Keep rolling your eyes, Stan. You might eventually find a brain in there," Sarah called after him.

This was definitely not the first impression I wanted to make with my new coworkers.

"Don't worry about that queef dumpster," Lionel said, patting me on the back. "He gets intimidated by anyone with actual talent and real-world experience since he's completely lacking in both."

The others at the table nodded in agreement, so I figured I might not be the problem here.

Just as I glanced up from the table, I recognized a familiar face heading our way.

"Incoming," Lionel said low, under his breath. "Cover your tits, ladies."

Dr. William Abel was making his way toward us with that same creepy smile he wore like a uniform, and his focus seemed to be aimed at the only new person at the table.

"Ms. Olivier," he said, eyes wide, mouth parted. "Nice to see you again."

"Hi, Dr. Abel." I stood, greeting him as politely as I could manage. "Thank you again for giving me this opportunity."

"We're happy to have you. And please, call me Will."

Yeah, I wouldn't be doing that.

"I see you wore your hair down for the evening," he noted.

I had my hair pulled back into a low ponytail in our interview but having the difference in my hairstyle choice pointed out rendered me speechless for a moment.

"Yes, that's true. I decided to change it up," I finally said.

"Sometimes you just gotta let your hair down, eh?" He laughed, nudging me with his elbow.

"Dr. Abel, isn't it lucky that we were able to snag Hadley for our team?" Lionel said, saving me from the awkward encounter. "Stanley was just saying how qualified he thinks Hadley is."

Sarah had to cough to cover up her laughter.

"He's absolutely right. We're quite lucky to have you." He put his arm around my shoulder, eyes zooming in on my chest. I made huge "help me" eyes at Sarah.

"You know, I heard Stanley saying he was going talk to the president. Something about wanting to update him on plans for the music department this year," Sarah said, distracting him.

"What?!" Dr. Abel cried indignantly. He let go of my shoulder, and I stepped away from him, hurrying to take a seat.

"We tried to tell him we didn't think that was his job," Lionel said, feigning innocence.

"I should think not!" he said, his face turning purple with outrage. His head swung around, searching for Stanley. As he marched away, we heard him muttering, "He thinks just because his father and Benson are golf buddies..."

When he was finally out of earshot, Lionel and Sarah burst out laughing, and I couldn't help but join in. Even the other ladies at the table seemed amused by the little show happening in front of them.

"Did you see his face? He hates the thought of someone else getting to be up Benson's ass!" Lionel said, still wheezing with laughter.

Dr. Richard Benson was president of the university and was seated at one of the tables near the stage at the very front of the hall. I recognized him from the university newsletters I started receiving once I was officially on staff. He was currently surrounded by a crowd of people trying to get a word with him, one of those people being Dr. Abel.

"Benson won't give him the time of day," Lionel noted, looking over at his table. "He's too busy walking his new show pony around for everyone to see."

"What do you mean?" I asked.

"Word on the street is the university acquired some uber-famous scientist," Lionel answered. "Everyone's been talking about this guy, but I've never heard of him."

"That's only because he's never been employed by the Bravo network," Sarah quipped.

"*Anyway*," Lionel said, shooting her a look. "Benson's been strutting around proud as a peacock all evening showing him off to everyone."

"I heard the peacock got into a bidding war over him with Yale and Columbia," Sarah added.

"Who is he?" I asked curiously.

"I think his name's Polinski maybe, I don't know," Lionel said. "All I know is that we paid a pretty penny to have him here."

"What are we talking?"

"Millions in grant money."

My eyes widened with shock. "Holy shit!"

"Yeah. Apparently, he's this super genius. And young too, only thirty-three. They think he has a shot at winning a Nobel Prize for his research in Alzheimer's, so I'm sure Benson wants to be able to claim Stanford had a part in it."

Sarah inclined her head toward Lionel. "Tell me again what the budget for our department was last year."

"You don't want to know."

"That's what I thought," she said, shaking her head. "Okay, well let's try and get some food before the other more important departments take all the good shit."

A few other faculty members from the department came and joined us as we ate the surprisingly good food from the buffet, including Stanley, who we saw Dr. Abel laying into while we were waiting in line. He spent the entirety of the meal looking down at his plate and appearing immensely disgruntled. I pretended not to notice as Sarah and I caught up on each other's lives over the past ten years with

Lionel interjecting to tell some amusing stories of his and Sarah's time together at Stanford.

About an hour into the evening, Dr. Benson took to the small stage at the front of the room where there was a lone podium with a microphone, and began his introductions.

"Good evening, ladies and gentlemen. For those of you who don't know me, my name is Dr. Richard Benson, and I'm the president of the university here at Stanford. I want to give a warm welcome to all of our faculty and staff and especially to our newest team members. It is my sincere hope that you find Stanford to be a home away from home and that we can all join together with the common goal of educating future generations of scholars."

He stood tall with both hands planted firmly on the podium, exuding a calm authority, his eyes sweeping across the crowd as he spoke.

"I'd like to introduce you all to one of our newest faculty members, who we were lucky enough to have join our team this semester. He's a world-renowned neurobiologist, acclaimed author, and winner of last year's *Fellowship of the American Association for the Advancement of Science*—Dr. Alexsander Strovinski. I am convinced that this gifted young man will be a tremendous asset to all of us here at Stanford, students and teachers alike."

Everyone applauded as Dr. Strovinski took the stage. Dr. Benson reached out to shake his hand, pulling him in for a half hug and whispering something in his ear.

"I think Benson's in love," Lionel whispered to us.

I knew Lionel said he was young, but I was still surprised to see just how young he actually was. For some reason, in my mind, all scientists looked like Doc Brown from *Back to the Future*. But this man had thick brown hair that was so dark, it could have passed for black in the right lighting. He wore a pair of simple, rimless, rectangle glasses, and a perfectly tailored gray suit with no tie.

The entire room grew quiet. Not even the sound of cutlery hitting dinner plates could be heard as he stood at the podium waiting to speak. I was just as intrigued as the rest of the room seemed to be.

"Hi, I'm Dr. Alexsander Strovinski." He paused, looking out amongst the crowd. "I'm grateful to be here with you all tonight and to have even been offered a position as an instructor here at Stanford, seeing as I've never taught a day in my life."

A soft murmur of laughter echoed throughout the room. Everyone seemed to be sitting up a little straighter, waiting for whatever he was going to say next.

"Despite the shortcomings in my resume, Dr. Benson asked me to say a few words to you all tonight about academia and the pursuit of higher learning. With no experience to draw from, this had me wondering what, if anything, I could bring to the conversation. What I can say is that I've studied and done research in the field of neurobiology over the last thirteen years of my life, and in that time, I've been able to draw a few steadfast conclusions I'd like to share with you all. So, in that regard, this is my first lesson and you are my first students."

He looked around, smiling modestly as more hushed laughter filled the room. He had a deep, rich timbre to his voice that commanded attention even though his manner seemed quite reserved.

"Our brains are composed of complex neurotransmitters that propagate electrical signals to neighboring neurons by the thousands, leading to what we know as thought formation. We spend nearly every moment of our lives wrapped in our own thoughts, often held hostage to the nature of those thoughts. They have led to mankind's greatest achievements as well as our greatest failures as a species. Our thoughts, however, are all we possess at any given moment and are all we really have to offer one another."

I couldn't stop my brain from putting him under a microscope and noting each of his mannerisms as he spoke—the subtle tilt to his head, the punctuation of certain words to emphasize a point, the way he brushed a lock of hair away from his brow. He had an effortless grace.

"To me, this idea forms the basis for what our true purpose as educators really is: the realization that there are truths to be known in this life, and the discovery of those truths can have a remarkable impact on society. Whether that impact is good or bad is yet to be determined, because the pursuit of knowledge is a uniquely human endeavor, and we are not without flaws. There must first be a willingness to have your beliefs modified by new evidence and an openness to controversy and self-doubt, which will ultimately lead to enlightenment."

He paused to look around the room, his eyes scanning the crowd as he moved away from the podium to stand at the center of the stage. The room was so quiet, we could all still hear him perfectly even without the microphone.

"I love science on principle because it is the most durable way of thinking. It transcends any cultural or political boundaries a person may have and does not limit itself to what can currently be proven but asks the question of what can potentially be proven. There is a phenomenon in neuroscience known as the Kanizsa triangle in which three spatially separated fragments give the impression of a bright white triangle. Your brain, when given this image, sees the breaks in the shapes, and if given no further input, will assume there is a figure in front of the lines. What this phenomenon demonstrates is that we have the capability to perceive objects that are not really there. We *want* something more. But it is only with a holistic approach that our brains display an infinite ability to be creative. This ability is what sets us apart from all other species, and you merely have to open your eyes to see it."

He was pacing back and forth across the small stage as he spoke, his movements so relaxed and engaging. There was a fluidity to them that mirrored the ebb and flow of his words, leaving me and the rest of the audience spellbound. I didn't even blink, my mind intent on catching every detail.

For a brief moment, we locked eyes, and I felt myself lean forward involuntarily. He froze mid-stride, abandoning his pacing to stand rooted at the center of the stage, his gaze fixed firmly on mine.

His lips moved, carrying on with the speech, but his focus never wavered—every word felt like it was meant for me. But perhaps he was making everyone else in the audience feel the same way.

"The materialization of mankind's genius is all around us: great feats of engineering, feats of architecture, music, literature... all of which did not come about without the help of those willing to share their thoughts and knowledge with others. It is with this understanding that I will treat my new responsibility as an educator with the utmost care and devotion required of such an important position, as I hope everyone in this room will. A little education and a great amount of kindness is what is required if we are to secure harmony in this life and the lives of those who will come after us. Thank you very much."

He concluded his speech, his eyes lingering on me. Or at least, it felt that way. Though, to be fair, I often had the starring role in my own delusions.

The room fell silent for a few moments after he finished, still and reverent, before bursting into thunderous applause. I watched him blink rapidly, breaking the connection, and shifted his focus to scan the crowd.

He was a beautiful speaker, that much was clear, but what made the whole thing even more impressive was that he never once looked down at any kind of notes during his speech.

I wasn't ready for it to be over. I felt like I could have listened to him speak all night, even if the topics were way over my head. I guess I wasn't the only one, because he was swarmed as soon as he stepped off the stage.

"Wasn't he incredible?" Dr. Abel said, walking up to our table. "Dr. Benson told me that he's the smartest person he's ever met. And that's saying something."

"Do you think he knows Taylor Swift?" Lionel asked.

Dr. Abel gave him an exasperated look. "Why in the world would you ask that, Mr. Vaughn?"

"Well, they have a lot in common... she's also a genius," Lionel said seriously. "And they both have a way with words with the same kind of dedicated fan base."

Dr. Abel shook his head. "I never have any idea what you're talking about."

"If I had a dollar..."

"I think I should go over and introduce myself," Dr. Abel said, ignoring Lionel and glancing over his shoulder. "He'll probably want to meet all the department heads."

"I don't think he's interested in us, Dr. Abel. Unless you think he's suddenly dying to learn about classical harmonic keys and chord progression," Sarah chimed in.

"Maybe not, Ms. Samaha, but Dr. Benson said he's new to this area and probably doesn't know too many people. We should make him feel welcome."

"Doesn't look like he's having trouble meeting new people to me," Lionel pointed out.

"Hadley, you're new too. Why don't you come with me?" he said, ignoring Lionel again. "It would probably make him feel more at ease to know he's not the only newcomer."

"Oh, I don't think—" I started.

"I insist," he interrupted, gesturing for me to follow. I sighed. Sarah and Lionel looked on sympathetically, but there wasn't much they could do now.

"See if he knows Taylor!" Lionel called out to me as we headed toward the mob.

I followed along after Dr. Abel as he pushed his way through the throng of people surrounding the Drs. Benson and Strovinski. After a lot of "excuse-me's" and "so-sorrys," we finally made it to where they were both standing. They were deep in conversation with a group of fellow admirers, so I was a little shocked when Dr. Abel tapped on Strovinski's shoulder as he was mid-sentence. He stopped talking abruptly and turned to see the cause of the interruption. He glanced down briefly at Dr. Abel, who was a great deal shorter than him, before he spotted me standing there, his gaze unyielding as he took me in.

Did he think I was the one who crassly tapped on his shoulder? He must have, the way he was staring at me so intently.

"Hi, Dr. Strovinski," my new boss said, trying to get his attention. "I'm Dr. William Abel. It's a pleasure to meet you, sir."

Dr. Abel stuck his hand out toward the man, who finally pulled his eyes from me and accepted the handshake.

"What do you need, Will?" Benson said, turning and looking annoyed by our presence.

"I wanted to introduce myself to Dr. Strovinski. As head of the music department, I thought it important he know that he can come to me for anything."

"Okay, that's great. Thank you, Will," Benson said dismissively.

Dr. Abel continued on anyway. "I'd also like to introduce you to my colleague, Hadley Olivier. This will be her first semester teaching as well, so you're not the only novice in the bunch."

"Hi, it's nice to meet you." I smiled politely, but he didn't return the gesture. He stood a little over six feet tall with warm, whiskey-colored eyes that seemed fixated on me once again. Up close, I noted his well-defined cheekbones and full lips offset perfectly with the squareness of his jawline.

"Your speech was really great," I said, trying again.

"Thank you," he said curtly. Man, he was really holding a grudge about this shoulder tap.

"I understand you're doing Alzheimer's research." I was determined to break the awkward silence that followed his short response.

Benson turned to face me. "Are you familiar with Dr. Strovinski's work?"

I shook my head. "No, the only doctor whose work I'm familiar with is Dr. Dre."

I felt Dr. Abel go stiff standing next to me, while Benson stared at me with a puzzled expression.

"Who is Dr. Dre?" Benson asked. "Is he also a scientist? I don't think I've ever heard of him."

I couldn't believe my ears.

"Dr. Dre," I said, staring in disbelief. And because I didn't know when to shut my big mouth, I continued to ramble. "You know…" I said awkwardly. "'The Chronic?'… 'California Love?'… 'Nothing but a G Thing?'"

Benson was looking at me like I'd grown two heads.

"I believe he's a rapper, sir," Dr. Abel said, looking like he wished he'd never brought me over here.

Wrong crowd, I guess. Although I could have sworn I saw Strovinski's lip quirk ever so slightly.

Benson narrowed his eyes at me. "What is it you're going to be teaching, Ms. Olivier?"

Shit. Should've flown under the radar.

"Music composition."

"I can assure you, she is more than qualified for the position, sir," Abel said, trying to save face for my little faux pas.

"I'm sure she is," he responded doubtfully.

Dr. Abel planted a big smile on his face. "Actually, Hadley hails to us all the way from The Big Apple."

Benson nodded slowly like he couldn't have found this topic any less interesting.

"Great cheesecake," I said, just throwing something at the wall of awkwardness and hoping it would stick. They all just stared at me, not saying a word.

"Dr. Strovinski, could I steal you for a moment for a few photos?" A man with a rather large camera had come up, saving me from the unpleasant encounter. I took that as a chance to escape, slipping out through the crowd and making my way back to our table, not bothering to wait for Dr. Abel.

I decided it was definitely time for me to be heading home before I embarrassed myself any further. I said my goodbyes to Sarah and Lionel and the rest of my new coworkers. As I was leaving, I dared another glance toward the photo-op area to see a pair of whiskey-colored eyes following me as I departed.

Chapter 4

"Marge, please!" I shouted, banging on the steering wheel. "No no no no no no! Not today!"

I couldn't believe this was happening. I was never late for anything, and now I was going to be showing up to work late on my very first day with the excuse of "car trouble." This was going to look so bad. After the way faculty night had ended, I knew I was skating on razor-thin ice with the Creepmaster General. And now Marge decided to make things even worse for me. I was definitely getting fired.

I got out of the car and ran across the street to Professor Dunbar's house, pounding on the door to see if he'd already left for work. He was my next-door neighbor who I'd met when the moving van finally showed up a couple of days after my arrival, and he'd graciously helped me move a few of my things in. He was a horticulturist who taught in the agriculture department of the university, and it showed. His small garden at the front of his home was absolutely stunning. I baked him a few of my homemade triple chocolate brownies as a thanks for helping me, and he offered to get my shrubbery looking just as good as his if I promised to bake more goodies for him. I had to concede another pro to California's column—the people here were a lot friendlier. I don't think my neighbors would stop to piss on me if I were on fire back in my old neighborhood.

When he didn't answer, I was about to give up and call for a taxi when suddenly, I saw a familiar face coming out of the townhouse directly across from mine.

My mouth fell open. There was no way.

Dr. Alexsander Strovinski lived in the faculty housing units? I guess it kind of made sense. He wasn't from this area, and I'm sure wasn't trying to put down roots in Stanford.

I decided I was going to have to take advantage of this opportunity, even if my ego would have to take a hit.

"Dr. Strovinski!" I called out, rushing over to him. He turned and found the source of the disturbance. He looked so taken aback at the sight of me that I thought he probably didn't remember who I was and just saw a crazy lady running toward him.

"Dr. Strovinski, hi! I'm Hadley Olivier. I don't know if you remember me, but we met the other night at the faculty banquet," I said, a little out of breath.

"I remember you," he said succinctly. *Great.* Guess he was still mad about the whole shoulder tap thing that wasn't even me!

"Well, I was hoping to ask for a favor. You see that car over there taking a cigarette break?" I pointed to poor Marge, who still had black smoke coming from her hood.

"That's my car, and I really would hate to be late on my first day of work. Could I catch a ride with you? If that's where you're heading, of course."

He stared at me blankly for a few moments, I'm sure trying to decide if I was really crazy or not before he replied, "Okay."

"Thank you, thank you!" Relief washed through me so much so that I had to hold myself back from throwing my arms around him in a tight hug. Bet that would have gone over about as well as a screen door on a submarine.

"I do have a roommate that I'm waiting for. He should be coming out shortly."

"No problem! I so appreciate this, you have no idea. I didn't think I'd have time to call a taxi and still make it there on time."

He nodded but didn't say anything further. Maybe he was on some kind of strict word diet because the silence seemed to stretch on and on. I found myself opening and closing my mouth like a confused goldfish, desperately trying to think of something to say.

As the silent standoff continued, my eyes went skyward, searching for someone to save me from the jaws of this awkward monster. I was about to break down and call on the hero of small talk to come and rescue me, but today's weather would have to wait because I finally saw my savior emerge from the townhouse.

"Well, well, well, who do we have here?" his roommate asked. He looked to be about the same age as Strovinski, but a lot smaller in stature, with a coy smile playing across his face.

"Hey, I'm Hadley," I said, overjoyed to be with someone who embraced verbal communication. "I was having car trouble this morning, so I asked your roommate for a ride. I hope you don't mind."

"Damsel in distress is my favorite kind of damsel." He extended his hand. "Stuart Benowitz. Pleasure to meet you, my lady."

I offered mine in return, which he brought to his lips, kissing the back of my hand. I laughed at the corniness of the gesture, knowing in my gut that he was harmless.

"Let's get going. We don't want to be late," Strovinski said tersely.

I was definitely on his bad side. Maybe if I searched high and low, I could find the roadmap to his good side. Then again, it would probably just keep rerouting me to the land of "do not disturb."

"So, do you guys work together?" I followed them to a shiny, silver Lexus GS that was only a few cars down from my vehicle, which thankfully no longer had smoke wafting from under the hood.

Stuart rushed ahead to grab the door handle to open it for me. "Going on ten years now."

"And you live together as well?"

Stuart paused, the door hanging open midway. "It's not what you think."

I smirked. "I didn't say anything."

Stuart's head whipped towards Strovinski. "I told you people would start to say that about us!"

His roommate seemed totally unbothered by the notion.

"Knew we should have gotten separate places," Stuart grumbled, opening the door the rest of the way for me.

"Thank you." I smiled and slid into the front passenger seat at the same time as Strovinski, who still hadn't said more than a few words.

"Thanks again, Dr. Strovinski. I really appreciate this," I said, trying to warm him up to me a little.

"Lex is fine." He put the key in the ignition and adjusted his seat back slightly to make more leg room.

Stuart got into the back seat and slid to the center so he could lean forward between us. "Yes, please! If I have to hear one more person around here say *Doctor* Strovinski, I'm going to blow my brains out. This is an Ivy League university. We all have doctorates."

"I don't have one," I pointed out.

"Well, what is it you teach?"

"I'll be teaching music composition to level one freshmen."

"Oh, so you're part of the college of fine arts... makes sense. I thought you were a work of fine art when I first saw you."

That was so cheesy, but I still couldn't help but smile. "And it makes sense that you're part of the biology department."

"Why's that?" he asked.

"Aren't there a lot of other tiny organisms there too?"

I turned to see Stuart staring at me deadpan, and I laughed out loud. Technically, he stood about the same height as me, around five-foot-five, but I still had to tease him a bit.

"I'll have you know dynamite comes in small packages," he replied, wiggling his eyebrows.

"Are you saying you should come with a warning label?" I asked. "Because I completely agree."

I spotted the barest flicker of a smile on Strovinski's lips before he started up the engine, which, unlike mine, was working perfectly.

Stuart fixed me with another blank stare before he turned to Lex. "Where did you say you found this one?"

As soon as Lex started the car, a loud blast of music came through the speakers blaring Cher's "If I Could Turn Back Time."

We all jumped as he hurried to shut the music off. There were ten seconds of complete silence before I couldn't take it anymore. I burst out laughing.

"Smooth, man," Stuart muttered under his breath.

"My aunt was visiting over the weekend," he explained. "I let her borrow my car yesterday to go pick up dinner."

I tried covering my smile when I saw how mortified he looked. "Whatever you say."

"Stuart can tell you. She stayed with us all weekend."

"It's okay to love Cher. She's an icon. No need to be embarrassed," I told him.

"Stuart?" he asked, looking for reinforcement.

Stuart clamped a hand on his shoulder. "We all have our passions, Lex. It's no use hiding them from the world."

He sighed, giving up the argument with the two of us ganging up on him, and pulled out of the parking lot.

"So Hadley, you're new to California, right?" Stuart asked, giving Lex a break.

"Yes. I just moved here from New York."

"Well, we've been here for a few months now. We'd love to show you around the city sometime, just so you can get the lay of the land. I mean, unless your boyfriend's already doing that."

I smiled, knowing what he was getting at. "Well, with his job, he really doesn't have time."

I glanced over to Lex, whose face remained expressionless.

"So you do have a boyfriend... figures," Stuart said with a hint of bitterness.

"Yes. His name's Bruce."

"*Bruce?*" he said as if the name were offensive. "What kind of a name is *Bruce*? Sounds like some meathead football player."

"He's actually a scientist too."

"What?" they asked simultaneously, both turning their heads to look at me. Their tone was incredulous. I had to work hard to hide my smile.

"Yeah, he's incredibly smart and a really nice guy. Well... most of the time, anyway."

Stuart's brows pinched together. "What do you mean?"

I sighed. "I can't explain it. He just has this dark side. Sometimes it scares me how angry he can get."

I could tell I had them eating out the palm of my hand. "Anyway, he's absolutely brilliant. The smartest guy there is."

Stuart scoffed. "I doubt that. I've never even heard of him. What's Bruce's last name?"

I had to bite my lip to keep the laughter from escaping. "Banner," I said, waiting for the joke to set in. When the realization finally hit, Stuart threw his hands in the air, and Lex actually smiled the first true smile I'd ever seen him wear. It changed his face completely. There was a crinkle at the edges of his eyes that made him seem warm and almost approachable.

"Okay... you're an asshole," Stuart said dryly, and I laughed even harder. "Are you really even from New York?"

My chin lifted in mock indignation. "I would never joke about that."

"Let me check to see if your pants are on fire."

I chuckled before turning to them. "What about you guys? Where are you both from?"

"I'm from Portland," Stuart answered. "City of Roses."

"Chicago," Lex stated. I wondered if he'd entered some kind of a contest to say as few words as possible around me.

"The talk of the town is Stanford gave you a heaping pile of money to do your research here."

"It's true," Stuart confirmed. "They offered *Doctor* Strovinski a deal we couldn't refuse. We were working at NIH, but they wanted too much of a say in what we were doing, so we started shopping around and found Stanford. The only requirement they had was that we teach a course each semester."

I tilted my head. "So, is it just you and Lex then?"

"No, the whole team moved here. There are eight of us who have been together since the beginning. But we've acquired a few more team members since we got here."

"That's pretty amazing that you've stuck together all these years."

"What can I say? Opens more doors when you've got the doc on your team." He said it mockingly, but it was clear he wasn't resentful.

"And have the two of you *always* lived together?" I asked, eyeing him meaningfully.

Stuart paused before shouting, "It's not what you think!"

I laughed even more and realized how good it felt. Even if it was just for this short drive, I was grateful for the brief escape from the heavy reality that had brought me here in the first place.

As we drove along, I took the time to admire the campus. It was absolutely stunning, but I was a little overwhelmed by the size of it. The defining characteristics of the university's architecture were the sandstone buildings with covered colonnades and half-circle arches stretching out in long corridors, giving it that historical Romanesque feel. I noticed a large portion of the campus was canopied by coastal live oak trees interspersed with different variants of eucalyptus trees. I knew if I stared at it for too long, I might start to think that living here wasn't so bad after all.

I told Lex what building I was supposed to be in, which he somehow found without having to look for any directions.

"Thanks again, you guys. I really appreciate it," I said when he stopped in front of the building.

"Don't be a stranger, Betty," Stuart said as I got out of the car.

I had to think about it for a moment, then it finally hit me. Bruce Banner's wife—Betty Ross.

I laughed and waved goodbye to them. Stuart returned the smile while Lex simply drove off without another word. He was definitely going to win that taciturn contest.

Chapter 5

I found the small office that was going to be mine for the semester and dropped off my things before heading to the classroom, where a few students were already waiting. It was a fairly large classroom with auditorium-type seating. In the corner of the room sat a parlor grand piano, while a large whiteboard and an extended desk stretched across the front.

I had mapped out my lesson plans for the semester with a little bit of help from Sarah, who had given me some pointers. I started writing a few highlights from the syllabus on the board and waited for everyone to get seated. The nerves and self-doubt started setting in, wondering if I really could do this, but I pushed them away. The worst that could happen was that I lose this job, which paled in comparison to the realities of what I was facing with my mom.

"Hello, everyone," I said, walking up to the front of the room to face them. "I'm Hadley Olivier, and this is Music Composition 101."

"Mommy!" one of the guys in the back of the room shouted, sinking lower into his seat as his friends beside him burst into laughter.

"Oh, I'm sorry, you must be in the wrong room. This is music com-position, not psychotherapy for out-of-control oedipal complexes," I retorted and the whole room erupted in laughter.

"What's your name?" I asked as he sat up a little straighter, knowing he was busted.

"John-Luke," he replied, grinning smugly. He looked like the son of a politician, with perfectly quaffed hair and a button-down polo shirt.

"How biblical." I walked over to that side of the room. "Let's try and keep the outbursts to a minimum, John-Luke. I'd hate to have any more Freudian slip-and-falls on my watch."

He gave me the same cocky grin. "I'll try, but I can't make any promises, Teach."

"Do give it your best effort," I said with a wry smile. "Mommy has a lot of work to do. And if you're on your best behavior, I'll let you go play frisbee golf when we're done."

His friends were laughing and elbowing him, but he didn't say anything further so I moved on.

"So, unlike a lot of people around here, I do not have a doctorate degree. But what I do have is a lot of real-world experience in writing and composition." I did have a Master of Fine Arts degree from Northwestern and had some pretty great internships, but I found that terribly boring, so I decided I was going to speak from the heart when giving introductions about myself.

"What I love most about composing music is the infinite possibilities." I thought of what Frank Zappa once said about composition. "There's something exciting about being given a piece of time, and you get to be the one to decorate it."

I looked around the room, and I seemed to have everyone's attention, despite frat boy's outburst. "Throughout this course, I'll be giving you the vocabulary necessary to speak the same language as those who are already in this business, but beyond knowing the parlance, you'll only be limited by your own creativity. So, let's get started."

I spent the next hour going over some introductory topics and tried to give real-world examples of where these things might apply, hoping it would have a greater impact. At some point though, I could see their attention drifting. Heads were resting sideways on fists, and there were one too many glazed looks on the sea of faces.

I abruptly stopped mid-sentence on my explanation of ledger lines and blurted out, "My god, you all look bored out of your minds."

They all started to chuckle and straightened up in their chairs.

"Why don't we change things up a bit?" I looked around and my attention focused on a young man sitting by himself midway up the auditorium. He had a kind face that resembled Chidi from *The Good Place*.

"You there," I said, pointing to him. "What's your name?"

He looked around to make sure it was really him I was speaking to, before deciding that I must be, since there was clearly no one else around him.

"Sam Matherne," he replied shyly.

I smiled encouragingly. "Sam, tell me what kind of music you like."

"Ummm... rhythm and blues."

"Nice," I said. "Who's your favorite artist?"

He pushed his glasses up his nose. "I don't think you've heard of him."

"Can you check your watch for me?" I eyed the Apple watch on his wrist.

"Why?" he asked, looking down at it.

"I just want to know how many calories you burned jumping to that conclusion."

He looked up, grinning from ear to ear.

"Why don't you try me?" I said confidently.

"Eddie Kirkland," he answered.

I grinned back at him before I sat down at the piano and started playing one of the few Eddie Kirkland songs I knew. Luckily, he had come up in my graduate thesis work so I got to show off a bit.

Sam could not wipe the smile from his face as I played "Meet Me on Sugar Hill" and sang along. I looked around to see I had piqued everyone's interest. I broke down the composition of the song piece by piece, going over basic rhythm patterns and harmonic intervals. I got a thrill out of seeing them scribbling furiously on their little notepads. Did I just crack the code to teaching? I decided to try again.

"What about you, John-Luke?" I asked when I noticed he was chatting with his neighbor and not paying attention. "What kind of music do you like?"

He gave me an arrogant smile. "Yeah, music's not really my thing, Ms. Olivier."

That answer took me by surprise. "You really are in the wrong classroom."

"Some of us have to be here," he countered. "For some reason, the University of Stanford thinks a music course is necessary for my law degree."

I turned and started to play the theme song for *Law and Order* as a chorus of laughter rang out. "A lawyer, huh? You plan to put the bad guys away?"

"I plan to defend them," he said, smirking.

Should have known.

I played the infamous dun-dun sound from the *Law and Order* scene starter, and he smiled despite himself.

"Well, there must be a reason you chose composition instead of another introductory course," I said, trying again to make a connection.

Another cocky grin played across his face. "Yeah, I heard the teacher was hot."

The kids were all trying to hide their faces or cover up their laughter with coughing, but it was no use. Eventually, the whole room was shaking with laughter.

"Alright, alright, settle down." I shook my head. I needed to get this lesson back on track before I had Chris Hansen walking through the door on my first day.

A curious thought suddenly came to my mind. "So, who here is actually a music major?"

I don't know why I never considered the fact that some of them might not even be interested in music. I looked around to see only about half the class had their hands raised. Now I just felt foolish for assuming they were all music majors. I went to a performing arts college so I'd always been surrounded by people in the same field of study. A very obnoxious teacher-esque idea suddenly sprang to my mind, but I was going for it.

"I just had a great idea, ladies and gentlemen!" I bounced on the balls of my feet excitedly. "I want all of you to pair up in groups of two or three to compose one single song, any genre. The catch is the group has to have at least one non-music major in it, and I want your composition to be about whatever it is that person is majoring in. I'll monitor each group's progress weekly and give feedback. It will count toward your final grade for the semester."

There were audible groans and sighs as they looked around the auditorium, starting to size each other up. I knew what a pain in the ass group projects could be, but I was actually excited by this. I dismissed the class for the day before any real complaining could start up.

"I guess it goes without saying this hasn't been the best first day so far," Sarah said as I met her outside the cafeteria for lunch. I had told her all about the morning I'd had, including the car breakdown and my biblical heckler.

"I don't know." I half-shrugged. "I think I made my point to polo shirt. And as far as the car goes, I'm counting myself lucky that someone was still there this morning that I was able to catch a ride from. Marge was on her deathbed. I should have looked into getting something sooner."

I still needed to call a tow company to come pick up poor Marge. I was hit with a twinge of sadness at the thought of having to part with her. It was always a hassle to own a car in New York City, but I never even considered giving her up. My mom could never bring herself to sell Dad's car and had kept it in a garage all these years. She gave it to me when I was old enough to drive, and I loved taking her out on the weekends. It was like a private getaway each time I got behind the wheel. I could drown out the noise of the city and let my brain be as creative as possible. Ironically, some of my best pieces of music had come about just through being silent and meditative. There was nothing I loved more than driving in complete and total silence—no music, no books on tape, no talking whatsoever. The white noise of tires moving along asphalt combined with the motion of the car always put me at ease and dissolved any tension I might be feeling.

"So, how was it being up close and personal with Alexsander the Great?" Sarah asked, interrupting my thoughts.

"It was okay, I guess. He didn't say a whole lot," I said, remembering his standoffish demeanor. "Honestly, I don't think he likes me very much."

"Ahhh, the shoulder tap thing." I had filled Sarah in on what happened with Benson at faculty night. She'd laughed her ass off when I told her about the Dr. Dre joke.

"It wasn't even me!" I protested. "Maybe I should tell him that." It *was* pretty rude. I think I'd be annoyed if someone did that to me while I was mid-sentence.

"Oh, who cares? He sounds stuck up if that's really what's bothering him."

"Maybe. But I think I need to make nice anyway. We might be seeing a lot of each other. We're neighbors, after all."

She shook her head. "I can't even picture it. Seems like they'd put him up in a chateau or something, not faculty housing."

"Don't hate. They're actually pretty nice."

"You're just saying that because you lucked out and don't have to share it with a roommate."

She might be right about that. On my drive over from New York, someone from the Faculty Advisor's Office called to let me know that my almost-roommate failed her background check, and they were unable to fill the vacancy last minute, which left me sans roommate. I had been disappointed at first until I saw the size of the upstairs bathroom we were meant to share.

"Did I tell you about Lex's roommate?" I asked her.

"Lex? You call him Lex?"

"He asked me to. What's so weird about that?"

"I don't know. It's the way you said it."

"How did I say it?"

"Like you've seen him naked."

Just as I was about to tell her she was nuts, I got distracted by who I spotted over her shoulder walking toward us with a man I'd never seen before.

"Well, if it isn't Betty," Stuart said with a sly grin. "We meet again."

"Yeah, long time no see," I smiled at him and his friend, who looked like he was breaking out in a cold sweat.

"Hey, I'm Hadley," I said, introducing myself to his friend.

"Hi, my Peter... Shit... I uh, what I meant was my name is Pete... Peter, actually. But my friends call me Pete. Whichever you want, really."

"Jesus, Pete." Stuart slapped his palm across his face and let it slide off his chin.

"This is my friend, Sarah," I said, chuckling. "Sarah, this is Dr. Strovinski's roommate—"

"Stuart Benowitz," she finished before I got the chance. "We've met.”

"You have?" I asked, perplexed.

Stuart's eyes darted around as he fidgeted with his watch.

"Yep. On faculty night right before you got there," Sarah said, fixing him with a steely glare. "He asked me what department I worked in and when I told him music and performing arts, he said he wasn't surprised because I looked like a work of fine art."

I narrowed my eyes at him. "Nice. Very original."

He put his hands up. "Okay, in my defense... it's a really easy connection."

"Not very clever," I chastised.

"Oh c'mon. What should I have said? 'Hi, I'm Stuart. I saw you from across the room, and I thought you were very beautiful.'"

"Uhhhh, yeah. That's perfect, actually," Sarah said.

"Please. That wouldn't have worked either. You barely glanced up from your phone when I first said hello."

"That's because I was waiting on my college roommate here, who I hadn't seen in over a decade, to call me so I could go meet her," Sarah said defensively.

His brow lifted. "You guys were roommates?"

"Not the same kind of roommates as you and Lex," I said with an exaggerated wink.

He shot me a disparaging look. "Lex should be so lucky. I'll have you know that I've had *several* women tell me that I'm the whole package, ladies," he said with an arched brow.

"Your mom doesn't count," Pete retorted, and I fought to hold back my laughter. I guess the opportunity to rib Stuart allowed Pete to find his confidence again.

"Also, you could be the whole package, but you're definitely at the wrong address," Sarah added. With that comment, there was no silencing the laugh that escaped me.

"Give it up, man," Peter said, slapping a hand on his shoulder. "It's not going to happen."

"I don't remember asking for your opinion, Pete," Stuart said, shrugging him off.

"You didn't have to," he quipped. "It's on the house."

"We were about to go in to grab lunch if you guys want to join us," I said, interrupting their bickering.

"Sure," Peter said quickly.

Stuart folded his arms across his chest. "I don't know," he said, pretending to be mulling it over.

"What's the problem?" I asked.

"I'm not sure I should give you guys the unbelievable pleasure of my company after the treatment I've had to endure here today."

"I wouldn't play hard to get when I can tell you're more hard to get rid of," Sarah said impatiently. "Now drop the Pepé Le Pew act and come have lunch with us."

She didn't wait for his response as she marched into the cafeteria ahead of us. I heard Stuart mutter, "Fine!" under his breath as he followed behind her.

A smile stretched across Peter's face as he turned to me. "I'd like to thank you both for this." He placed his hand over his heart. "Putting Stuart in his place is not a service many provide, but one I'll gladly pay for."

I shook my head, chuckling. "No need. Our services are complimentary."

We walked in behind the bustling crowd of students, making our way toward the serving station. I braved the chef's special of the day, chicken marsala, which looked pretty decent, before joining the others at the table.

I took a seat next to Sarah. "So, where's Lex?"

"Still working," Stuart answered.

"Does he not eat lunch?"

"Actually, I think the boss man just periodically shuts down until we have time to put a little oil in him and get him plugged into a socket to recharge," Peter answered, looking more relaxed now.

"Workaholic?" I inferred.

"That's an understatement. He never stops."

"Sounds like a tough person to work for."

"I wouldn't say that," Peter said thoughtfully.

"No?"

"There's a reason we follow him all over the country."

Besides being crazy smart, I wondered what else there was.

"His outgoing personality?" I teased.

"Not exactly," he said, smiling. "He's dedicated to his work but when you're that gifted, it's hard to shut your brain off. He works harder than anyone I've ever known, but it's more inspiring than it is frustrating."

I considered what he said and thought that was actually a nice sentiment. I would love to feel inspired by my superiors rather than creeped out.

"It's all about helping the world to be a better place. He really does want to make a difference."

"Yeah, well from what we've heard, you guys are saving the world and getting a huge budget to do it," Sarah said. "Meanwhile, I have to go ten levels up the chain of command to get a new eraser, and I'm pretty sure my piano's from 1985."

"So, you guys both work in the music department?" Pete asked.

"Composition," I answered.

"Musicology," Sarah said.

Peter had a woeful look. "Damn, my mom was right. I should have stuck with those clarinet lessons."

"Yeah, the music department's hogging all the good-looking

women," Stuart said. "All we've got are AARP members and that chick that says "knock, knock" before entering every room."

"Sounds like you'll be able to stay more focused on your work while you're, you know... working," I pointed out.

"Wow, seems like Lex was able to join us for lunch after all," he said, tone laden with sarcasm. "You sound just like him."

I stuck my tongue out at him, and he gave me a wry smile in return.

"So, how was your first day teaching?" he asked, changing the subject.

I looked down at my food, pushing it around a bit. "It was okay."

"Some kid tried to throw her off," Sarah said, answering his questioning look at my lukewarm response.

"What'd he do?"

I waved him off. "Just yelled something inappropriate."

It wasn't even what he said. It was the fact that I clearly seemed like an easy target to them. Could they smell rookie on me? Darling little bloodhounds, trying to sniff out incompetence.

Stuart shook his head. "I can imagine."

"What about you? When do you start your classes?" I asked, trying to divert the conversation.

"Not until Thursday."

"And you'll be teaching a neurobiology class?"

"No, I'm not technically a neurobiologist. Lex needed a chemist for his team, so that's how I started working with him. After all these years, I've absorbed enough to get by, but my PhD is in chemistry, so that's what I'll be teaching."

"And then what? You do your research on all the other days?"

"Yeah, we got started in the lab today."

"What kind of research are you guys doing exactly?" Sarah asked.

"We're trying to create an implantable device for Alzheimer's patients to deliver medication to the affected segment of the brain to delay neuronal death and possibly even reverse it.”

"Wow, that's pretty amazing," Sarah said, and I nodded in agreement. "I hate to admit it, but you're kind of impressive."

"Yeah, I could barely pass basic algebra in high school," I added.

He straightened with a hopeful gleam in his eye. "Wait, I did tell you guys I was single, didn't I?"

He just couldn't help himself.

Sarah used her hand as a fake phone and started to dial. She nodded at me to pick up.

I played along. "Hello?" I answered.

"The delusion's coming from inside the house," she whispered dramatically.

At that, I broke into a fit of laughter, with Peter joining in. Stuart just rolled his eyes, sagging back down in his chair.

When the laughter finally died down, I got an uneasy feeling in the pit of my stomach. It took me a few minutes to identify what it was: guilt. Here I was, sitting around laughing and carrying on with my life, while my mom was going through one of the hardest times in her own life. She said this was what she wanted for me when we talked about moving here, but it still didn't sit right with me.

As we got up from the table to leave, Stuart asked, "Betty, before I forget to ask, are you going to need a ride back home?"

"I can just take an Uber." I didn't want to burden anyone.

"I'll take you. It's on my way home," Sarah offered, and I accepted.

"Great," Stuart said. "Now I can officially report back that your transportation has been covered, and I can stop hearing about it."

I wondered what he meant by that. Was he talking about Lex? It didn't seem likely that he would care how I was getting home, but maybe he was just being courteous. I could picture the relief on his face when Stuart told him that he wouldn't have to bother with me and could practice remaining as quiet as humanly possible.

Chapter 6

"So, who is this Lex fellow I keep hearing about?" my mom asked as we sat in the back seat of the taxi on the way to her doctor's appointment. She hadn't been cleared to drive yet with the medication she was taking, and since I was officially car-less, we would have to resort to getting around this way for now.

I could see her studying me from the side while I deliberated on how to answer her. I sometimes hated how well she knew me. Even though I barely mentioned his name in the stories I'd told her from the past few days, she had somehow zeroed in on the fact that there were mixed feelings there.

"Remember, I told you he's the one who gave me a ride yesterday." I decided to keep it simple. "He's the same guy who gave the commencement speech at faculty night."

"And how do we feel about Lex?" she asked oh-so-casually.

"I don't really know," I answered honestly. "By all accounts, he's a great guy, doing amazing work, but I don't think he likes me too much."

"That's impossible. Everyone likes you."

She said it so seriously, I had to laugh. "You might be a bit biased."

"Maybe. But he doesn't even know you."

"It's okay. Not everyone has to like me."

"You're right," she agreed. "But I don't trust anyone who doesn't like you. Something's clearly not right with him."

I smiled because she meant that wholeheartedly and not as a joke at all.

"I feel like we might have gotten off on the wrong foot," I said. "We're neighbors, so hopefully if we get to know each other better, it won't be so awkward. His roommate seems to like me well enough."

"Well, I'm glad you at least have Sarah. I remember the two of you were pretty close when you lived together."

"Yeah, we kind of fell back into it like no time had passed. And I've met some of her friends. They all seem great."

"Oh, that's good. I want you to have people here," she said before growing quiet. "You know I still want you to live your life, Hadley. You're only twenty-eight years old. No matter what's going on with me, you still have to keep living."

I knew what she was getting at. I couldn't bring myself to have this conversation. She'd been trying to go there with me over the past few weeks, but I wasn't ready.

"We're here," I announced as we pulled up to Dr. Gremillion's office, not acknowledging her words.

We didn't have to wait long to see him.

"Ms. Olivier, I heard your surgery went really well," Dr. Gremillion said as he entered the exam room.

She smiled. "Yes, both doctors were great."

"Good, I'm glad to hear it. Now as you know, the cancer had already spread to the lymph nodes and surrounding tissue by the time we found it. The reports from the surgeon show that they got most of it when they removed your breasts and a large portion of the lymph nodes, but there are still cancer cells that remain. The next step is going to be chemotherapy. I'd like for you to begin next week. The sooner the better, now that you've recovered from surgery. The treatments will be twice a week for the next few months, at least. We'll monitor you throughout the treatments to see how well your body is responding to them."

My heart beat nervously. "There's still a pretty good chance for remission, isn't there?"

"Yes, absolutely," he answered. "You're in good health, so I'm optimistic that this course of treatment will be successful."

Every muscle in my body felt tense. "And if it isn't?"

"We'll cross that bridge if we get there. Let's take it one step at a time for now."

I sighed. "Fair enough."

He was right. I didn't want to get too far ahead of myself. *One step at a time.* That would be my new mantra.

It was Friday night, and I found myself home alone with nothing but profound boredom to keep me company. My mom had found a canasta group to join, and they happened to play on Friday nights. While I applauded her newfound social life out on the West Coast, I was disappointed at being left to my own devices for the evening. Didn't an ejection from the womb grant me automatic dibs?

I decided to bake some of my kitchen sink cookies, which were made up of chocolate chips, pretzels, potato chips, toffee bits, and M&M's. I chose it because it was a really time-consuming recipe, and I needed a way to occupy both my mind and palate.

It was times like these that I wished my almost-roommate would have worked out. I would have taken being housed with a violent criminal if it meant I wouldn't be spending Friday night alone, daydreaming about joining the all-ladies Canasta Clique. Alas, I'd been dealt a different hand (pun intended). Even though Sarah told me to call her anytime, I didn't want to always bother her just because she was the only other person I knew here.

As I prepped the ingredients, I realized I hadn't heard from Garrett again besides a few texts asking how my mom was doing. I had rarely even thought of him since we got here, which was just further confirmation that I did the right thing by breaking things off. Now that things had slowed down a bit, and I was spending a lot more time alone, my mind started drifting back to him.

I didn't think it was even him that I was missing, but more the companionship. There wasn't any part of me that wanted to be romantically involved with him any longer, but I sometimes missed the way he could make me laugh. I remember the last time he made me laugh so hard, I cried. We were hanging out at his apartment, and I was watching random videos on my phone and there was one of a colorblind kid who received those glasses that allowed him to see in color. I showed Garrett the video and said, "Isn't that sweet? He's so happy," because the kid was so overcome with emotion, and he said, "I would be too, if I could finally play Twister." I think I laughed for a full five minutes straight. When I thought about moments like that, it made me want to pick up the phone and call him just so we could talk, but I didn't think that was fair. I didn't want to send the wrong message so I sucked it up, realizing I couldn't reach out just because I was feeling lonely.

I meticulously assembled my circles of sweetness with the precision of a brain surgeon. But even after all was said and done, it was barely past the time for early bird dinner at the Golden Corral when they finally emerged from the oven. I figured I could take some over to Professor Dunbar's since he had liked my brownies so much. I packaged a few of them up and walked them over to his house, knocking on the door.

"Well, hello again, Hadley," he greeted me warmly when he opened the door. He had the same kind of gentle disposition that you'd imagine any grandparent would. It automatically made you feel comforted.

"Hey, Professor Dunbar. I just wanted to bring you some of my kitchen sink cookies." I held up the bag. "Do you guys have any allergies? They have nuts in them."

"That is so kind of you. And no, we don't," he said, taking the bag from me. "Mira is going to be so thrilled. She still raves about those brownies you made. Did you want to come in?"

I shook my head. "No, I don't want to interrupt your evening. I just wanted to come say hello and drop them off."

"Well, thank you so much. You've definitely found your target audience."

I smiled and said, "Enjoy!" before walking down the steps of his porch.

"I see you've been keeping up with the rhododendrons," he called out to me as I was passing the garden he'd helped me plant.

"I'm trying. None of it looks as good as yours, though."

"That's a good thing. People would start to think I'd lost my touch if yours looked better," he said, winking. I laughed, and we waved goodbye. Just as I was about to head inside, I heard a familiar voice calling my name.

I turned to see Stuart and Lex coming up the walkway, both holding armfuls of takeout.

"What are you guys up to?" I asked, chuckling.

"Just getting off work. We picked up some Thai food," Stuart said.

"You guys leave any for the rest of Stanford's population?"

"I'm starving and everything they have there is amazing," he replied. "I couldn't decide so I got one of everything."

"I see that. Very practical."

"Come join us."

Lex, who had remained his normal reticent self up to this point, was looking at Stuart like he wanted to wrap one of the bags he was holding around his head.

"Oh no, that's okay."

"Why not? You have plans?"

"No, but I don't want to bother you guys." I declined even though I *was* pretty hungry.

"Come on, Betty. As you can see, we have plenty." He lifted the bags, shaking them.

I looked back and forth between Lex and Stuart. If it was just Stuart, I would have accepted the invitation without hesitation, but the look of horror on Lex's face made me think twice. Then again, maybe this was my chance to show him I did actually have manners, and he could stop looking like he wanted to crawl out of his skin when I was around.

"Okay, I'll come over in a bit."

Lex's face turned to disappointment, which almost made me tell them I changed my mind, but I figured with Stuart there as a buffer, it would be fine.

I went back inside and packaged up the rest of my cookies to bring to the guys' house before heading their way.

When I arrived, it was Stuart who let me in. I didn't see Lex anywhere in sight, and the suspicion kicked in that he was avoiding me. The setup of their home was identical to mine, save for the decorations, which they had kept to a minimum.

I noticed they had unboxed the food and had it spread across the table. They had gotten so much that it took up nearly every square inch of the table.

"Wow, it does look amazing," I said, taking a seat. "How much do I owe you for my share?"

"Don't worry about it." Stuart waved me off. "It's on the house."

"Well, in that case, dessert's on me," I said, setting the bag on the table. "Fresh baked cookies, right out of the oven."

"Great. I was worried we weren't going to have enough food," he teased.

He handed me a plate, and I started pulling a little from each container. Lex joined us after a few minutes. He spared me a glance that lasted about as long as a sneeze, and then ignored me completely as he started fixing his plate.

Must have left all my appeal in my other pants.

"So, how was your first day of classes?" I asked Stuart, remembering he had told me he was starting yesterday.

"Bunch of spoiled prima donnas who wouldn't know the difference between optical isomers and enantiomers if it slapped them in the face."

"That's crazy!" I said with a look of indignation. "It couldn't be more obvious. I don't know how they expect you to work like this."

"I KNOW!" he agreed emphatically.

"Maybe you could petition the Department Head. Request a whole new group of students," I suggested.

"You really think I could do that?" he asked sincerely.

"No," Lex answered, giving me a chastising look. I tried hiding my smile while sipping my drink.

Stuart huffed. "Probably would just give me another batch of morons anyway."

"Yeah probably," I said in mock agreement before digging into my food. It was absolute bliss.

I kept sneaking glances over at Lex, who kept the perfect mask of indifference on for the entirety of our dinner. I wondered if he ever got tired of being perpetually aloof. I didn't think Scooby Doo and the mystery gang could even rip the mask off that one.

"So how are you liking California so far?" Stuart asked. "Big change from New York."

"That's an understatement," I said between bites.

"What brought you here in the first place? Sudden urge to meet Arnold Schwarzenegger?"

"My mom," I said, deciding to give them the truth. "We found out she has a rare type of breast cancer and there's a doctor here that specializes in it. He's supposed to be the best there is."

"Are you talking about Dr. Gremillion?" Lex asked.

My eyebrows furrowed. "You know him?" Lex speaking to me at all was shocking enough, but him knowing the name of my mom's doctor nearly had me on the floor next to my jaw.

"Yes," he answered, looking just as surprised. "We did cancer research together many years ago. His specialty was breast cancer. He left to start his own practice. I thought I remembered him saying he was coming to this area."

"I'm sorry, Hadley," Stuart said. "I didn't mean to be flippant." It was odd to see him looking at me so sincerely. I was used to his playful nature.

"I know that. It's okay," I reassured him. "She had her surgery about a month ago. She starts chemo next Tuesday."

Stuart gave me a tight smile. "I hope everything goes well."

I nodded. "Me, too. What do you know about Dr. Gremillion, Lex?"

"He earned his reputation," he answered. "He knows what he's doing. Your mom's in good hands."

"Thank you. That's good to hear." Coming from him, it really meant a lot. If a man as accomplished as Lex thought he was good, then he must be.

I got caught up looking at him from across the table. It felt completely disarming to see that he was actually making eye contact since he usually avoided it. His face didn't hold the same frustrated expression it normally did as he looked back at me. If anything, his eyes seemed almost warm as they swept across my face. The tiniest bit of hope started to bloom in my chest that he might not despise me after all. A loud knock at the door made me jump.

That annoyed expression returned to his face almost immediately as he got up to answer the door.

As he opened it, I saw a woman about my age standing there. She smiled at Lex in a way that could only be described as intimate.

"Hey, I think I left my glasses here the other night," she said, still looking only at Lex.

Her hair was a dark shade of pink, and she was sporting a sleeve of tattoos down her right arm and a septum piercing. Despite her somewhat unconventional appearance, it was clear she was a very beautiful woman.

Stuart groaned loudly, drawing her attention to the two of us. She narrowed her eyes at me, looking like she had suddenly smelled something sour.

"Where do you think you left them?" Lex asked impatiently.

Her expression changed back to friendly almost instantly. "Maybe in the guest bathroom."

"I'll go look," he said.

"Who's this?" she asked as soon as Lex was out of earshot.

"This is Hadley. She's our new neighbor," Stuart answered. "Hadley, this is the pizza burn on the roof of everyone's mouth, a.k.a. Nicky."

Her eyes narrowed. "Either roll a condom over your head, Stuart, or stop acting like a dick."

"Hey, it's nice to meet you," I said, trying to diffuse the spat. "Do you work on Lex's team as well?"

"Something like that," she said dismissively.

Lex re-entered the room, holding the glasses. "Here, I found them."

"Thanks," she responded sweetly. The personality changes were truly impressive. "Can I talk to you outside for a minute?"

He remained silent as he followed her outside.

I turned to Stuart. "Who was that?"

"Nicky Balderas." He said her name as if it left a bad taste in his mouth. "She's Lex's ex and the bane of my existence."

"You don't like her, I take it?"

"Nope. Never have. Never will," he said. "And she does work with us, unfortunately."

"Why'd she say 'something like that' then?"

"Who knows? Probably wanted to seem more important than she actually is. They broke up a year ago, but she still always seems to be hanging around. Always 'forgetting things' at our apartment."

"Why'd they break up?" I couldn't resist asking, even though it was none of my business. I just couldn't imagine someone like Lex in a relationship, but maybe this Nicky was fond of silence.

"I don't really know. When he told me they broke up, I didn't ask questions. Just took him out to celebrate."

"Why don't you like her?" I asked, though I could definitely pick out a few reasons on my own.

"I don't trust her," he said. "I've seen her do and say some pretty nasty things when she thinks Lex isn't looking."

"It must be hard for them to work together," I mused. "Having to see your ex all day, every day... Sounds more than a little complicated."

It definitely gave new meaning to the term "close working relation-ship." I don't think I could pull that off with any of my exes. Well, maybe I could if I came prepared with a muzzle and an oversized stress ball featuring their face.

"He seems fine. But like we told you, he's a workaholic with one train of thought. Not much will distract him in the lab."

Since Stuart was clearly in the mood to gossip, I figured now was as good a time as any to ask the question that had been plaguing my mind for days. "Stuart, can I ask you something?"

"Shoot," he said, shoveling pad Thai in his mouth.

"Does Lex not like me?"

His brows furrowed. "Why would you say that?"

I shrugged. "Just a vibe I get sometimes. Like he really doesn't want me around."

He smiled to himself and continued eating more of his dinner. "That's not it. Trust me," he finally said.

"How do you know?"

"I just do," he replied matter-of-factly. "I promise your presence doesn't bother him."

I really had my doubts about that, despite how confident Stuart seemed to be.

Lex came back inside a few minutes later looking extremely irritated as he sat down, not looking up at either one of us as he began eating.

"This food is delicious," I said, testing out the waters and trying to gauge Lex's mood. "Probably the best Thai I've ever had. How'd you guys find this place?"

"Well, once we heard we were getting the grant, we asked to move into the housing units early. They agreed, so we've been here a couple of months already. We've scoped out pretty much all the great food spots," Stuart said. "Actually, if you're free this weekend, we could show you around town so you could get acquainted as well."

That was a really nice offer. "I'd love to, but I really need to find a car before next week. I was going to go look tomorrow."

"Well, we can take you. Right, Lex?"

"I need to go into the lab this weekend." He still hadn't looked up from his plate.

I made eyes at Stuart as if to say, "See? I told you so." He motioned at me with his free hand, making a face like "I got this."

"Yeah, no problem. Peter has a car, Hadley. We can ask him to take us. I'm sure he wouldn't mind."

"No," Lex said, finally looking up. "I'll take you."

Stuart grinned. "Schedule suddenly clear up there, buddy?"

"No, I just realized I can finish the work next week," he said, getting up from the table and bringing his dishes into the kitchen.

Stuart folded his arms across his chest and gave me a smug "what'd I tell you" look. I shrugged, not convinced that this guy didn't hate my guts.

"It's settled then. Ten a.m. tomorrow?"

"Sure," I agreed, wondering if this was going to be as awkward as it sounded.

Chapter 7

The next day at 10 a.m. on the dot, there was a knock at my door. I was expecting to see Stuart when I pulled it open, but it was only Lex standing there, hands stuffed in his pockets.

"Ready?" he asked. No smile. No hello.

"Yes," I said, looking around behind him. "Where's Stuart?"

"He couldn't make it. Said his IBS was flaring up from all the Thai food."

"Wow, that's…. TMI." I was trying very hard to think of anything else besides Stuart's IBS. "You don't have to bring me, though. I know you said you had work to do. I can just call a taxi or an Uber."

He shrugged. "If you want," he replied noncommittally. "But since I'm already here, we might as well stick to the original plan."'

I scrutinized him for a moment, trying to figure out what his motivations might be, but then I decided I was overthinking it. "Well, thanks. I appreciate it."

I followed him to his vehicle, thinking the whole way that I could still make a run for it. Against my better judgment, I got in the car and just hoped for the best.

"Where are we heading?" he asked.

"I looked up a few places last night. There's a used car dealership called Esteban's Auto Sales on Monterrey that seemed to have a good selection."

He plugged it into his GPS and pulled out on the roadway without another word.

"How's work in the lab going so far?" I asked, casting out the conversational line, hoping to reel in something pleasant.

"Fine."

And with that response, let the awkward games begin.

"What about your classes? Stuart was telling me they're packed."

"Yes, they're full."

Internal sigh.

"So, Strovinski... That's Polish, right?"

"Yes."

And he wins! First place for the most awkward car ride goes to Alexsander Strovinski. The silence seemed to drag on and on until I couldn't take it anymore. I had to do something.

I sucked in a sharp breath. "Ow," I said, clutching at my lower back. "Oww. OWWW!"

"What's wrong?" he asked, startled.

"It's my back. It just started hurting all of a sudden." I massaged the spot. "OUCH!" I called out, putting my hand on the dashboard.

He pulled over onto the side of the road. "Might be a kidney stone. I'll turn around."

"No, that's not it," I said, peeking over at him. "I think it's just hurting from having to carry this whole conversation."

He stopped the car and was staring over at me in disbelief. I couldn't help it. I immediately broke out into laughter.

"That was a terrible joke," he said, but he had a slight smile on his face as he said it.

"Well, it is painful trying to talk to you right now. Like pulling teeth. I promise that despite what you may think, I'm really not that terrible of a person."

His eyebrows pinched together in confusion. "I never said you were."

"Then let's do this... Let's small talk," I said, giving him my warmest smile.

He held my gaze wordlessly for a moment, then sighed. "Okay, you're right. I'm sorry."

As he pulled back out onto the roadway, he began to talk. "Let's see... the lab work is always stressful. Trying to coordinate a team of people, most of whom have become close friends after working together for so long, adds an extra layer of difficulty."

He looked over at me, and I smiled encouragingly at him to continue.

"I've never had to teach classes before, but so far, I'm surprised by how much I'm enjoying it. I'm also grateful that my classes have seemed to garner so much attention. And lastly, my father was from Poland and my mother is from Russia."

It was like he was going down a mental checklist of everything I had asked. It was the longest I'd heard him speak besides the speech he made at faculty night. I decided to go with the last little piece of information he gave in his info dump. I noticed he said his father *was* Polish and his mother *is* Russian.

"Are your parents still living?"

"My mother is, but my father died in a car accident when I was two," he said, confirming my suspicions.

"I'm sorry to hear that. My father died too, when I was eight... Drug overdose."

I didn't tell many people how my father died, so I didn't know why I was sharing. Even though he'd been acting as if I were harboring some highly contagious disease, for some reason, I just innately knew I could trust him. Maybe it was his reserved nature. He was probably holding a lot of people's secrets in that giant brain of his.

"Anyway, he was this larger-than-life guy and an amazing father, but he had his demons."

He looked over at me thoughtfully before speaking. "I don't remember mine."

I studied him. "I'm sure you remember some things."

"No. Episodic memories don't convert to long-term memories until much later in childhood when the hippocampus and frontoparietal regions of the brain are more developed."

Wow. Okay then.

"I just meant that even if you don't have perfect recall of the events from your childhood, it doesn't mean your heart doesn't remember him," I explained. "You might not remember exact details, but I'm sure he still loved you, still held you in his arms. That bond doesn't just go away. My memories of my dad have definitely faded over the years, but I always remember how he made me feel—loved, cherished. There must be something similar for you."

He stared out at the road ahead of us, brow furrowed in concentration.

"I suppose you're right," he finally said. "Though I don't think I feel his absence as acutely as you feel your father's."

I thought he was probably right about that. I was painfully aware of my father's absence from my life and still thought about him almost every single day. I wished I could call him and hear his voice just one more time. More than anything, I wished I had him to lean on, especially now. It might have been a little easier if we were going through this whole thing with my mom together as a family.

If we didn't switch gears soon, I was definitely going to start crying. We were venturing too far away from small talk.

I straightened. "So, how did your family end up in the US?"

"My mother and I moved here when I was ten. My mother's sister left Russia to come to the US a few years before we did. When the conflict in Russia started getting worse, my aunt begged my mom to get out and bring me here."

"Is this the Cher-loving aunt?"

The side of his mouth reluctantly turned up into a half grin. "Yes, that's the one."

"And do you see her here now, Lex?" I asked with my best therapist-like voice.

"HA-HA," he said with an eye roll for good measure. "She's real, I promise. Her name is Polina and she lives in Santa Barbara with her husband Stan."

"Sure, whatever you say." I gave him a doubtful look, and a smile tugged at his expression again. "And you didn't leave until you were ten? That must have been really hard for a ten-year-old," I remarked.

"It was definitely a big adjustment for us."

"Do you still speak Russian?" I asked curiously.

"Konechno."

"I'm going to assume you said yes and not F-off."

He grinned. "I said *of course*." His tone was light with humor. "I really only get to practice with my mother and aunt regularly. Otherwise, I'm sure I would have forgotten it."

"It's crazy that you came here at ten years old but don't seem to have any kind of accent at all."

"Ten-year-olds from Chicago aren't the nicest kids in the world. I had to adapt pretty quickly so I'd stop having my face beaten in."

"I bet." I could only imagine how much he was probably picked on.

"We're here," he announced.

He pulled into the gravel driveway of a parking lot with the sign labeled *Esteban's Auto Sales*. We were approached almost immediately by a salesman in a clean gray suit.

"Hola, amigos!" He greeted us in a thick Spanish accent. "My name is Rodrigo. How can I help you today?"

"I'm looking for a used car," I told him. "I'm not especially picky. Just something reliable and preferably with low mileage."

"I'm sure that we can find you something. What is your name, hermosa?"

"I'm Hadley, and this is Lex."

"Such a beautiful couple. I'm sure we'll find the perfect car for the perfect couple," he said, laying it on thick.

"We're not—" Lex started to say, but I cut him off.

"Thank you. That would be great," I said, looping my arm through Lex's.

We followed behind Rodrigo toward the corner of the lot, and I kept my arm wrapped around Lex's. I tried not to register the warmth of his skin or the curve of his muscles pressed against my nonexistent ones.

"What are you doing?" he asked, low enough so only I heard.

"Just go with it," I whispered. "Men always respond better if they think another man is involved in the purchase of a vehicle. Otherwise, he'll think I'm easy prey."

"Now this one would be perfect for you." Rodrigo stopped and pointed to a gray Nissan Altima. "It's got great gas mileage and is only eight years old."

We both circled the car once before Lex popped the hood open to inspect the engine. I slid into the driver's seat to check out the more important features, like how many cup holders and USB ports there were.

"What do you think, snookums?" I asked Lex, who raised an eyebrow at me but didn't comment on his new nickname.

"Well, there's oil on the engine." He swiped his finger across it, coming up with a black stain. "And the spark plugs look like they're in really bad shape."

I was suddenly really grateful that Lex was here because there wasn't a chance in hell I would have noticed any of that even if I had bothered to pop the hood.

"Oh my! We'll definitely have to have the mechanic take a look," Rodrigo said, trying his best to look shocked but not quite pulling it off.

"Your husband has a good eye," he said. "It is your husband, yes?"

I looked adoringly toward Lex. "Fiancé, actually. We just got engaged last month. Had to get the ring sent off to get resized." I held out my hand and looked longingly at my empty ring finger.

"So lovely," he said. "You are a lucky man, amigo."

He turned to bring us to more vehicles, and I giggled at the dismayed look on Lex's face. He would make a terrible actor.

"Now this one," Rodrigo said, pointing to a midnight blue Chevy Impala. "This one I know has been through a thorough inspection and is in great condition. You wouldn't need to worry about your wife driving this one around. She'd be very safe."

Lex looked at him doubtfully but didn't respond.

"Thank you, Rodrigo," I said. "My sugar bear would just be beside himself if I were to get stranded on the side of the road." I leaned my head against Lex's shoulder, and he went stiff as a board.

"I can assure you this one is perfectly safe, señorita."

We performed the same ritual of Lex looking under the hood while I checked out the interior. I really, really liked this one. I stuck my head out the window ready for the verdict as Lex slammed the hood back down.

"This one looks fine," Lex announced.

I couldn't contain my excitement. "Awesome! Let's take it for a test drive."

Rodrigo clapped his hands together. "Fantástico! I'll get you the keys."

As he left to go get the keys, I told Lex, "Come on, get in."

I ran my hands over the steering wheel and checked out more of the car's gadgets while Lex slid into the passenger seat. Rodrigo came back with the keys and told us the best route to take.

As we buckled our seat belts, Lex turned to me. "Sugar bear?" he asked, obviously still mulling over his new nickname.

I batted my eyelashes at him. "Yes, sweetums?"

He shook his head. "There's no way this guy believes we're a couple."

"No thanks to you. You could try to be a little more convincing there, Strovinski."

He sighed. "Alright, let's just take this thing for a test drive. Hopefully, he's not trying to pass off another lemon on you."

We made the loop around the block and everything seemed fine as far as I could tell. I was still a little nervous there might be something I was missing, so I made Lex switch places with me and drive it the rest of the way back to the dealership.

"Everything seems okay," Lex said as we pulled up. "But maybe you should have a mechanic look at it before you buy it."

"I don't really have time for that. I'd like to have a car before my mom's first chemo appointment so that I can take her."

Something gentled in his expression as he looked over at me. "Okay. But let's check out a few more. And try not to look so excited about this one when we get out."

I gave him a quick salute. "Yes, sir."

"Well, what did you think, my friends?" Rodrigo said as soon as we stepped out of the car.

"We're interested, but we'd like to see a few more," Lex said, answering for "us."

We walked around for twenty more minutes or so and test drove a smaller Honda Civic, but I knew I wanted the Impala.

"Alright, let's go see what kind of deal we can get," Lex told me.

We went inside while Rodrigo gave us his best sales pitch on why we were getting a great deal on the Impala. "And as you can see, this car is in great condition. I spoke with my boss, and the lowest we can go is $6,000."

"That's over what the Blue Book even puts it at," Lex said sharply. "There is no way we're paying that."

Another Hispanic gentleman walked up, having heard the tail end of what Lex had just said.

"Hello, my name is Miguel Diaz. I am the manager here at Esteban's. I saw you guys looking at the blue Impala. A very nice choice."

"Yes, and I was just telling your colleague here that there is no way we are paying $6,000 when the Blue Book lists it at $5,500 in great condition."

"Which it is, I can assure you, sir."

I remained quiet, letting Lex take the lead. I hated this kind of stuff. I probably would have just forked over the six grand. When did he even have time to look up the Blue Book value?

The two gentlemen started speaking Spanish to one another, going back and forth for a few minutes while we waited quietly. When they seemed to be reaching the end of their conversation, Lex all of a sudden jumped in rattling off a stream of full-blown, fluent Spanish.

My head whipped around towards him, my eyes widening as big as an owl's—Any more shocked, and I'd have been hooting. The stunned looks on their faces must have matched mine, and it was absolutely priceless. I felt a swell of affection for Lex in that moment and was beyond grateful for his presence.

Once the manager regained his composure, he smiled ruefully and said, "Okay, best offer is $4,000, and we'll do an oil change and full tune-up. What do you say, my friends?"

I looked at Lex to see if he had any objection, and he tilted his head slightly as if to say it was my call, but he must have thought it was a good deal or else he would have said something.

"Yeah, that sounds great," I said, unable to keep my enthusiasm under wraps.

"Excellent! Let's go get all the paperwork signed."

Lex stayed with me until all the Ts were crossed and the Is dotted. Rodrigo handed me the keys to my new, used car. I'd miss Marge, but I thought Agnes and I were going to get along just fine.

Together, Lex and I walked over to the Impala. Once we were out of earshot, I turned to him and said, "So I guess you speak Spanish, too?"

He smirked. "Didn't I mention?"

I chuckled. "What were they saying?"

"They were just talking about what price they thought the dumb Americans would go for. They settled on $5,000 before I jumped in."

I shook my head, grinning. "That was amazing."

"It was nothing."

I was so filled with gratitude that I threw my arms around him before I had the chance to think about what I was doing. He made an "oof" noise as I hugged him tightly, his arms pinned to his sides.

"Thank you, Lex," I said sincerely. "I mean it. I don't know what I would have done without you today."

He patted me awkwardly on the back before I finally let go and wiped a tear that formed in the corner of my eye. My emotions were hardwired to my tear ducts. I had to stay somewhere between a four and a seven on the emotional scale. Too happy and I'm blubbering. Too sad and I'm sobbing. Couldn't really manage to get embarrassed about it anymore. I just had to go with it as one of the many character flaws I possessed.

"You're welcome. Glad I could help." He put his hands back in his pockets, his cheeks burning a bright shade of red.

"I guess I'll see you later then?" I sounded a little more hopeful than I intended.

"Yeah, see ya," he said before turning and practically sprinting to his car.

I got into my new-used car and continued to wonder all the way home if Dr. Alexsander Strovinski really even liked me at all.

Chapter 8

I was enjoying my third cup of coffee and scribbling down lesson plans for next week's classes the following morning when there was a knock on my door that sounded like "La Cucaracha," so I had a pretty good idea of who I'd find there.

"Mon chéri. Please forgive my absence yesterday. That Thai food performed the second coming of Chernobyl on my intestinal tract," Stuart said, bowing in front of me before handing me a long-stemmed pink rose that looked awfully familiar.

"Stuart," I said, taking the rose from him and bringing it to my nose. "Did you take this from Professor Dunbar's yard?"

"Oh, so what?" he said, making a swatting motion in front of him. "He's got plenty and knows exactly how to grow more."

I chuckled. "Well, thanks."

"As part of my apology for missing yesterday, I'd like to make it up to you and invite you out to lunch today. I can show you around the area like we talked about. There's this amazing Mexican restaurant that I just know you'd love."

"And how would you know that?" I asked.

"Because who doesn't like Mexican food?"

He had a point. "Can't argue with that."

"Great. You want to leave in an hour or so?"

"Yeah, that sounds good." I was already picturing the chips and salsa. "Are your intestines up for Mexican, though?"

"Oh yes. Completely emptied, as a matter of fact."

"Shouldn't have asked," I mumbled to myself. "Is Lex joining us?"

I probably shouldn't have cared, but I was hoping we'd made some progress toward building a friendship, or at the very least, not having him look as if it were a razor-scooter-to-the-ankle type situation whenever I was around.

"I planned on asking him, but I think he's out on one of his runs. If he's back before we leave, I'll see if he wants to come along."

"Alright. I can drive us. I'd like to break in Agnes."

"Agnes?" he asked.

"My new car! She's beautiful, Stuart. I can't wait to show her to you."

"Oh yeah. Lex told me you found a car."

"Yes, and she's pretty great."

"Can't wait to meet her." He smiled, walking down the porch steps.

I got ready for our outing, throwing on a pair of jeans and a plain emerald scoop-neck fitted top that brought out the green in my eyes. I brushed my hair out and gave the ends a slight curl, adding a light amount of makeup. I took a look at myself in the mirror, deciding I looked decent before making my way over to the guys' house.

I knocked a few times on their door and waited until it swung open to reveal a sweaty, shirtless Lex, looking very surprised to see me standing there. He'd obviously just gotten back from his run as he pulled his earbuds out.

"Hey," he greeted, still a little out of breath. Through a valiant effort, I kept my eyes averted from his bare chest, but then I decided YOLO! I gave in and took a quick peek at the smooth planes of his broad chest that had little beads of sweat glistening over perfectly tanned skin. There was a small patch of hair right at the center that I stared at for a few seconds before moving down to his toned abdomen. His body wouldn't be described as ripped but was certainly sculpted enough to make any girl drool.

"What are you doing here?" he asked, snapping me back from my ogling.

"Oh um," I stammered, trying to pull my thoughts out of the gutter and remember what I was doing there. "Stuart asked me to lunch."

Stuart walked up right at that moment, slapping Lex on the back.

"Hey, you made it back. Go hop in the shower. We're heading to La Carreta for lunch."

I held my breath, waiting for his response, unsure if I wanted him to accept or not. He glanced at me for a brief moment before saying, "Give me five minutes."

I relaxed a little as he walked away and realized I needed to get a better grip on my reactions if we were going to be spending more time together.

Stuart invited me inside, and we chatted about our classes before Lex came back down not long after, looking freshly showered and thankfully fully clothed. He was also wearing his glasses, which I found to be quite endearing. I had only seen him in them on faculty night, and I decided they suited his face nicely.

"Alright, let's go meet Agnes," I said to Stuart.

"Who's Agnes?" Lex asked.

"How dare you?" I said, feigning offense. "The two of you met yesterday. How could you forget her so soon?"

"The car, dude," Stuart explained.

"Right," Lex said, probably questioning my sanity as we walked toward the parking lot.

"Here she is!" I announced like a proud mother.

"Nice." Stuart walked around, giving her a once-over. "She looks dependable. Well done, Hadley."

"Oh, it was all Lex," I told him as we all got into the car, Stuart in the passenger seat and Lex in the back.

"Is that so?"

"Yes, you should have seen him!"

I proceeded to regale him with the previous day's events as we drove into town with Stuart interjecting briefly to tell me where I needed to turn. I explained the whole story of how Lex caught that the engine in the first car was leaking oil and then about how they were trying to sell us Agnes at a much higher price.

"...then that's when Lex jumped in, speaking full-blown, perfect Spanish. You should have seen these guys' faces!"

I glanced in the rearview mirror to see Lex sitting quietly, looking out the window with his elbow leaning on the door frame. His fist was resting on his cheek, partially obscuring his face, but I could have sworn I saw a small smile there as I was telling the story.

"And can you even believe that?" I said to Stuart. "The guy speaks three languages. Even I had to pick my jaw up off the floor."

Lex coughed and shifted around in his seat while Stuart grinned like the cat that ate the canary.

"What? What am I missing?"

Stuart cocked his head. "Well, I hate to make Lex's ego any bigger since you already have stars in your eyes, but he actually speaks five languages."

"What?" I asked deadpan, looking at him in the rearview mirror.

"I told you my father was Polish. I used to spend summers with my grandparents. I picked it up from them."

This guy was just full of surprises.

"And the fifth language?"

"Japanese," he answered. "Our team worked on a project there a few years ago."

"Yeah, we lived there for about a year and all I can remember how to say is 'pass the sashimi,'" Stuart said. "Meanwhile, Lex learned to speak fluently within a few months."

"Now I'm just freaked out. Who speaks five languages?" I asked, disgruntled. "Seems to me like you have something to hide, Strovinski. Are you actually a Russian spy sent here to learn government secrets?"

"Actually, now that you mention it, I have heard him say a lot of anti-American things," Stuart said.

I gasped. "Like what?"

"Just the other day, he said he hates watching football."

"NO!" I cried out in mock outrage.

"YES! And I've never once seen him eat a hotdog."

"Well, there you go," I said. "That proves it, Lex... if that's even your real name! We're turning you in."

Lex rolled his eyes. "Knowing five languages does not make me a spy."

"Exactly the kind of thing a spy would say, don't you think, Stuart?"

"A regular Stierlitz if you ask me," Stuart agreed.

"Are you two done? I'm not a spy," Lex said, exasperated.

I narrowed my eyes at him in the rearview mirror. "Prove it! Eat a hot dog and we might believe you."

He made a face of disgust. "I'd rather take my chances getting turned into the government."

I spotted the sign for the restaurant and pulled in while the guys continued to argue.

"I've never seen you eat a hot dog either," Lex accused as we got out of the car.

"That's because I'm Jewish."

"I saw you down three shrimp tacos last Friday."

"Shhhh! My mother can hear you." Stuart whipped his head around, scanning the parking lot. "Way to go, Lex! I just got off the prayer list at my mom's temple and now you're going to get me put back on."

"Your mother lives in Sacramento," Lex pointed out.

"There's a secret Jewish mother's network that they're all tapped into. They hear everything, especially when their sons aren't keeping kosher."

"Alright, let's go eat." I grabbed both their arms, pulling them toward the restaurant. "Lex, we won't make you eat a hotdog, and Stuart we'll say a little prayer that no one in the Jewish community overheard."

"Fine," Stuart huffed. "It's too late anyway. She already knows."

We got seated with Lex sitting next to me and Stuart across the table from us. We were looking over our menus when our waiter came over, stopping at our table and staring at me awkwardly for a few seconds before greeting us.

"Hey guys, my name's Zack. I'll be taking care of you today. Can I get you started with anything to drink?"

"I'll take a water," Stuart said.

"Same for me," Lex added.

"Water's good for me too," I said, rounding things out.

"Great, um, is there anything else I could get you right now?" he asked, only looking at me.

"No, I think we'll look over our menus for a minute," I told him, smiling, and he beamed back at me.

"So, where are you guys from?" he asked, his eyes trained on me.

"New York," I answered even though it seemed unusual for him to ask.

"Wow, I'd love to go there someday," he said, not waiting for the guys to respond.

I nodded. "Yeah, it's pretty great."

"No doubt, no doubt," he said in a California accent, nodding his head and standing there for a few more seconds. "Well, I'll give you guys a minute. I'll be right back with those drinks."

When he finally left, Stuart started to laugh while Lex just stared stone-faced into his menu.

"What's so funny?"

"Did you not witness the same thing we just did?" Stuart asked.

"What? The waiter?" I guess he *was* acting odd.

"Yes, he was practically drooling on your shoes. Did you not notice or are you just used to men swooning and batting their eyelashes at you?"

He was a little off, but I figured people here were just friendlier. "I think he was just nervous. Maybe it's his first day."

"Hadley, we're men. We know these things." Stuart gestured between himself and Lex. "Trust me on this one. Most guys turn into blundering buffoons around beautiful women."

"You two seem fine," I pointed out.

"That's because you're way out of my league, and I've accepted that," he said, placing his hand on his chest. "And Lex has yet to figure out that he's good looking. He has Clark Kent syndrome."

"What's that?"

"He thinks because he wears glasses sometimes, he looks like a totally different person," he explained. "My guy here could pull whoever he wanted, but he never tries because he's usually too busy working to even notice the opposite sex."

"I'm right here," Lex pointed out.

"You sure are, buddy. Now tell her I'm right about the waiter."

"He's right," Lex said before going back to perusing his menu.

Stuart leaned forward. "I bet you any amount of money he's going to try and find a way to ask if you're single."

I leaned forward as well. "You're on." I wanted to take Stuart down a peg and get that smug look off his face.

"Loser pays," he said, extending his hand across the table to me.

"Deal." We shook hands.

Zack, the waiter, came up and gave us our drinks, continuing to focus his attention on me, and I started to get nervous that Stuart might be right.

"So, are you guys ready to order?" he asked (me).

"I'll take the shrimp tacos," Stuart said.

Lex shot him a look of annoyance. "Really?"

"What? All that talk about them made me really want them again."

Lex sighed. "I'll take the chicken fajitas."

"And I'll take the Baja chicken," I said, passing him the menu, not making eye contact.

"Great choice," he said, and I spotted Stuart smirking.

"And how will the checks be divided? Will you and your boyfriend be on one ticket?" he asked, looking between Lex and I.

Ughhh. Really? I snuck a glance over at Lex, who was trying to hide his smirk.

"No, we'll all be on one ticket." I avoided looking in Stuart's direction. "Apparently, it's on me."

At that, they couldn't hold back their laughter. Lex at least had the decency to try and hide it, but Stuart jumped up, laughing triumphantly.

"HA! Thank you, sir." He shook the waiter's hand. "I'll save you the trouble. She's single."

"Stuart!" I chastised. "I'm sorry, Zack. My friend here's an idiot."

"No, he's right. I was trying to see if you were single," he admitted, not ashamed at all. "You're very beautiful. It's hard to look away."

"That's very kind of you to say." I didn't know how else to respond.

"I know you must get that all the time, but I still had to say it. I'll go put in your order."

He walked off, and I continued avoiding looking Stuart's way, but I could see him staring at me with a devilish grin out the corner of my eye.

Stuart folded his hands on the table. "Say it, Hadley."

"Say what?"

"Say that I was right. I need to hear it."

I sighed, admitting defeat. "You were right."

"There it is," he said, drumming his hands on the table.

I rolled my eyes. "You probably embarrassed the hell out of that guy."

"Yeah right. You didn't properly turn him down... 'That's very kind of you to say,'" he said in a girlish voice, trying to mock me. "He still thinks he has a chance. You played nice and now he's coming for your number."

"Oh, come off it," I said, contemplating a kick to his shin.

"You want to go double or nothing?"

"No," I answered quickly, realizing Stuart may actually have some insight into this guy.

"That's what I thought," he said, smirking. "Don't take it too hard, Betty. I took advantage of you. I could tell you were one of those women who's oblivious to how insanely hot they are."

"Thanks, Stuart," I said. "That's sweet in a twisted sort of way."

"Sure, and if you ever feel like lowering your standards and dating down a league, I'm always available."

"I'll keep that in mind."

Lex chose not to comment on our conversation, and mercifully, another server came to drop off our food.

"Oh, it's not over," Stuart said when he saw how relieved I probably looked. "He's definitely coming back for your number."

"You really think he's going to ask?"

"Uhhhh yeah. That's what I've been telling you."

"What should I say?"

"Well, do you want to give him your number?"

"No, but I don't want to embarrass him or hurt his feelings either."

"Then just say whatever you normally tell guys to let them down," he said through a mouth full of shrimp tacos.

"Believe it or not, this doesn't happen to me that often. I'm from New York. No one there tells you you're beautiful and politely asks for your number. Heckling and catcalling are practically an Olympic sport in our state."

He shrugged. "I'm sure you'll think of something."

We finished our lunch, and I realized Stuart was right again—the food was delicious.

Zack dropped off our check without saying anything, and I paid for mine and Stuart's after Lex insisted he had nothing to do with the bet, so he wasn't letting me pay for his. I thought I was home free as we made our way to the exit until Zack stopped me just as we reached the door.

"Hey, could I talk to you for a minute?" he asked.

"We were just leaving," Lex said impatiently, stepping in front of me.

He looked around Lex at me. "It will only take a second."

"Okay," I said, not wanting to be rude.

"Alone?" he asked, eyeing Lex.

Lex didn't budge as he turned his head to me. "I'll stay if you want me to."

"It's fine," I told him, knowing Zack wasn't a threat.

Lex looked at me for a few seconds before turning to glare at Zack as he pushed the door open to leave. Stuart followed behind him, winking at me as he left.

"So, I know you don't know me very well or at all really, but I was hoping we could change that. Maybe you could give me your number, and I could call you sometime." Just as Stuart predicted. I hated that he was right.

"I'm sorry, but I don't think it's a good idea," I said.

"Is it because of that grumpy-looking guy out there?" He nodded toward Lex.

I smiled. "He's not always so grumpy," I said, though the evidence was stacked against him. "But no, that's not it. I'm not really ready to date right now. Thank you, though. I know it's not easy putting yourself out there."

He nodded, accepting defeat. I hated the feeling of disappointing someone.

"Well?" Stuart asked as I walked outside to meet them. "Two for two?"

"Oh, that?" I said, sticking my thumb out toward the restaurant. "He just wanted to make sure I knew I could save 15% by switching to Geico."

"He *so* asked for your number," Stuart said, ignoring my bad joke.

"Where to next?" I asked as we all got into the vehicle.

"Hadley, you are now in the heart of Silicon Valley, and the only true way to appreciate it is with a visit to The Tech Interactive."

"Oh no," Lex mumbled.

"What's that?" I asked curiously.

"I'm glad you asked. It's a science and technology center where you can build robots, explore space, and sit in a jet-pack chair! You can even visit the bio-design studio where they discuss bioengineering and have the distinct pleasure of hearing Lex point out its inadequacies."

"Is it really that bad?" I asked Lex.

"No, it's just that we've been there five times already."

"Each time funner than the last. What do you say, Hadley?"

"Sounds interesting. I'm up for it if you guys are."

"YES!" Stuart yelled. "Lex?"

"Fine," Lex said with a sigh.

Chapter 9

"Where to first?" I asked as we strolled through the front doors of The Tech Interactive.

"Let's hit the robot exhibit," Stuart said excitedly, already heading in that direction as Lex and I followed behind. Lex was looking like the indulgent parent of a toddler.

The exhibit was actually pretty interesting. Stuart, who obviously had an aptitude for it, tried explaining to me the mechanisms behind building a robot and why it was such an important feat of engineering. I could appreciate why it was impressive, but the particulars were completely lost on me.

"Dr. Strovinski?" I heard someone say from behind us. I turned to see a young guy, scrawny and bespectacled, standing there, looking wide-eyed at Lex.

"Yes?" Lex replied politely.

"I thought that was you! Tompkins, get over here. It's him!" he yelled out to another guy hiding behind a column. "You have no idea how thrilled I am to meet you, sir. Your paper on the development of quantitative measurements to distinguish between hypothalamic tanycytes and radial glia literally changed my life!"

"Thanks, man. I appreciate it," Lex said kindly.

The guy named Tompkins ran over, looking like he spotted Mick Jagger himself.

He extended his hand to Lex and introduced himself. "Hi, I'm Robert Tompkins. It's an honor, Dr. Strovinski."

"Lex is fine."

The two men exchanged looks of barely contained excitement.

"And I'm Nathan Segura." He and Lex shook hands as well.

"We heard you were at Stanford now. What are you working on?"

I didn't want to keep eavesdropping on their conversation, so I went to find Stuart, who was arguing with what looked like a ten-year-old about the best way to assemble the robot's arm.

I walked around the exhibit for a little while longer. They had an entire section dedicated to the use of robots in different movies like *Star Wars* and *The Terminator*, and I listened to a short video about the engineering behind it. It may have been interesting if I'd understood a word of it. I circled back to where I started feeling more confused than a cat at a laser show.

I noticed Lex's fan club was still going strong. They were both chatting excitedly while Lex just smiled and nodded along politely. He noticed me looking at him and gave me eyes that said "help, please."

I jumped into action, walking over and interrupting the guy named Tompkins telling Lex about his own paper he was writing.

"Sorry to interrupt, guys. I'm Dr. Strovinski's assistant. We need to get going if we're going to make that meeting," I said, putting my hand under his elbow to usher him away.

"Oh yeah, no problem!" Nathan said, buying my assistant act.

"Nice to meet you, fellas," Lex called over his shoulder as we walked away hurriedly.

"Thank you," Lex whispered as we left the robot exhibit area.

"Anytime," I said.

"I like fake assistant better than fake fiancé," he remarked. "Comes with less pet names."

He caught me off guard, and I paused to stare at him. "Did you just make a joke, Lex?"

He smiled and shrugged. "Happens every now and then."

I laughed out loud, coming to a stop in the hallway when we were out of sight of his admirers.

He looked around behind us. "Wait, where's Stuart?"

"I tried to get him, but he was in the middle of an argument with a preteen about operating a robot."

"Sounds about right," he said, shaking his head. "Anything else you want to check out?"

"The space exhibit sounded interesting."

He pointed down a side hall. "It's this way."

I followed him down the hallway, and as we entered the exhibit, I was immediately captivated.

Large projectors were casting rotating images of the night sky above earth, creating a beautiful simulation of the stars and galaxies. I walked around, taking it all in while Lex followed behind quietly. There was a voice coming from the speaker, giving a history of Earth's creation and different facts about the stars visible in our night sky. It felt humbling to see that we were all just a small, insignificant piece of the puzzle.

I turned to find Lex watching me. I thought he would have looked away quickly, but he continued to stare at me with the lights casting shadows across his face and reflecting in his glasses. His blended parentage gave him such an interesting and beautiful look. His full mouth paired seamlessly with his high cheekbones, and his light brown eyes were so perfectly clear, it was as if you could see all the way to their depths.

"What are you thinking?" he asked softly.

I didn't want to admit that I'd just been admiring him, so I smiled and said, "Just your typical existential wonderments. How did we get here? What does it all mean?"

He gave me a small smile in return.

"It's beautiful, don't you think?" I nodded toward the sky dome.

"Hmmm," he answered noncommittally, pulling his gaze up toward the lights.

"How *do* you think we got here?" I asked. "I mean, do you think it's really all some colossal accident or do you think there's more to it?"

"Are you asking me if I believe in God?"

"Yeah, I guess I am."

"That's hard to answer," he said, pausing to think about it. "Do I think there's a guy in a robe with a long beard and a clipboard taking attendance on Sundays? No. But I don't think we're here by mistake." He looked up toward the artificial sky once more. "Once you study any type of science and learn more about our existence as a species, the less it all makes sense. I tend to think of it more as a question we'll never know the answer to. Kind of like trying to teach a dog calculus. It's not something we'll ever be able to understand, and we're probably not supposed to."

"That's oddly comforting," I told him, still looking up at the stars shimmering above us. "Sometimes when I think about it too much, it scares me. I just want to know that this wasn't the end for my dad. That there was more for him than the life he had here."

"What was he like?" he asked.

"That's the thing... I remember him being so happy and just full of life. He was always laughing. Everyone loved him, and he never met a stranger. It's hard to reconcile the person I remember with the one who was addicted to drugs. But I know he wasn't a bad person."

"Being an addict doesn't make you a bad person. Addiction is truly an illness of the brain just like any other illness. You can take my word for it," he said. "It has nothing to do with who we are as people."

"Thanks, Lex," I said, my voice cracking a bit. Why was it that every time I talked to him, I was on the verge of tears?

"What about your mom? What's she like?" he asked, probably sensing how emotional I was getting talking about my dad.

"She's the absolute best," I told him, smiling. "She never has a bad word to say about anyone. If someone stole her purse, she'd probably say they needed the money more than she did."

Talking about her was likely to bring on the waterworks as well.

"Maybe you could meet her one day if you're not too busy answering fan mail," I said with a wink. "She'd probably have a million questions about your work and your life and then would badger you about why a handsome guy like you is still single."

Just picturing Lex sitting at my mom's dining room table while she pestered him about his love life was enough to make me smile.

"I'd be happy to meet her," he said. "And if the questioning gets to be too much, I'll just have my assistant rescue me again."

I laughed. "If that's the case, your assistant might start asking for a raise."

I never got to hear what he was about to say next, because I spotted his fan club walking through the door. "Crap! Hide!" I said, pushing him down by the shoulders and ducking behind the projectors.

"Let's go this way," I whispered, crouching down and crab-walking toward the door like we were on a military operation.

We burst into the hallway, laughing together at our narrow escape. The sound of his laughter echoed all around me, and I stopped to listen. It was a deep, rumbling sound that already felt familiar even though he rarely used it.

"Close one." I wiped fake sweat off my brow. "Does that happen to you often? People giving you the celebrity treatment?"

"Sometimes," he admitted. "Mostly it's people just wanting to give a kind word to say they admire my work."

I looked at him, wishing he was always this way with me, preferring this to his usual guarded demeanor. As he stared back at me, I watched his eyes rove over every inch of my face. I wanted so badly to know what he was thinking. The silence wasn't overpowering or awkward as it had been in the past. This time it felt like there was subtle contentment moving between us in the stillness of the moment as we stood there taking each other in.

Loud voices carried down the hallway, sounding like they were coming closer.

I cleared my throat. "Should we go find Stuart?"

He gave a slow nod in agreement, his eyes flicking across my face in a way that had my insides squirming. My breathing felt a little tighter as we walked the short distance back to the robot exhibit where we found Stuart still arguing with the young kid.

"You ready to go, buddy?" Lex asked him.

"Not yet. I'm trying to explain to young Billy Pham here why the conductor belongs on this side of the switchboard."

"Okay, but didn't you say you wanted to take Hadley to that ice cream shop on Frontage Road?"

That seemed to pique Stuart's interest. "Blake's?"

"That's the one. You know they close at three."

"Fine," Stuart said, putting down a robot part and getting up to join us. "This isn't over, Pham."

The little boy stuck his tongue out at Stuart as we walked away.

We finally made it to the ice cream shop after listening to Stuart tell us the whole way there why Billy Pham was completely incompetent, and that they probably shouldn't even let kids in there.

I got my usual cookies and cream and was surprised to see Lex ordering rocky road. I would have thought he was a vanilla guy through and through. I was not at all surprised to see Stuart order the cotton candy flavor. It felt like it suited him since no one over the age of eight probably ever ordered that particular one.

We strolled along the boardwalk, eating our ice creams, and I caught myself reveling in the beautiful weather. California was really doing a number on me.

"So, what did you think of The Tech Interactive, Hadley?" Stuart asked as we walked down an alleyway toward a spot that had great views of the bay.

"It was great," I said. "Actually, I was thinking everything about today was great. Thank you both for this. I didn't know how it would be moving to a new city and not knowing anyone, but you guys have really made me feel welcome."

I inevitably started tearing up.

"Are you crying?" Stuart asked, sounding horrified.

"No," I said, sniffling.

"The people in New York must be really bad if all it takes is a little ice cream and you start sobbing like a baby."

I swatted his arm with the back of my hand and turned to look for a garbage can to throw away the rest of the ice cream that I couldn't finish. I cut across the alley when I spotted one on the corner, only to find a rare gem hiding in plain sight.

I squealed and ran straight toward it.

"Ouch! Eardrums, Hadley," Stuart told me, covering his ears.

"Sorry, but look!" I pointed at my discovery.

"Are we looking at the same thing?" Stuart asked, perplexed. "It's a well," he said, pointing out the obvious. "What's so great about a well?"

"Acoustics," I told them, hanging over the side. "Come here."

I gestured for them both to lean over the side with me. They indulged me, leaning over the edge apprehensively.

I was trying to decide what song I wanted to use to demonstrate the sound when a lightbulb went off.

"Do you believe in life after love?" I sang into the abyss and the effect was perfect. My voice echoed around, bouncing off the walls of the well in an eerily beautiful sort of way. "I can feel something inside me saying I really don't think you're strong enough, no."

"Holy shit!" Stuart exclaimed, laughing. "You can fucking sing!"

I thought Lex might laugh or at least crack a smile at the song I'd chosen, but he didn't say a word. He continued staring at me with the tiniest part between his lips.

His gaze was piercing.

"Great song choice." Stuart looked over to Lex. "You know my guy here is a big fan."

"Keep going," Lex finally said in a low voice.

"More Cher tunes?" I asked lightheartedly, trying to distract from the intensity of his gaze.

"Anything," he said.

I leaned over, staring into the well for a few moments, thinking about what I should sing next before looking up into those whiskey-colored eyes. Inspiration hit in the span of a single breath.

I chose "The Scientist" by Coldplay.

I closed my eyes through the beginning, trying to focus on remembering the lyrics. When I was about midway through, I opened them to see Lex's impenetrable gaze was still trained on me. I felt ensnared by those eyes as they burned brightly with an almost overwhelming intensity. I continued to sing the heartbreaking words, unable to look away. We may as well have been the only two people there as the outside world seemed to fade away.

When I finished the last note, I heard clapping coming from behind us, breaking the spell.

"You drew a crowd, Hadley," Stuart said, looking over his shoulder. "We should have put a cup out to try and get tips."

"Yeah, we probably could have made a whole three bucks," I said, walking toward the bay, trying to shake off the odd feeling I was having. I was always comfortable singing in front of people so I don't know why this time just felt different.

We spent another hour walking along the bayside, checking out the local shops, and admiring the view. Lex didn't say much the rest of the afternoon or even look my way, really.

I hated that I noticed.

Luckily, Stuart was great at filling the void in the conversation department. He chatted happily, and I chimed in enough to keep the conversation going. I wondered if that's how they maintained such a great friendship over the years. Their personalities were so different. Complete opposites really, but it seemed to work for them.

We made it back home in the late evening, and I thanked them again for such a great afternoon.

"Let's do it again," Stuart said. "You didn't even get to see half of what The Tech Interactive has to offer."

"And whose fault is that?" I accused.

"Billy Pham's."

I smirked at him and rolled my eyes, but my attention quickly shifted to a tall, bearded man approaching us. He was dressed in dark jeans and a black Henley, the sleeves pushed up to reveal an array of tattoos on his forearms.

He was smiling with his gaze focused on Lex.

Lex turned to see what I was looking at before his face broke out into a wide grin.

"Merrick?" His tone was full of surprise.

"Strovinski!" he responded, laughing as the two embraced. Did the whole town of Stanford know who Lex was?

"What are you doing here?" Lex asked.

"I'm living in San Francisco now. There was talk of some world-renowned neurobiologist who came to work at Stanford. I knew it could only be one person, so I thought I'd look you up," he said. "What have you been up to, man?"

"Working."

He shook his head. "Same old Lex." That's when he noticed Stuart and I standing there.

"Introduce me to your friends," he said with his eyes locked on me.

"This is my roommate and coworker, Stuart Benowitz," Lex said, and they shook hands.

Lex's eyes then turned to me reluctantly. "And this is Hadley Olivier, a music composition professor here at Stanford and our neighbor."

"Nice to meet you," I said politely, shaking his hand. He was even taller than I first thought. At least six-foot-four, with dark brown hair and hazel eyes. He was definitely good looking, and he knew it.

"Merrick Callahan," he introduced himself. "Lex and I grew up together."

"Is that so?" I grinned mischievously at Lex. "I bet you have some pretty embarrassing stories then."

"You bet I do. Maybe we can get together sometime, and I'll tell you about the time Lex found out it was 'a blessing in disguise' and not 'a blessing in the skies' in front of the whole fifth grade class."

Merrick laughed, and Lex rolled his eyes, smiling.

"You have plans, Merrick?" Lex asked. "Can you stay for dinner?"

"I'd love to... Hadley, will you be joining us?" he asked with that confident smile.

"No, I think you two need some time to catch up. Maybe another time. Thanks again, guys," I said, waving and walking toward my house.

"Later, Betty," Stuart called after me.

A flush crept its way up my neck when I made it to the foot of my porch. I dared a glance over my shoulder, instinctively knowing what I'd find. Lex's steady gaze was following me up the steps of my porch, all the way into my home.

Chapter 10

I met Lionel and Sarah for coffee Monday morning before our classes that day. Lionel had texted that he wanted to meet to tell us a crazy story that just couldn't wait until later. We ordered our coffees and sat down before Lionel launched into the tale.

"So, I go to meet up with this guy Saturday night that I've been chatting with for almost a month on The LuPone Zone"—which was apparently a dating app for die-hard Patti LuPone fans—"and he seemed perfect. We love all things musical theatre, we detest Lea Michele, and we both listed brunching as our favorite hobby."

"Clearly soul-mate level status," Sarah said, sarcasm front and center. "Continue."

"Anyway," he said, giving her the side eye. "He messaged me to say he had made it to Café JoJo's and was sitting in the corner booth. I arrived fashionably late, only to walk in and see a student from my Sound Engineering class—sixth row, great biceps—sitting in said corner booth."

"What?" I gasped.

"Yes! He was looking down at his phone, so I hightailed it out of there before he spotted me."

"So you ditched him?" Sarah asked.

"You bet your ass I did. Daddy can't afford a lawsuit. I'm still paying off those Julliard loans from way back when I was going to be the next

Baryshnikov," he said, pointing his nose in the air. "All that got me was a couple hundred grand in debt... that and really great calves."

"How did you not recognize him before that?" I asked.

"His profile was a shirtless pic. I didn't pay much attention past his pecs. I knew those biceps looked familiar though..."

Sarah shook her head. "Why am I not surprised?"

Lionel responded by flipping her the bird.

"Also, how did he not recognize his own teacher?" I asked. "Didn't you have your picture on there?"

He grinned sheepishly. "I may have put a *slightly* older photo on there."

"How much older?" Sarah asked, her eyes narrowing.

"Let's just say we both had our most recent college photos as our profile pictures."

Sarah made a *tsk-tsk* noise. "Patti would be ashamed."

"Patti got me into this mess in the first place. I should have just stuck with Queeries."

"You're still on Queeries? Isn't that the app that lets you give your date a bedroom rating afterward?"

"Yes," he answered, taking a sip of his coffee. "But I never pass up an opportunity to hurt my own feelings."

"Why won't you let me set you up with my friend, Mitch?" she asked.

"Because if I go on one more terrible blind date, I'll be headed for a grippy sock vacation," he said to her. "Besides, you lost your setting-up privileges with baby-talk Mike."

"Mike's not that bad," she said without any conviction behind it.

"I showed you the text messages. Are you going to deny that you saw the words 'sowwy' and 'pwease' typed out and sent by a grown-ass man?"

Sarah didn't deny it, and I was sure I had a disturbed look on my face. *Ick.*

"Exactly," Lionel said. "But while we're talking about it, I think you should try getting on a dating app, Ms. Samaha. You've been single for almost two years now, and you've gone on like three dates."

"No, thanks," Sarah said. "The only dating app I plan on using is my calendar."

"How are you ever going to meet anyone? You stayed in your pajamas all weekend and watched The Bachelor."

"Food Network, actually," she corrected. "And I'm just in a dry spell. But it's not enough to get me on an app where I might accidentally get set up with a student."

"Two years isn't a dry spell. That's a drought. The Native Americans are going to start doing rain dances around your lady garden."

"Gross." Sarah scrunched her face. "Can we talk about something else? Hadley, what'd you do this weekend?"

Aw, crap. She had shifted the hot seat over to me.

I didn't want to confess I'd been hanging out with the guys, because I knew they'd turn it into something it wasn't. Maybe I could skirt around the truth.

"A couple of my neighbors helped me get a new car on Saturday because my old one finally crapped out. Then we went to lunch on Sunday and walked around the city a bit."

"Don't you live in the faculty housing?" Lionel asked. "What neighbors did you go with?"

Busted.

"One of the chemistry professors, Stuart Benowitz. And the other one you already know, Alexsander Strovinski."

"Don't try acting all formal now, missy," Sarah teased. "She was calling him *Lex* just a few days ago."

"Wait, are we talking about the hottie who gave the commencement speech at faculty night? Benson's new show pony?" Lionel asked.

"Yep, that's him. And he *asked* me to call him Lex," I said huffily, wrinkling my nose at her. "Anyway, they're nice guys. We went to eat at this really great Mexican restaurant, La Carretta. We should go for margaritas one night. It didn't feel right getting one at noon on a Sunday."

"It's never *not* the right time for margaritas," Lionel replied. "But that's beside the point. Tell us more about this poly date you went on."

"It wasn't a date. They were just being nice, showing me around town. We're friends." *I think.*

Sarah and Lionel exchanged "yeah right" looks.

"Wake up, Chita Rivera," Lionel said, snapping his fingers at me. "They're definitely trying to get in your pants."

"No, they aren't," I said, dismissing the notion completely. "I mean, Stuart's always over the top with the flirting, but you can't take him seriously. And Lex barely manages to tolerate me most of the time."

I looked to Sarah for backup.

"I'm with Lionel on this one," she said. "You're right about Benowitz, but there's no way two straight guys are carting you around town 'just to be nice.'"

"Maybe we're completely missing the point, Sarah," Lionel interjected. "I don't know about this Stuart fellow, but Dr. Tall, Dark, and Brooding could definitely get it. Maybe our friend here *wants* him to find his way into her panties."

"I gotta get to class," I said, looking down at my watch to see if it really was time for me to go.

"Ooooooo," they chanted together. "I think she does!"

I rolled my eyes. "Can we go back to talking about how Lionel might be a borderline criminal?"

"Hey! All parties involved were over the age of eighteen!" he shouted indignantly.

"How can you be sure? I hear people misrepresent their real age all the time on those apps." I gave him a pointed look.

"Don't you have to get to class?" he said, narrowing his eyes at me.

"Sure do," I replied. I checked the time again and realized I did have to get going. "See you guys later. And don't talk about me when I leave."

"We definitely will," Lionel called out after me.

I underestimated just how long it would take me to get across campus to my classroom at Braun Music Center. I made it to class with only a few minutes to spare and most of the students were already seated.

Once I finally caught my breath from rushing over, I looked around the room and smiled. "So, who wants to go first this week?"

The group project I had assigned was going really well so far. It had been just the thing I needed to engage them in the lessons and had the unexpected benefit of helping me reconnect with composing again. I had essentially stopped writing since my mom's diagnosis. All my guitars and journals had been sitting abandoned in the spare bedroom since I first moved here. I only recently picked them back up again, feeling little sparks of creativity that I hadn't felt in a long time.

I spotted a red-headed girl who couldn't have been older than twenty tentatively raising her hand.

"Ms. Kennedy, right?" I knew she was the music major in her partnership because she was also in one of Sarah's classes. Sarah had told me she was an incredible violinist.

"Yes, that's right," she said shyly.

"Who's your partner?" I asked.

Another young female, who was so small I could barely see her seated behind the taller gentleman in front of her, stood up.

"What's your name?" I asked her.

"Maya Chen," she said.

"What's your major, Maya?"

"Nursing," she answered.

"Wow. That's amazing," I said. "One speck of blood and I'd be on the floor."

She smiled and stood a little more proudly.

"Show me what you guys came up with." I gestured to the board.

They made their way to the board and wrote out the loose structure of a 32-bar form. I was genuinely impressed by their composition, especially since half the group couldn't even decipher musical notations. I sat at the piano and played the first two A-sections and discussed how they could clean up the second half of the song.

"Overall, very nice, ladies! It has a little Jerry Lee Lewis thing going for it," I told them.

"Who's that?" Maya asked with a puzzled expression.

I clutched my chest like I was injured. "Maya, thank god you're a nurse. I may need medical attention after the way my spirit was just crushed harder than the 'I' in Pixar."

She giggled, and I started playing the one Jerry Lee Lewis song most people knew, "Great Balls of Fire."

"Oh yeah," she said. "I do know that one. My dad likes all that old stuff too."

I gave her a deadpan look. "Anddddd that'll do it for team Kennedy and Chen." I shuffled them back to their seats.

Maya continued to giggle. "I didn't mean it like that, Ms. Olivier."

"Huh? What was that?" I said loudly, cupping my ear. "You'll have to speak up. I don't have my hearing aids in."

They were both chuckling as they made their way back to their seats. I was about to call for my next set of volunteers when I saw John-Luke raising his hand with a mischievous grin on his face.

"Ms. Olivier?" he called out. *Internal sigh.* What was he up to? "Is it true you know Phoebe Bridgers?"

I could tell he was working some angle, and that this wasn't just genuine curiosity. I hesitated to answer, knowing the other shoe would eventually drop.

"Yes, it's true," I confirmed when excited murmurs broke out. "I helped write a few songs on her last album."

I could see his faithful lackeys gearing up for the joke to come. "You think you could give her my number? I think we'd really hit it off," he said, bravado on full display.

There was that other shoe. "And what makes you think that?" I asked, flexing my sarcastic muscle.

"My dad and I bumped into her at a restaurant in LA once. He told her I was in law school, and she said she could always use a good lawyer. I think she was giving me the green light, Teach. What do you think?"

"I think that's a bigger stretch than MJ's arm at the end of Space Jam. Now, you and your partner come up here and show me what you've been working on."

He grinned wider than the Cheshire cat as he and his partner made their way to the board. Their composition was actually decent, but I hurried to give them their feedback to avoid any more flare-ups.

When class finally wrapped, some of the students stopped to thank me and asked a few more questions about my work with Phoebe. Despite John-Luke's continued attempts to distract me, I still felt really content about the day as I drove home. It was the first time I considered the possibility that I might actually be able to pull off this teaching thing.

"You have all the paperwork Dr. Gremillion gave you, right?" I asked my mom when I called to check in on her later that evening. She had an appointment first thing in the morning, so I wanted to be prepared.

"What paperwork?"

"Mom…"

"Just kidding. Lighten up, kiddo. It's just a little chemo."

I sighed. I was glad she was feeling so lighthearted about the whole thing, but I was feeling more anxious than ever, not that I wanted her to know that.

"I can't wait to show you Agnes," I said. "She has a lot of character."

"If she's anything like her namesake, I'm sure we'll get along splendidly." Agnes was the name of her eldest sister, who passed away a few years ago, but they were always extremely close.

"I'll be there first thing in the morning, okay?"

"For what?" she teased.

"Good one," I said, eye roll implied. "See you tomorrow. Love you, Mom."

"Love you too, baby girl."

I tossed and turned all night, unable to get even a few minutes of sleep. Statistics, survival rate numbers, and every other daunting fact about my mom's prognosis were on a continuous reel running through my mind. The 65% five-year survival rate was the number that seemed to stick out the most. Was she destined to be a part of the other 35%? I pushed the thought away before I worked myself up into a full-blown panic attack. I decided I might as well get out of bed since sleep eluded me.

I looked at the clock to see I had plenty of time to get coffee and breakfast before heading to my mom's. I walked outside to find it was still pretty dark out, the sunlight barely peeking out over the horizon. I crossed the street and saw a figure in the distance jogging toward me, and I thought I recognized the silhouette.

It seemed pretty early to be out, but I guess I wasn't one to talk. As the figure came closer, there was no mistaking who it was. I waved at Lex when I thought he spotted me, but he crossed the street and continued up a different path. I guess he didn't see me, or the more insulting but also more likely scenario was that he did see me and ignored me anyway. I didn't have the energy to decipher Strovinski's behavior today, so I moved on without giving it another thought.

Chapter 11

Pulling into my mom's driveway, I made a mental note to call a landscape company to take care of her yard when I saw how long her grass had gotten. She would never admit to me that her illness was making her more tired, but I could hear in her voice some days how drained she sounded. I had a spare key so I let myself in, carrying the coffee in the crook of my arm and the bagels in the other.

"Mom?" I called out for her. "I'm here."

"Hi sweetheart," she said, rounding the corner of the hallway.

"What did you bring?" she asked, noticing my hands full.

"I stopped at that little café on the corner. They had a great selection. I got you some coffee and bagels."

"I'll have to check it out. Thank you."

"No problem. Let's eat and head out. I don't want to be late," I said, buzzing with nervous energy.

"We have plenty of time," she said. "Sit down and talk to me for a few minutes and let me enjoy my breakfast."

I checked my watch and decided we did have a few minutes to spare.

"How are you settling in to the new house?" I swirled my coffee around anxiously.

"It's been great. I have the friendliest neighbors. There's a gentleman a few houses down from me. His name's Carl Howser. He's been helping me get some things put up around the house. He hung those pictures on the wall over there and even got the TV mounted in the bedroom. He used to be a history professor at Stanford, but he's retired now. I told him all about you and how you had just gotten a job there. He's a widower too."

"Oh yeah? What's this Carl look like, Mom?" I wiggled my eyebrows at her.

"Oh, stop that," she said. "He was just being neighborly."

I couldn't help but notice the similarities between this conversation and the one I'd had yesterday with Lionel and Sarah. My mom and I each having the same response—denying these men had any interest in us.

"Well, what's so wrong with that anyway? I don't think I remember ever seeing you go on a single date after Daddy died."

"I went on dates. Just nothing that ever stuck, that's why you never knew anything about it. Besides, Daddy was the love of my life. It doesn't feel right to even try when you've experienced a love that big."

"You still miss him?" I asked.

"Every day," she said solemnly while sipping her coffee.

"Me, too," I admitted. "I've been thinking about him a lot lately."

I wanted to ask her something that had been on my mind but didn't want to upset her before her appointment.

"What is it?" she asked, picking up on my hesitancy.

I knew she'd know if I was holding back, so I gave in and asked what I'd been wondering. "Does it ever bother you the way he died? I mean, did his addiction ever come between you or did you not know?"

I couldn't believe we'd never talked about this before. We shared everything about our lives, but we often tiptoed around anything related to my father, especially about his death.

"I knew," she admitted. "He was pretty good at hiding it. Mostly because he never did drugs around you. He was always straight as an arrow when it came to you. I thought he kicked it completely after you were born."

"But did it bother you?" I asked because she didn't fully answer my question.

"Everyone has their demons." She looked out toward the window like she was getting lost in her memories. "For a while after he died, I would lie awake at night wondering why we weren't enough, why he didn't love either of us enough to stop. But then I realized that was foolish. He showed me he loved me in so many ways, and I knew he hated that part of himself that felt pulled to his addiction. That terrible compulsion was a part of him, but it didn't define him. He was an addict, but he was also all the wonderful things you remember—funny, compassionate, loving, and he had the kindest heart. He would take the shirt off his back for any stranger. He made me want to be a better person, and I loved him for who he was. All of him, good and bad."

I could feel my emotions bubbling to the surface, lingering in my throat. We hadn't talked about him in so long.

"That's mostly what I've been thinking about... How the person I remember feels nothing like the kind of person who would abandon his family to get high."

"It's only natural to think about these things. You're about the age he was when he passed. But he didn't abandon us. He was sick and couldn't find his way to a cure."

That reminded me of what Lex had told me—that it was truly an illness of the brain.

"Don't let it darken your memories of him. He was every bit the wonderful man you remember. And there was no one he loved more than you."

And it still wasn't enough, I thought. I didn't want to say it out loud and upset her, so I did something I rarely ever did—I lied to my mom.

"You're right. Thanks, Mom."

She smiled, but it didn't reach her eyes, which gave me the distinct feeling that she knew I was placating her.

"We better get going," I said. "We don't want to be late."

"Sure. Let me grab all that paperwork you've been fussing about."

When she came back with the thick manila envelope full of all her bloodwork, scans, and doctor's notes, we headed out the door.

Walking through the glass atrium of the cancer center, I looked around at the building that would be a fixture in our lives for the foreseeable future. It was a busy area, completely surrounded by windows, and had a glass ceiling that let in the sunlight, giving it a warm and inviting appearance. Even so, I didn't think anyone could forget why they were here, no matter how pleasing the design.

We got into the elevators, pressing the button for the third floor. The doors opened to reveal a large room with individual suites sectioned off along the walls. Each suite contained a large recliner, a second chair for guests, and televisions at each station. There were several people already at various stations receiving their infusions.

An elderly woman greeted us as we walked up to the desk. "Can I help you?"

"Yes, I'm Gail Olivier. I'm here for my first treatment."

"Yes, I've got your information right here. You'll be at station nine, right over there." She pointed to a suite in the corner of the room. "I'll need your paperwork from the doctor, and I'll also need you to fill out a few forms."

"I'll take care of that," I said, giving the envelope to the desk clerk. "Mom, why don't you go take a seat while I finish this up."

"Alright," she agreed, making her way over to suite nine. I finished filling out the forms, knowing my mom would have gotten me to do it anyway. She was way too impatient for that kind of stuff.

When I got to my mom's suite, I noticed she had already managed to make friends with the people at station ten.

"Hadley, this is Mary and her husband Phil," she told me as soon as I walked up.

"Nice to meet you." I smiled at the elderly couple, both with graying hair. They appeared to be in their late 70s with Phil sitting close to Mary's side, holding her hand.

"Mary has breast cancer just like me, Hadley. This is her third week of treatment. She's seeing a different doctor than me, though."

Leave it to my mom to already know this woman's life story in the five minutes I was gone. It used to embarrass me how forward she was with people, but I eventually embraced it when I realized she was willing to give as much as she took. She'd always been an open book and was surprised when anyone else wasn't the same way.

"How have your treatments been so far?" I asked Mary.

"Not too bad. It tires me out for a few days after. I'll start to find my strength again, but then it's time for another treatment. Small price to pay, I suppose."

"My Mary's a fighter. She's going to be just fine," her husband Phil said, taking her hands and bringing them to his lips, planting a kiss on her knuckles. The gesture was so sweet and his adoration shined brightly.

The nurse walked up at that moment and introduced herself. "Hi, Ms. Olivier. My name's Amber. I'll be your nurse today."

"Hi, Amber. It's nice to meet you. This is my daughter, Hadley." She and I exchanged greetings before she began opening a kit at the bedside table.

"So, I'll start your IV and go over some information about the treatment you're receiving," she said, putting on a pair of gloves. "The infusion will last about two hours, and I'll be with you through most of it. But some things to look out for will be bleeding around your gums, soreness or ulcers in your mouth, nausea, fever, or trouble breathing. Let me know immediately if you start to experience any of these symptoms. You can expect to be tired afterward and probably won't have the best appetite. You may also start to have hair loss after a few treatments."

She explained all of this while starting Mom's IV. The doctor had already gone over most of this with us at her last visit, so we felt prepared.

"Do you have any questions before we get started?"

"No, I don't think so," Mom said, looking to me. I shook my head.

The nurse came back after a few minutes covered with a biohazard gown, face shield, and heavy-looking gloves.

She started the infusion pump, and we looked on, not saying a word. I think it all became a little more real for both of us, watching the bright red medication slowly drip into her veins.

"Where are you from, Nurse Amber?" my mom asked, probably needing a distraction. She loved gathering the details of the lives of everyone she met.

"Minnesota," she answered, taking down some information in Mom's chart.

"Wow, that's a pretty big change. What brought you here to California?"

She paused for a moment before sighing. "A guy."

The three of us laughed together, appreciating her candor.

"It always is," my mom said. "In fact, that's how I ended up in New York. My James was a musician, and he was so passionate about it. I moved to New York so we could be together, and I've been there ever since. Well, up until a month ago."

I'd heard the story of how they met several times over the years. My dad was a folk singer and was in my mom's hometown for a gig filling in for another band that had cancelled last minute. She followed her sister out to a bar that night and the rest was history. They fell madly in love that same night, and she left with him to go to New York the next week.

"Well, my story doesn't have as happy an ending. He dumped me less than two months after I moved here," Nurse Amber said.

"You didn't think about moving back home?" I asked.

"I thought about it, but I ended up falling in love with California. If I'm being honest, I really hate the snow," she said, and we laughed at the irony. "I do miss the Swedish meatballs, though. They're hard to come by here."

"Everything happens for a reason. I wasn't even planning to go out the night I met James, but my sister begged me," my mom told her. "Trust me, you're exactly where you're supposed to be."

"Thanks, Ms. Olivier," she said, her shoulders softening.

My mom smiled at her reassuringly. She stayed with us for the first thirty minutes before leaving to check on another patient.

Mom turned her head and gave me the same reassuring smile she'd given Nurse Amber. It was the teacher in her. She had taught sixth grade at Valman Elementary for almost thirty years before she retired a few years ago. I could still spot those nurturing mannerisms she once used on her students now subtly resurfacing in her interactions with everyone else.

"I'm sorry I couldn't go car shopping with you," she said. "I hate to think of you going out into the city all alone."

"I didn't go alone," I told her. "Lex came with me. We went to lunch the next day at this really great Mexican place."

"How wonderful! It's about time you went on a date since you dumped old stick-in-the-mud Gary."

"His name's Garrett," I said, giving her a dry look. She just smiled, knowing exactly what his name was. "And it wasn't a date. His roommate came with us. We went to a museum and walked around the city."

"I thought you said Lex didn't like you. Has something changed? Did he finally come to his senses?" she asked.

"Not really," I said with a half-shrug. "I think he might be tolerating me a little better now."

She was about to say something when a look of slight discomfort came across her face.

"What is it?" I asked.

"Nothing. I'm fine," she said. But then she closed her eyes and squirmed in her seat a little.

"Mom, tell me," I pressed.

"I'm just a little queasy is all."

I shot up out of my seat and walked over to the nurse's station to let her know.

"She's going to get some medicine for you," I said, sitting back down next to her, taking her hand, and rubbing my thumb over the back of it.

Nurse Amber came back and hung a bag of medicine, hooking it up to mom's IV. "This should start working soon," she said, and I thanked her.

My mom kept her eyes closed, probably trying to stave off the nausea.

"What can I do?" I asked helplessly.

"Sing one of my favorites," she said in a quiet voice without opening her eyes.

I used to do that all the time for her when I was a kid when she was feeling sad or ill. She always said it made her feel better. I thought about it for a second and decided on "Moon River" from *Breakfast at Tiffany's*.

I started to sing softly, pulling my chair closer to hers and stroking her hand. She kept her eyes closed, but the tension around them seemed to slowly dissolve after a few minutes. When I finished "Moon River," I went straight into "Let It Be" by the Beatles. She opened her eyes midway through and watched me finish out the song.

"Better?" I asked.

"I should say no so you keep going, but yes. It's much better."

"Good," I told her, smiling.

"That was lovely, dear," I heard Mary say next to us.

"You have a beautiful voice," her husband added. "Next time a little louder, please. We're not spring chickens over here." He winked and I smiled at them, nodding in agreement, even though I was hoping there wouldn't be a next time.

I continued to watch her closely for the rest of the infusion, looking for any other side effects, but nothing else happened as she chatted happily with our neighbors. When it was finished, we said goodbye to Mary and Phil and walked down to the lobby.

I didn't know what I was expecting to find as I looked her over. She didn't appear any different as far as I could tell, maybe a little tired, but nothing that seemed overtly worrisome. She didn't say much as I drove back to her house, and I kept glancing over at her.

"Stop doing that," she said a few minutes into the drive.

"What?"

"You keep staring at me," she complained. "You look like that kid that was always popping up behind Helga Pataki."

"Maybe I'm waiting for you to hand over your chewing gum so I can finish my closet shrine."

"Is that why you won't let me go anywhere near your closet?"

"No, it's because you steal all my shit."

"What have I stolen?" she said, putting on an air of offense.

"How about that pink Banana Republic sweater?" I accused. "Not only was it stolen, but it was also damaged. Forensics concluded that it was pizza sauce. I should have you charged with theft and vandalism."

"I would get off on a technicality because you didn't get your facts straight. It was actually spaghetti sauce," she said as we pulled into the driveway.

I chuckled lightly. "What about the confession you just made?"

"Coerced. No jury would convict. Especially not after seeing how pitiful I look after my first round of chemo."

"You'd play the cancer card?"

She shrugged. "Whatever it takes."

I walked her inside, and the fatigue was now plainly evident on her face. "Go rest, I'll have something for you to eat when you wake up. I'm thinking spaghetti as a form of retribution." I heard her laugh softly as she headed to the bedroom.

I tidied up the house and made a few meals for her that were easy to reheat so she didn't have to cook. She was still sleeping when I was finished, so I went and sat with her while she slept.

When she finally woke a few hours later, I closed the book I was reading and sat on the side of the bed to look her over.

"You're getting dangerously close to Forrest-Gump-level obsessed with your mom," she said, yawning.

"But you're my best good friend," I said, trying out my best Gump impression and patting her arm.

"Hadley, while I appreciate your concern, they told us it would be normal for me to feel tired afterward. You can't stay and watch me sleep after every single treatment. Besides, you need to get going, you have classes in the morning."

I could tell by the look on her face that she was resolute, so I didn't argue. "Okay, I have some food in the refrigerator for you if you get hungry."

"Thank you. I'll be fine."

I kissed her on the cheek. "I'll call you later to check on you."

I got in my car, and the tears started to fall before I made it out the driveway. My mom was always so vibrant and stoic. It was hard for me to see her suffering. I allowed myself a few more minutes of sadness before I resolved to do better. I vowed to never let her see me this way. I would be a source of strength for her as she had always been for me.

Chapter 12

I was pretty sure the daylilies and snapdragons sprouting from my garden weren't there when I left for work this morning. I smiled to myself, thinking I would have to make something really special to thank Professor Dunbar for this, when I heard, "Psssst, Hadley!" coming from behind me.

It was Stuart, running up the sidewalk from his front porch. "Hadley!" he called out, still trying to whisper.

"Why are we whispering?" I asked, matching his tone when he reached me.

"I was trying to catch you without the guys hearing me."

"What guys?" I asked, looking around.

"Lex and Merrick. They're inside right now. We're all about to have dinner, and I need you to come over."

"Why?" I asked, turning my key in the door as he grabbed a couple of the grocery bags I was carrying and helped me inside with them.

"Because I can't sit through another dinner with that guy, and you'll be the perfect distraction."

"Gee, thanks," I said. "What's wrong with him?"

"He's a grade-A asshole, but as usual, Lex doesn't see it."

"What do you mean?"

"The guy sort of looked out for Lex when he first moved here from Russia and stopped the other kids from picking on him. So, I guess he feels like he still owes him loyalty or something. But I'm telling you, he's a prick."

"Is there any chance you're wrong about him?" I asked, wanting to give him the benefit of the doubt.

"I don't think so. He keeps calling me Stuey and tousling my hair like I'm a member of the Rugrats."

I chuckled. "Maybe you should give him a chance. He's obviously important to Lex."

"I'm trying. I agreed to have dinner with them again even after I sat through the first one with him talking incessantly about how he was a star lacrosse player in college. Then he proceeded to explain the rules of lacrosse to me."

"Well, did you know the rules?"

"No, but it somehow felt anti-Semitic when he did it."

I laughed and continued putting away my groceries.

"Please, Hadley. Please please please please please…"

"Fine," I said to get the begging to stop. "Let me go change."

"Yes! Thank you! They think I'm taking out the trash, so I'll just say I bumped into you, and you begged and pleaded to come over for dinner, and I couldn't say no."

"Don't you dare," I threatened.

"Fine. I'll just say that I saw you going out to dinner all alone and being the kindhearted soul that I am, I took pity on you and invited you over."

"Or you could just tell them the truth. You stalked me and then begged me to come over, so you didn't have to third wheel."

"My version's better," he said, rushing out the door. "See you in a bit. And don't take too long."

I blew out an exasperated breath before heading upstairs to change into something more casual than my work clothes. Being in the classroom today really helped pull me out of the funk I'd been in when the day started.

I had called to check on my mom a few more times after I left yesterday and then again this morning. She insisted she was fine, and she honestly sounded better, but I still felt unsettled.

Teaching served as a great distraction from worrying so much, and my mood improved dramatically by the end of the day. That was probably a good thing for Stuart, because otherwise, I don't think I would have agreed to go over and be a dinner distraction. I wondered if he was right about Merrick. Stuart had a flair for the dramatics, but he also had a knack for seeing people's true colors.

I finished putting away the last of my groceries before heading to the guys' house. I had barely knocked once on the door before it swung open with Stuart standing there to greet me.

"Hadley! Come on in. Glad I caught you before you went out and wasted all your hard-earned money when we have plenty of food for you here."

"Subtle," I muttered to him as I walked through the door.

I didn't see Lex anywhere, but Merrick got up from his chair at the table and walked over to me with a huge grin on his face.

"Nice to see you again, Hadley," he practically purred at me.

"Yeah, you too. I hope I'm not interrupting guy's night."

"No, we're glad to have you. If I'd have known Lex had such beautiful neighbors, I would have invited myself over sooner."

"Hope you're hungry, Hadley," Stuart said, saving me from having to respond. "Lex said it was almost ready."

"I am."

"Would you like something to drink?" Merrick asked even though it wasn't his home.

"I can get it," I said.

"There's soft drinks and water in the fridge," Stuart said, hooking his thumb toward the kitchen.

I walked through the swinging door into the kitchen to see Lex taking a pan out of the oven. He didn't look surprised to see me, so I figured Stuart must have told him I was coming over.

"Hey." I smiled at him.

"Hey," he said, setting the dish down on the stove.

"Smells delicious. What is it?" I asked, trying to look over his shoulder at whatever smelled so heavenly.

"Swordfish."

"Wow," I said, impressed. "I didn't know you could cook."

He gave me a half-shrug like it was nothing. I waited for him to say something more, but instead found myself in the company of his silence, as usual. I had hoped we'd made some progress during our last outing, but his demeanor seemed just the same as when I first met him.

I decided to leave him in peace and went to the refrigerator to grab myself a drink. Just as I was about to leave the kitchen, I heard him say, "How was your mom's appointment yesterday?"

I turned to look at him, surprised he remembered. I had only mentioned it once that I could recall.

"It was hard, but she's doing okay. I'm just praying the treatment works," I said. "It will all be worth it then."

"Dr. Gremillion is the best oncologist I've ever worked with. Your mom's going to be fine."

He said it so earnestly that it was easy to believe every word he said.

"Thank you, Lex." A knot had formed in my throat. I cleared it, feeling the emotions of the past few days wanting to spill over.

"How often does she have to have treatments?" he asked.

"Twice a week for now. We go back on Friday."

"Any side effects so far?" he asked with a clinical tone.

"Just nausea and fatigue," I answered. "Which I know doesn't sound that bad, but I'm just not used to seeing my mom like that.

She's always been so strong. I think I'm going to have to toughen up."

I smiled even though I felt like crying again.

"You seem pretty tough to me," he said, taking another dish out of the oven.

"Oh yeah? What gave me away... all the crying?" I chuckled lightly.

"No." He shook his head. "It's the fact that you picked up and moved across the country, changed careers, left everything and everyone you know behind, all to take care of your sick mother."

I gave him a half smile. "Well, when you put it like that..." Maybe I did have a little bit of toughness in me and didn't even realize it. I was surprised to hear he saw me that way. He just had a way of speaking—when he chose to speak at all. I thought he could convince me of anything.

"We all make sacrifices for the people we love. It's not anything more than what your mother did for you," I said, thinking about how the two were similar. Her journey of moving to a new country and not knowing the language with a fatherless ten-year-old seemed immensely more difficult, however.

"Yes, and she's a tough lady," he said with an affectionate smile, obviously fond of her.

I was about to ask him more about his mother when Stuart poked his head through the door. "How's it coming along in here, guys?" he asked, clearly dropping the hint to hurry up.

"Everything's ready. I'll bring it out in a second," Lex said, his words clipped.

"Great. I'll just be right over here... in the dining area...right outside this door... waiting." He slowly closed the door behind him.

"I guess we better get out there," I said. *Before Stuart drags us out.* "Do you need help with anything?"

"No, I got it," Lex replied stiffly as he began plating the food.

"Okay." I could already feel the subtle shift in his demeanor. It was like our private bubble had burst, and now we had to get back to the status quo—small glances and as few words as possible.

I walked out to the dining area where Stuart and Merrick were already seated. I sat down next to Stuart, hoping to offer him some kind of support for his dislike of the man sitting across from us. Lex brought out the rest of the food, which consisted of swordfish, roasted potatoes, and broccoli, when my mouth started to water.

"So, where are you from, Hadley?" Merrick asked as we all dug in.

"I just moved here from New York," I answered while trying a bite of everything on my plate. I was starting to think there wasn't much Lex wasn't good at. The food was incredible.

"What brought you to California?" he asked. Lex and Stuart both had their forks suspended in midair as they peered over at me. It wasn't a secret that my mom was sick, but I didn't feel like getting into it with this guy, so I told him a half-truth.

"I accepted a teaching position at Stanford as an adjunct music composition professor. Mostly introductory courses."

"Music, huh?" Merrick asked, accepting my vague answer. "That sounds interesting. Not sure I'd be able to concentrate if you were my teacher though," he said with that lazy smile. He definitely had flirting down pat.

"What is it that you do for a living?" I asked, trying to be polite.

"I work for a shipping company. Loading and unloading containers from overseas," he said. "It's a lot of physical labor. Never really had the brains like my friend here to do much else." He shoved Lex's shoulder playfully. "He was always the smartest guy in our school. The smartest guy in every room, really."

Well, that seemed kind and actually quite genuine. Hopefully, Stuart was reading him wrong.

"How long have you two known each other?" I asked.

"Since the fifth grade," Merrick answered. "He was just this scrawny kid from Russia. Barely spoke English. I had to fight off a couple of jackasses who bloodied his nose one day. We've been friends ever since."

"That's nice that you looked out for him." I looked to Lex, who seemed happy to let Merrick tell the story.

"I remember this one time freshman year of high school, Lex was tutoring this gorgeous blonde a few years older than us. Her boyfriend was a senior and captain of the football team, and he didn't appreciate all the after-school hours his girlfriend was spending with her new tutor. He cornered Lex in the locker room one day and warned him to stay away from his girlfriend. Well, Lex flat-out refuses... I think he had a thing for Ms. Stephanie Akers." He looked over at Lex. Lex didn't look up from his food, but I noticed his shoulders had tensed. He remained silent, chewing with deliberate care. "So, the meathead boyfriend decides to get a couple of his football cronies together and planned to jump Lex in front of her in the parking lot after one of their tutoring sessions to teach them both a lesson."

"Where did you guys go to school... Rikers?" Stuart chimed in, which Merrick ignored.

"I caught wind of the whole thing and got a couple buddies of my own from our old neighborhood to join me after school that day. The look on these guys' faces when these kids from the south side of Chicago walked out with Lex, carrying bats and crowbars, was priceless," he said, laughing heartily. "They tucked tail and never messed with him again. Can't say the same for the girlfriend though. I think he roughed her up a bit."

Lex had gone completely still, staring down at his plate. I could tell how much this memory still bothered him even though he hadn't said a word.

"That's horrible," I said.

Merrick slapped a hand on Lex's shoulder. "Tell the truth man. Did you ever have anything going with that girl?"

"No," Lex replied bluntly. "She was a nice girl in a bad situation."

Merrick let go of his shoulder and continued eating. "You were always such a chicken with the ladies," he said through a mouth full of potatoes. "Remember Mindy Davies?"

Lex's eyes narrowed a fraction. "What about her?"

"She was practically in love with you, and you still never made a move."

"Mindy and I had nothing to talk about. When I told her I moved here from Russia, she said she would love to take a road trip there someday."

"Who said anything about talking to her?" Merrick said, smirking.

And with that, I was pretty much convinced Stuart was right about Merrick.

"Now that you mention it, Mindy did tell me you tried hooking up with her on multiple occasions," Lex said, staring directly at Merrick.

Stuart and I froze, looking between the two of them, feeling the tension turn up a few notches.

Merrick seemed to be fumbling for a few seconds before he recovered his cocky grin. "Yeah, well, you said it yourself—you didn't think she was smart enough for you," he said before turning toward me. "Careful, Hadley. If you don't know the capital of Florida, Lex may never speak to you again."

Lex ignored that last comment. "Mindy turned you down though, right?"

"Yeah, so?" Merrick said, his irritation breaking through that confident façade.

"So maybe she's smarter than I thought."

I was biting my lip, trying not to laugh, but Stuart gave no such effort as he howled with laughter.

"No, I think you were right about her," Merrick said, trying to save face. "The few times I talked to her, I was thinking there must be a village somewhere missing an idiot."

"I don't know. I think we should give her more credit. After all, she was able to see straight through your bullshit," Lex said, still fixing Merrick with a hard stare. "I think most women can."

Lex glanced pointedly toward me with that last remark. Merrick followed his gaze until both men were staring at me. I grinned at Lex, and I thought I saw his lip quirk before he resumed eating.

"Man, you've changed," Merrick said with a forced laugh. The underlying implication was clear as day—you're not as complicit as you once were.

"That's funny. I was just thinking you haven't," Lex said, like he wasn't bothered in the least.

I could see the glaring difference between the two of them in that moment. Merrick was all smiles and bravado while Lex had a quiet indifference that seemed even more lethal.

"Thanks again for having me over, guys. I haven't had food this good in a long time." I said, mostly to Lex, trying to steer the conversation in another direction.

"Now you understand why I keep rooming with him," Stuart said.

"Can your boyfriend not cook, Hadley?" Merrick asked, shaking off his awkward interaction with Lex.

"No, he has a hard time picking up the spatula with his giant hulk hands," Stuart said, making me snort as I was taking a sip of my drink.

"What was that?" Merrick looked completely lost.

"It was a joke," I explained. "I'm single."

"How's a girl like you single?"

"Isn't it obvious?" Stuart said. "Her hideous appearance runs them all off. They call her the Quasimodo of Stanford."

I put my middle finger up against my cheek, pretending to scratch it.

"I know damn well that's not true," Merrick said with his self-assured demeanor fully restored. "You weren't seeing anyone back in New York?"

"Yes, I was dating a guy for a while before I moved here," I answered.

I glanced over and noticed Lex's eyes were squarely on me, sending an inexplicable wave of nervousness through me.

"What happened with that?" Merrick asked.

"He's a great guy. We got along really well, but I knew long distance would never work," I answered. "I don't think it ever really works for anyone, but especially not for us."

"He didn't want to move here with you?" Merrick asked.

"No, he loves his job. And I'd never ask that of him."

He shook his head. "It's a good thing you got rid of him. He's obviously not right in the head. I'd follow you all over this damn country."

I gave him a tight smile, trying to accept the compliment gracefully.

"Hey, you know what animal really gets the shit end of the stick?" Stuart asked, looking around the table at everyone. We all just stared back at him, wondering where he was going with this.

"Cows," he said, answering his own question. "We raise them, slaughter them for the meat, but not before we take the milk meant for their offspring and give it to our own babies to fatten them. The final blow comes when we take their babies and charge fifty bucks a plate for veal."

The silence in the room was deafening. We all continued to stare at Stuart as the seconds ticked by. The change of subject was so random, and the confused look on Merrick's face was so comical that I couldn't help it. I covered my mouth, trying to stifle my laughter, but failed miserably. I started laughing and continued to laugh until tears ran down my face. I knew Stuart had done it to get Merrick's attention off me and for that I was grateful. Lex was shaking his head, trying to hide his grin.

"Do you think about cows a lot?" Merrick asked, still appearing bewildered.

"Oh, I think about all sorts of things. The spatiotemporal profile of altered neural reactivity… presynaptic spike drive plasticity… women's volleyball."

Merrick continued to look at Stuart with his eyebrows knitted together in confusion. He shook his head and muttered, "Whatever you say, Stuey."

Hearing Merrick call him Stuey sent me into another fit of laughter.

"How's your mom, Lex?" Merrick asked, probably done with Stuart and I's antics.

"She's great. She moved back to Russia a few years ago to take care of my grandfather."

"No shit," Merrick said. "That lady sure could cook. What was that dish she used to make? The one she'd grill with the skewers on Friday nights?"

"Shashlik," Lex answered with a smile. It was a real, genuine smile that he seldom used. His happiness at the memory was contagious, and I realized I was smiling too. I wished I could bottle up that exact feeling I saw on his face.

"Yes, that's the one," Merrick said. "You should make that next time I come over."

"Next time?" Stuart asked, looking horrified.

"I never could get it exactly right," Lex said, ignoring Stuart. "I've tried many times over the years, but it never turned out as well as hers."

"I'd never had Russian food before I met you guys. Mrs. Strovinski converted me into a true disciple though. There's a really great place in downtown San Francisco that I go to at least once a week. Nowhere near as good as your mom's, but it's still pretty damn good."

"My mom used to say she was going to have to take out a second mortgage if I kept bringing you over for dinner," Lex said, smirking.

"Yeah, well, it was YOYO night at my house every night, so she pretty much kept me alive all those years. I can't cook for shit."

"What's yoyo night?" Stuart asked.

"It stands for 'you're on your own,'" he answered.

Our faces both fell at this revelation. I grew up with a single mom for most of my childhood. Money was always tight, but I'd never experienced neglect in this way.

"Don't start pitying me, gorgeous," he said when he saw the look on my face. "It was pretty common in the neighborhood I grew up in. Nobody's parents were ever around."

"I'm sorry," I said, not knowing what else to say.

He waved me off. "Don't worry about it. I was just lucky Lex's mom took me in. I ate at the Strovinski's almost five nights a week all throughout junior high."

"She's from a pretty impoverished part of Russia," Lex said. "She knew what it was like to go hungry. She would never turn anyone away. Especially not her son's personal bodyguard."

They started to laugh together, and it was evident just how deep their roots ran. They were thrown together out of necessity and eventually learned to survive together. I wasn't Merrick's biggest fan, but I could see now why Lex had chosen to ignore the more grating aspects of his personality.

When dinner was finally over, Merrick made himself comfortable on the couch with a beer. I helped Stuart and Lex clean up before I decided to head home.

"What? You're leaving already?" Stuart followed me to the door like a stray puppy.

"You'll be fine, Stuey." I patted him on the shoulder. "Thanks for dinner, Lex. It was really delicious."

Lex gave me a quick nod, his eyes following me out. Merrick winked and waved goodbye from the couch. I closed the door on Stuart as he stood in the doorway, looking like I was trapping him in there. I smiled all the way back to my house, picturing him going to the window and pressing his face to it like he was watching a prisoner escape.

Chapter 13

"What's in the pan?" I asked as my mom came out to meet me at the car, carrying one of those large disposable aluminum foil pans. I was there to pick her up for her second chemo appointment.

"Swedish meatballs," she answered. "I called around to a few restaurants in Minnesota, and they gave me some of their recipes."

"You made those for that nurse? Mom, that's so nice."

"Well, it sounded like she needed a little taste of home… literally."

I don't know why I was surprised. It was on brand for my mom to try to cheer someone else up for her own chemo appointment.

Amber was our nurse again, and my mom gave her the dish once we got there. She held it for a few seconds before she broke out in tears. My mom hugged her, and she cried for a full five minutes and said it was the nicest thing anyone had ever done for her. I smiled, thinking my mom really was the best person I knew, but the sobering reality of why we were here sunk in as we sat down and watched the red bag being hung again.

She handled the treatment much better this time in large part because Nurse Amber gave her the nausea medicine before and after the infusion. Mary and Phil weren't there this go-round, so my mom and I chatted, and I caught her up on the dinner I had with the guys on Wednesday.

"I think I'd like to meet these young men you seem to be spending all your time with," she said.

"I think they'd like that," I told her. "Why don't we plan a day for you to come over? You haven't seen the campus yet. It's really nice. I could show you around, and we could all have dinner."

"That sounds perfect."

As we drove home, I could see the fatigue starting to set in again. I pulled into her driveway and put the car in park. When I went to turn off the engine, my mom put her hand out. "Uh-uh, Edward Cullen. You're not coming to watch me sleep again."

"I'm just going to stay with you for a little while to make sure you're okay, and then I'll leave."

"No, we talked about this. Call me a hundred times again if you want, but it's Friday. You need to go out and enjoy being young."

"Mom, all I'm going to—"

"No," she cut in. "I'm going inside to take a nap and then hopefully I'll be feeling well enough to make it to canasta tonight. I met some great ladies the last time I went. And you'll be out with your friends having a great time yourself."

I sighed in defeat as she got out of the car and walked inside. When the door closed behind her, I picked up my phone and called her.

"Really?" she answered.

"You said I could call as many times as I wanted."

"I'm hanging up now, you freak. I promise to call as soon as I wake up to give you a full report on my REM cycle."

"I'm going to bang down the door if you don't," I warned.

"I believe it," she said and hung up.

Once I got home, I decided to make my mom happy. I texted Sarah and Lionel to see if they wanted to go to dinner, and they accepted. I called my mom on the way, and she said she was feeling perfectly fine and was heading out to her canasta group.

I suggested La Caretta to Lionel and Sarah so we could finally try the margaritas. I was a little nervous to run into my old friend, Zack the waiter, but thankfully he was nowhere to be seen. We had a really fun evening together, and I called my mom several more times throughout the night.

"Would you give it a rest already?" she said after the tenth call. "I told you, I'm fine. I'm trying to enjoy my game."

"You explicitly stated I could call as many times as I wanted," I said. "And I never received that REM cycle report, missy."

"You're psychotic."

"I think it's best if I come over tonight."

"I'm locking the doors and bolting the windows shut."

"That never stopped Edward Cullen."

"This is me explicitly stating not to call anymore," she said.

"Does texting count?"

"I'll see you tomorrow, Spider-monkey."

"Be there bright and early, Loca," I said before hanging up.

I went to bed early on Sunday night and woke up much too early Monday morning. I looked over at the clock to see it was only 5 am. After a few unsuccessful attempts at falling back asleep, I dragged myself out of bed and headed downstairs toward the coffee pot. I pushed open the door to the kitchen, still a little bleary-eyed, when suddenly I heard the flapping of wings and turned to see a black mass of feathers swooping straight toward me. I ducked, letting out a scream, and sprinted out of the kitchen.

I ran all the way out the front door, still yelling and swatting at my hair. My heart was hammering in my chest when I finally stopped to take in my surroundings. Of course, *of course*, Lex was outside on one of his jogs and was heading straight for me. I thought of how ridiculous I must have looked—shoeless, sporting my old Christmas pajama set, and my hair a tangled mess from trying to keep it from becoming a literal bird's nest.

"What's wrong? What happened?" Lex asked when he reached me a few seconds later. He sounded genuinely concerned as he scanned me from head to toe.

"It... kitchen... thing flew... bird!" I said through gasping breaths, pointing at my house.

"A bird?" he asked, trying to decipher what I was saying. "A bird is in your house?"

I nodded fervently, still trying to catch my breath. Relief seemed to wash over his expression. Why he appeared relieved, I couldn't begin to imagine. After all, I'd just been attacked by a psychotic bird in my own kitchen!

"What kind of bird?" he asked.

"Hawk... eagle... pterodactyl! I don't know! It was huge and flew straight at my head, trying to peck my eyes out."

A smirk played across his face during my rambling. "Do you want me to take a look?" he offered.

"Yes, please," I said in a small voice.

He started walking toward my house, and I followed close behind. I felt like clapping and chanting, "Hercules! Hercules!" but thought better of it.

"Be careful, Lex. It had murder in its eyes."

He continued smiling and pointed at the kitchen. "In here?" he asked.

"Yes! Scene of the crime."

He pushed open the door and I closed my eyes, ducking behind him, ready for another attack.

"That monster right there?" He pointed to an innocent-looking robin perched on one of my cabinets. I guess it wasn't exactly pterodactyl-sized, but still.

"Don't let him fool you. That miscreant likes to attack when you least expect it."

He chuckled lightly. "Do you have a spare blanket or bedsheet?"

"Yes!" I said, elated that he was going to take care of this for me.

I went to the hall closet and pulled out a bed sheet and handed it to him. He walked slowly into the kitchen with the sheet spread wide between his hands. The little beast wasn't paying attention. It was too busy pecking at its feathers when Lex threw the sheet over it. I yelped when I heard the sound of it trying to fly again, but Lex secured the sheet around it and walked the little demon outside, releasing it once he reached the threshold.

I threw my arms around him, hugging him from behind. It started out innocent enough, but my brain immediately registered the hard lines of his muscles as I held him.

Down, girl.

"Thank you! Thank you!" I cried.

That was the last time I'd leave my windows open to let the cool night air in. The birds in New York would never have tried to pull something like this.

"No problem," he said with laughter in his voice.

He handed me back the bed sheet once I finally let him go. I could still feel the heat from his body as we stood there staring at one another.

He cleared his throat. "Alright well... have a good day."

"You're leaving?" I asked pitifully. I was still feeling keyed up from my near-death experience and didn't want to be alone.

"I was going to go for a run... unless you think he had a partner in crime you need me to check for."

I shook my head. "No. There's no way a creature that evil managed to make any friends. He was definitely flying solo."

"So then...?" he asked, wondering what more there was.

"I guess I'll be okay," I muttered pathetically. I just needed a minute to pluck up the courage to go back inside and try to shake off the feeling of bugs crawling all over me.

"You could come with me... if you wanted to," he added quickly.

"You want me to go for a run with you?"

He shrugged. "If you don't feel like being alone."

Well, there was an idea... A bad one, but still.

"I have the endurance of a panda," I told him. "You'd have to go much slower than you're used to."

"I don't mind."

"Are you sure? I don't want to hold you back."

"It's fine," he said. "Besides, I'm a little afraid I'd come back to you putting up scarecrows all around the neighborhood."

"You think you're joking."

He smiled a warm, almost tender smile, and I felt like that bird might have gotten lodged in my stomach and was flapping around in there.

"Okay. I'll go change."

I ran up the stairs and put on my workout gear that still had the tags on it. I met Lex back outside and noticed the weather was starting to cool off. Perfect weather to go for a run. That is, if you're into the whole 'gasping for air while your legs turn to jelly' kind of vibe.

"So, how far do you normally run?" I asked, giving my legs a stretch.

"Usually about four to five miles."

"Oh, is that all?" I asked, tone dripping with sarcasm.

"I usually head up Perkins and turn on Bleaker. I like to run by that park with the big lake. It's really nice in the morning. No one's ever around."

That's because all the sane people are probably sleeping.

"Okay. Let's do it," I said.

We started to jog up the path he had laid out, and I was drenched with sweat and wheezing within ten minutes while he looked like he'd just been lounging on the sofa.

"I think I'm dying," I gasped as we finally reached the lake.

It actually was a really beautiful area. The lake itself looked to be about fifty square acres in size with old oak trees casting shade around the entire pathway. Lex had been right—there wasn't a soul in sight. I would have found the scene quite peaceful if I hadn't been about to hack up a lung.

I crumpled like a Jenga tower onto the grass underneath one of the oak trees and decided running was definitely not for me. The only time I'd ever been in any kind of decent shape was when I had to perform on the big stage. After the last show, I'd always head straight for my rightful place on the couch. It had been years since I'd done any kind of onstage performance, and it was showing here and now.

Lex hadn't complained once about my pace or the number of times I had to stop.

I lay out dramatically on my side, resting my head on my outstretched arm, and peeked up at him with one eye open. "Go on without me. I'm dead weight. Dead being the operative word."

He laughed as he looked out toward the lake. "It's nice to get a chance to look around a little. I don't ever stop to take it in."

What a gentleman. I could tell he was letting me off the hook. "Glad I could be of assistance."

"You know, running actually increases your lung capacity and helps improve breath control. Might arguably be the best workout for a singer," he teased.

So much for letting me off the hook.

"Thank you, doctor," I said, still feeling like I might die. "Is that why you jog, Lex? To keep up your singing voice?"

"No. I think you might prefer getting attacked by that bird again than having to listen to me sing."

"So, what is it then? You just enjoy running?" I asked, finding the idea ridiculous.

"I didn't at first, but now that I've been doing it for a while, I enjoy it more."

"Why so early?" I leaned on one elbow while he crouched down next to me, picking at the grass.

"I never sleep for more than a few hours a night. It's been that way for as long as I can remember. I can never seem to shut my brain off," he explained. "I used to toss and turn wide awake until I got the idea one morning to go for a run. Now it's just become this thing I do to pass the time when I'm restless."

I nodded. That made sense.

"Why were you up so early?" he asked.

"Same reason as you—couldn't sleep. I haven't been getting much sleep since my mom's diagnosis. Every time I close my eyes, my brain conjures up images of her dying, and I work myself up into a panic."

"I'm sorry, Hadley." The tendons of his hand flexed. It looked like he was about to reach out to comfort me, but changed his mind at the last second.

I nodded. "Thanks. I just can't picture my life without her. I want her to be there for the things that matter. Like if I ever got married or had kids," I told him. "She'd be such a wonderful grandmother."

He smiled sympathetically at me. I needed a subject change before I turned into a walking ASPCA commercial.

"Do you picture yourself ever getting married? Would you want kids?" He'd always been such an enigma to me. I decided to try and satiate my curiosity while he was still being relatively open before the inevitable shutdown occurred.

"I haven't really thought about it that much. I think I'd have to find someone I'd actually want to marry before considering it. It would definitely make my mom happy, though."

I tilted my head. "Did you want to marry Nicky?" I hoped I wasn't overstepping.

"No," he said, shaking his head.

I couldn't read his expression properly, so I pulled myself up to a sitting position. "It must be hard having to work with an ex," I said. "I'm not sure I could do it."

He stretched his long legs out on the grass in front of me before answering. "Some days are worse than others. We seem to manage for the most part."

Since he didn't immediately shut me down, I decided to push a little more. "How long did you work together before you got together as a couple?"

I knew I was being nosy, but his romantic life was just another facet of Alexsander Strovinski that I was deeply curious about for reasons I wasn't quite ready to admit to.

"A few years," he answered simply.

"And what? All those late nights in the lab you realized you were made for each other?"

"Something like that," he answered vaguely.

With that response, I figured he was ready to drop it. But to my surprise, he continued after a beat. "She sort of... propositioned me one night. She told me she knew I wasn't seeing anyone and that she wasn't either. She said it would be mutually beneficial because our schedules were too busy to ever meet anyone else or go out on dates."

"Wow, that's not the romantic story I was hoping for."

"No, I guess it really isn't. But she was right. We never had time to meet anyone, especially back in those days. And I liked her well enough. Over time though, her feelings grew, and she wanted more from me than I could give her."

I tilted my head. "What do you mean?"

He looked off toward the lake like he was thinking carefully about what to say next. "Work always comes first for me. It always has. I can get obsessive about it. It's sort of been the story of my life—work coming between me and the person I'm dating. I thought my relationship with Nicky was the perfect solution. I thought she understood, but I guess I was being selfish. She needed more from me and from our relationship than I could give her, so I eventually broke things off."

Well, now I just felt sorry for her. She was a rude toad of a human being but giving your heart to someone and having them reject it really hurts. And on top of that, having to still see them and work side by side, day after day, I could see why she'd be jaded.

He inclined his head toward me. "You must think I'm an asshole."

I shook my head. "No, you did the right thing. It would have been worse for you to string her along when your heart wasn't truly in it."

He sighed. "I don't recommend dating coworkers."

I shrugged. "Who knows, maybe you'll end up back together someday." I felt a knot twist in my stomach at the thought, but second-chance romances were a personal favorite of mine.

He gave me a disparaging look. "I sincerely doubt it."

"You guys still spend time with each other outside of work... There must still be something there."

He looked away again, his eyes squinting in the sunlight. "I've tried very hard since our breakup to make sure she wasn't being ostracized by the group to the point of doing things I wouldn't normally do."

"Like what?"

He chewed on the inside of his lip. "I never want anyone to treat her badly simply because we're not together anymore. It's difficult because we all spend so much time with each other. So when plans get made, I make it a point to have her included."

"I get it."

I felt like I was getting a rare insight into who he was. Despite his somewhat cold demeanor toward me in the past, I had still always suspected he was a good guy. Now, I was beginning to think he was one of the really good ones. I don't think many men would go out of their way to make sure their exes were being treated well by mutual friends after a breakup.

"What about you?" he asked, straightening slightly out his relaxed posture. "You never wanted to marry New York man?"

I shook my head. "No, we weren't together long. And we weren't really in love. Well…" I stopped short of finishing that sentence. I had assumed Garrett and I were on the same page, but after our conversation, I realized I had underestimated his feelings.

"Well, what?" he asked curiously.

I guess I had to confess.

"When I told him I was moving here, and that I didn't think long distance would work for us, he didn't say too much. He agreed with me, as a matter of fact, and even hugged me and wished me luck. He didn't seem upset, so I definitely thought we were on the same page. But when I first got to California, he called me and told me he loved me."

His face was set in stone. "He had never said that before?"

"Not once. I don't even know if it's true or if he thought maybe I'd change my mind and head back to New York if he said it."

He paused, his expression becoming thoughtful. "Would you have stayed in New York if he meant it?"

I shook my head. "No. But I might have tried to make long distance work. I didn't even want to try though, which told me everything I needed to know about the relationship," I said. "But he told me on that same phone call that he was going to fly out here to visit me. He made it a point to say that my mom would be better in no time, so we'd be back together again in New York soon enough."

"What did you say?" he asked, leaning forward, causing his forearm to brush against mine.

I quickly crossed my hand over my arm, hoping to conceal the goosebumps that had suddenly made an appearance.

"I said my mom was going to be here for a while, and I didn't expect him to wait for me."

"But when she does get better, you plan to move back and pick things up with him?"

It didn't escape me that he said *when* she gets better and not *if*.

"Not exactly. I know I'll be back in New York eventually, but I won't be getting back with Garrett."

"Does he know that?"

"He sort of hung up on me before I could say those exact words."

"You haven't spoken to him since then?"

"Just a few texts asking how my mom was doing, and I asked about his sister. But no, nothing else about our relationship. I'm hoping he realized it's over between us."

Because I guess the whole breaking up thing wasn't clear enough.

He was quiet for a few moments, and I took the opportunity to admire his profile as he looked out on the lake. The cool breeze pushed around his dark hair, and my fingers itched to find out if it was as soft as it looked.

Eventually, he turned toward me. "Make sure he knows," he said in a low voice that made my toes curl.

I looked into those crystal clear brown eyes, wishing I could know what exact thoughts were crossing through that brilliant mind of his. It was easy to imagine there was something between us, especially in moments like this when he was being open and vulnerable with me when no one else was around. It suddenly dawned on me that the only time he was ever this way with me was when we were alone. I had to look away as my thoughts took a dark turn. Was he embarrassed by me? That was a depressing thought.

"What is it?" he asked, picking up on the sudden change in my disposition.

I thought about brushing it off and telling him it was nothing, but I really wanted the truth. "Can I ask you something?"

"Of course," he said curiously.

"Why are you only nice to me when we're alone?"

His smile faded, and I could almost see the conflicting thoughts warring around in his mind. I expected him to play dumb or deny that it was true, but he didn't.

"I don't mean to," he said, his shoulders hunched. "I promise I'll do better."

I wanted more of an explanation but didn't want to push too hard. "So, we're good? Friends, even?"

He wrinkled his nose a bit like the thought was distasteful, but then he smiled and said, "Yeah... We're friends."

I smiled back, thinking how silly it seemed to need a declaration of friendship, but with him, I could never be sure.

"Great, because we're going to have to get really close to each other very soon."

A flash of intrigue played across his features. "Why's that?"

"Closeness is essential when friends are engaged in the ancient and noble art of piggyback rides."

He looked at me for a beat before his head fell back in laughter. It was such a beautiful thing to witness. His laughter had the same velvety richness to it that any bass singer would be jealous of.

He stood up, extending a hand to me, and I took it as he pulled me up.

"I may be able to manage on my own two feet if you can stand my snail's pace for the rest of the way home," I said, limping along.

"Kind of an insult to snails, don't you think?"

I swatted his arm playfully. When we made it back to the townhomes, I saw Stuart sitting on the front porch of their home, drinking coffee.

The second he spotted us walking back together, a huge smile spread across his face.

"And what are you two up to at this early morning hour?" he called out as we approached.

"Engaging in multiple forms of torture, apparently," I answered.

"How so?"

"First off, I was attacked by a giant bird in my own home. Then Lex decides the best way for me to shake off the unfortunate incident is to take part in a grueling five-mile hike around Stanford."

"It was an innocent baby robin," Lex stated. "And we maybe made it a mile before she collapsed."

I opened my mouth wide, pretending to be shocked. "*Innocent*?! That lunatic of a bird would have given even Edgar Allen Poe nightmares."

Stuart laughed, while Lex just smiled and shook his head.

"Sounds like you're having a rough morning," Stuart said.

"I am," I said, pouting a bit.

"Would coffee help?"

I perked up. "Coffee always helps."

"I just made some," he said, walking up the steps.

Just as we were about to follow him inside, I spotted pink hair flying down the center walkway. She was looking between Lex and me with a scowl on her face.

"God, it's too early for Satan's spawn," Stuart groaned.

"You're going to be late." Nicky aimed her comment straight at Lex. "The whole team needs to be on time today if we're ever planning on finishing this experiment. Or don't you care about our work anymore?"

She glanced at me with that last comment.

"Calm down. We still have another thirty minutes before we start the simulations," Lex replied, seeming irritated.

Normally, it was hard for me to tell what he was thinking. But lately, the subtle changes in his voice or shifts in his expression was something I was starting to pick up on.

"It's my fault," I said, hoping to run interference. "I asked Lex if I could join him on his run this morning, but I slowed things way down with my general out-of-shapeness."

I was thinking that might smooth things over, but it only seemed to irritate her more that I spoke at all.

"Dr. Strovinski has an extremely important job that has to be completed on a strict timeline. He doesn't have time for distractions." She gave me a look of such contempt that I pictured steam coming out of both ears.

"What about me?" Stuart asked. "Does Dr. Benowitz have time for coffee or am I not an important part of the team too?"

"You could shrivel up and die, and we'd all barely notice," she said scathingly.

Stuart's head turned to Lex and me. "You ever meet someone and think the world would have been a better place if their mom had just swallowed?"

"Sounds like you all really need to get to work, and so do I," I said quickly. "See you later, guys."

I waved and walked off hurriedly, but I heard the bickering start back up again. Normally, I'd be annoyed when someone acted like such a petty asshole, but all I felt was pity for Nicky. Especially now that I knew the story behind their relationship. I'd probably be a little insane too if I had to work with someone I once loved, and they dumped me because I asked for more from them. And not to mention the fact that she can't get away from him without giving up a career that she worked hard for. Lesson to take away from all of this is to never, under any circumstances, date your coworkers, people.

Chapter 14

"So, what do you think of the campus?" I asked my mom as we took a break in one of the gardens. The weather was perfect to finally show her around Stanford's campus. She was feeling up to it after her chemo appointment, so we walked around the grounds while I acted like a professional tour guide, giving her all the highlights.

"It's absolutely beautiful here. I can see why you love it," she said as we sat down on one of the benches near the live oak trees.

"How are you feeling?" I asked for about the hundredth time that afternoon. "If you're too tired, we can head back."

"No, I just need to sit for a few minutes. You can give me a lecture on this bench and its historical significance though, if you like."

"In 1891, Leland Stanford himself sat on this very bench..."

She laughed and closed her eyes, leaning her head back to let the sun hit her face. I watched as she unwrapped the scarf from her newly shaved head. She was handling the chemo treatments better and better. However, after the fourth or fifth round, she started to lose her hair, so I helped her shave it off one afternoon. We shopped around and got a few wigs, but she mostly wore head scarves, saying the wigs were too itchy.

She didn't seem bothered by the hair loss, so I didn't dwell on it. As long as she was here with me, nothing else really mattered.

The smell of fresh flowers and the cool breeze on my skin gave me a feeling of such serenity. I was basking in it until I looked over to see my mom watching me.

"Can I tell you something you might not want to hear?" she asked.

"What is it?" I asked cautiously.

"This place suits you."

"This bench?" I pointed to it, smirking.

"California," she said seriously. "This job, this place, your friends. You're different here."

My brows pinched together. "What do you mean?"

"You were always so restless in New York. Jumping from one project to the next. You never felt settled," she said. "But here... you just seem content."

Where was this coming from?

There was no denying that I enjoyed a lot about my new life in California, but it wasn't home.

The more I thought about it, the more I realized that everything about my life looked completely different here. Teaching had been something I never in a million years thought I'd be able to pull off, so I'd been shocked to find that not only was I able to pull it off, I actually looked forward to it each week. I'd made some real connections with the students, and my writing had never been better.

I'd pitched a few songs to different artists that I thought might be good fits for their records, and the feedback had been amazing. Many of them had asked for me to come out and help with the production, but I hadn't been able to get away with my mom's treatment course. Production could be a grueling process, so I had to admit I wasn't exactly heartbroken about not being involved with that side of things. I was more than happy to stay put and fuel my creative outlet from a distance.

The friendships I had here were also nothing like the ones I'd left behind in New York. Back home, most of my relationships were built around business, and the conversations rarely strayed from work. But with Sarah and Lionel, there were no strings attached, just easy, effortless fun. And something about the friendships I'd made with Lex and Stuart felt more like family than anything else. I would have dinner with them most nights if they didn't have to work too late, and the time I spent with them felt comfortable and familiar, as if we'd known each other for much longer than a few months. All that being said, hearing my mom say those words out loud made me feel defensive of my old life in New York.

"I know you have your roots there," Mom said, pulling me out of my train of thought. "And I know it would be hard to give up because of how much Daddy loved it, but I want you to think about it."

"Think about what, exactly?" I could already feel my guard going up.

"About making this your permanent home."

I scoffed at the idea.

"All I'm saying is to think about it."

I didn't need to think about it. When she got better, we were going back to New York. Unless... maybe that was the problem. Maybe *she* was the one who didn't want to leave.

"Do *you* not want to go back to New York?" I asked.

"I can make a home anywhere," she said with a shrug. "It's you I'm thinking of."

She was right about that. You could drop her anywhere in the world and she'd be perfectly content, but I still wasn't convinced this was all about me.

An errant thought suddenly and irrationally crossed my mind. She'd told me her neighbor who was always helping out around the house had asked her on a date earlier in the week, and she had accepted.

I had met him once after I dropped her off from her chemo appointment a couple of weeks ago. He seemed like a really nice guy and looked at my mom like she hung the moon. I'd teased her mercilessly about it, but I was actually thrilled that she had finally taken that step. It was long overdue.

But now that I was being confronted with leaving New York behind, suspicion about her true motives burrowed its way into my mind. A sudden wave of anger came over me, and I blurted out what I was thinking. "Is this about Carl, mom?" That serene feeling I was having was now smashed to bits. "Are you so in love now, you don't want to leave?"

"Hadley," she said reproachfully.

That was all she needed to say. I immediately felt like shit.

"I know. I'm sorry," I said, already regretting it. I knew I crossed the line, but I was feeling protective of the life we had in New York. My whole childhood—memories with my dad, with us as a family—they were all in New York.

"You and I have already planned a trip to go back during the Christmas holidays. New York will always be there," she said, putting her arm around me. "This doesn't have to mean what you think it does."

It was so difficult for me to wrap my mind around what she was saying. New York felt like such a huge part of my identity. Even thinking about leaving it behind was painful. It felt like a betrayal for reasons I couldn't quite put into words.

"You want to grab some coffee?" I asked, trying to avoid talking about this subject any further.

"Sure," she said with a smile. I could tell I was already forgiven for my outburst.

We walked over to Peet's and ordered our coffees. As I looked over my shoulder to find a place to sit, I spotted Lex and Stuart walking in together. Lex smiled when he saw me, and the breath I'd just taken got caught somewhere in my chest. He had never been generous with his smiles, so this one took me by surprise. I became even more distracted when I noticed he was wearing his glasses. I stood there staring at him awkwardly for a few moments, preoccupied by how good he looked in them.

When I was finally able to drag my gaze away from Lex's face, I noticed Stuart standing next to him, his eyes sparkling with mischief when he caught sight of my mom. I wished they could meet under different circumstances since our little spat was still weighing on me, but it was too late now. They were walking over to us.

"Mom, these are the guys I was telling you about," I said when they finally reached us. "This is Stuart Benowitz."

I introduced him first since he had practically jumped in front of Lex to extend his hand to my mom.

"It's so nice to meet you, Stuart," my mom said, taking his hand.

Instead of a quick handshake, he held her hand in his. "Pleasure to meet you, Ms. Olivier," he said with one eyebrow arched. "It's clear where Hadley gets her ravishing good looks."

My eyes rolled around involuntarily in my head.

"You should've seen me with hair," my mom replied.

Lovely. I wasn't sure this could get any weirder.

"I don't know. I think this look works for you. It's definitely working for me," he said, still not letting go of her hand.

Guess it could get weirder.

My mom laughed, not bothered in the least with how forward Stuart was acting. "Outside Demi Moore, I'm not sure many women can pull off the bald look."

"Hey now." He patted her hand with his free one. "Will Smith wouldn't allow that kind of talk and neither will I."

She smiled even wider. "I think I'm being charmed against my will."

"Okay, that's enough, Stuey." I pulled him away from her. He grumbled a little as Lex was finally able to step forward.

"Mom, this is Alexsander Strovinski." I got a nervous feeling in the pit of my stomach as I introduced the two of them. I told myself it was because I wanted her to like all of my new friends, but I knew deep down there was more to it with this particular friend.

"The scientist," she said inscrutably. He nodded and smiled at her.

"It's a pleasure to finally meet you, Ms. Olivier," Lex said politely as they shook hands. "I've heard a lot about you."

"Likewise." She turned her head slightly, examining him. I thought she might still be holding a grudge from the time I told her I didn't think he liked me very much.

"Do you two gentlemen have time to join us for coffee?" she asked.

They glanced quickly at one another, which told me they definitely didn't. But Lex smiled and said, "Of course."

"Wonderful!" my mom said excitedly.

As she turned to find a table, I said to Lex, "You don't have to do this. I know you guys are busy."

"We have some time," he said, not meeting my eyes. I knew he was lying, but I didn't argue any further as they got their coffees and we sat down at a table together—Lex and Stuart on one side, my mom and I on the other.

"Boys, Hadley has already told me so much about you, but I must know more." She absolutely loved meeting new people.

"Fire away. We're open books," Stuart said, leaning back in his chair.

"First, I want to know why you chose Alzheimer's to study."

Hell of a first question, I thought. No "How's your day going?" or "Where you from?"

Stuart took it in stride. "I'm just along for the ride. You'll have to ask Lex about that one."

All eyes turned to Lex. I realized I was actually curious to hear his answer.

He took a sip of his drink before responding. "I couldn't think of anything worse." His fingertip traced the lid of his cup. "It's one thing for your body to fail you, but the mind seemed like a far greater loss to me," he said almost shyly. "I hope that doesn't come off as insensitive. I realize it's a terrible thing you're going through."

He looked at my mom apologetically.

"Not at all!" she said. "I couldn't agree more. I'd choose this fate any day over a disease like Alzheimer's."

Stuart leaned over to me and said, "Well that got deep pretty quick."

"Buckle up. She's just getting started," I told him.

My mom ignored that last comment. "Did you always want to be scientists?"

"Not really," Stuart answered. "I was just always good at chemistry, so I got my degree in it. I didn't know what I was going to do after I graduated, but I ended up seeing an advertisement for this job. I've been a part of Lex's team ever since. Luckily, I enjoy this work."

"That's so lovely," my mom said. "You've been friends and coworkers all this time."

"Don't forget roommates as well." I smiled sweetly at Stuart. He shielded my mom from the middle finger he was giving me behind a napkin holder.

"What about you, Alexsander?" she asked. "Did you always know you wanted to be a scientist?"

"Yes," he nodded. There was a chord of intensity in his voice as he said, "I've always been someone who was sure of what they wanted."

His eyes shifted to me, and our gaze locked for a brief moment. In those few seconds, I felt the overwhelming urge to reach over and touch him. If we'd been sitting on the same side of the table, I don't know if I would have been able to stop myself. I got lost looking into the clear brightness of those whiskey-colored eyes that seemed to burn even brighter behind the lens of his glasses. He blinked rapidly, and I snapped out of it, suddenly finding the lid of my coffee cup fascinating.

"Well, you two have that in common," my mom said as she scrutinized us both. "Hadley knew from a very young age that she wanted to be involved in music."

I turned to her and smirked. "I may have had a little encouragement along the way."

My mom laughed. "That's true. My husband, James, was teaching her to play the piano before she could even walk."

"Probably should have stuck with the basics before moving on to piano playing," I said. "I still struggle with not tripping over my own two feet."

"I couldn't tear you away," she said, smiling. "Not that I wanted to. Even at that age, it was clear you were gifted."

I chuckled. "Your opinion might be a bit biased."

"It absolutely is not," she said defiantly before turning to Lex and Stuart. "Has she ever played for you?"

"No, but we've heard her sing," Lex said in a low voice. I glanced over to see him looking at me in a way that made me feel... edgy.

"Isn't she incredible?" my mom said proudly. "You should have seen James and I's faces when our five-year-old belted out "Proud Mary" in perfect pitch one evening after dinner."

"'Proud Mary?'" Stuart gave me a questioning look.

"What's wrong with that?" I asked.

"Nothing. I just can't think of many five-year-olds who are into soul music."

"My dad loved it," I explained. I can't remember a time when there wasn't music playing in our house growing up. He especially loved classic rock and old R&B.

"Are you boys into music at all?" my mom asked them.

"Actually, Lex is a huge Cher enthusiast, and I happen to be a big fan of dubstep," Stuart said. "Have you ever heard of Skrillex?"

"I can't say that I have," my mom said, sounding genuinely interested.

"Did Hadley get any of her musical abilities from you?" Lex asked, interrupting Stuart before he got carried away on a dubstep tangent. My name on his lips had some unmentionable parts of me standing at attention.

"Oh no! I wish." She guffawed. "No, I was the odd man out in my house. Hadley got all her talent from her father. He was an amazing singer and musician. It's the reason I fell in love with him... Well that, and he was great in bed."

Stuart nearly had a spit-take as he grabbed a napkin and started coughing up the sip he'd just taken. I laughed, shaking my head. I looked over to see Lex smiling as well.

When Stuart finally recovered, he asked, "How did he die, if you don't mind me asking?"

"Drug overdose," she said as casually as if she were announcing the time. They both froze mid-sip and were looking at me, trying to gauge my reaction, but I was used to this. She wasn't ashamed of anything. Lex already knew this piece of information, but he appeared tense as his eyes worked over my face.

"He was really a remarkable guy. Very talented. And the kindest man you could ever meet... but he had his demons," my mom continued despite everyone's uncomfortable reaction. "James was a great husband and an even better father. And there was no one he loved more than Hadley. He would have done anything for her."

"Except quitting drugs." It slipped out before I had the chance to think about what I was saying.

"Shit... sorry guys," I said when I saw the looks on their faces. It was a stupid thing to say. I wasn't sure I even meant it. I think I was still feeling off after the disagreement my mom and I had earlier. We rarely argued and talking about my dad now felt like we were picking at the wound we had opened earlier with the New York discussion.

"Don't worry about it," Stuart said, waving me off.

Lex didn't say anything but was looking at me with his eyebrows pinched together, seeming concerned.

"Hadley, you know that's not true," my mom said, looking just as concerned.

"I know," I told her. "I said it without thinking. I didn't mean it."

The way everyone was looking at me in this moment, like I needed a "handle with care" stamp on my forehead made me want to run out of this place as fast as possible.

"Mom, the guys are really busy. They need to get back to work."

I looked to them pleadingly, hoping they wouldn't argue. They picked up on my subtle dismissal and stood with their coffees to leave.

I mentally kicked myself the whole way back to the car.

"You want to talk about it?" my mom asked once we were inside the vehicle.

I shook my head. "Not right now."

She didn't push me on it, and we drove back to her home mostly in silence. I dropped her off and spent the rest of the evening alone. Stuart had texted to invite me over for dinner, but I ignored him. I knew he was probably worried about me because he texted a few more times to check on me, so I told him I was fine, and that I was just going to bed early.

I didn't know what was bugging me exactly. I was feeling out of sync with everyone around me, and now more than ever, I wished I had my dad to talk to about it.

Chapter 15

My class ran late the following Monday, so I had to sprint through the quad and cut through one of the science buildings just to make it on time to our faculty meeting on the other side of campus. By the time I reached the entrance of Roble Hall and hurried to the designated room on the third floor, I was sweaty and out of breath.

I managed to slip in through the back just as Dr. Abel was getting to the podium and setting up for his presentation. Sarah and Lionel had saved me a seat near the rear of the conference room, where we'd spend the next thirty minutes listening to Captain Creeper give a presentation on ethics and sexual harassment in the workplace.

"You think he knows the irony of what he was saying?" Sarah asked as we all left the meeting together.

"No, he thinks he's just being friendly when he tells us we should smile more," I answered. "Although, the Captain seemed a little off his game today. He didn't even crack a smile when he talked about the penal code."

"I heard his wife just left him," Lionel said.

"Are you surprised?" Sarah asked. "Even his hair abandoned him."

"I swear he looked straight at me when he got to the part about dating students being an ethical code violation," Lionel said.

Sarah rolled her eyes. "You're imagining things."

"A guilty conscience will do that to you," I said, piling on.

"Go play in traffic, both of you," he said. "I've got to get to my next class."

"Biceps in that class?" Sarah asked with a smirk.

"I haven't the slightest clue who you're referring to," Lionel said, walking away. "But yes," he called over his shoulder.

"I've got to get going, too. I'm meeting my sister for lunch, so I can listen to her complain endlessly about her deadbeat husband that she should have left years ago," Sarah said.

"Yikes. Have fun!"

"See ya," she said with a wave.

I cut through the same building as a shortcut to get back to the music department. I don't know how I missed it the first time, but right through the entrance was a huge eucalyptus tree that was surrounded by glass on all four sides. It stretched all the way to the top of the exposed ceiling so that it was technically outside even though it was placed indoors. I stood admiring the construction of it for a few minutes when I heard a familiar voice carrying down the hallway.

I grew curious so I followed the sound until I found the source emanating from a large lecture hall. The door was partially ajar so I peeked in. It was twice the size of my classroom, but nearly every seat was taken as its occupants studiously observed Dr. Alexsander Strovinski pacing back and forth at the front of the auditorium.

I listened in on his lecture about some complicated process in the brain that made my own brain hurt just trying to decipher all the advanced words and scientific jargon. But he spoke with such confidence and had absolute command of the room. You would normally see at least a few students dozing off or looking bored, but this group was hanging on every word.

"Automatic detection of an unexpected change in the sensory input is a central element of exogenous attentional control. Stimulus-specific adaptation is a potential neuronal mechanism for detecting such changes and has been strongly identified across sensory modalities and different instances of the ascending sensory pathways..."

Yep, definitely over my head.

But he was so magnetic up there that I, along with everyone else, had trouble looking away. It was as if he were the center of gravity, and we all couldn't help but be pulled in.

I thought it was probably best if I didn't lurk by the door and possibly disturb the lesson. Common sense told me the best thing to do would be to leave, so naturally, I waited for him to turn and write something on the board before I dashed to one of the few open seats along the aisle. He seemed to be none the wiser as he turned and continued his lecture.

I felt a slow smile spread across my face as I watched him. He was completely in his element, and I had to admit I was a little jealous. He was just as new to teaching as I was and yet here he was doing it so naturally and with such conviction. It was like he'd been doing it all his life.

I'm not sure how I captured his attention since I was sitting as low in the seat as possible in such a large crowd, but eventually, his gaze inexplicably found me, and we locked eyes. I smiled, knowing I was busted. He raised an eyebrow questioningly but didn't miss a beat as he continued on with his lecture, pacing from one side of the room to the other.

Every time he turned to my side of the room, his eyes always found their way back to me. After a while, he stopped the back-and-forth pattern and stood directly in the center of the room. We were locking eyes so often that the rest of the room began to blur, leaving the two of us caught in a quiet exchange that made the crowded room seem distant and unimportant.

His voice carried a rich timbre, the kind you could sink into like a warm bath, soothing and all-encompassing. His face remained an enigma, a mask concealing every trace of his thoughts. But his eyes—those whiskey eyes—told stories his lips never would, and I clung to every single word.

The intensity of his gaze held me captive, making it impossible to tear my eyes away. He continued speaking but never turned his attention away from me. Eventually, I became distracted by the fullness of his mouth. My eyes lowered to those sumptuous lips as I watched them forming words but didn't hear a sound. I thought of everything he might be able to do with those lips. How perfectly soft they would feel brushing across my skin. How much I wanted to feel them pressed against my own. My mouth suddenly went dry, and I felt a warm flush creeping up my neck. Holy crap, was I actually getting turned on... in a room full of students?

I pressed my legs together and realized yes... yes, I was. I still didn't look away, though. I continued to picture his mouth on mine... fingers threaded in my hair... our bodies pressed together...

"Alright, that'll be all for today, guys," I heard him say, snapping me back to reality.

I slowly let out a breath I didn't know I was holding. As the crowd of students started to make their way out, I thought I might be able to slip out without being seen. That is, until I heard my name being called.

"Ms. Olivier, can I see you after class, please?"

Well, there went that brilliant plan.

I hoped he wasn't angry with me for sitting in on his lecture. I waited until most of the students had left before I made my way to the front where he was still talking with a few stragglers.

Once everyone had departed, I asked, "You wanted to see me, sir?" I was trying to be funny, but it sounded more like a line from a bad porno.

He raised an eyebrow but didn't comment on my bad joke or even question what I was doing there. He simply asked, "Are you busy right now?"

Just picturing us rolling around in bed together like a couple of rotisserie chickens... but besides that, no.

I cleared my throat. "No, why?"

"I'd like to show you something."

"Okay," I agreed, feeling curious.

He gathered his things, and I followed him up the stairs to the second floor. We headed down a side hallway, passing a few offices, when I noticed one with *Dr. Alexsander Strovinski* labeled on the door. It looked to be about twice the size of all the others.

When we got to the end of the hallway, Lex flicked on the lights of a completely vacant laboratory. There were several long tables in the center of the room with microscopes, beakers, and other lab equipment scattered across them. The walls were lined with floor-to-ceiling shelves stacked with far too many books to count as well as different models of the brain.

"Take a seat right here," he said, pulling out a stool that had a microscope sitting on the table directly in front of it.

"Is this your lab?" I asked, looking around.

"I wouldn't call it *my* lab," he said, smiling. "But it's the one Stanford is letting me use for my research for the time being."

I rolled my eyes. "Semantics."

I took a seat on the stool, swinging my legs back and forth. "So what is it you wanted to show me?"

"Hold on one second," he said, rifling through a few boxes in the corner of the room. "I just need to find... here it is."

He opened the box as he walked over to me and took out a small glass slide before slipping it into place under the microscope. "Take a look."

I leaned forward, now extremely curious about what he wanted to show me.

"It's a bit fuzzy," I told him. I remembered from high school biology that I probably just needed to adjust the knobs on the side to bring it into focus, but I didn't want to take the chance and break his fancy lab equipment.

He leaned over my shoulder, looking through the lens and adjusting the knobs. Our faces were mere inches apart. He smelled like clean laundry and general maleness. I breathed in slowly, savoring the scent of him, until he pulled away, allowing me to look through the lens again. The image was crystal clear now, but I still had no idea what I was looking at.

"Umm Lex, I hate to break it to you, but the only thing I remember from biology class is to steer clear of the kid who was overly excited about frog dissection day."

He laughed. "Sorry. You're looking at a tissue sample from a part of the brain called the pre-frontal cortex."

"Okay?" I said, continuing to look at the image.

"Do you know what the pre-frontal cortex is responsible for?"

"Decision making?" I guessed, thinking that sounded familiar.

"Exactly," he said excitedly, though he couldn't hide the surprise in his tone. "But not just decision making. It's responsible for impulse control, emotional reactions, as well as our focus."

"Should I be taking notes?" I teased.

He chuckled again. "Does anything seem unusual about this image?"

"Not really, no." It looked okay as far as I could tell but that wasn't saying much.

"That's because this is healthy tissue," he said. I could sense him coming closer. I inhaled that familiar scent again, feeling the warmth of his body as he leaned over to change out the slides, his chest brushing against the side of my arm.

"Now, look at this one," he said, remaining close to my side.

As soon as the fog of lust cleared, I was able to focus on the new image before me. I could definitely see a noticeable difference. The cells appeared more shriveled and distorted and just had a sickly look to them.

"This one looks much worse," I said.

"It is." He was silent for a few moments. "This is the pre-frontal cortex of a heroin addict," he said quietly.

I froze. It suddenly dawned on me why he was showing me this.

This was about my father.

"I wanted you to see it," he said almost apologetically. "I wanted you to know that no matter how much you love a person, addiction alters your brain on a cellular level to the point where you lose almost all impulse control. The person you're looking at had virtually no willpower. We like to think we're in control, but ultimately, we are at the mercy of our brain and how well it's functioning on any given day."

I didn't move an inch as I continued looking at the fragmented picture. Tears started to fill my eyes, distorting the image even further. He was trying to show me what he and my mother had been attempting to tell me all along—my father had been ill. No matter how much it hurt that he wasn't able to overcome his addiction, I couldn't deny what was staring back at me through the lens—proof that addiction was as real as any other illness.

I blinked away my tears before I finally looked up at him.

"Thank you, Lex," I whispered, knowing if I spoke any louder my voice was going to crack.

His forehead wrinkled. "You're not mad?"

I shook my head before getting down off the stool and standing before him. His eyes roamed over my face like he was looking for any hint that I was lying. I could almost see the wheels working overtime in his mind.

"You're going to hug me, aren't you?" he guessed.

I nodded and waited a moment to see if he was going to refuse me.

"Ready?" I asked softly.

He gave a quick nod in response. I stepped toward him until we were toe to toe. I looped my arms around his waist, pressing my cheek to the center of his chest. I could hear his heart hammering wildly as he tentatively wrapped his arms around me. He was probably uncomfortable with the close contact, but I selfishly didn't pull away. I could think of no other way to show him how grateful I was that he cared enough to show me this.

I stood there quietly holding onto him until his heart slowed to a normal rhythm. He had one hand pressed against the center of my back, while the other slid slowly to the nape of my neck. I didn't have a single clue how long we stood that way, but I knew in that moment as I held him and he held me back that I couldn't deny how I felt any longer.

I was falling for him.

I'd *been* falling. The time I'd spent pretending we were nothing more than friends had been a complete and utter waste of time. The truth had always been there, no matter how hard I tried not to see it. He was more than a neighbor, more than a friend, he was just... more. In every single way.

With so much at stake, this realization should have felt more frightening than it did. But I just couldn't find it in myself to be scared. There's a certain calmness that the truth always brings when it's finally revealed, and I was ready for it.

I pulled back a fraction, still not letting go as my eyes lifted to meet his. He peered down at me through thick lashes, his gaze feeling like a caress to my soul. I felt his grip on me tighten, and his breathing seemed shallower as we stood there taking each other in.

I leaned in further without thinking. Everything in me was pulled toward this man. His eyes became fixated on my mouth at the same moment my gaze found his.

"Lex?" I heard a female voice call out to him.

The feeling of being doused in icy cold water hit me as we pulled away just as Nicky walked through the door. We weren't doing anything wrong, but I'm sure we still looked guilty as hell.

"I was coming to see why you weren't in your office, Lex, but I'm glad to see you're hard at work here," she sneered, looking between the two of us.

"I was just leaving." I wasn't in the mood to deal with her attitude today.

"No, don't let me interrupt. I can see you've developed a serious interest in neurobiology lately."

"That's enough, Nicky," Lex warned.

"What? Were you two just pondering the mechanism of renin-angiotensin inhibitors and their capacity for suppressing neuronal cell death?"

I knew she was trying to make me feel small for not knowing anything about neuroscience, the one thing that held them together.

"What we were doing is none of your concern. In fact, you should worry more about your own work rather than wasting time tracking my every move," he said crossly. "Your work might even be a little better if you gave it the same attention."

Ouch. I didn't want to see the look of hurt on her face that I knew was there, not that she didn't deserve it. She had no response as she stood in the doorway, looking shell-shocked. I would have bet my life he had never spoken to her that way before.

I knew it was time for me to leave. "I'm going to go," I told Lex.

"I'll walk you out," he said, still sounding annoyed. I wasn't expecting him to, but maybe he didn't want to deal with her either.

She said nothing as we brushed past her, still frozen in the doorway. I almost apologized for causing such a rift between them. I didn't have any ill will toward her, even though she acted like a total twat every time I encountered her.

Once we made it out of the building, I stopped and turned toward him. "Thank you again, Lex. You don't know how much this meant to me."

He nodded. "I'm sorry about Nicky. I know she can be tough to deal with sometimes."

I gave him a tight smile. "Go easy on her. I'd probably be the same way if you dumped me."

He looked taken aback by that statement and seemed to be fumbling for something to say.

"Anyway, thanks again," I said, saving him the effort.

He continued to stare blankly at me, the shock never leaving his face as he mumbled, "You're welcome."

I walked away with an overwhelming, undeniable realization—I really, really liked California.

Chapter 16

"Hm," was all my mom said after I told her about what Lex had shown me in the lab while sitting together at her chemo appointment.

"What?" I asked, knowing there was more.

"Nothing," she said vaguely. "That was very kind of him."

"Mhmm. What else?"

"He seems like a really great *friend*," she said, putting emphasis on the last word.

"Just spit it out."

She smiled before chanting, "Lex and Hadley sitting in a tree..."

"Oh my god." I rolled my eyes, smiling. "You're so childish."

"Admit it," she said. "You like him."

"I admit nothing."

"That's too bad because he definitely wants to be sitting in that tree with you."

"How would you know?"

"Please. A blind man could see the way that man looks at you."

"And how is that?"

"Like you invented blowjobs," she said, cracking up at herself.

"Wow." I shook my head. "I knew we never should've gotten you that medical marijuana."

She continued to laugh. She was in such a great mood these days, and I wondered if I had her new friend Carl to thank for that.

"All jokes aside, it's pretty obvious how he feels about you. His eyes barely left your face in the ten minutes I spent with him. If you moved even an inch, his attention was on you."

That seemed like an exaggeration. "I don't know about that."

"Why are you fighting this? He seems great."

"He is," I agreed. "It's just that we're both so busy. I don't think we'd ever see each other if not for the fact that our homes are directly across from one another. Plus, I don't even know where we'll both be in a year's time. I might be back in New York, and his next grant might take him to Antarctica, for all I know."

"Do penguins get Alzheimer's?" she joked.

"I don't know if it's worth all the heartache."

She smiled warmly at me. "Only one way to find out."

I got uncomfortable thinking about how much it would hurt to not be able to see him anymore, and we weren't even together. I didn't know if I would ever be ready to take that risk.

"Let's talk about your love life," I said, ready for a change of subject. "You and Carl still sitting in a tree?"

"Oh honey, Carl and I have moved from the trees to the gardens."

I made a gagging noise, and her laughter rang out playfully like a child's. I loved seeing her this happy. My mom had never been unhappy per se, but I hadn't seen her *this* way in so long. Had she been lonely this whole time? I had a feeling leaving California was going to be an even bigger challenge now.

"So, what are your plans for the evening?" she asked.

"Actually, Sarah invited me to her friend's bachelorette party tonight. I was thinking about going. It's not until much later though, if you want to grab dinner before your canasta group."

"Yeah, that sounds good."

We ended up at that same sushi place we went to when we first came to California, where she continued to pester me about my love life, and I had to plug my ears when she talked about hers.

After dinner, I still had plenty of time to spare before the bachelorette party was set to kick off, so I decided to head home. I figured I could get a little writing done before we headed out since the plan was just to go bar hopping in downtown Stanford.

As I started up the footpath toward my house, I heard the sound of rock music and laughter filling the air. I could see a party going on a few doors down from mine at Sanjay's, one of the guys from Lex's team.

I recognized some of the other guys from the team hanging out on the front porch, sipping from plastic cups, including my endlessly entertaining comrade, Stuart. I was about to go over to say hello but hesitated when I saw who else was there. Jace, another of Lex's coworkers, was also one of the porch dwellers.

I'd met him a few times when I'd been over for dinner at the guys' house. Our interactions had always been friendly, but I think he must have misread our exchanges because he ended up asking me on a date yesterday when I saw him at the coffee shop. I was reminded of what my gran had once told me—women always flirt best with men they aren't interested in.

My disinterest was through no fault of his. He seemed really nice and was definitely cute, but I wasn't sure I was ready to date just yet, which is exactly what I told him.

"Hadley! HADLEYYYYY!" Stuart bellowed, waving his arms around wildly, gesturing for me to come over.

This should be interesting. I sighed and headed toward them.

"Hey Stuart," I said, walking up the stairs of the porch.

He pulled me in for a tight hug like we hadn't just seen each other yesterday.

"It's my favorite gal pal, Hadley!" He reeked of booze. "Hadley, this is Dan, Friedrich, and you already know Peter."

"Hey guys," I said. They all gave the guy version of a hello—a quick head nod.

"And apparently you already know this asshole." Stuart hooked his thumb toward Jace.

Jace gave me a kind smile. "Nice to see you again, Hadley."

Stuart threw his arm over my shoulder. "We need you to clear something up, Betty," he said. "Jace went around telling everyone at work today that he asked you out on a date and you said maybe."

I looked over at Jace, who didn't appear embarrassed in the least.

"That's not exactly what I said," Jace explained, grinning. "I told them you said you weren't ready to date yet, but I'd be here when you were and that it would be worth the wait." He winked, and I smiled back at him, thinking he must not have an insecure bone in his body with the way he was talking about this so openly in front of all his friends.

"What a schmuck," Stuart said dramatically. "Are you seriously going to entertain this, Betty? Just get it over with and tell him you're not interested."

I wished I was interested in a guy like Jace. He seemed easygoing and not afraid to say exactly what he was thinking. Unfortunately, my feelings seemed to be tangled up in the silent, cryptic type lately.

"No, he's telling the truth," I said, not wanting to embarrass him. Though I was starting to think that wasn't even possible. "I'm not ready to date yet, but he's a perfectly good option for any woman in their right mind...which I'm clearly not."

Jace smirked at my roundabout rejection, and I was happy to find it wasn't a blow to his ego.

"Ridiculous!" Stuart said ten times louder than was necessary.

"Okay, good buddy." I snatched his cup from him just as he tried to take another sip. "I think you've had enough."

Peter rolled his eyes. "He had two beers and a shot but he's acting like he did a whole keg stand."

"I'm fine," Stuart slurred.

I patted him lightly on the back. "I know you are, but you should probably give it a rest for now."

"You're right," he said, touching his index finger to the tip of my nose. "We're having a poker tournament, but I got cleaned out an hour ago, so all that was left to do was drink!"

I wondered if he had gotten any food in his system before this drinking binge. I might have to get something in him or else he was going to be extremely hungover.

"I guess what I'm really trying to tell you is we lost, Hadley... ergo, you are hanging out with a group of losers." He made the L shape against his forehead. "You should go inside where the winners are."

"Boy, you really can't handle your liquor," I said to him.

"Like a teenager on spring break," Dan added.

I gave a small sigh. "I think *I* might need a drink." I was definitely going to need one if I was going to deal with this fool.

"Your wish, my command," Stuart said, bowing down low in front of me and almost falling over.

"'E looks like a baby 'orse trying to valk for the first time," Friedrich commented as he watched Stuart trying to right himself.

"Can it, Freddy!" Stuart shouted.

"I'll get you that drink," Jace offered.

"Thanks," I told him, helping Stuart inside.

They had quite the party going. There were around twenty guys and a few women gathered around four poker tables. Some were playing while others just stood by watching. The couches had been pushed up against the wall, where more people were hanging out and drinking. It didn't take long for me to spot Lex (not that I was looking) facing away from us at one of the poker tables, his chips stacked a mile high. I came to a halt when I saw him, staring like a deer caught in headlights.

The shocking part wasn't seeing him socializing with a large group of people. What had my complete, undivided attention was the fact that Nicky was draped over his shoulder, whispering in his ear. The blood boiled beneath my skin. I didn't even know I was capable of such rampant, irrational jealousy, but here I was picturing taking her head and bashing it into the table over and over.

Jace had come back from the kitchen and handed me a drink. I thanked him and took a large swallow, trying to cover up my anger.

"Everyone! Listen up!" Stuart started shouting. Everyone turned to look at him including Lex, whose eyes went wide with surprise when he saw me standing there.

"This divine lady here who looks like she should be carved into the front of a pirate ship is my good pal, Hadley. Not a one of you is good enough for her," he said, pulling me to his side. "And that includes you, Jace... so hands off!"

"For fuck's sake," I mumbled. "Thanks for that."

"What? I was making sure they knew you were off limits."

Dan rolled his eyes. "No one was planning on jumping her, Benowitz."

The party recommenced with everyone ignoring Stuart and getting back to their conversations and the card game. Everyone except Lex, who was glaring in our direction, his eyes flitting between myself and Jace.

I wasn't sure if I should go over and greet him or not while he was in the middle of playing, so I settled for just waving and smiling, but he didn't return the gesture. *Rude.* He turned back to the game as I watched Nicky playfully trying to peek at his cards with her hand wrapped around his bicep. I must not have been able to hide my revulsion, because Stuart stopped to look at what I was staring at.

"Oh, you noticed that horrible smell too? Looks like you found the source," Stuart said loud enough for Nicky to hear. That got her attention.

"He can't even have a couple drinks without acting like a sloppy mess," Nicky said just as loudly, glancing at Stuart. "Pathetic."

"Anyone else think it's no coincidence that Nicky's name has the word 'ick' in it?" Stuart asked, looking around at everyone.

That got a laugh from a few of the other guys in the room, which made me wonder how well-liked she really was.

"Fuck off, Stuart," Nicky snapped.

"Love to! The smell was getting to me anyway," he retorted. "Come on, Betty. Let's get you that drink." He grabbed my arm, trying to pull me toward the kitchen.

I held up my cup in front of him. "I already have a drink."

"Then come with me so I can get another."

"I don't think you need any more," I protested, but he pulled me with him to the kitchen anyway.

I looked back apologetically at Jace, who smiled and shrugged like he was used to Stuart's antics. I dared a glance back at Lex just to see him scowling in our direction. What was this night turning into?

I took a few sips of my drink while I watched Stuart clumsily make himself another one.

"I think you should eat something first," I told him, trying my best not to sound like a mother hen.

"All Sanjay has is stale Tostitos and leftover vindaloo, and you know what curry does to my IBS."

Boy did I. I made the mistake of eating Indian food with them one night and suffered for it the whole car ride home.

"You literally live a hundred feet away from here. You could go grab something."

"And miss the fun of seeing you and Lex having a standoff from across the room? No, thank you."

"We're not having a standoff." I didn't know what to call what was going on between us.

"He's not interested in her anymore. I promise," he said, digging in the freezer for more ice for his drink.

"Who?" I asked, pretending like I didn't know exactly who he was talking about.

He ignored my bad attempt at feigning ignorance. "I mean, did you see her?" he asked, dropping the ice cubes into his cup with a clink. "She's been hanging all over him all night. He's been trying to shake her off, but she just keeps coming back around like some kind of evil, desperate boomerang."

It didn't seem that way to me, but I could hardly think straight through the blinding jealousy I was feeling.

"Let's get back out there," I told him, not wanting to talk about this anymore.

There were a few open chairs near the couches, so he and I went to sit with the rest of the guests not participating in the card game. Unfortunately, these seats were directly across from Lex's table so I was getting a front-row seat to Pinky and the Brain. I tried not to look their way, but I would catch glimpses of him out the corner of my eye looking up at me from his cards every so often. Dan, Peter, and Jace came to sit with us, and I was happy for the distraction.

"Lex looks like he's cleaning up over there," Dan noted, taking a seat on the edge of the couch. So much for the distraction. All eyes turned to Lex's table.

"He always does," Peter commented.

Lex was watching our little group, looking more annoyed by the minute.

Dan heaved a sigh. "Why does he have to be good at everything?"

"I'd kill for his brain," Peter said. "Did you see how fast he worked that Nernst Equation today when we were looking at the ion concentrations?"

"UGHHHHH." Stuart rolled his eyes and slid down in his chair dramatically. "We get it. Lex is the second coming of Christ. Can we talk about something else please?"

"Sure," Peter said before turning toward me. "Hadley, you think you might change your mind about going out with Jace?"

"Absolutely not," Stuart cut in before I had the chance to respond. "Jace is an idiot."

Jace raised his glass. "Thanks, man."

"If you want to go on a date, then I'm going to choose the guy," Stuart said, pretending like Jace wasn't sitting right there.

Dan raised his hand. "I volunteer as tribute."

Stuart rolled his eyes. "That's actually a good option for you, Hadley... charity work. You could claim it on your taxes."

"Fuck off, Stuart," Dan said, flipping him the bird.

Stuart's eyes widened with surprise. "Why does everyone keep saying that to me tonight?"

"Because you're a dickhead, that's why." Peter shrugged. "Not that you've ever cared."

"Not only do I not care, I actually prefer it." Stuart took a large swallow of his new drink, smacking his lips. "Sets people's expectations a lot lower."

"Well, it's working. My expectations of you are always ridiculously low," Dan remarked.

Stuart grabbed my chair, pulling it close to his, and threw his arm around my shoulder.

"We'll find someone for you, Betty. Don't worry. I already told you, none of these assholes are good enough for you anyway."

"I doubt she needs your help finding a date," Peter commented.

"Of course she doesn't. Look at her! She's the face that launched a thousand ships, for god's sake. But I'm just trying to help my friend out of the goodness of my heart."

"Mhmmm," I said doubtfully. "What is it you really want?"

He pretended to be thinking about it for a moment, tapping his index finger against his lips. "Well, if I'm able to find you the man of your dreams, then there is one *teensy* thing I'd like in return."

"What is it?" I already knew this was going to be absurd.

"Reciprocity," he answered. I was surprised he could even say the word without slurring.

"You want *me* to set you up with someone?"

"It's only fair," he said.

"This room is occupied by a large majority of the people I know here in California."

"Hadley, you work in the liberal arts department. You're surrounded by women who are morally opposed to the brassiere. I'm sure you could find at least one who would be interested in a lovable, five-foot-eight, Jewish neurobiologist."

I raised an eyebrow. "Five-foot-eight?"

"Fine, five-foot-six... whatever."

I chuckled. "I'll see what I can do." Hopefully, he'd forget about this conversation by tomorrow.

I tried glancing up inconspicuously at Lex's table only to find him glaring holes in the arm Stuart had around me. My immediate reaction was to pull away, but I stopped myself. My relationship with Stuart was the epitome of platonic. Meanwhile, the esteemed Dr. Strovinski was letting his ex attempt to fuse her body with his.

The dealer must have called for his attention because he abruptly pulled his gaze away from us. He seemed flustered as he looked down and played one of his cards. I heard the grating sound of Nicky's giggle before she leaned over and rested her head against his shoulder. A buzzing sound filled my ears before my mind went completely blank.

Without thinking, I shot to my feet. The guys all stared at me with puzzled expressions. I'm sure they were wondering what the hell I was doing, but I couldn't stay here any longer. My skin felt like it was crawling, and my drink turned sour in my stomach as I looked at them.

"What's wrong?" Stuart asked.

"Nothing," I said curtly. "I just told Sarah I would meet her out at the bars downtown tonight, so I think I should get going."

"You could just say these guys are boring you. They bore me all the time," Stuart said, sloshing his drink around.

"No, I'm having a good time." Or at least I *was*. A thought suddenly sprang to my mind. "You guys should come with me." I thought I might like the distraction of having a big group with me.

"You want us to go out to the bars with you?" Stuart looked even more confused.

"One of Sarah's friends is having a bachelorette party, and they're just going bar hopping downtown. She told me to bring some friends if I wanted to." It was a joint bachelor/bachelorette party, so there would be guys there too.

"Are you kidding me?" He stood up so quickly, he swayed a little. I grabbed his arm to steady him. "Sarah's hot."

"Okay?"

"So, it's a known fact that hot girls travel in packs and they've been drinking! I'm a solid seven to a drunk girl."

"Whatever you say," I said with a shrug. "You guys coming?"

"I'm in," Peter said excitedly.

"I'm in too," Dan agreed with a smile.

"I can't," Jace said, looking disappointed. "Sanjay would kill me if I left him here to deal with the whole party and its aftermath alone."

I had forgotten that Jace was Sanjay's roommate. I thought it was respectable that he wasn't ditching him.

"Awww bummer," Stuart said, not looking disappointed at all.

"Let's go." He started heading for the door.

"Wait. Let me just go home and change."

"Fine," he grumbled, falling back in his chair. "Meet us back here when you're done."

"Okay, we can call an Uber then."

Stuart perked up. "This is going to be awesomeeee," he said, dragging out the last word. I laughed at his enthusiasm about going to a bachelorette party, but the smile quickly faded when I turned to see Nicky's head still leaning against Lex's shoulder. I walked out past their table hurriedly without giving them another glance.

Maybe I'd been reading Lex wrong this whole time. The feelings I was having were probably all one-sided. I just needed to take a giant step back and not let this Nicky thing bother me. The reality was he wasn't mine to be jealous over. But that didn't mean I had to sit there and watch them canoodle right in front of my face. Going out with the girls—and now the guys—was going to be the perfect distraction. I was single and going out with a group of really great friends. Conditions were ripe for a good time, which meant I should dress the part.

Up in my room, I teased my hair into a tousled, wavy look. I wanted to spice things up a bit so I gave myself a smoky eye and red lip. My closet was a mess, so I had to dig for a while to find a bachelorette party-worthy dress. I pulled out a tiny black number that I never wore, because the last time I did, I spent the entire night trying to tug it down. I slipped it on, and it was as short as I remembered, coming to about mid-thigh. It hugged me in all the right places though, so I decided to go with it. It was a bachelorette party, after all. I found a pair of black pumps that had straps across the toes and around the ankles that I knew I'd deeply regret wearing tomorrow, but I was living life for today.

I checked myself in the mirror, thinking I'd probably aged out of wearing something like this about five years ago. *Oh well.* I'd come this far. I wasn't turning back now. I grabbed my ID, cell phone, and some cash, stashing them in a small handbag, and headed back out the door to meet the bachelors.

I walked back inside and found my crew still sitting in the spot I left them, except for Jace, who was nowhere to be seen. As I approached, Dan and Peter's eyes grew so wide, they resembled cartoon characters, and Stuart's mouth was hanging slack-jawed.

I grew a little self-conscious looking down, worried I'd accidentally walked out in my underwear, and then realized the outfit was so short, it could have passed for underwear.

"You guys ready?" I asked when I reached them. They continued to stare blankly.

"Stuart?" I snapped my fingers in front of his face.

"Sorry." He shook his head like he was trying to clear his thoughts. "I got distracted by the Jessica Rabbit impersonation you're doing."

"You guys ready to leave?" I asked again, wanting to get out of there as quickly as possible.

"Yep. Just not going to look straight at you. Maybe that will help," he said, standing. We started making our way to the door when Lex stepped in front of me, blocking our path. His jaw was clenched so tight, I thought his teeth must have been grinding down to nothing.

"You're really taking these morons out to the bars downtown?" His face was flushed with anger. Stuart must have filled him in on our plans while I was gone.

"Yeah, what's the problem?" I asked, matching his tone.

"The problem is you're all faculty members, and your plan is to go out drinking at the college bars that will be crawling with students. You really want your students to see you drunk and dressed like that?" he said, waving his hand in front of me.

You could have heard a pin drop in the room. The music was still playing, but no one said a word.

I narrowed my eyes at him. "You have a problem with the way I'm dressed?"

"I don't," Stuart said, stepping in front of us. "I mean, if you were about to use your lifeline to poll the audience... that's my vote."

I ignored Stuart. "Answer the question," I said, glaring at him. A muscle in his jaw ticked as he glared back at me. Wisely, he chose to remain silent.

"That's what I thought," I snapped. "Go back to your poker game, Lex." I picked a piece of pink hair off his shoulder and held it briefly in front of his face before letting it drop to the ground. "Looks like you're going to get lucky tonight."

I glanced pointedly at Nicky, who was still seated at the card table, so he knew exactly what I was implying, before I turned and marched out of the house.

Chapter 17

"Everything okay?" Jace asked as I stomped down the steps of their porch.

"Yes, everything's fine. Your boss is just being a dick," I grumbled.

"Yeah, he's been like that all day," he said, chuckling. "Although I think I'm starting to see why."

He was looking past me toward the house, and I turned to see Lex glowering at us from inside the doorway.

"Maybe you could explain it to me then, because he basically just told me I looked like a slut."

Jace looked stunned. "He did?"

"He didn't use those words, but yes."

He shook his head. "That doesn't sound like him. He usually doesn't bother to notice anyone, much less how they're dressed."

"Great," I said sarcastically. "I love being the exception to *that* rule."

Jace chuckled. "We've worked together for a long time. He's a good guy. I'm sure he didn't mean it. He's just not used to feeling this way."

"What way?" I asked.

He looked back at Lex once more and then grinned at me as if it were obvious. "Jealous."

Before I could tell him how ridiculous that was, Stuart, Dan, and

Peter all came running out the door. "Let's go before daddy puts us in timeout," Stuart said, throwing on his jacket.

I waved goodbye to Jace as Stuart pulled me along.

"Shotgun!" Peter called out as the Uber driver pulled up.

I got in the car as carefully as I could without flashing anyone, which proved to be quite the challenge, while Stuart sat between Dan and me in the back seat.

"Where we heading?" Stuart asked.

"Sarah said they're at the Whiskey Cowboy," I answered.

Dan turned to me. "Isn't that the bar with the mechanical bull?"

"Yeah, I think so," I told him.

"You plan on trying it out, Dan?" Stuart asked.

Dan shook his head. "No. You know my carpal tunnel's been flaring up."

"For the love of god, if you're talking to a woman tonight, please don't bring up your dainty wrist problems," Stuart said, exasperated.

"It's a serious condition, dude," Dan retorted.

I was too distracted by what Jace had just told me to pay attention to the rest of their conversation. Was it possible that Lex was actually jealous? I knew I was. Thinking about him and Nicky sitting together at that table made me see red, and the irrational thoughts took over. I hated being jealous. It was an emotion that inevitably made people act out of character. Normally, I would have brushed off his comment about the way I was dressed, but the damn jealousy made me act like a petty jerk.

Stuart had his phone sitting on his lap when I saw it light up, but he was too busy arguing with Dan to notice. When I saw who the message was from, I couldn't help but peek at what it said.

Alexsander Strovinski: Don't let anything happen to her or I'll kill you myself.

My heart stuttered. Was this about me? I had no way of knowing for sure who he was talking about, but just the possibility that he was talking about me was enough to assuage my anger.

We arrived at the bar in no time.

I let Sarah know we had made it after giving my ID to the bouncer. I waited inside the door for the guys to come in when I spotted Sarah walking over with a beautiful blonde, dressed in a short white dress with a pink sash that read *BRIDE*.

"You're here!" Sarah had to shout over the music playing. "You look so hot!"

"So do you!" I said, laughing and giving her the once over. She was dressed in a strapless, sequin number with her long legs on full display.

She pointed to the blonde at her side. "This is my friend, Emily."

I smiled at her. "The bride, I presume."

"What gave me away?" she said with a curtsy.

"You look beautiful. Congratulations," I told her.

"Thank you, but I'd kill for your tits," she said. "Just thought I'd let you know because I can't stop staring at them."

I started to laugh, taking a liking to her immediately. "Are you having fun so far?"

"I was until I discovered I started my fucking period just now. Great time to be wearing all white." Emily took a large swallow of her drink.

"We talking periods?" Stuart walked up behind me flanked by Dan and Peter. "Medieval's my favorite."

"Benowitz," Sarah said curtly.

"Samaha," he said in return with a coy smile. "You're looking lovely as ever."

She smiled sweetly back at him. "And you're looking... delusional as ever."

"Come on. I just got here," Stuart whined, dropping the flirting act.

"Emily, these are my friends. This is Stuart, Dan, and Peter. We all live in the faculty housing units together," I said, introducing the guys to the bride. "They're all neuroscientists doing research at the university."

"What in the Big Bang Theory?" Emily said, looking between the four of us.

"Nice to meet you, Emily." Stuart put his game face back on. "The groom is a lucky man."

"Damn right he is," she said, raising her glass.

"Should we get a drink?" I looked around at everyone. "First round's on me."

"Yes!" Sarah exclaimed. "Let's do a round of shots."

"I'll go get them. Be right back."

I made my way over to the bar through the crowd of people. I leaned over to get the bartender's attention and got a big surprise when he finally turned around. Merrick started making his way over to me with a roguish grin on his face.

"Hey," I said, surprise coloring my tone. After our memorable dinner, I had seen him a few more times at the guys' house when I'd been over, but it had been a while. "What are you doing here? I thought you worked for a shipping company."

"I still do. I work here on the weekends sometimes to make extra cash." His eyes moved over the length of me. "You here alone?"

"No, I'm here with some friends." I motioned to where they were standing.

"Where's Lex?" he asked.

"Poker tournament."

"Huh," was all he said.

"What does that mean?"

"Nothing. I just thought he'd be here with you."

"Why would you think that?"

"Just thought you guys were kind of a package deal."

That hit a nerve. "Well, we're not," I said sharply, unable to hide my annoyance.

"So, you're telling me that he'd rather be hanging out with a bunch of guys playing poker than be out with you?"

"Oh, there are girls there too," I said before I could stop myself. Nicky's head leaning against his shoulder was still burned into my retinas at the moment.

His eyes flared with excitement when he noticed my jealousy.

He leaned over the bar toward me. "Men can be idiots."

"I noticed." I eyed him meaningfully.

He chuckled. "Look, I've been wanting to apologize for how I acted when we first met. I know I came on strong."

"I'd say a wrestler's entrance is more subtle," I said, to which he laughed again.

"I really am sorry." He sounded sincere. "But in my defense, you really are that beautiful."

I looked at him doubtfully.

"I think I was just trying to find my place with them," he said, surprising me.

"What do you mean?" I asked curiously.

"I mean there are times when we hang out that I don't understand half the things they're saying. It's like they're speaking a different language. I just got excited thinking I would finally have someone on my side that night. Someone who wouldn't look at me like I was an idiot for not knowing what a presynaptic, astrological krypton cell is."

I smiled despite myself. "I get it."

Sometimes they would get deep into conversation about things happening at work or in the science world, and I'd find myself totally lost. It was hard to keep up. But it wasn't a blow to my ego the same way that it seemed to be to him.

"Anyway, when Stuey stops glaring at me, I'll apologize to him too."

I glanced back to see Stuart was indeed glaring at the two of us, but mostly at Merrick. It suddenly occurred to me that Merrick had been intimidated by Stuart. Not physically, but mentally. Sweet, tiny Stuart made Merrick feel about two feet tall.

"I wouldn't call him Stuey in that apology if I were you," I suggested.

"Noted," he said, chuckling. "So, what'll it be?"

"Six shots of Patrón, please."

"You got it," he said with a wink.

Sarah came over to help grab the shots he had poured for us.

"Well, have a good night," I said before walking back to the rest of the group.

"Who was that?" she asked as we made our way through the crowd.

"One of Lex's childhood friends. We've hung out a few times."

"He's gorgeous." She was glancing conspiratorially over her shoulder at him. "And he's staring at you like you're solely responsible for global warming." She laughed, nudging me with her elbow. "Or are you too caught up with the scientist to notice?"

I ignored her mention of Lex. I didn't feel like talking about him after our little spat tonight.

"Obviously he's hot, but he's kind of a jerk." Although now that he laid out his insecurities about the way being around the guys made him feel, I was starting to see the situation differently.

She sighed. "Shame."

We handed the shots out to everyone when I noticed Stuart still glaring at Merrick. "What's *he* doing here?"

"He's working," I told him.

"There are plenty of bars in San Francisco."

"Maybe he was hoping he would run into you," I said. "Seeing as you two are such good friends."

"I don't think it's me he was hoping to run into," he spat.

"Let's kick this bachelorette party off!" Sarah raised her shot glass. "To Emily and Liam!"

"Emily and Liam!" we all said, toasting our glasses together. My eyes watered as the tequila burned its way down my throat. I welcomed it.

We met the rest of the bridal party, including the groom, to whom I was first introduced after he was flung from the mechanical bull. They were all very welcoming and all very drunk.

We bar-hopped over the next few hours but ended up back at the Whiskey Cowboy once the live band started playing. I was worried the guys would feel out of place not knowing anyone, but they were having the most fun out of any of us. At one point, Sarah and I looked on horrified as Stuart drunkenly made out with one of Emily's bridesmaids. Peter and Dan jumped on stage with the other groomsmen and sang along with the band as they played AC/DC's "You Shook Me All Night Long."

Sarah and I were dancing and laughing together until our stomachs hurt as we watched it all unfold. The alcohol made everything seem a million times funnier than it really was. I could *almost* forget about what had happened earlier with Lex.

When the band started to play a slow song, I felt a tap on my shoulder. It was Merrick, holding out his hand to me.

"I'm a terrible dancer, but I'm willing to risk it all for you," he said, smiling. I scrutinized him for a moment, wondering about his motivations before I finally relented. One dance couldn't hurt, right? I sighed before placing my hand in his. Sarah winked at me as she walked off the dance floor.

"Is this even allowed?" I asked. "Will you get in trouble?"

"I don't think there are any rules about dancing in the bartender code of ethics," he teased. "Besides, I'm on my break."

He pulled me in close, putting one hand around my waist and

holding the other out by our chests. I could feel the warmth of his body pressed against mine. It felt like a betrayal even though logically I knew the only person I was betraying was myself. I may be unattached, but my feelings definitely were not. I didn't want to give him the wrong impression, so I tried to put some distance between us.

"Are you having fun?" he asked close to my ear.

"Yes," I answered truthfully.

"I was watching you out there. It looked like you were having a good time. It was nice seeing you smile like that. Lex is a fool to miss it."

"I'm sure he's fine." I regretted letting him see that I was jealous earlier. I could already feel he was going to try and zero in on it.

"It was that coworker of his, wasn't it? The one with the pink hair?"

That shocked the hell out of me. How did he know it was Nicky? I pulled back to look him in the face. "Do you know her?"

"I've met her a few times when I've been over hanging out with them. She always seemed to be dropping by. I didn't know if something was going on between them."

I shrugged, pretending like I didn't know and didn't care.

"They say he's a genius, but I'm not so sure. No man in his right mind would prefer any other woman over you."

"I don't really care," I said. He laughed, obviously not believing me. He pulled me in even closer. "A little piece of advice?"

"If you must." I was ready for this damn song to be over.

"Don't waste your time. Nothing is more important to him than his job... or should I say no one."

Before I could respond, I felt someone wrap their hands around my right arm, tugging at it clumsily. I turned to see Stuart, his eyes glazed over from the alcohol but still determined.

"What the fuck, man?" Merrick scowled at Stuart.

"What are you doing?" I asked as he continued trying to pull me away.

"I'm s'posed to be takin' carof you t'night," he slurred.

"I'm fine," I told him.

"You o'viously drunker thn I thought if yur dancin' with dis ass-hole."

"I think it's you who's shitfaced." I was watching him now using my arm to keep himself upright.

"Yeah, man. I think you should head on home now, Stuey," Merrick said.

"Stuey will kick your ass!" He balled his fists up in front of his face, the move causing him to start tipping over.

"Okay, okay. I think you're done." I grabbed Stuart and held him up, looking around for Dan and Peter. I spotted them talking to a few girls in the corner of the room.

I put Stuart's arm over my shoulder and turned to Merrick. "I've got to go. Thanks for the dance."

"Remember what I said, Hadley."

I didn't bother responding as I walked off. I found Sarah and told her I was taking Stuart home.

"You need help?" she asked as she watched Stuart barely able to keep his eyes open.

"No, I'm good. I just need to talk to Dan and Peter."

"I'll go get them," Sarah offered, making her way towards the guys. Dan and Peter walked away from their company begrudgingly.

"Do we really have to go?" Peter whined.

"There's still a few more hours until the bars close," Dan added.

"Stuart here won't make it a few more hours," I pointed out. "But I'll take him. You guys can stay and have fun."

"You sure?" Peter asked. He couldn't hide the excitement in his voice.

"Yeah, I was ready to go anyway." Merrick had effectively killed my buzz.

The night had grown cooler, and I began to really regret my choice of outfit. My arms and legs were covered in goosebumps as Peter and Dan helped me get Stuart to the car.

"Thanks, Hadley!" they called to me before slamming the car door shut and heading back inside.

Stuart fell asleep on my shoulder and was snoring in less than thirty seconds. I had to shake him awake when we made it back to the townhomes. He could barely stand as I held up most of his weight, walking him back to his house. He couldn't answer me when I asked if he had his keys, so I had to do what I was dreading and knock on the door to see if Lex was home. I decided if he didn't answer, I would just haul Stuart over to my house so he could sleep it off on my couch.

Thinking ten seconds was plenty enough time to wait, I hurried to leave like the coward I was. Just as I turned to depart, the door swung open to reveal Lex standing there, looking wide awake despite the late hour. My traitorous eyes let the amorous part of my brain know that he was shirtless. *Think, Hadley, think.* I was still mad at him, right?

My heart beat a little more rapidly when our eyes met. We stared at each other wordlessly as the seconds ticked by. His gaze was full of longing as it caressed the edges of my face. I couldn't look away. That is, until Stuart groaned loudly.

"Damnit," Lex said, finally noticing Stuart. He grabbed Stuart from me and helped him over to the couch. "The idiot shouldn't have drank this much."

"No kidding," I huffed.

"Best. Night. Ever!" Stuart yelled out to no one in particular from the couch. Within seconds, the loud snoring started up again.

"Where are Dan and Peter?" Lex asked, looking around.

"They weren't ready to leave just yet."

"Some friends," he muttered.

I drank in the sight of him, the alcohol making me stare at his bare chest without restraint. Rational Hadley was working overtime trying to remember that he had insulted her earlier and that we'd gotten into a fight over it. But carnal Hadley kept pushing the memory down.

"Thanks for bringing him home." His voice was low and mesmerizing.

"No problem," I heard myself say. We continued staring at one another. Against insurmountable odds, I kept my eyes from slipping down to his chest.

I blinked rapidly, allowing the cogent side of my brain to finally slip back in the driver's seat. I needed to leave before I did something incredibly foolish like confessing to what I knew were unrequited feelings.

"Hadley," he said just as I reached the door. I turned to look at him.

"I'm sorry for what I said earlier. I didn't mean it." His tone was full of sincerity. "You look beautiful tonight. You always do."

I let the compliment wash over me, feeling my heart constrict at his words. I wanted to walk over and throw my arms around him, but something was nagging at me that I couldn't keep to myself. The words sat on my tongue, desperate to get out.

"I danced with Merrick tonight." I wanted to slap my hand over my mouth for letting the words escape.

"You what?" he asked, his eyes narrowing a bit.

"Your friend, Merrick—" I started to try and explain myself, but he cut me off.

"Yeah, I know who he is," he said curtly. "What was he doing out tonight?"

"He was the bartender at one of the bars we went to. He said he was working there on weekends to make extra money," I explained. His entire body appeared tense. "Anyway, he asked me to dance... So we did... but just for one song." Apparently, I was unable to stop more words from spewing as I dug myself deeper into the hole.

"Is that all you did?" His voice was eerily calm.

"Yes! Of course!" I said, a little insulted that he would even have to ask. The tension around his eyes softened a little.

"Are you interested in him?" he asked, sounding accusatory.

"What? No!" I said defiantly.

"Because he's definitely interested in you... along with all the others. Jace, Peter, Dan, Zack from La Caretta. Just take your pick."

What was he implying? For the second time tonight, it felt like I was being called a slut by the man standing in front of me.

"I'm not interested in any of them." I was actively trying to rein in my temper. "I'm going home alone, just like I always do. Not sure you can say the same." I looked up the staircase toward his bedroom, wondering if Nicky was there between his sheets. The thought made my stomach roll.

"There's no one up there," he said.

"You sure? Pink seemed to be your favorite color tonight." The alcohol was making the filter between my brain and mouth nonexistent.

His eyes sharpened. "I told you it's not like that anymore."

"Whatever you say. It's none of my business anyway." But there was a small part of my heart that was elated to hear him say it. It wasn't enough to make me forget what he'd just said about me and all the guys I could get with as the anger burned through me once again. This whole conversation had been an exhausting dance of sidestepping landmines, and I could feel how close we were to an explosion. It was like being on an emotional roller coaster, one that I desperately wanted to get off of.

I was suddenly physically and emotionally spent from this entire night. The only thought going through my mind at the moment was getting out of this ridiculous outfit so I could crawl into bed and be blissfully unaware of all my problems for the next eight to ten hours.

"Look, can we just pretend this night never happened so we can get back to being friends again?" I asked, deciding that was probably best. It wasn't at all what I wanted, but clearly, something wasn't working between us. He hesitated to answer, looking as if he wanted to say something more.

"Sure," he finally said, sounding as defeated as I felt. "Whatever you want."

Chapter 18

"Are you going to tell me what's been going on with you?" my mom asked, picking up on my sour mood as we waited in the exam room for Dr. Gremillion. It had been a few weeks since that awful night, and things between Lex and I had changed dramatically. I still had dinner with them most evenings, but he seemed resigned to keep things cordial and nothing more. If anything was going on between us before that night, it was officially dead in the water now. That realization was weighing on me a lot more than I ever thought it would.

"Nothing's going on. I'm just tired," I answered.

"You know you can tell me," she said, clearly not believing me. "I promise to keep my opinions to myself."

I grinned. "I don't know if you're physically capable of that," I replied, and she narrowed her eyes at me.

It wasn't that I didn't want to tell her. I just knew the moment I said it out loud, I would have to admit to myself that things were over, and I wasn't ready.

"Hello, ladies," Dr. Gremillion said, entering the room with my mom's chart.

"Hey doc," my mom greeted. "How's everything looking?"

I waited for his usual "things are looking great" speech that he'd given each time we'd come before, but my heart sank as he paused before looking up at us.

"I'll cut right to the chase. Your numbers look worrisome this month, Ms. Olivier. They had been on a steady decline since we began the treatment, which is what we expected to see," he stated. "But now they've more than doubled in a month's time. I'm afraid the chemo has stopped working."

My mind and body no longer felt connected. I seemed to be having trouble staying grounded in the room and in reality itself. It felt like a dream... a bad one that I'd wake up from any moment now.

"We can try upping the dosage and frequency of the chemo, but the reality is your body has stopped responding to it." I stared at him, waiting for him to say this was some colossal joke. "Your cancer is so rare that most of the other traditional treatment options would just be a Band-Aid for the larger problem at hand. There isn't much else we can do at this point."

"I understand," my mom said softly. I'd felt suspended in mid-air up until that moment, but hearing her say those words brought me crashing back down to the ground. The anger flared in me, scorching through my veins.

"This can't be it." I stared at him, irate. "You're supposed to be the best! We came here because you're the best. Everyone said so. You can't tell me there is nothing else you can do!"

"I'm sorry. I truly am."

"No." I started shaking with fear or with anger, I didn't know which. "There must be something else you can do."

"Hadley," my mom said, reaching out to comfort me, but I shook her off.

"There must be something else. Another treatment...anything!" I shouted as I shot to my feet.

"There may be another treatment option," he said calmly. "A drug trial that I'm conducting for your mom's specific type of cancer, and

I've been having promising results."

"So put her in it," I said sharply, unable to rein in my temper. The anger felt better than the devastation that loomed just below the surface.

"It isn't that simple. The FDA only allows a certain number of patients per trial. It's possible that if enough people drop out or choose other treatment options, we could get your mom in. But those chances are slim, and your mom can't wait much longer."

This wasn't happening. I could hear the words he was saying, but it was like I was hearing them through a glass enclosure. They seemed muffled as my attention came in and out of focus. The anger I'd felt was quickly fading, morphing into something far worse.

As I listened to him going through all the options she had, none of which would get her to a cure, the paralyzing fear started to set in.

We walked out of the office together enveloped in silence, neither of us knowing what to say. I wanted so badly to be there for her in this moment, to be a source of comfort, but I couldn't seem to find the words.

When we drove up to her house, I went inside with her, and we settled on the couch together. I stared blankly ahead, the shock still setting in.

"We'll find another doctor, Mom," I said, finally breaking the silence. "He obviously isn't as good as we thought."

"No, Hadley. We've been down this road. We've done the research. He's the best there is. This isn't his fault."

"How can you be so calm about this?" I asked, fanning the flames of anger.

"Because I'm not afraid to die," she said gently. "I've lived a good life. I always knew this was a possibility since I first got diagnosed. I'm only scared of leaving you without either of your parents."

"Stop!" I cried, shooting up from the couch. I couldn't listen to this.

"Just… stop."

"Hadley…" She tried to reach for me, but I turned and bolted out of the house, fleeing through the front door, and collapsing onto my knees in her yard. A loud, piercing scream tore from my throat and didn't cease until my lungs started to burn. My head was spinning. Thoughts collided, nothing seemed to hold meaning, and nothing ever would. My world felt irreparably shattered.

Not a single tear fell as I sat in her front yard for what felt like an eternity, my eyes fixated on the empty driveway ahead.

"Come inside, Hadley. It's getting dark out," I heard her voice call from the doorway.

I knew I was being selfish, but I remained immobilized, unable to muster the strength to rise. The sound of the door closing echoed in the distance, yet I was still unable to scrape all the battered pieces of myself off the ground.

Time drifted by, and eventually I summoned enough strength to drag myself back inside where I found her lying in her bed. I didn't know if she was sleeping, so I pulled back the covers as gently as I could and lay by her side. Once my head hit the pillow, she reached over and took my hand, and we fell asleep like that without another word.

The next morning, I drove home in a daze, my body going through the motions of existing, but I felt numb through and through. I needed to go home to shower and change before my morning class, but I wasn't sure I'd be able to put one foot in front of the other, much less teach a class.

I vaguely heard the sound of voices as I walked up the steps of my home.

"Hello? Earth to Hadley!" It was Stuart. He and Lex were standing in the walkway. I must have passed right by them, but it didn't register.

"You get wasted last night or something?" He smiled as he took in my haphazard appearance.

"No, I didn't." I didn't even realize I'd spoken until I heard my voice say those words.

I turned to walk up the stairs when a moment later I felt someone grab my forearm to stop me.

I spun to see Lex standing there on the steps below me. "What's wrong?" he asked, his eyebrows pinched together.

I looked down at my arm encircled by his hand and thought of how just a few days ago this would have sent chills down my spine... but I felt nothing.

"Hadley..." His voice was rough with impatience, his eyes pleading with me.

"It's my mom," I said without a single ounce of emotion in my voice. "The chemo stopped working. The doctor said there isn't much else he can do."

"Fuck," I heard Stuart say from behind Lex.

The devastation in Lex's eyes matched mine, and I felt like I was looking at my own reflection as I stared into their depths. A sharp stab of despair shot through me, momentarily breaking through the numbness as I looked at him, but it dissolved as quickly as it had come on.

I pulled my arm away and said, "You need to get to work. I'll talk to you guys later."

I turned without looking back at either of them and walked into my home. I wasn't ready to face the pain, so I pushed it down and tried like hell to make it through the rest of the day.

Over the next week, I spent every second of my free time searching for different treatment options that might help my mom as well as other doctors who specialized in her type of breast cancer. I begged her to let me take her to MD Anderson for a second opinion, but she flat-out refused. I went through cyclical phases of either being extremely angry or completely numb.

Since I was staying over at my mom's most of the time, I didn't see much of the guys even though they both called and texted often to check on me. Lionel and Sarah also offered to help in any way they could, but there wasn't much anyone could do.

It was a Thursday right after lunch when things took a sudden, unexpected turn. My cell phone started ringing, and I hurried to pick up the call from my mom. She never called when she knew I was at work, so I was instantly filled with panic.

"Mom?" I breathed.

"Hadley, Dr. Gremillion's office just called. They want me to go there right away. They didn't say what it's about. Do you think you can come?"

"Of course!" I stood, hurrying to gather my things. "I'll be right there."

We made it to the office in less than ten minutes and waited anxiously for him to come into the room. My mind was going through every possible scenario of what he might tell us, most of it grim.

He finally walked in, his face unreadable.

He pulled the rolling chair closer to his body and sat down in front of my mom before his face broke into a wide grin. "I've got good news, Ms. Olivier." My pulse quickened at those words. "A spot has opened up in the drug trial. I'd like you to start today. The sooner, the better."

My mom and I looked at each other with twin looks of shock.

"H-How?" my mom asked, her voice shaky.

"A great stroke of luck," he said, smiling. "Here's the paperwork I need you to bring over to the cancer center. I've called ahead, so they're already expecting you."

"Thank you so much," my mom said, her voice cracking at the end.

My heart continued pounding in my chest as he went over what she could expect with this new drug and warned us not to get our hopes too high since this was not a proven drug. It was impossible *not* to feel hopeful though as we made our way to the cancer center together.

I gave the paperwork to the front desk attendant as my mom got settled in at one of the treatment suites.

"Ms. Olivier!" It was Nurse Amber, who walked over excitedly and wrapped her arms around my mom in a tight hug. "I was so worried," she said. "When you didn't come on your normal treatment days, I called Dr. Gremillion's office to see what was happening. I hope you don't mind."

"No, of course not. That was sweet of you to worry," my mom said, patting her hand.

"I can't believe this happened. Thank god they were able to expand the trial."

My mom's forehead wrinkled. "What do you mean?"

"Dr. Gremillion's drug trial," she said, sounding confused. "Didn't they tell you? They expanded it. We were able to take on ten more patients, including you."

"We were just told a spot had opened up," I said, just as confused.

"I guess, technically. But so did nine more spots. I spoke with Dr. Gremillion's nurse earlier. She called to tell me the good news because she knew I was worried about you. She said there was some famous researcher who came in and petitioned the FDA to expand the trial. Apparently, he had some connections there, because it took them less than a week to give the green light."

Lex. This had to be him. It was too much of a coincidence. I had told him what Dr. Gremillion said about the drug trial when he had texted me last week. My heart felt caught inside a fist. I wasn't sure how much harder I could fall for this man, but it was starting to feel like a freefall.

"It was Lex, wasn't it?" my mom asked when Nurse Amber walked away.

"I think so," I told her. It came out as a whisper as I was choked with so much emotion. "I can't believe he did this for you."

She smiled warmly. "I don't think it was for me."

I had an overwhelming urge to see him. Once her treatment was finished, I dropped her off at her house and hurried back to the townhouses. My heart lurched when I spotted Lex's car in the parking lot. I ran over to his house, and the tears started to fall before I made it to the door.

I knocked impatiently. After only a few seconds, I started banging on it, unable to wait any longer. I had to see him. I was about to push the door open myself when it finally opened to reveal the warmest brown eyes looking back at me. I had fully planned to shove Stuart aside if it had been him and not Lex who answered.

I walked in and threw my arms around him without saying a word. His eyes widened momentarily before he caught me without hesitation. He wrapped his arms around me tightly as I started to sob into his neck. My knees had buckled so much, he was practically holding me up.

"What is it, Hadley?" he asked softly after a few minutes of us standing like that. "Is it your mom?" His voice was full of worry.

I couldn't answer just yet. I continued to cry into his neck, letting out every emotion that I'd been holding in since we were told the treatment wasn't working.

"Whatever it is, I'll do everything I can to fix it," he said into my hair, pulling me in even tighter. "I promise."

I pulled back to look him in the eyes and said through the tears, "You already have."

Chapter 19

The treatments were working.

After only a few weeks, Dr. Gremillion had told us her numbers had dropped drastically. Her body was responding to the chemo just as it should. This drug was taking a much harsher toll on her body, however. She could barely keep anything down lately and started to lose even more weight. We had to be extra cautious because it also wreaked havoc on her immune system. She stopped going out in public completely, and I wore a mask and kept my distance as best I could any time I was at her house.

Carl came over often and took the same precautions. My respect for him was at an all-time high. He hadn't tucked tail and ran when my mom started to become more frail. If anything, he seemed to be just as worried as I was and was so gentle and caring with her. When she made it through all of this, I knew they were going to become even more serious about each other.

I hadn't seen much of the guys lately. I was spending most of my time outside of work checking on my mom and taking care of things for her. But I was really starting to miss them. Stuart had texted me that he was throwing a party this Friday for the big Stanford vs. Berkeley football game. I knew they both could not have cared less about football, so I saw it for what it was—an excuse to throw a party. I checked with my mom, and she said that she and Carl could use some alone time. *Bleh.* So, I decided I was going to attend.

I'd been thinking a lot about my relationship with Lex. Uncertainty lingered over where we stood now, and whether there was anything beyond friendship from his end. But I'd made my decision. Life was too short, and I didn't want another day to go by without him knowing how I truly felt about him... even if he didn't feel the same way.

Friday night rolled around, and it was freezing out. So much for the vaunted California weather I was promised. I dressed in Stanford colors and threw on a large jacket and ran over to their house, banging on the door for someone to let me in before I froze to death.

"You made it!" Stuart said excitedly as he opened the door. He pulled me in for a hug that wasn't playful. It was reassuring and kind.

Lex walked up behind him, appearing just as happy to see me. He didn't make a move for me as we stood locked in a silent gaze. The world around me began to blur, the sounds fading to the background as I drank in the sight of him. It bordered on painful just how badly I wanted to reach out and touch him.

"How's your mom doing?" Stuart asked, snapping me out of it.

I blinked rapidly a few times, trying to clear my thoughts before turning to him.

"The treatments are working," I answered with a smile. "Her numbers are a lot better, but she's been much sicker."

"She's going to beat this," Stuart said solemnly.

I nodded in agreement. The alternative wasn't something I could fathom.

I followed them inside the house, where Lex stopped to help me remove my overcoat. The soft brush of his fingertips across my arms sent goosebumps in their wake as a nervous flutter beat through my chest. I needed a drink ASAP to settle these nerves, or I'd never make it through this night.

I looked around to see they had quite a few people in attendance for their "football" party. Most of the guys on their research team were there as well as some other faculty members, none of whom were watching the game. I also spotted Nicky in the corner talking to Jace, sipping a beer, and looking at me like I had the plague.

Glad to see everything was back to normal.

"We were just about to play another round of beer pong. You in?" Stuart asked.

"Beer pong? Am I at a frat party?" I asked, chuckling.

"Most of us didn't have a typical college experience. We're trying to do things right this time now that we're back in college again," he said, smirking. "Look, we've got the football game on and everything." He pointed to the TV that no one was watching. "What do you say?"

I smiled. "Alright, I'm in."

"Awesome!" he said. "Since it's your first time, you get to choose your partner."

"Whoever I want?" I looked around, pretending to be sizing everyone up.

"Whoever you want," Stuart repeated. "But just so you know, I've been undefeated this entire—"

"I choose Lex," I said, cutting him off. I turned to look at Lex, my face splitting into a wide grin. Surprise flickered across his expression, but he smiled back at me.

"What?!" Stuart said, outraged.

"Lex doesn't drink," Nicky spat from the corner, obviously listening to every word.

"I'll play," Lex said, his eyes never leaving mine.

Nicky scoffed and walked away to join the others in the living room.

"Really?" Stuart deadpanned. "*You're* going to play?" His tone was doubtful.

"You said she could choose whoever she wanted. I'm respecting the rules."

"That's right," I said, smirking.

"Whatever," Stuart said. "He's never even played before. I don't know why you'd choose him over someone like me with a proven track record of success."

"Simple," I stated. "Height advantage."

Lex's grin widened, and everyone around us began laughing. Stuart resisted at first as he stared me down, then a slow smile spread across his face. "Good to have you back, Betty."

"Thanks," I said, feeling choked up all of a sudden.

After the cups were set up, Lex and I stood across from Stuart and Peter. Our team went first, with Lex lining up and sinking the first shot.

Stuart rolled his eyes. "Beginner's luck."

I sank the second shot, and we watched as they both drank the contents of the red cups. By the fourth round of us both making all of our shots, Peter turned to Stuart and said, "We're fucked."

"You think?" Stuart said in annoyance as he drank his fourth cup of beer.

I giggled, looking up at Lex, who was looking back at me with a soft expression, almost as if he was enjoying the sound of my laughter. I got distracted by the warm, tingly feeling that was spreading through my chest. I missed my next shot, causing us both to have to drink several cups of the lukewarm beer as Stuart and Peter went on a three-shot winning streak.

"This is disgusting, by the way," Lex said as he downed his beer, grimacing the entire time.

I laughed. "Sorry," I told him sincerely. It really was gross.

The game was pretty evenly matched after that as we all started to get more tipsy, but our team eventually won, with Lex sinking the final shot in the remaining cup. I yelled out, throwing my hands over my head in victory. I jumped into Lex's arms, and he caught me as I laughed, feeling so carefree and happy.

He chuckled at my exuberance before he put me down, a sweet smile on his face. We were so close, I got lost looking into his lustrous brown eyes. Somehow, I'd forgotten how beautiful they were. They seemed to be shining so brightly tonight.

"I have a confession," I said, low enough so only he could hear me.

"What's that?" he said, still smiling.

"I didn't choose you just because you were tall."

He tilted his head. "No?"

"Nope," I answered, shaking my head. "I figured the KGB had special training in hand-eye coordination."

His grin stretched even wider across his face as he started to laugh from deep within his chest. The sound reverberated in my ears and in my heart.

I had to tell him. Tonight.

"Lex, come look at this." One of the guys was calling him over from the living room to look at something on his phone. He shot me a sidelong glance before he walked away, a small grin lingering on his lips. I chewed on my lip nervously as I headed toward the kitchen to pour myself another drink. I was going to need the liquid courage if I was ever going to tell him.

The sharp fear of rejection was something that was front and center in my mind. The more crippling fear, though, was the possibility that our friendship might be ruined once I confessed. If he didn't feel the same, then things might never go back to the way they were if he started to feel uncomfortable around me. Stuart came in as I was mulling it all over.

"I'm happy you came," he said. No joking, no teasing, just genuine kindness.

"Thanks, so am I."

"And I'm glad your mom was able to get into the trial," he added.

I smiled. "Thanks to Lex."

I could tell by the look on his face that he already knew, but he tried to play dumb. "What do you mean?"

"It's okay," I told him. "The nurse at the cancer center let it slip that some famous researcher got the trial expanded. I used my considerable powers of deductive reasoning and figured out who it was."

He gave me a half-smile. "He told me not to say anything. He didn't want you to know."

Lex had told me as much the night I cried in his arms. He wouldn't even talk to me about it, seeming uncomfortable whenever I attempted to tell him how grateful I was. He refused to even acknowledge the role he played in helping her get into the trial anytime I brought it up.

"I know," I said. "Did he have to go through a lot of trouble?" I'd been wondering if it was as simple as the nurse made it seem. When I asked Lex about it, he brushed me off, telling me not to worry about it before changing the subject.

"Not really. The company sponsoring the trial was happy to get a big name like Lex's attached to it." He looked away as he said it, so I had a hunch there was more.

"Is that it? He just had to let them use his name?"

He shrugged. "Pretty much."

I narrowed my eyes at him, and he sighed. "I mean there's a *little* extra paperwork that's needed."

"How much is a little extra, exactly?" I asked.

"It's no big deal."

"Stuart," I pressed.

"What?" he asked innocently.

"He doesn't have time for dinner most evenings. I hate to think of him taking on any more of a workload when he can barely keep up with what he has on his plate now."

"He's fine. We're all helping."

My eyes widened with surprise. "What do you mean?"

"I mean he came to all of us and asked if we would help."

"The whole team?"

"Yes. He said this project was really important to him and asked if we would help take some of it on. He never asks us for anything, so everyone said yes right away. No one even questioned it. I'm the only one who knew it was for your mom."

I started to tear up immediately. "Thank you, Stuart," I managed to choke out.

He pulled me in for a hug and said, "It's nothing. I'd take on a hundred times this amount of work if it meant your mom got better." He sounded like he was getting choked up himself.

We stood like that crying silently together for a few minutes. I wondered what I ever did to have such amazing friends.

"Well, don't you two look cozy," I heard the unmistakable sound of Nicky's voice say as we broke apart.

"Oh Nicky, you bring such joy to a room... specifically when you exit," Stuart said, trying to covertly wipe his eyes.

She had a smug look on her face as she fixed herself a drink. "I'll leave you two alone," she said, walking back out the door.

Stuart rolled his eyes. "You ready to get back out there, Betty?"

I dabbed at the last of my tears and straightened my shoulders. I came to have a fun evening. No more waterworks tonight. "Let's do it."

I followed Stuart into the living room, where Peter was setting up the cups again. I did a quick scan of the room but didn't see Lex anywhere.

"I say we have a rematch, Betty," Stuart said. "Although, it looks like your partner may have run off scared. You'll have to pick again."

I laughed. "Okay, let me just go to the bathroom first." I started to head down the hallway.

"Dan just went in there," Peter said. "He might be in there a while, too... I saw him eating a bowl of Sanjay's vindaloo earlier."

Yeah, definitely didn't need that visual.

"Just use the one upstairs," Stuart offered.

Thankfully, the upstairs bathroom was unoccupied, because I'd had way too much beer at this point. After I washed my hands, I was about to turn the knob when I heard Lex's voice say, "What are you doing up here?"

My brain automatically thought he was talking to me, so I cracked the door open, ready to explain myself, when I heard Nicky respond, "When did you get so jumpy?"

I closed the door again as softly as I could. I knew it was wrong to eavesdrop, but I couldn't help it.

"What do you want, Nicky?" Irritation colored his tone.

"Why are you being so uptight? I just wanted to talk to you."

"About what exactly?"

She made a noise of derision. "God, you don't even realize how much you've changed," she said. "I don't even know who you are anymore."

"What the fuck are you even talking about?"

"Playing beer pong?" Her tone was full of disgust. "In the eight years we've known each other, I haven't seen you take a single sip of alcohol. And now you're suddenly playing drinking games?"

"I know you like to think you know everything about me, but you don't," he shot back.

"I'm not the only one who's noticed. Everyone on the team can see how different you've been acting these last few months. You rush out the door every evening after work to have dinner with a certain neighbor." The disdain in her voice was evident. "Every other project we've worked on, you would stay later than everyone else and be back the next morning before we even got there. Hell, some nights you wouldn't even leave the lab at all."

"You're mad that I don't sleep over in the lab anymore? Is that what you're saying?"

She scoffed. "What's happened to you? You used to take this seriously," she said. "You've been so distracted lately, you even mixed up those ion permeabilities yesterday."

"Everyone makes mistakes, including you."

"I've never seen you so much as put a decimal in the wrong place."

"Are you done?"

"No. I want you to admit it," she said, her voice growing darker. "Admit that the reason you've been acting so different is because of Broadway Barbie down there."

"Don't go there," he warned.

"I knew it," she said with a snicker. "What is it, Lex? Is it that you think you actually have a shot with her? Pathetic."

He didn't say anything.

"I promise you're not that girl's type. Barbie wants a Ken who watches football in his spare time. Not one who's trying to discern membrane capacitance."

"You don't even know her." His voice sounded calm, but I could tell she was getting to him.

"I know her type—chest full of silicon, face full of botulin." She laughed derisively. "Apparently, it's *you* that I don't know because I never took you for the kind of guy to think with the head that's not on his shoulders."

I pressed my ear to the door, waiting for Lex to say something back to her, but it was dead air.

"Honestly, what do you even see in her?" she continued. "Our team is doing *real* work here, trying to make an actual difference in the world, and what is she doing? Singing show tunes and writing crappy pop songs for the glitterati of Hollywood. You know… the kind of shit we used to make fun of. But here you are fawning all over her with the rest of those idiots down there. When are you going to wake up and realize that she's not waiting for you, Lex? She's waiting for the latest sale at Sephora."

I waited for him to defend me… to say anything at all as the seconds ticked by, but he said nothing. Not a word. His silence spoke volumes, and I'd heard enough. I swung the door open to see them both standing in Lex's doorway with twin looks of shock.

"Don't mind me. I was just leaving," I said to them. Lex stood there stunned with his mouth slightly open, eyes wide with surprise. I could barely look at him, I was so hurt.

I turned to Nicky. "Give my compliments to your hairdresser, Nicky. The pink really distracts from the horns you have growing underneath."

I looked to Lex and said, "I'll let you get back to your conversation. You two actually have way more in common than I thought."

I started for the stairs.

"Hadley, wait!" Lex said, trying to step around Nicky, but I could see her blocking his path.

"Where are you going?" she cried.

I was down the stairs, grabbing my jacket before he could say another word.

"I'm leaving," I told Stuart when he looked at me questioningly. "Thanks for having me."

The cold air stung my face as I ran across the walkway back to my house. The tears started to well in my eyes. I couldn't believe this was happening. I felt like such an idiot for letting myself believe there was something more between us when the truth was he couldn't even be bothered to defend me against his snake of an ex.

"Hadley, stop!" I heard Lex calling from behind me. I hurried to fish my keys out of my pocket to get inside, so he wouldn't see my crying.

When I finally wrenched the door open and went inside, I caught a glimpse of Lex running across the walkway in nothing but his jeans and a navy, button-down shirt. He wasn't wearing a jacket in what felt like 30-degree weather. I closed the door and leaned my head back against it. The guilt was riding me hard as I thought of him out there in the freezing cold when a second later, there was a loud knock at my door, making me jump.

"Hadley, please open up!" he called out, continuing to pound on the door.

"There's nothing we need to talk about, Lex. Go back home and get inside."

"I'm not leaving until you talk to me. Please, just let me explain."

My first instinct was to ignore him or tell him to go to hell, but I sighed, knowing I didn't have it in me to leave him out there to freeze. I opened the door to see his body shivering and steam filling the chill air from his heavy breathing.

"Jesus, Lex. Get in here." I grabbed his arm, pulling him inside. "Honestly, what were you thinking running out there without a jacket in this weather?"

"I don't care. I needed to talk to you," he said breathlessly. His cheeks were flushed from even that brief time in the cold.

I crossed my arms, feeling protective of my heart. "There's nothing left to say."

"Hadley—" he started, but I didn't want to hear whatever excuse he was going to give me.

"Look Lex, what you did for my mom… there aren't enough words to express how truly grateful I am for what you did for us. I'll owe you in every lifetime, but right now, I can barely stand to look at you."

He flinched, his eyes lowering to the ground. "I'm so sorry about what she said."

My anger and hurt boiled over. "I couldn't care less about what she said! It's what you didn't say. You just stood there and let her say hateful shit about me," I fumed.

I spun away from him, bringing my hands to my hair just as the tears started to fall. "God! I'm such a fucking idiot," I said more to myself. "The worst part is that I was planning on telling you tonight and in the end, it would have all been for nothing!"

His brows knitted together as he stepped closer. "Telling me what?"

I could feel the alcohol still coursing through my veins as I paced back and forth across the entryway of my home. I had wanted it to help give me the courage to tell Lex how I felt, but now I was fighting to get control of that filter that drinking always made me lose.

I stopped and turned toward him. "Can you just answer one thing for me?" I swiped away the trickle of tears. "Why did you do all of this? Stuart told me how much more work the trial is for you... Did you just feel sorry for me?"

"Feel *sorry* for you?" he questioned, disbelief evident in his tone. "Is that really what you think?"

"No! I thought—" But I couldn't finish.

"What? You thought what?" His voice was low and tortured.

"It doesn't matter," I said, shaking my head.

"You thought what, Hadley?" he pressed. His tone was desperate, and I knew it was no use hiding anymore.

"I thought this was real!" I cried, gesturing between the two of us. I put my hand over my heart, pressing it against my chest, trying to soothe the hurt. "I thought you felt the same way. I thought you wanted me as badly as I want you. But now... Now, I just feel like a fool, because I don't think you ever wanted me."

I was unable to stop more tears from falling, so I turned away, trying to hide my face.

"Don't say that," he said sharply. It came out barely above a whisper.

"Why not? It's true," I said, unable to meet his gaze.

"No, it's not," he said roughly. He took my face in his hands before tilting my chin up toward him so that I was looking him squarely in the eyes as he said, "It feels like that's all I do. From the moment I met you. It feels like all I do is spend my time wanting you. Every second of every fucking day. I've never wanted anything so badly in all my goddamn life."

He was breathing heavily as he said it, his eyes boring down into mine.

For the second time tonight, I'd heard enough.

I didn't think. I just acted. One second, I was standing there, and the next, I was closing the distance between us as I crashed my lips to his. I wrapped my arms around his neck as he pulled me in close. It was better than I could have ever imagined. His mouth fit perfectly against mine. One hand was pressed against the small of my back while the other drifted to tangle in my hair, securing my mouth to his. The kiss deepened, and I couldn't stop the whimper that escaped. The sound only seemed to ignite him further as he pulled my body even closer to his. Our tongues tangled and the faint taste of the beer we'd drunk combined with the stronger flavor of something minty lingered on his tongue. I wanted more of it. I wanted more of him.

I let my hands drift over the hard muscles of his chest that I'd been itching to touch since the first day I'd seen him shirtless. As I frantically explored every inch of that beautiful chest, I could feel him backing us up until my back hit the wall with a thud. His hands moved over my waist and hips as his body pressed further into mine, all while kissing me like he was born to do it.

I lifted my leg to hook around his hip and he took the hint, grabbing me under the thighs and lifting me as I wrapped my legs around his waist. We were more evenly matched in height this way, so I took advantage and swept my tongue across those perfect lips, savoring the taste and feel of him. He let out a hiss, and I moved my hips to press our perfectly aligned pelvises together. He pressed his hard length back into me, and I gasped.

Our bodies moved together like they were already thoroughly familiar with one another. I didn't think I would ever get enough of this. Every touch, every taste had me wanting more. I never wanted to come up for air.

The sound of kissing and heavy breathing filled the room until suddenly I heard my phone ringing loudly from my back pocket. It wasn't my mom's ringtone so I ignored it, unwilling to move even an inch away from him. He was content to do the same as his tongue never ceased the sweeping motions across mine. A minute later, however, his phone started to ring just as loudly, and we both paused, realizing the same person was probably calling us and was probably going to keep calling us. He let the call go to voicemail as he set me down, looking irritated.

I smiled. I had a pretty good guess of who it was.

Our gazes were locked, and my eyes drifted to his swollen lips. I already missed the feel of them on mine. He was breathing heavily as he asked, "What are we doing, Hadley?"

I put my hands on my knees, trying to catch my breath. "Well, I'm no biologist, but I think it's called kissing."

He stepped closer. "I mean about us." I could see the intensity of his emotions crackling right below the surface. "You have no idea how long I've wanted this."

"Me, too," I said. "I had it all planned out. I was going to tell you how I felt about you tonight, but then..."

The memory of what had happened outside the bathroom with Nicky came crashing back.

"But then I fucked it up," he said, finishing my sentence, looking regretful. "I'm sorry. I know I should have said something to her, but

I was barely listening after she said I was pathetic for thinking I had a shot with you. I believed her. I never thought this would happen."

"Why?" I was genuinely curious.

"Have you seen you?"

I exhaled a laugh. "Yes," I said. "And I see you. You're unbelievably handsome, freakishly intelligent, and you have the kindest heart. I've wanted this for a long time now. I just didn't know how to tell you."

He was looking at me like he couldn't believe the words coming out of my mouth. I was looking at him like I wanted a repeat performance of what we were just doing. We started to draw closer together. As we leaned in tentatively, there was a loud knock at the door, making us both jump.

"Lex, you in there?" It was Stuart, and I smiled widely when Lex let his head fall backward, hitting the wall behind him with a thud.

"He's not going to give up," I said, still smiling.

He gave me a frustrated look. "I know."

"Maybe we should let him in."

"I'd really rather not," Lex said.

I giggled at the look on his face, and his features softened.

"This won't be the last time we do this, I promise," I said. "No need to rush things." And I meant it. I wanted to do this right.

He let out a rough exhale before he finally nodded. "Will I see you tomorrow?"

"That depends," I said.

"On?"

"If we can go somewhere where Stuart can't find us."

His mouth split into a breathtaking smile. He was so incredibly beautiful. I bit my lip, wanting to grab his face and pull it back down toward mine.

"Deal," he said. "But you need to stop looking at me like that, or I'll never be able to walk out this door."

"Hadley, it's Stuart," Stuart called out like I didn't know who he was. "Are you guys alright?"

Lex gazed at me for a few seconds longer before he finally opened the door to find Stuart standing there, shaking in his huge overcoat.

"What the hell is wrong with you two?" Stuart yelled, running inside. "Hadley, you ran out of the party without any explanation, and this moron ran out into the frozen tundra wearing a T-shirt. Are you two fighting?"

"No, we're fine," I told him. "Just a misunderstanding."

"Come on, let's go home," Lex said, still sounding frustrated. He grabbed Stuart's arm, pulling him back toward the door.

"Wait! At least let me grab you a jacket or a blanket," I called to Lex.

"I'll be fine." His eyes moved tenderly across my face as he said it. "I'll only be outside for a few seconds."

"Lex—" I started to complain, but he cut me off.

"So, I'll see you tomorrow?"

"Definitely," I said, smiling. He grinned back at me before walking out into the freezing night air.

"What are we doing tomorrow?" I heard Stuart ask as they jogged back to their house.

I couldn't wipe the smile from my face. It was really happening. I wore that same smile to bed that night, all the way into the next morning.

Chapter 20

The butterflies were setting in as I rifled through my closet the next evening for something to wear for our date. Lex had texted me when he got home last night asking if he could take me somewhere after he got off work. Of course, I'd agreed. He'd been working most Saturdays lately, which now made me wonder with a pang of guilt if that was because he was having to take on extra work for the trial.

I didn't know what to expect or how to dress because he wasn't giving away what we were doing. He had called earlier that morning while I was still in bed, and he was already at work.

"We still on for tonight?" he'd asked when I answered the call. I guess we weren't mincing words. I smiled. Was he really that unsure of how I felt about him?

"Who's this?" I couldn't help teasing him a little.

"HA-HA. Answer the question."

"So bossy." I laughed, picturing him impatiently waiting for me to answer. He would need me to say the words to really believe it. "What time are we leaving, boss?"

"I'll pick you up at six." His tone seemed more relaxed now.

"By pick me up, do you mean walk across the grass?"

He ignored my joke. "Dress warmly."

"Are you going to tell me what we're doing?"

"It's a surprise."

"I think Ted Bundy said the same thing to all his victims."

He laughed, and I relished the sound.

I smiled and said, "But if this has really all been some elaborate plan to get me alone in the wilderness somewhere to finally get rid of me then at least have the decency to take your shirt off while doing it. I might not even notice it's happening that way."

I could almost see the smile on his face through the phone as he said, "I'm really glad we're doing this."

"Me, too," I agreed.

That conversation was playing over again in my mind as I tore through my entire wardrobe, unable to find a damn thing to wear. I finally settled for a tight-fitting, long-sleeved sweater dress that hugged each and every curve. It was on the shorter side, so I paired it with some over the thigh, high-heeled boots so that a little bit of skin was peeking through around my thighs. It wasn't as cold tonight as it had been last night, but I grabbed my overcoat from the downstairs closet just in case.

Lex knocked at the door precisely at six o'clock. Hopefully, I was dressed okay for whatever he had planned.

I opened the door to see him standing there in dark jeans and a soft, cream-colored pullover, looking like a whole snack. His eyes took in every inch of me, starting from my face and moving down, stopping at the exposed skin on my thighs.

"Fuck," I heard him mutter under his breath. "You look incredible, Hadley."

"So do you," I said. I usually hated first dates. They were always so awkward, but I already knew this man, and I was eager to explore all the parts that I didn't know.

As we got into the car, he wasn't saying much. He never did, but his energy seemed a little off. It suddenly occurred to me why that might be.

"Are you nervous?" I asked.

"Yes," he admitted with a chuckle. "But I always am around you." I smiled at him and he said, "If I'm being honest, I kept waiting for you to change your mind all day."

"Why would I do that? I'm finally living out my mother's dream for me—going on a date with a hot doctor."

He laughed, and the tension in his posture seemed to relax a little. "I don't think I'm the kind of doctor she meant."

I shrugged. "Tomato, tomahto."

I studied his profile as we drove along the highway. The squareness of his jawline, coupled with his straight nose and those thick, beautiful lashes framing his brilliant brown eyes had me wanting to crawl into his lap and taste him all over again.

"So, can you tell me what we're doing?" I asked as a distraction from my own ogling.

"We're going to dinner first, but then after is the surprise."

"Am I dressed okay?"

He looked over at me, his eyes zeroing in on my legs again. "Not really," he said with a swallow. "But I don't think I want to stop looking at you in this outfit."

My cheeks flushed at his words. "Is it the boots?" I asked playfully.

"No." He was looking at me out of the corner of his eye. "It's you."

Now my whole body felt flushed.

Once we got seated at a small Italian restaurant downtown, I ordered wine, trying to fight the nerves as I looked over the menu. My eyes bugged out when I saw the prices.

"Holy crap!" I said.

His brows rose. "What?"

"These prices are insane," I told him. "There's no way I'm ordering anything."

"Don't be ridiculous," he said.

"I think I'll just stick with the wine and some bread," I said, grabbing a piece from the basket.

"Hadley…"

"If it was good enough for Jesus, it's good enough for me."

He sighed. "I'm just going to order something for you if you don't choose. We've had dinner together a thousand times. I know what you like."

"Fine," I said, choosing the cheapest option I could find. He ordered for himself and added two more dishes to the order that I knew were for me: pan-seared scallops and a black truffle pasta. *Yum.*

I looked over at him, still in disbelief that we were actually doing this. I was nervous but for the most part, I was absolutely thrilled. His expression was unreadable as he looked back at me.

"Can I ask you something?" His tone had me a little worried.

"What is it?"

"Did the fact that I helped your mom get into the trial have anything to do with you agreeing to come tonight?" He looked so dejected at the thought. "I-I never wanted you to feel obligated to me. I didn't do it for this. I never even wanted you to know."

"I know you didn't." The desire to comfort him was overwhelming. I reached out and placed my hand on his, making the butterflies spark to life even with this simple touch. "But I already told you how badly I wanted this to happen. I'm so grateful for what you did for my mom, but me being here has nothing to do with that."

I wished I had told him before everything happened with my mom. I didn't want him to have any doubts about how I felt.

"I can't pinpoint exactly when my feelings started to change, but I've always felt drawn to you. Since I first heard you speak at faculty night, I've wanted to know you. And the more I did, the more I knew it wasn't just friendship I was feeling." I smiled at him, threading my fingers through his. "But then you were only nice to me when we were alone, so I figured you were embarrassed by me, or you weren't really interested."

"That wasn't it," he said, looking down at our entwined hands. He stared at them for a moment before he finally pulled his eyes up to meet mine. "There hasn't been a single day since we first met that I haven't thought about you. At times, it seemed like that was all I could think about. I'd spend almost every day counting down the minutes until I could see you again. But I didn't think there was a chance in hell you felt the same way, so I tried to keep my distance. I felt like it was written all over me how badly I wanted you. I was always trying to hide it, but people noticed anyway."

"Stuart," I guessed.

He smiled. "He was always pushing me to tell you how I felt. But then I wasn't sure if you liked him."

I shook my head. "Not in that way."

"He said the same thing. But I was still jealous of how easy your friendship seemed to be."

"We care about each other, but it's never been like that," I said. "You're lucky to have such a good friend."

"So he's always telling me," he said with a wry smile, and I laughed.

The dinner was amazing, especially the dishes he had ordered for me. *Damn him.* I tried arguing for him to let me at least pay for my half of the dinner, but he rolled his eyes and ignored my plea.

The drive to our mystery activity took about thirty minutes, and I grew even more curious as we approached the shoreline of the Pacific Ocean. He held my hand as we walked along the dock of the Safe Harbor Marina to a small fishing boat that apparently was waiting for us.

"We're going on a boat?" I asked.

"Yes." He nodded. "I want to show you something."

"Again, probably a phrase Ted Bundy has uttered," I said. "I knew you were trying to get rid of me!"

He laughed. "I wouldn't have to go through all this trouble if I wanted to get rid of you. I'd just set a bird loose in your house."

"You wouldn't dare!"

"Hola Alexsander!" a Hispanic gentlemen greeted him from aboard *The Lady Kriller* as we walked up.

Lex greeted the gentleman, who evidently was the captain of the boat. They started speaking in Spanish to one another, still not cluing me in on what we were doing.

"How did you manage to find someone with a boat in less than twelve hours anyway?" I asked.

"He owed me a favor," he said with a smile.

"Do I even want to know?" I asked, and he chuckled.

There was a ladder to climb aboard the boat, which Lex used first before holding his hands out to help me. I shivered with pleasure when he put his hands on my waist to steady me as I descended the ladder onto the boat. The fact that I managed to do it even in this outfit was a small miracle.

The captain spoke in Spanish to Lex again before he entered the small cabin onboard that could only fit one person, so I knew we'd be taking the only remaining seats at the front of the boat.

"Sorry, he only speaks Spanish," Lex said to me.

"That's okay. I know you guys were just discussing the best place to dump a body."

His eyes widened, and he gave a small gasp. "So you do speak Spanish."

I laughed before tugging on his pullover. "Just remember our deal—shirt needs to come off that way I won't realize when my time's up."

He rolled his eyes, a grin playing across his lips. "Just keep your coat buttoned. It might get pretty chilly on the ride. But it should only take about ten minutes to get there."

I started humming the funeral march, and he shook his head, his eyes sparkling with amusement.

We couldn't really talk anymore when the boat got up to a higher speed as we made our way toward the open ocean. He was right. It did get pretty chilly as the wind whipped across my face. I pulled my coat in even tighter around me.

He leaned close to my ear so that I could hear him above the noise of the boat, sending shivers down my spine that had nothing to do with the chill in the air. "Are you okay? Are you cold?"

"I'm fine," I told him, but my traitorous teeth started to chatter.

"Take mine." He started to unbutton his own coat.

"No," I said, grabbing his hand. "I have a much better idea of how to keep warm."

I took his arm and wrapped it around me. He smiled, pulling me in close. I breathed in the scent of him—clean laundry and that earthy maleness. It started as a ploy just to get him close to me, but it really did help to keep me warm.

True to his word, in about ten minutes, the boat started to slow as we pulled up next to a cluster of large rocks about a mile out from the shoreline. The sun had completely set at this point, and the only light being cast was from the countless number of stars shining brightly above. They were so breathtaking. I was never able to see the stars in New York.

"So, I know it's been hard for you adjusting to living in California," he said, leaning close to my ear, the warmth of his breath fanning over my face. "But I wanted to show you something that you can't see much of on the East Coast."

We walked to the side of the boat as the captain anchored next to the rock cluster. After finishing, he went back inside the small cabin again, leaving the two of us alone again.

"Look just over there." He pointed to the far side of the rock cluster where the waves were crashing over. I looked in the direction he was pointing and tried not to focus on his hand pressing against my lower back.

I had to blink a few times to make sure what I was seeing was real. The water shimmered with an iridescent blue glow all along the line of rocks. Even the waves seemed to emit a faint luminescence as they crashed against the rocks, each splash adding to the surreal spectacle.

My eyes went wide and my lips parted. "What is it, Lex?"

I could see out of the corner of my eye he wasn't looking at the water. He was watching me. "It's called bioluminescence. It's pretty easy to find along the coast of California."

"How?" I asked breathlessly. It was so incredible. It was like someone had plunged neon glow sticks right under the surface of the water.

"It's a chemical reaction from various organisms living in the ocean. It causes them to emit this blue light near the surface of the water. It's usually triggered by motion, which is why you can see it so well near these rocks."

My eyes were completely transfixed on this impossible phenomenon happening right in front of me. I couldn't tear my eyes away. It looked like something out of a fairytale.

"It's so beautiful." The smile I was wearing felt fixed to my face. "I don't think I'll ever want to leave."

"We have some time. Look as long as you want," he said in a hushed tone.

Second only to helping my mom get into the trial, this was the most amazing thing anyone had ever done for me. Both gifts were from the man standing next to me. I looked up at him, and his eyes seemed to be shining just as brightly as the water, but they were even more beautiful to me.

"Okay, but I think I'm starting to get cold again," I lied as I took his arms and wrapped them around me, my back pressing into his chest. He laughed softly, pulling me in closer as I looked out, watching the bright blue water dancing across the rock line. The moment was so perfect with the ethereal glow of the moonlight shining above us in the stillness of the night... I couldn't help myself. My brain was always thinking musically, and there was one song in particular playing through my mind.

"When the night has come," I started to sing softly. "And the land is dark. And the moon is the only light we'll see. No, I won't be afraid. Oh, I won't be afraid. Just as long as you stand, stand by me."

He leaned down and his breath tickled my ear as he said, "I could listen to that sound all my life and never grow tired of it."

I turned in his arms to look up at him. His eyes moved over my face with infinite tenderness before his gaze locked with mine.

"I know I've already said it and so has everyone else at this point, but would it be crazy if I told you again how incredibly beautiful you are?"

I smiled. "Not when it's coming from the only person I want to hear say it."

He lifted his hand to cup my face and stroked his thumb along my cheek. I closed my eyes briefly at the softness of his touch, and my heart started to beat rapidly in my chest. I could feel my pulse throbbing all the way up my neck. I took his free hand and placed it over the center of my chest so he could feel how fast it was beating.

"Tell me why it does that," I whispered.

His lips were parted, and he was breathing a little more heavily as he lifted his fingertips to brush along the side of my head just above my ear. "Your amygdala, just here, is readying your body for fight or flight," he said softly. He brushed my hair back and smiled before saying, "Which will it be?"

I looked down at his mouth, aching to have it on mine. "Well, I'm definitely not going anywhere."

He leaned down and captured my lips with his. This kiss was different from the first one. It wasn't rushed or full of the same overpowering intensity. It was gentle and slow-burning, leaving me aching all over.

One hand held my neck, while the other grasped my waist. I placed my palms against his chest and took my time memorizing the way his lips moved against mine. The kiss deepened, and I wrapped my arms around his neck as he pulled me in close. I exhaled raggedly through my nose as he took his time kissing me, our tongues dancing slowly across one another. I don't know how long we stayed like that, but after what only felt like minutes, I heard the captain behind us clearing his throat. We pulled apart, laughing.

I assumed he told Lex in Spanish that it was time to get going because Lex took my hand and walked us back to our seats at the front of the boat. He wrapped his arm around me without me having to ask this time, and I leaned my head against him, feeling happier than I'd felt in a very long time as we made our way back to shore.

Chapter 21

My mom's birthday was tomorrow, and I still hadn't found anything for her. The three of us—me, my mom, and Carl—were just planning on having dinner together at home since she couldn't really go out. She was tolerating food a little better these days, so I decided I was going to make her favorite—chicken and veggie stir fry. I had tried all week to find her a gift but to no avail.

When Saturday came around, Lionel and Sarah offered to go shopping with me. We spent the morning on the hunt at some of the more eclectic shops until I stumbled on the perfect thing, an antique watch that looked just like the one my grandmother used to wear. I knew she would love it.

Lex was working again today, but he still texted me throughout the day.

Alexsander Strovinski: I'm usually the one having to tell everyone to put away their phones and get back to work. But now I've got mine glued to my hand, thanks to you.

My face split into a stupid, sappy grin.

Hadley Olivier: You're the boss. You can do whatever you want.

Alexsander Strovinski: I'm serious. This time I'm really putting my phone away.

Hadley Olivier: No, you hang up first.

Alexsander Strovinski: ....

I guess I should let him get back to work. He had been trying to do so for an hour now, but I kept sending him suggestive texts and dirty emojis.

I smiled and put my phone down to see Lionel and Sarah watching me with a matching pair of mischievous grins on their faces. We were having lunch at a little bistro downtown, and I was ashamed to admit I was caught up talking to Lex instead of paying attention to my friends.

I cleared my throat and pretended to be looking at the menu.

"It's too late now," Sarah said.

"Yeah, bitch. You're busted," Lionel added.

I pulled the menu up higher to cover my face.

"I have a guess of who put that smile on her face, Lionel," Sarah teased.

"Do tell," Lionel replied.

"It's the scientist, isn't it, Hadley Marie Olivier?" Sarah snatched the menu from me.

I sighed before looking up at them, grinning. "Yep."

"Oh my god!" Sarah cried out, tossing her napkin at me. "How could you not tell us?!"

I laughed, throwing the napkin back at her. "It just happened."

"When? Where? How?" Sarah stuttered.

"Yeah, this isn't lunch anymore, it's tea time. Spill!" Lionel demanded.

"Wellllllll," I said, dragging it out a bit.

"Spit it out already!" Lionel shouted. "Shania Twain and I want the same question answered—he's got the brains, but does he have the touch?"

I laughed. "Okay, fine. We went on a date last weekend. That was after we got into a fight the night before and ended up making out against the wall of my living room until Stuart interrupted."

"In the immortal words of Paris Hilton... that's hot," Lionel said. "How was the sex? Was it freaky? I bet it was freaky."

"We haven't had sex yet."

"Why not?" Sarah demanded. "You've been pining away at each other for months now. What's the holdup?"

"It just hasn't happened," I said, taking a sip of my water.

"You nervous his dick is crooked or something?" Lionel asked. "Because that only makes it better. Trust me."

"No, you freak," I said. "I'm not worried about that."

"Then what are you worried about?" Sarah asked.

"I don't know. I think I really like him," I replied. "Actually, I know I do. And I also know there won't be any going back for me once we cross that line. I'll really be in deep."

"So will he," Lionel said, wiggling his eyebrows. Sarah swatted him.

"What?" he said, rubbing his arm. "It was too easy."

"He's right," Sarah said, looking over at me.

"I regretted it as soon as I said it."

Sarah grinned, leaning forward. "From what I've seen and from everything you've told me, this man has it just as bad for you. It's going to be worth it."

"Yes. And when you do, come back and give us all the dirty details," Lionel said, winking at me.

I chuckled. "Thanks, guys."

"Is he at least a good kisser?" Sarah asked.

I smiled. "The best," I answered, remembering each time over the past week that things had gotten hot and heavy between us. I didn't want to rush things, but that was proving to be more difficult than I could have ever imagined.

Lionel sighed dramatically. "I swear, every day of being single brings me closer to a life of crime."

◆◆◆

I went to my mom's around five to start cooking dinner. She was looking so much better today and was able to tolerate eating half a plate of food. We had dinner and cut the cake before she opened her presents. She loved the watch I'd gotten her, and Carl had given her a beautifully bound collection of poems from her favorite author, Oscar Wilde. It was a wonderful evening, and I just kept thinking of the one person who had made it all possible on the drive home.

Hadley Olivier: *Hey, you up?*

Alexsander Strovinski: *Yes, how was dinner?*

Hadley Olivier: Great. Can I come over?

I started knocking on his door without waiting for a response.

He opened the door wearing nothing but gray sweatpants with his bare chest on full display. His face broke into a smile, and I started to gawk.

"What is wrong with you?! Who answers the door shirtless?" I gaped, unable to pull my eyes away from all that perfectly tanned skin.

"I was about to go to bed," he said with laughter in his voice. "I don't sleep fully clothed."

"Sure. Likely story! The truth is that you're trying to seduce me, and it won't work."

But it was working, and I couldn't stop staring at his broad chest and toned abdomen. He continued to laugh.

"You came here," he pointed out, but I waved him off.

"This can't happen. We've only been dating a week," I told him, slapping my hands over my eyes.

"I understand." He tried sounding contrite but failed miserably. "I'll go put on a shirt."

"No! Wait." I put my hand out to stop him. "Just one more quick peek." I pulled my fingers apart, peeking through my middle and ring fingers, taking in all his smooth skin and that small patch of hair right at the center of his chest that I was itching to run my fingers through.

He stayed where he was, grinning. I leaned forward, gently placing my hands on his pecs, feeling the steady rhythm of his heartbeat beneath my touch. I thought about running my tongue all along his chest, down those abs, and even lower...

I abruptly pulled my hands back.

"Now look what you made me do!" I accused. I turned and ran down the porch steps.

"Where are you going?" he asked, laughing.

"Back to my house to take a cold shower. Really, Lex, I'm ashamed of you!" I called out over my shoulder. "You can't even control yourself. Trying to ruin my darling reputation. What would our mothers think?"

I had already jogged across the walkway before he could answer. His laughter followed me the whole way back to my house.

I really did take a cold shower to try to calm down. I was in over my head with this man. I didn't trust myself not to take it too far, and there was some part of me that didn't feel ready. But I felt bad for the way I left him. I texted him ten minutes later, deciding to give it another try.

Hadley Olivier: *Whacha doin?*

Alexsander Strovinski: Trying to remember the neural pathways between the irrational center of the brain and one's libido.

Hadley Olivier: What did you come up with?

Alexsander Strovinski: *Definitely connected.*

Hadley Oliver: Can I come back now? I promise to behave.

Alexsander Strovinski: Sure. I'll make sure to be fully clothed this time.

Hadley Olivier: I appreciate that.

I made my way back to his house and knocked on the door a few times. He answered in what looked like three pairs of sweatpants, five shirts, a jacket, scarf, and beanie, and I burst out laughing.

"Better?" he asked.

"Much!" I laughed before launching myself at him. I wrapped my arms around his neck, and he wrapped his around my waist, smiling down at me.

"I just came by for a goodnight kiss," I told him, gazing into those beautiful eyes. "I missed you today." I pulled the beanie and scarf off, taking the time to appreciate how handsome he was.

"I can tell," he said in a husky voice.

I closed the last bit of distance between us until our chests were pressed together, and I tilted my face up to his. The mood quickly shifted away from being playful as I ran my hands across his chest and even with all the extra layers, it wasn't doing much to kill the desire I felt rising up. It felt like this palpable thing between us that I didn't even try to suppress.

He remained silent as his hands kneaded at my waist before he leaned down, and our lips finally met. The kiss was slow at first, our tongues sliding leisurely against one another, but as it started to build, my rational thoughts went out the window. I unzipped his puffer jacket and began tugging at the extra layers he had on. We both started to laugh when the layers got stuck as I tried to pull them over his head. We quickly resumed kissing once he was down to a single layer of clothing.

After a few minutes, I made the bold decision that the last T-shirt needed to go as well, so I swiftly removed that one too. *So much for my darling reputation.* He didn't object. He just continued to kiss me like he never wanted to stop. My breathing felt tighter as he led me backward toward the sofa, his hands trailing along my waist. My skin came alive underneath his touch. He settled onto the sofa, pulling me with him until I was straddling him. I could feel his erection pushing into me, and I pushed back.

His hands slid underneath my shirt, pressing along my back before venturing toward the front of my body, and I felt him starting to palm my breasts in tandem with our kisses. Realizing he needed better access, I broke the kiss and pulled off my own shirt in one quick motion. He took the hint, leaning forward and pulling down the straps of my bra until my breasts were exposed, and his mouth covered my nipple. I groaned softly as he ran his tongue along my breasts, cupping them both gently in his hands.

"Maybe we should go to my room. I don't know when Stuart will be back," he whispered, but I was too caught up in a haze of lust. I barely registered the words he had spoken as a dull roaring sound filled my ears.

"Mhmm," was all I managed to respond. Apparently, I was incapable of human language. I continued to grind down on his erection, needing more. I pulled his face back to mine, already forgetting what he had just said to me. He seemed just as lost in the moment as he turned my body, laying me flat on the sofa. Hovering just inches above me, our kiss resumed, igniting a blaze of desire that threatened to consume me.

After a few minutes, I was so worked up that I had to break the kiss just to catch my breath, but he took that as an invitation to start kissing my neck. Hot, aching desire flooded my system.

He moved down even further to give attention to the other breast. His tongue slid around my other peaked nipple as I tangled my fingers in his hair, urging him on. My hips began to roll, and I started groaning with each sweep of his tongue across my sensitive flesh. I felt his weight shift, followed by the gentle brush of his fingertips along my abdomen. His hand trailed even lower, slipping under the waistband of my pants, delving further into the fabric of my panties until he found the exact spot I needed him to.

My breathing picked up speed as he worked two fingers in, and I'm sure it was now crystal clear to him just how turned on I was. His thumb pressed along that bundle of nerves as his fingers pumped into me, all while kissing along my chest and neck. It was all too much and not enough. I grasped the wrist of the hand that was pressing into me in all the right ways and wound my free arm around his neck as my eyes fluttered closed in pure ecstasy.

"The noises you're making are driving me crazy," he said, low in my ear. I couldn't concentrate on anything else but the feel of his fingers guiding into me with an expertise that I'd only dreamed of, and the sensation of his lips on my skin.

"Don't stop," was all I managed to breathe out.

His hand started to move a little faster, and I squeezed my eyes shut from the onslaught of pleasure. He pressed his forehead to mine, and I placed my hand around the back of his neck to hold him there and kissed him briefly until all I could do was moan against his mouth as I felt myself getting closer. He pressed his thumb in a little more firmly, and that propelled me over the edge.

I writhed underneath him as he watched me climax, breathing heavily with his lips parted and a look of pure desire on his face, doubling my own pleasure. When I finally came back down, I stared up at him in a blissful daze. All I could think about was how incredible he was going to be in bed if that was the kind of orgasm I got just from his hand.

"I feel like I could hammer nails after watching you come undone like that," he said a little breathlessly, his fingers still slowly moving in and out as little aftershocks of pleasure rippled through me. I felt his erection pressing into my leg, and it did feel hard as a rock.

"Let's fix that." I pushed him back up to a sitting position and knelt in front of him.

His eyes were trained on my face as I tucked my fingers into the elastic waistband of his sweatpants and boxers and moved to slide them down. He lifted so I could pull them down all the way, and his cock sprang free. It was as beautiful as the rest of him. But it looked painfully hard, so I didn't waste any more time.

He appeared spellbound as I grasped the base and ran my tongue along the side, swirling around the tip a few times before bringing him fully into my mouth. I heard his sharp intake of breath, his head falling back onto the sofa as I glided my mouth up and down his shaft, coordinating the movement with my hand. He muttered something in Russian, sending it skyward before his gaze finally lowered. His breathing became more ragged as he watched me heatedly. I stared back into his eyes as I pulled him deep into my mouth, sucking and tugging at his hard length.

"You're so fucking beautiful," he whispered, threading his fingers into my hair and moaning as I started to move faster. I felt him grow harder inside my mouth, and I could tell he was close. I picked up the pace for a few moments longer until he pushed himself even deeper into my throat, and I watched him cry out.

I tasted the sudden explosion of warmth flowing into my mouth, and I took it all in. I was thinking that he might be on to something because I wasn't sure I'd ever seen anything sexier than this man coming apart in front of me. Knowing it was me who put that look on his face only heightened my arousal.

He caressed my cheek before lifting his bottom to pull his underwear and pants back into position. He stood up, pulling me with him. In typical Lex fashion, he didn't say anything, but instead brought both hands up to cup my face and gazed into my eyes with a look that told me everything I needed to know. He kissed me with such tenderness that I could have melted right where I stood.

The next thing I heard was the sound of the door unlocking. I crossed my arms over my exposed breasts while Lex pulled me quickly into his chest. He wrapped both arms around me, trying to cover my half-naked body.

"Stuart, get out, will you!" he shouted gruffly over his shoulder with his back facing the door.

"What the hell is your problem? This is my house too, dude," Stuart retorted but then stopped short when he realized that Lex clearly had someone in his arms.

"Hey Hadley," Stuart said suggestively.

"Hey Stuart," I called back, smiling into Lex's chest at the thought of how silly we probably looked.

"Could you give us a minute, please?" Lex asked a little more calmly this time.

"Fine, but I'd like to point out that you both have bedrooms, you voyeuristic freaks." He shut the door behind him, leaving us alone again.

Lex grabbed my shirt and helped pull it over my head as I pulled my bra back into place.

"That was some goodnight kiss," he said, grinning wickedly.

"I blame you," I said.

One shoulder lifted. "I'm okay with that."

I laughed, grabbing my coat and slipping it back on.

"You don't have to leave, you know. You could stay the night."

Heat flooded my system just hearing those words. I shook my head. "There's no way I'd be able to hold back if we were in a bed together."

His thick lashes lowered. "Does it matter that much after what we just did?"

"Well, we didn't go all the way, so I'm still considering this relationship un-christened. General rules of dating for women clearly state not to give it up too soon or the guy might think you're easy."

"Except that I would never think that and now that I've had a taste, I won't be able to think about anything else," he said, lowering his voice and stepping closer to me. I could feel the heat radiating from his body as he pressed his chest to mine before leaning down to kiss me again. I didn't even try to resist.

"Stay," he whispered against my lips, and I could already feel my self-control waning.

I don't know why I was holding back. I knew this wasn't some one-night stand, but my instincts told me this wasn't the right moment for us.

"I promise to keep my hands to myself," he added, pressing his forehead to mine.

"It's not you that I'm worried about," I replied, smiling but completely serious.

"Hey guys! It's pretty friggin' cold out here, if you wouldn't mind wrapping it up!" Stuart yelled from outside the door.

I laughed and pulled away from him.

"I'll see you later. Thanks for the goodnight kiss." I winked at him before opening the door to let Stuart in.

"Oh, hey Stuart!" I said, pretending to be surprised that he was standing there.

"Don't 'Hey Stuart' me. You and your lover boy need to keep your carnal activities to the confines of your own bedrooms," he scolded, but the look in his eye told me he was genuinely happy for us.

"I don't know what you're talking about. Lex was just checking me for errant moles."

I could hear Lex laughing from behind me. I patted Stuart's shoulder before making a quick exit.

"See you guys later," I called out as I made my way back to my own home, trying to put distance between me and the temptation of Lex's bed.

Chapter 22

I was armed and ready to drop a bombshell on my class this week, and I wanted nothing short of Mentos in a soda bottle-type reaction. I was practically tap dancing with excitement as they took their seats.

Cue drumroll, please!

"Good morning, everyone," I greeted with a smile as ridiculous as the Grinch. "We're halfway through the semester and your compositions are coming along beautifully. The talent and creativity you've shown has far surpassed any of my expectations. So today, I'd like to try a little something different. I brought in a special guest to review your compositions and give feedback."

I ushered my special guest in through the side door and had the pleasure of seeing their jaws hit the floor harder than a Looney Tunes piano drop when they caught sight of who strolled in.

I'd worked with Jimmy Blackmore a handful of times over the years, so when I heard he was in town, I couldn't resist calling him up to ask for this favor. Jimmy was a world-renowned guitarist and lead singer of the rock band, DeRidder, and just so happened to be from the Bay Area.

With his sleek hair, dark jeans, and faded black T-shirt, Jimmy oozed rock star. He strolled casually to the center of the room, looking around at the sea of wide-eyed, young faces. "Hey, guys. I'm Jimmy."

Boom, suckers! Bombshell detonated. Favorite teacher award this year was going to a one Miss Hadley Marie Olivier for providing a celebrity encounter of epic proportions. Sarah was always bragging about her collection of vintage Mozart music sheets that the kids were always fawning over. Well, in your face, Samaha!

Alright, let me rein it in. I was getting a little carried away by my own awesomeness.

"Surprise! Jimmy's the one who will be giving the feedback this week for your compositions. Who wants to go first?"

Normally it was like pulling teeth trying to get volunteers, but nearly every hand shot in the air.

"How about Sam's group?" I said, pointing to him, his arm practically coming out of socket.

He and his partner descended the stairs quicker than a *Price is Right* contestant to stand in front of Jimmy.

"Sam's an engineering major and a big Eddie Kirkland fan," I explained to Jimmy as they reached us.

"Great taste, Sam." Jimmy extended his hand, and Sam shakily accepted. "Eddie was one of the greatest guitarists to ever live."

Sam was rendered speechless for a moment as he fumbled for something to say. "It-it's such an honor to meet you, Mr. Blackmore. I heard you play at Austin City Limits last year. The show was incredible."

"Appreciate it, man," Jimmy said kindly.

"And this is his partner, Elizabeth Warner," I said, introducing them. Elizabeth was the music major in this group—audio engineering.

Jimmy took her hand. "Pleasure to meet you, Elizabeth."

Elizabeth started to giggle like a schoolgirl, her cheeks reddening. Jimmy had that effect on most women. He was a few years older than me and extremely handsome with his always perfectly styled chestnut brown hair and bright blue eyes. I bet even his mirror blushed at the sight of him.

Jimmy folded his arms across his chest. "I'd love to see what you guys have been working on."

They stood immobilized with fear. I could tell their thought process when volunteering didn't make it past meeting Jimmy to actually having to play their work for him.

"Here, I'll take it." I reached out for their composition notes.

They handed it over nervously. Their composition was best suited on the guitar, so I grabbed one and started playing while Jimmy listened closely, nodding along. When I finished, Sam and Elizabeth stared at Jimmy with bated breath.

"Very nice," Jimmy said, smiling. "The bridge is so unexpected. You guys really nailed it. The only thing I would say is that you have the harmony in C-minor, which is giving it a somewhat darker feel than I think the song intended. Maybe think about changing it up."

Sam was nodding fervently. "Yeah, yeah, that's a great idea."

"Overall, it's a great piece of writing though, guys." Jimmy gave a quick nod.

"Thank you, sir," Sam said while Elizabeth continued to giggle.

"And you're an engineering major?" Jimmy asked with surprise in his voice.

Sam shook his head. "Not anymore."

"What?" I asked, confused.

"I changed to music technology last week," Sam said proudly, beaming at me. "I love music. I just never thought I could do it as a career... until now, that is."

"Sam, that's amazing." My throat felt tight. "You really have the talent for it."

"You were the first person to ever tell me that." Sam pushed his glasses further up his nose. "My whole life everyone always told me that there was no future for me in music, and I believed them."

"Well, I was told my whole childhood I wouldn't always have a calculator on me and yet here we are." I patted the phone in my pocket. "People are wrong all the time."

Sam chuckled. "Thanks for everything, Ms. Olivier."

Tears pricked my eyes as I walked over and gave Sam a hug. This was the feeling my mom always talked about when she tried explaining why she loved teaching so much. She said it only took one student in one moment to make it all worth it.

"Ms. Olivier," I heard John-Luke call out. I sighed. *Here we go.* "Do I have to switch majors too to get that kind of hug?"

He and his entourage were the only ones laughing. I rolled my eyes, refusing to let him get under my skin today.

I directed Sam and Elizabeth back to their seats before Jimmy turned to me and asked, "What's up with that kid?" while eyeing John-Luke.

"The wheel's spinning, but the hamster's dead," I told him.

Jimmy scoffed. "You couldn't pay me enough to do this shit. I'd get fired the first day for knocking that kid on his preppy ass."

"Not necessary." I waved him off. "For their final assignment, I'm having each of them write a comparative analysis of various artist's compositional work... my special friend over there will be getting The Spice Girls."

Jimmy's face split into a wicked smile. "Nurture that side of yourself and never let it go."

Once the class ended, Jimmy and I ventured out to a local lunch spot to catch up. It proved to be quite the challenge, however, as word that Jimmy was on campus spread like wildfire. Despite his attempts to stay incognito with sunglasses and a low-hanging hat, he couldn't evade the constant interruptions from adoring fans eager for a photo op. He refused to take me up on my offer to wear the fake nose/mustache/glasses combo, so technically this was his fault. In the end, we resorted to eating our club sandwiches in the car before returning to campus.

"Thanks again for doing this, Jim," I told him on the drive back. "It really meant a lot to the kids."

The class had hummed with excitement from start to finish, and I knew a barrage of Jimmy-related questions awaited me at next week's lecture.

"Thanks for hitting me up. It was a lot of fun." In the sanctuary of my car, he was finally able to remove his hat as he shook out his hair. "You've got a really talented group in that room."

I beamed with pride. "That's for sure."

"The teaching thing really suits you," he noted.

"I've definitely been enjoying it." Now that I got over my imposter's syndrome, I actually looked forward to my classes each week. Might just be something in the gene pool, because my mom still talked about how much she missed teaching.

I could see him eyeing me from the passenger seat.

"What is it?" I asked, wondering if I had a bat in the cave.

"Nothing... You're just so different here," he said thoughtfully.

"How so?"

He pushed his sunglasses to the top of his head like he was trying to get a better look. "I don't know. You've just got a look about you that I've never seen before."

I feigned offense. "And what look is that?"

He smiled. "Contentment, maybe. I don't know." He let his sunglasses fall back into place. "I just know you never looked like this when we worked together in New York."

My forehead wrinkled. "How did I look in New York?"

"Overworked," he stated dryly.

I laughed because it was true. "We were all overworked," I said. "Didn't mean I didn't love it."

"I'm not saying you didn't. Life's just different out here." He looked out toward the road. "This business is a grind and will wear down even the best of us."

"So, you're saying I looked both overworked *and* worn down? Appreciate it, Jim," I teased.

He chuckled. "No, I'm just playing devil's advocate here."

I smiled. "The devil doesn't need any more advocates." I already had enough people trying to tell me what a great fit me and California were.

"Whether you want to admit it or not, the Cali life looks good on you, my friend."

Spoken like a true Californian. "I'm starting to think all you Californians made a pact at some point to try and convert as many people to your way of life as possible."

He gave me a cocky grin. "We know what we have."

"Well, you can't have me," I said obstinately.

He smiled and shook his head. "Shipley's been trying to reach you," he said, changing the subject.

I sighed. "I know."

Logan Shipley was a producer friend of mine who'd been calling and texting incessantly over the past month trying to get me to go to New York for a job, but I'd been dodging him. "I've just had a lot going on." I hadn't told anyone in the business about my mom except for a few really close friends.

"Logan's been telling everyone that he doesn't think you're going back to New York either."

I turned into the parking lot. "Then he needs a new fact checker."

He chuckled. "I don't know, Olivier. Now that I've seen you in action, I think there's a shot at conversion."

"Not a chance in hell." My chin lifted. "If you ever catch me touting the benefits of matcha or complaining about the gridlock, just take me out."

Jimmy burst out laughing.

From the first day I'd met Jimmy Blackmore, I'd always felt comfortable around him, despite his bad-boy reputation. I learned later on that it was carefully cultivated by his PR team because he was honestly one of the nicest guys I'd ever met. He didn't allow drugs in the studio or on tour, and he had a long-time girlfriend that he was crazy about. None of that was a good fit for a rock star persona, however.

I thanked Jimmy again and said my goodbyes before dropping him off at his vehicle. I thought about what he said on the walk back to my office. He was now the second person to tell me that I seemed different here, and I wasn't sure what to make of it. I could definitely think of one reason why I'd been feeling happier these days that had nothing to do with the state of California. I was seeing the human equivalent of a bottle of Prozac, so it was impossible *not* to feel happy. But my identity was woven so tightly around New York, I wasn't sure it could ever be unraveled.

I checked my watch and realized I had lost track of time grading papers. I had told Lex I would be at his house at 6:00 and it was already 6:05. I gathered up my things and raced home, ridiculously eager to see him. As I made my way up the walkway, my phone started to buzz, and I checked to see that it was Lex.

"Hey, you still coming?" he asked as soon as I answered.

"Yes, sorry." I picked up the pace. "I got caught up at work. I'm almost to your door, actually."

The door to his home swung open just as I made it to the foot of their porch. Lex was standing there in the entryway, and we both hung up at the same time. I smiled like an idiot and ran up the steps, jumping into his waiting arms. He lifted me so that I could wrap my legs around him. One arm snaked around my waist to hold me there, and the other tangled in my hair as our lips found each other. I sighed at the relief of having his hands on me again even though it had been less than twenty-four hours since I'd seen him.

My eyes closed as I let him kiss me right there in the doorway, our tongues already sliding together. I was addicted to this feeling of him kissing me and was already thinking of when I could get my next hit. Running my fingers through his soft hair, I nipped playfully at his bottom lip. His answering growl made me giggle as he pulled back with a grin on his face. He kissed me softly once more before setting me down on my feet. I was still looking up at him, marveling at his handsome features, when I heard someone cough loudly next to us.

Stuart was standing there with a look of pure mischief gleaming in his eyes. It was a testament to how preoccupied I was with Lex that I hadn't even noticed Stuart standing there until that moment.

"Is this how we're doing greetings these days?" Stuart asked. "Because if so then... how do I put this delicately... my turn!"

"Stuart, I have something to tell you." I gave him a serious look. "It's going to come as a bit of a shock, but here it is... Lex and I are no longer platonic."

"What?! No!" Stuart said, gasping, placing his hand over his chest. "Is it because he's a neurobiologist and I'm just a chemist?"

"You caught me." My chin dipped. "I'm a neurobiology-only kind of gal."

"Figures," Stuart said, but he was smiling looking between the two of us. Lex just shook his head, not bothering to get involved in our repartee.

We sat down for dinner together, and I wondered how much of our dynamic would change now that Lex and I were seeing each other. I didn't want to make Stuart uncomfortable or feel like he was third-wheeling, but that didn't seem to be a concern in Lex's mind as he sat down right next to me, placing his hand on my thigh. Lex had always participated in our conversations in the past when we had dinner, but there was always some part of him that seemed reserved, and now I knew why. He held no such reservation tonight, however, as he ate with either his arm draped over my chair or his hand resting on my legs.

I glanced at Stuart throughout the dinner to see if it ever seemed like he was getting uncomfortable, but he just smiled like he was enjoying seeing his friend so happy. As usual, the food Lex cooked was absolutely delicious. A thought sprang to my mind that I'd been contemplating over the past few days that I'd just remembered to ask.

"Hey, do you guys know if Jace started seeing anyone?" I felt Lex stiffen next to me, and I realized how that must have sounded.

Stuart grinned at the irritated look on Lex's face. "Why? You sick of Lex already?"

"What? No!" Obviously, that's not what I meant. "I'm asking because I think he might be a good match for Sarah."

Lex's posture relaxed a little as he resumed eating. I placed my hand over the one he had on my leg, holding it there.

"What?!" Stuart said, outraged. "Why wouldn't you try to hook *me* up with Sarah?"

I popped another roasted carrot in my mouth. "You lost your chance when you tried to pull that cheap line on her at faculty night."

"So, I'm just supposed to sit by and watch while all my friends get paired up and I get bupkis? I thought we had a deal. I set you up and you set me up in return."

"How exactly did you set me up?" I swished my fork at him. "Lex and I managed to get here all on our own. I don't remember you being involved."

"Oh, I was involved!" he said indignantly. "I'm the one who's had to put up with his wallowing over these past few months. And it was *me* who was always telling him to quit being a baby and make a move because there were more guys like Jace and Merrick lining up. Or didn't he tell you?"

I bit my lip, trying not to laugh. "He never mentioned it."

"What?" He narrowed his eyes at Lex. "Tell her!"

"I don't recall you ever saying anything like that," Lex said with a shrug.

"Oh, this is rich!" Stuart exclaimed. "My contribution to Halex is going to go completely unrecognized." He got up and stormed off to the kitchen with his plate, while Lex and I burst out laughing.

"Wait! Stuart, come back! We were just teasing," I called to him from the dining room, still laughing. "We definitely would not be here without you!"

He poked his head through the door. "So, you'll set me up?" he asked, grinning with his eyebrows raised.

"Sure," I said, shaking my head. "For your contribution to Halex, I will *try* to set you up with someone."

"Thanks, Hadley." He took his seat again. "I knew I could count on you... unlike some people..." He narrowed his eyes at Lex.

"*Halex* isn't going to become a thing, is it?" Lex asked me with a look of true concern.

Between taking care of my mom, driving her to all her appointments, and our busy work schedules, I had barely seen Lex over the past week. We hadn't been able to spend more than a few minutes each day together and that was only in passing since he had worked late almost every day this week.

I was growing antsy.

When I noticed his car wasn't in the parking lot after I got home from my mom's chemo appointment on Friday evening, I decided to give him a call.

"Hey," Lex answered on the first ring.

"Are you sick of me?" I teased. "Is that why you refuse to spend time with me?"

"Of course not," he said quietly. I could hear a shuffling noise and then the sound of a door shutting, and I knew he had walked away from the others at work. "I'm sorry about this week. We're just at a critical point in the project. As soon as this part's over, things will be better. I won't have to be here as late."

"Sure, whatever you say," I said in a pitiful voice. "I'll just have to find a way to occupy myself since I'm all alone." I sighed, laying it on thick. "Don't worry. I've been here before. I know just what to do. My hand and I are old friends."

His voice deepened as he said, "You don't need to do that. I can take care of it for you."

I made a *tsk* noise. "Promises, promises."

"Give me an hour," he said huskily.

"I *guess* I can wait," I said, digging in my purse for my keys as I made my way up the sidewalk. "But don't take too long or..."

I stopped short when I noticed there was a man standing on my porch very near the door. The evening had grown darker, and I couldn't make out who it was from this distance, but my heart started pounding. There was no one else around, and my mind started calculating the distance between him to me and me to my car.

"Hadley?" I heard Lex saying on the phone. He could hear my heavy breathing. "What is it?"

I was frozen to the spot. "There's a man on my porch," I whispered.

Chapter 23

"H ang up and call the cops," Lex said sternly. "Get back to your car. I'm on my way."

Just as he said those words, the man walked out from under the shadow of the porch. I recognized that face instantly.

My eyes widened with shock. "It's Garrett."

"What?" Lex said, sounding just as shocked. "As in your ex-boyfriend Garrett?"

"Hey, baby," Garrett called out to me, smiling as he walked down my porch steps.

"*Baby?*" Lex said with quiet fury.

"I'll call you back." I hung up before things got worse.

"What are you doing here?" I asked right before he swept me up in a hug and spun me around.

"I'm so happy to see you," he said in my hair.

"Garrett, what are you doing here?" I asked again, extricating myself from his grasp.

"I came to see you, of course!" He said it as if it were a ridiculous question.

"I haven't heard from you in almost five months," I said. "Why would you just show up here?"

"I was trying to give you space. I thought that's what you wanted."

"We. Broke. Up." I couldn't believe I was having to spell this out for him.

"I realize that, but…" He looked around at some of my neighbors walking up the sidewalk to their homes. "Look, can we go inside and talk? There are some things I want to say to you."

I sighed. I guess I owed it to him since he came all this way. "Fine," I said, leading the way. "How did you even know where I lived?"

"My sister gave me your address. She had it from when she mailed you that stuff for your mom."

Sophie. I forgot I had given her my address so she could send my mom some essential oils that were supposed to be for healing. I really didn't believe in all that crap, but I figured it couldn't hurt.

As I got to my porch, I noticed a suitcase sitting next to the door. "Really?" My eyes rolled in frustration. "You were planning on staying here?"

"Well, yeah. I flew all the way to California to see you."

I shook my head as we walked inside. "Garrett, you should have called."

"I wanted to surprise you," he said, shutting the door behind him. "And besides, I thought you'd say no if I told you."

Irritation spread down my spine, and I fought the urge to lash out at him.

"If you thought I'd say no, then you shouldn't have come," I said more calmly than I felt.

He looked over my face as we stood in the foyer of my home. "I'm sorry." He pushed his sandy blonde hair out of his eyes before stuffing them in his pockets. "I really was trying to give you space. I guess I was hoping you would change your mind. It's been tough for me not having you anymore to talk to every day. You were my best friend. I miss you, Hadley."

My heart squeezed sympathetically. "I've missed your friendship too, Garrett." I chose my words carefully, not wanting to give him an inkling of false hope.

"Is that all you've missed?" he asked, his blue eyes showing his devastation. I hated this feeling. I hated this, but I nodded, because it was the truth.

"You didn't even give us a chance. We could have made it work. I still think we can."

I stopped him before he went any further. "I'm sorry you came all this way, but there's nothing you can say to change my mind. I don't want to be with you anymore."

He still seemed determined. "You're going to come back to New York eventually. What then?"

I paused for a beat, knowing what I was about to say next was going to sting. "We still won't be getting back together."

He stared at me blankly for a few moments before his chin dipped. "Jesus, Hadley. Was I really that horrible?"

"Of course not," I said quickly. "You're a great guy, and you're going to make some other lucky woman really happy one day."

He looked crestfallen. "Some other woman, huh?"

I wanted to look away from the hurt I saw plainly on his face, but I made myself meet his stare. "I'm sorry, Garrett."

He nodded like he finally understood. "At least I got to see your face one more time." His eyes softened as he looked over at me. "I don't know if it's because I haven't seen you in so long, but you look... different," he said softly. "You were always beautiful, Hadley, but now... I can't explain it. You just look radiant." I didn't know what to say, so I stood there and let him take me in. He stepped closer, lifting his hand to my face. "It makes it even harder to look at you... seeing what I lost."

His fingertips barely skimmed my cheek before I registered what he was trying to do. Discomfort prickled at my skin, and I jerked back, but the movement halted as the front door suddenly swung open. Lex stood in the doorway, his expression cold and unreadable, but the quiet menace in his eyes was unmistakable.

His gaze went straight to Garrett's outstretched hand, sharp and unyielding, as though calculating exactly how to remove it.

"Take your hand off of her," Lex said, his voice dark and measured. "Now."

Garrett dropped his hand quickly as if it had been burned, confusion pulling his brows together.

"Lex, nothing happened," I said, knowing how bad this looked. "And nothing was going to happen, I swear," I added quickly.

Lex's expression shifted for a moment, softening as his eyes met mine. "I know that," he said, his voice steady. But as his gaze shifted to Garrett, his features hardened once more. "Does he?"

"Hadley, who the hell is this guy?" Garrett demanded.

I moved to stand between the two men, feeling like I'd willingly trapped myself inside a thundercloud.

"Garrett, this is Alexsander Strovinski. He's a researcher here at the university." I paused, unsure if I was ready for the fallout of my next admission, but I had to be honest with him. "And he's the man I've been seeing."

Garrett peered at me with a look of betrayal. "Are you serious? You're seeing someone else?"

I nodded. "Yes. And I'm sorry you had to find out like this, but we aren't together anymore, Garrett. We've been apart for almost as long as we were together. It's over. It's been over."

His frustration mounted, his hand raking through his hair in an agitated motion. "Unbelievable. I told you I *loved* you."

The words tugged at something in me, but I couldn't shake the suspicion that it was an attempt to manipulate my emotions. It felt eerily familiar, the same uneasy feeling I had the first time he said it.

"And I told you that I didn't feel the same," I said with a calmness I didn't feel. "I'm sorry, but this was never going to work."

He stepped forward, desperation creeping into his movements as he grabbed my arm, fingers digging into my skin. "How can you say that? We were so good together, Hadley," he said urgently. "You never gave us a real chance."

"Garrett, don't," I said, trying to pull my arm out of his grasp.

In an instant, Lex was between us, forcing Garrett back without so much as a push. He didn't raise his voice, didn't snarl. Instead, he leaned closer to Garrett, his voice quiet but deliberate.

"I'm only going to say this one more time," Lex said, his tone so devoid of emotion, it sent an icy chill down my spine. "Keep your hand off her, or I'll make sure you never use it again."

Garrett appeared visibly rattled, but he stood his ground. "I would never hurt her."

Lex scoffed. "You've made it clear there are very few lines you aren't willing to cross," he said, low but cutting. "You showed up to her house without bothering to ask if she even wanted you here. You refused to listen when she's told you multiple times that it's over. And twice you've laid a hand on her without permission. Forgive me if I'm not inclined to take your word for it."

Garrett stood there for a moment, his eyes flicking between me and Lex, trying to process what had just unfolded. Lex's words seemed to stir something in him, and for the first time, I saw a flicker of realization in Garrett's eyes—an understanding of just how far he'd pushed.

"I'm sorry, Hadley," he said quietly, the fight draining out of him. "I shouldn't have done that."

"It's okay," I said reflexively, even though Lex was right. None of this was okay.

"No. It's not," Lex said coldly. "I think you need to leave."

Garrett's brows shot up. "Where am I supposed to go?"

"There's a bus stop in town," Lex said. "Start there."

"It took me forever just to find this place. I have no idea where to go."

"You probably should have thought of that before showing up here uninvited," Lex answered flatly.

"Lex, can I talk to you for a minute?" I asked, my conscience tugging at me despite everything. I couldn't help feeling a little sorry for Garrett. As much as he was an idiot for coming here and not even bothering to call, I still didn't want to throw him out without any place to stay.

Lex let me lead him to the kitchen where Garrett couldn't overhear us, but before I could get the words out, Lex turned and said, "He's not staying here with you."

He appeared resolute, but I still pled my case. "Lex, he's not from here, and it's getting late. I have the spare bedroom, or he can take the couch. He can find a hotel in the morning."

"No," he said, clearly unmoved. "There's no way he's sleeping here with you. He's obviously incapable of keeping his hands to himself."

I didn't fear Garrett, not in the way Lex was implying. But I couldn't deny that if the situation were reversed, I'd be uneasy too, especially given the stellar first impression Garrett had just made.

"Then what do you suggest?" I asked.

He thought about it briefly. "He can stay at my place with Stuart. I'll stay in the spare bedroom."

My heart beat unevenly. Neither of us had spent the night at each other's place yet, so I knew he was trying not to be presumptive by suggesting the spare bedroom. But I also knew there was no way in hell this beautiful man was going to be under my roof, but not in my bed. Especially since I could practically hear my mattress begging for his company. But I didn't mention that little detail.

"Okay," I agreed, swallowing thickly.

He gazed at me curiously for a moment before nodding and taking my hand to walk back to the foyer.

"You can stay at my place tonight," he said to Garrett. "I need to check with my roommate first, but I don't think he'll mind."

Garrett seemed to find the idea distasteful. "*Your* place?"

"It's either that or a park bench," Lex replied casually. "Your choice... Truly, I couldn't care less either way."

I shot Garrett a look of annoyance. Didn't he know fishing for scraps meant no complaining about the seasoning?

"Fine," he grumbled.

Lex didn't bother to respond. He kissed the top of my head and said, "I need to get back to work to tell Stuart what's going on."

"Okay," I said again. I didn't know if I should thank him or apologize for dragging him into something that wasn't his fight.

"You can wait outside," he said in Garrett's general direction.

Garrett hesitated, looking to me for support, but I shook my head. Garrett sighed heavily, his shoulders slumping in defeat. Without another word, he stepped outside, the door shutting behind him with a soft click that felt heavier than it should.

"I'm sorry," I said quietly, breaking the silence.

"For what?" Lex asked, turning to me. The hardness in his features eased, though the edge of protectiveness remained.

"For Garrett showing up here. For dragging you into this. For all of it."

"Hadley, it's not your fault that he came here uninvited, put his hands on you, and then tried to guilt you into something you didn't want."

"I know," I said softly. "I just didn't want things to end like this. He's not a bad person, Lex. He's just... lost. And I feel responsible for that."

Lex stepped closer, his hands brushing my arms before settling gently on my waist. "Garrett isn't your responsibility," he said intently. "I know you care about him, but you can't set yourself on fire just to keep someone else warm."

His words hit their mark, unraveling something inside me. "You're right," I whispered, closing my eyes and resting my forehead against his chest as he wrapped his arms around me.

As he held me, the contrast between these two men became glaringly obvious—Garrett was a storm, unpredictable and consuming, while Lex was the calm after, steady and grounding, like the earth beneath my feet.

"You okay?" he asked when I finally pulled away.

"Yes, I'm fine," I said, quickly wiping a stray tear from my cheek.

He put a finger under my chin, tilting it up to his face as he scanned my features for any sign of distress. "I'll stay if you want me to."

I shook my head. "I'm okay, I promise." I gave him my best reassuring smile.

He stared at me for a moment longer then pressed a soft kiss to my forehead. "I'll be back. I just need to make sure Stuart's okay with Garrett crashing at our place."

I nodded. "Okay."

He turned to leave, pausing with his hand on the knob. "Lock this behind me. I won't be long."

I felt the urge to defend Garrett, to push back at the implication that he was dangerous, but I realized Lex was right. Garrett wasn't my responsibility anymore, and I didn't owe him protection or defense.

After Lex left, I threw myself into making dinner, using the steady rhythm of chopping and stirring to distract myself from the storm of thoughts swirling in my mind. By the time I started plating the chicken Florentine, Lex had returned to pick up Garrett, who had indeed stayed outside on my porch as instructed.

Once the food was ready, I carried a couple of plates over to Stuart and Garrett. Guilt pricked at me for leaving Stuart to play host, but I thought it was best that we not all have dinner together for obvious reasons.

Stuart didn't seem the least bit bothered as he was practically doubled over, laughing his ass off at the absurdity of the whole situation."You're going to owe me big time for this one, Betty," Stuart said, still trying to catch his breath from wheezing with laughter.

I sighed, rubbing my forehead. "I know. I'm really sorry I had to ask you to do this."

"Hey, what are friends for if not to babysit your ex-boyfriend while your new boyfriend channels his inner hall monitor?"

I shook my head. "I think you need new friends."

"Never," he said with a wink. "Not when my old ones are so endlessly entertaining."

"Ready?" Lex's voice interrupted as he walked down the stairs, a small overnight bag slung over his shoulder.

I nodded before turning to Stuart. "You sure you're okay with this?"

"Don't worry, Betty. I used to babysit my three-year-old nieces all the time. Tears, tantrums, and full-blown meltdowns are all well within my wheelhouse. If he shits his pants, though, he's all yours."

With a shake of my head, I followed Lex out the door.

When we got back to my place, I grabbed our plates from the kitchen, and we sat down to eat together. The room was quiet, the only sound coming from the faint clink of utensils against plates. Lex sat across from me, barely touching his food, his gaze fixed on some distant point beyond his plate. I could almost see the wheels turning in his head, the quiet intensity of his thoughts filling the space between us.

I shifted uncomfortably, trying to read his expression, but it was too guarded, too thoughtful. Was he upset? Did I push him too far? I couldn't shake the feeling that I'd done something wrong, that he was angry with me for letting Garrett back into my life in any capacity. The thought gnawed at me as each passing second amplified my uncertainty, until I couldn't stand it any longer. I had to say something.

"Are we okay?" I finally blurted out.

Lex's eyes snapped to mine, surprise flickering across his face. "Always," he answered without hesitation. "Why would you ask?"

"I don't know." I shrugged, unable to meet his eyes. "You seem... distant."

"I'm sorry," he began, his voice softer now. "I've just been having some doubts about a few things."

My stomach tightened. "A-about us?"

"Of course not," he said firmly.

"Then what is it?" I asked hesitantly.

He sighed. "I've just been thinking... I don't know if I handled this whole situation with Garrett the way that I should have."

"What do you mean?"

He rubbed his jaw, his expression becoming thoughtful. "I'm still angry that he showed up here uninvited, and I stand by what I said—he shouldn't have put his hands on you," he explained. "But I started thinking on the way over here that I might have more empathy for him than I care to admit."

I blinked, surprised. "Empathy? Why?"

He hesitated, his expression tightening. "I realized that could've been me," he said, his voice barely above a murmur. "If you ever left me, I don't think I'd be above showing up at your door, desperate for another chance... It would be just as hard for me to accept that things were over." His gaze drifted downward as he let out a heavy sigh. "I guess what I'm trying to say is I understand his motivations, even if I don't agree with his methods."

A swirl of emotions rose in me—surprise, tenderness, and a deep ache for the vulnerability he rarely showed. Without thinking, I crossed the room and folded myself into his lap, wrapping my arms around him. His arms encircled me tightly, holding me as if I might disappear.

"You're a good person," I whispered, my voice thick with emotion.

"I don't know about that," he replied with a soft, self-deprecating smile. "But I've watched you be kind to people who didn't deserve it. That's what made me start thinking about all of this in the first place. I wondered how you would've responded if you were in my shoes, and I realized you would've handled it with kindness."

I shook my head. "You're giving me way more credit than I deserve."

"I don't think I am." He smiled faintly, brushing a lock of hair away from my face.

I pressed my forehead to his, and we sat in silence for a moment, the weight of everything starting to lift. His arms were strong around me, grounding, and I let myself sink into that warmth, feeling safe in a way I hadn't in a long time.

His gaze lifted to mine, raw and unguarded. "I don't want to lose you," he murmured.

The heartache in his voice brought tears to my eyes. I tightened my hold on him, pressing my lips to his forehead. "You're not going to lose me."

He closed his eyes, and I could see the tension around the edges had relaxed a little. I stroked my thumb across his cheek, my heart breaking for how unnerved he had become. I then kissed each of his cheeks before pressing my mouth against his. I'd meant it to be reassuring, but my body immediately reacted to the taste.

After a few moments, I coaxed his lips to part so that I could feel his tongue against mine. He obliged, opening to me, and our tongues tangled. His hands pressed into my back, holding me to him as I ran my fingers through his soft hair. Heat pooled at my core with each passing sweep of his tongue across mine. I turned to put one leg on each side of his hips, and a low moan escaped from the back of his throat as I pressed our hips together.

"I want you," I whispered against his lips, and it was true in every way. I wanted this man, body and soul, and I realized how much time I'd been wasting. Lex and I belonged together. Unfortunately, it had taken seeing Garrett again for me to realize just how true that really was.

He stood with me wrapped around him, never breaking our kiss as he walked me up the stairs to the bedroom as if I weighed nothing. When we reached the foot of the bed, I let my legs drop down and I stepped away from him. I pulled my shirt over my head and dropped my pants down to the floor until I was in nothing but my lacy black underwear and bra. His eyes were smoldering as they raked slowly over my entire body.

Never breaking our eye contact, I reached behind my back, unhooking my bra, and let it fall to the floor. I watched his lips part, his eyes fixated on me as I pulled my underwear down and stepped out of them. There wasn't any part of me that felt shy or uncertain as I stood there stark naked in front of him. I couldn't help but feel like a goddess with the blazing look he was giving me.

I walked backward until my legs hit the bed and looked at him expectantly.

His tongue slid slowly across his bottom lip. "Somehow, you look even sexier than every fantasy I've had about you," he said brusquely.

I smiled, scooting myself back onto the bed. I got up onto my knees and started to pull him toward me.

"Do you think about me naked?" I asked in a low, husky voice that I barely recognized as my own.

"Yes." He swallowed thickly. "A lot more than I probably should," he finished quietly.

I slid my fingers beneath the hem of his shirt, my fingertips brushing lightly against his skin. I felt him shudder as I pulled it over his head.

"Good," I said, running my hands over his chest through that small patch of hair at the center. "Because I think about you inside me," I whispered, kissing along his chest. "A lot more than I probably should."

He groaned at my words as another Russian expletive escaped his lips. My mouth found his, and we began kissing in earnest. I fumbled with the buckle of his pants until his hands replaced mine as he rushed to unfasten his belt before letting them drop to the floor. Sitting back on the bed, I leaned up on my elbows, waiting for him to follow. He stood at the foot of the bed, his eyes moving slowly along every inch of my bare skin. His gaze became fixed on the spot between my legs, staring at me hungrily until I was pulsating with need.

"Come here," I whispered and his eyes flared.

The bed dipped under his weight as he climbed on, his irises blazing in the dull light. My breath seized in my chest as he hovered just above me, my peaked nipples grazing sensitively across his chest. Our lips found each other again, and I let my hands explore his body, moving down his chest, over his toned abdomen, and slipping into his underwear. He groaned into my mouth as I stroked his hard length. A wave of aching need swept through me. He pulled back a fraction and said, "If you keep doing that, this is going to be over before it even starts."

I smiled against his lips. "Do you have a..."

He nodded, reaching for his wallet and pulling out a condom. I took it from him before pushing on his chest for him to lie back. The tendons in his neck became strained as I kissed my way down the length of his torso before curling my fingers into the elastic waistband. He lifted for me, and I tugged his underwear all the way down, tossing them with the rest of our discarded clothes.

I stroked him leisurely, taking my time and admiring his fully naked form as he watched me with hooded eyes. I tore the condom wrapper apart between my teeth, our eyes locked together as I rolled it over him slowly. His cock twitched and a throaty rumble came from deep within his chest. I knew he'd reached his limit.

His hands gripped my waist almost painfully as he flipped me onto my back. He used his knees to part my legs and lined himself up at my entrance. My heart was pounding as he leaned down and kissed me for a few minutes longer until I was panting with need. Slowly, deliciously, he slid inside, inch by inch, stopping when he reached the hilt.

I watched his eyes squeeze shut as a raw, breathless groan escaped his throat. My head fell back, and I moaned his name, savoring the stretching sensation. My hands moved over his broad shoulders and down the muscles of his back, holding him to me. I needed him to move before I combusted.

"Lex..." I pleaded, starting to move my hips, but he pinned them down, not letting me move an inch.

"Wait," he said, low in my ear. "It feels too good." His voice was strained, so I remained still. The only movement was that of our chests rising and falling heavily together. His face was tucked into my neck, and I could hear him mumbling something in Russian.

After a few moments of feeling like I might die if he didn't start moving soon, he pulled back to look me in the eyes before unleashing his full potential. I held on, digging my fingers into the hard planes of his back as he picked up the pace. He hooked an arm under one of my legs, pushing it up and changing the angle before slamming into me as a ragged moan tore from my throat. He did it again, eliciting the same guttural response.

"Fuck, Hadley," he groaned. "I think I could come just from hearing the sounds you're making."

My fingernails dug into his shoulders as I looked up at him. "You like hearing what you do to me."

He grinned devilishly. "I like watching it more," he said before slamming into me again, and I cried out.

Lex watched me closely—every flutter of my eyelid, every gasping breath, every tremor coursing through me as he thrust into me over and over. I hooked my other leg around his waist, wanting the feel of his weight on top of me. He knew what I wanted without me having to say it as he lowered himself down until his chest was pressed against mine.

"It used to keep me up at night," he said as his hands moved continuously over my body, touching, teasing. "Thinking of all the things I want to do to you," he murmured against my throat.

I took his face in between my hands, shivering at the intensity and raw emotion I saw burning in his eyes. "Show me," I whispered back. His head suddenly dipped to capture my lips.

It seemed that Lex knew my body better than even I did because every twist and turn, every angle explored, had me engulfed in a sea of ecstasy.

I reached my hands up above my head to push against the headboard, trying to provide resistance as he rocked into me.

He sat up abruptly, gripping his hands tightly around my hips, and lifted them up off the bed before pulling me down onto his hard length as he pushed in deep. The movement caught me by surprise as the mounting pleasure suddenly crescendoed. The tension exploded and I shattered around him, my back arching off the bed. His name came out as a strangled moan as he continued pumping into me.

As I floated down from the highest peak, my body was pulsating with pleasure as I gazed up at his beautiful body still pushing into me. He was in rapture watching our joined pelvises and his breathing became more labored. It wasn't long until his movements became jerkier, and he sucked in a sharp breath before collapsing on top of me with one final stroke, groaning into my neck.

We lay together, still joined, waiting for our breathing to slow. I stroked my fingers up and down his spine. My body felt languid and incredibly satiated. He rolled onto his side, pulling me close to his chest. He gazed at me for a while, whispering my name as he pushed the hair out of my face.

I felt a tear escape from the tenderness of the moment. My emotional scale wasn't even registering. His forehead wrinkled as he swiped the tear away with his fingertips. He propped himself up on his elbow, his eyes searching my face. "Tell me you're okay," he said, concern plainly on his features.

"Better than okay," I breathed. "That was... you were... it was incredible," I rambled, unable to form a coherent thought.

Amusement played across his lips. "I thought so, too."

I let my fingertips drift across his neck. "So does that mean you're ready for round two?" I asked, my body somehow already aching for more.

He grinned, his eyes moving tenderly across my face. "Three and four as well."

Chapter 24

There was a knock at my door the next morning as Lex and I were sitting at the kitchen table drinking coffee. I got up and opened it to find Garrett standing there. He looked at me briefly before his eyes moved to Lex, who had walked up behind me with his rumpled hair and naked torso, looking like morning-after sex. He was leaning against the wall, casually sipping coffee while staring down Garrett.

"I just came to say goodbye," he said to me, refusing to acknowledge the man hovering just behind me.

"Okay," I said, feeling unbelievably awkward. "Goodbye, Garrett."

His expression faltered, disappointment crossing his features, as if he expected more. "I still have a few of your things at my place. Do you want me to send them to you?"

I didn't remember leaving anything there. "What is it?"

"Just some of the things you wore on our trip to Cancun—a couple of dresses, some shoes... that red bikini." He stared down Lex. "You know, the one with the all the strings."

Lex fell right into the trap. I watched his expression darken with anger as he took a step toward Garrett.

I put my arm out to block him. "No, I'm good. Thanks," I said quickly.

He cocked his head. "You sure?" he asked, still eyeing Lex. "I remember you telling me that night in the hot tub that it was your favorite."

Lex's jaw flexed. "I'd be happy to help wipe that from your memory."

I put my whole body in front of Lex as he took another threatening step forward.

A smug expression came over Garrett's face, knowing he'd succeeded in getting a rise out of Lex.

"I think it's time for you to leave, Garrett," I said.

Garrett grinned. "Alright, I'm going." He pulled the handle up on his luggage. "Once you get back to New York, you should give me a call. Maybe we could try to be friends again. I know Sophie misses you."

I felt Lex stiffen. "Yeah, maybe," I said, trying to hurry this along.

Garrett gazed at me with a torn expression. "I never thought this is how things would turn out for us." His eyes flicked to Lex momentarily before settling back on me. "I guess I just have to accept that this is what makes you happy now."

"It does," I confirmed.

He nodded. "I'm sorry that I couldn't."

The look of hurt on his face had my stomach clenching. I never meant to hurt Garrett.

Lex curled his hand gently around my waist, pulling me into his chest. Garrett took the hint and turned to leave. I exhaled a long breath as he closed the door behind him.

He ran his hand down my arm soothingly. "You alright?"

"I'm fine," I said. "I just hate hurting people. I didn't love him, but I still cared about him."

"I know," Lex said, and I was grateful for his understanding.

"Are you okay?" I asked, wondering if he was still annoyed at Garrett for bringing up our history.

"Yes... feeling pretty good, actually, now that he's finally gone and I won't have to hear about any more bikini-clad trips the two of you took."

I sighed. "He just said that to get a rise out of you."

"Oh, I know," he said with a smile. "Sorry if I was a jerk. I was struggling to muster any of the empathy I once had for him."

I shook my head. "I need some coffee," I said, wanting to move past this whole Garrett thing. "I'm dragging a bit this morning... Any idea why that might be?" I asked innocently as I wrapped my arms around his neck.

A slow, knowing smile spread across his face. "Can't say that I do," he replied, his hands sliding down my backside. "Though, for the record, I'm feeling pretty energized this morning."

"Oh, really?" I brushed my lips along his jawline, the feel of his scruff grazing against my mouth in the most tantalizing way. "Got any specific plans for how you're going to burn off all that extra energy?"

"I can think of a few things," he said roughly as I traced my tongue along his throat.

He pulled my mouth up to meet his, but just as he started tugging at my clothes, there was a loud knock at the door. Lex let out a noise of irritation as I pulled away, chuckling. I went to the door, opening it to find exactly who I thought would be there.

"Well, that was an interesting night," Stuart said, chuckling as he walked in and made himself at home on my couch. "Your ex-lover and I stayed up late talking and playing video games. Lex never plays video games with me." He shot Lex an annoyed look. "I even let him cry on my shoulder over this whole mess. I think I've finally found a replacement best friend."

I smirked. "Is that so?"

"Yep," he said. "Although it got a little awkward when he asked how serious things were between the two of you."

Lex fixed him with a look that said he was clearly not in the mood.

"Chill! I told him he needed to give up. I said you guys have a nickname and everything."

I sighed. "You told him you call us Halex?"

"It's going to catch on like wildfire. You'll see." Stuart winked.

"God, I hope not," Lex grumbled.

"To answer your question Hadley—yes. He's always this grouchy in the morning."

I laughed and kissed my grouch on the cheek before going into the kitchen to fix Stuart and I a cup of coffee.

When I came back, they were arguing.

"Hadley, tell Lex you'll come over tonight. The guys want to have a Spitzer tournament, and we're one player short," he whined, frowning at Lex.

I handed him his coffee. "What's Spitzer?"

"It's a card game. But you have to play in teams of four and we only have eleven. Lex is the last piece of the puzzle."

"You don't want to go?" I asked Lex.

"I want to be with you," he said, unabashed. "I don't care where we are."

"It's settled then," Stuart piped in. "You'll come, right Hadley? Especially since your very good friend Stuart, who took care of your weeping ex-boyfriend last night, is asking so very nicely."

Didn't need that reminder.

"Sure," I agreed. "I'm going to my mom's for dinner tonight, but I'll come over after."

"Yes!" Stuart shouted before I had finished the sentence. "I'm going to tell Pete the tournament's on." He shot to his feet and ran out the door toward Peter's house. I locked the door behind him, and Lex laughed.

"We don't have to go, you know," he said, pulling me into his lap.

"I'd rather have you all to myself anyway."

He tilted his head up at me. I kissed those perfect lips that had touched every part of my body last night and whispered, "Greedy," against his mouth. He smiled at me before resuming the kiss. It started out innocent enough, but the fire was licking through my veins in no time. He grabbed my hips and lifted me onto the table, yanking my clothes off before making love to me right there on the dining room table.

Chapter 25

"Garrett showed up last night," I told my mom as we dug into our chicken alfredo later that evening.

"What?!" She gaped, her fork suspended in mid-air. My gaze went to the sharp lines of her collarbone and jaw. I still wasn't used to how thin she looked now, but I never commented on it. I just encouraged her to eat as much as possible whenever we were together.

"I know," I said. "Lex showed up and pretty much kicked him out."

Her eyes widened. "Where did he go?"

"I didn't want him wandering the streets of Stanford late at night, so he stayed at the guys' house with Stuart, and Lex stayed with me." A warm flush crept over my cheeks as the memory of last night replayed in my mind. "He took an Uber back to the airport this morning."

"I can't believe you waited this long to tell me!" she protested.

"It was quite a scene," I said.

"Was Lex upset?"

"A little," I disclosed. "It bothered him how pushy Garrett was being."

My mom's face hardened with concern. "What do you mean?"

"He didn't hurt me," I assured her. "He didn't know I was seeing someone else, and I think he expected me to be thrilled that he came all this way to see me."

"But you haven't even talked to Garrett in months, right?"

"No, I haven't," I said. "Which was the reason I think Lex was so annoyed. Garrett kept pushing for me to give him another chance instead of accepting that things were over."

My mom shook her head. "You really had quite the evening."

"I wish that had been the end of it, but the scene continued into this morning when he came to say goodbye," I told her. "He was trying to get a rise out of Lex, talking about that trip we took to Cancun and asking if we could try to be friends once I got back to New York."

"What did you say?"

"I said 'maybe' just to get him out the house, but there's no way. I don't think we could manage it after all this."

Her expression became unreadable. "Interesting," she said cryptically.

"What's interesting?"

"Have you thought any more about what I said?" she asked, not answering my question.

"You'll have to be more specific," I responded. "You talk *a lot.*"

She smirked. "I don't think you're allowed to speak like that to a woman with no eyebrows."

I chuckled. "I've actually enjoyed that particular side effect. Your reactions to my insults have become more subdued."

She gasped, placing her hand over her heart. "I am shocked you would say such a thing, Hadley Marie Olivier."

"I would have no way of knowing that from your expression."

Her mouth slowly spread into a wide grin. "The woman who raised you must have been truly appalling."

"Truly." I smiled back at her. "So, what is it you want to tell me, mommy dearest?"

She had that teacher look on her face, so I knew I was about to hear a life lesson.

"Now, I don't want you to bite my head off again, but I know you,

Hadley," she started. "I can tell you and Lex are only going to get more serious about each other."

My brows pinched together. "Is that a bad thing?"

"Not at all. Lex is a great guy," she said. "The whole saving my life thing really convinced me of that."

I shrugged. "I'm still on the fence."

"Tell me something," she said more seriously. "Do you miss New York?"

"Of course I do," I answered automatically. I knew where she was going with this, and I could already feel my defenses going up. I wasn't sure if I was ready to revisit this conversation just yet.

"What is it you miss, exactly?" she asked.

"Everything," I said. "Sunday picnics in Central Park, walking the pier at Coney Island, ice cream in Chinatown…"

She nodded her head. "All the things you used to do with Daddy."

I stared straight ahead. I could feel the raw emotions wanting to take over for the logical side of my brain that was telling me she was right. If I thought of what I truly missed about New York, it was the memories I had with my dad, and how it always made me feel closer to him to still do those things.

"I get what you're saying," I said, trying to be diplomatic. "But leaving New York permanently… I just don't know if I can do it. It feels like I'm abandoning Daddy."

"Daddy would want you to be happy. That's all he ever wanted." She placed her hand over mine. "Can you really tell me that Coney Island and picnics in Central Park will make you happier than what you've found here? And I'm not just talking about Lex… Your writing has been even more incredible since you've been here, and you should see the look on your face when you talk about the students in your classes. I'd recognize that look anywhere. It's rewarding in a way you can't describe. I see how happy it makes you."

"Okay, but why is everyone acting like I was some miserable troll in New York?" At last count, that made three people—my mom, Jimmy, and now Garrett—all telling me that I was so different here. How could I not be different when my life had changed so drastically in a matter of months?

She shook her head. "I'm not saying that at all. I'm just afraid that trying to keep Daddy's memory alive is going to keep you from making memories of your own."

I couldn't meet her eye, knowing I would start crying if I did. Was she right? Was I just living in the past and destroying any future happiness I could have by holding on to the idea of New York so strongly? I wanted to tell her she was wrong, but my mom had always known me better than I knew myself.

Admitting the truth felt disloyal to the depths of my soul. But the truth was there regardless, just as it had been when Lex showed me that my dad was truly ill. This time I had to face the uncomfortable possibility that it wasn't New York itself that I was missing these days… it was my dad.

A single tear trickled down my face before I quickly swiped it away.

"This is your fault, you know," I accused.

She smiled, already picking up on my sarcasm. "How so?"

"You and your defective breasts got me into this mess."

Her hands flew to cover her breasts. "Shhhh! Romy and Michele can hear you."

I rolled my eyes. "You named them?"

"Of course. They're my new breast friends."

"And what am I?"

She smirked. "Old news," she said before wrapping her arm around me.

I sighed, leaning into her small frame. She was the one who was sick, but I still needed her support more than ever. I was never going to figure this out on my own.

"What am I going to do, Mom?"

She kissed the top of my head and smiled. "You tell me."

I went home and changed before heading to the guys' house for the Spitzer tournament. I thought of cancelling because I was still in a weird mood after talking to my mom, but I knew Stuart would throw a fit. More than that though, I wanted to feel Lex's arms around me and the mind-numbing happiness that always brought.

I could hear the party going on from outside the door. I tried knocking, but I doubted they could hear it over the loud music and everyone's conversations, so I let myself in. There were more than twelve of them here, it seemed, as people were scattered about their living room and dining area. Lex and Stuart were seated at a table in the center of the room, and Stuart spotted me as soon as I walked in.

"Oh, thank god!" Stuart shouted. "Hadley's here now, Lex. You can finally stop pouting and concentrate on the game."

Lex's head whipped around, his eyes brightening when he saw me. He shot out of his chair and walked over to me, pulling me into a tight embrace right there in front of everyone and kissing me intently.

"Guess you don't mind a little PDA then," I said, smiling against his mouth.

"Didn't even realize anyone else was here," he said, grinning back.

This. This is exactly what I needed. All the confusion and self-doubt disappeared in an instant the second I was in his arms.

"What. The. Fuck," I heard a guy at Lex's table say. I had only met him once that I could recall. I was struggling to remember his name.

"What?" Stuart said. "I told you Lex and Hadley were fornicating now, Louis."

Louis. That was his name.

"I thought you were bullshitting me! Hadley freaking Olivier. How could you not tell me, Lex?" Louis accused, gaping at him. "We spend countless hours piled on top of each other in a lab, and you didn't think to mention you were seeing Hadley freaking Olivier?"

Lex shrugged. "It never came up."

Louis scoffed. "This explains so much. He looks like he's been walking on clouds lately... I guess it makes sense. I would be too if I were dating Hadley freaking Olivier."

"You know 'freaking' isn't actually my middle name," I said as Lex walked me over to their table, where Peter was seated across from Louis. Dan and a few other guys I recognized at the adjacent table had started to laugh. I smiled at them in hello, and they gave me their usual nod in response.

"Sorry. I think my brain is hemorrhaging from this revelation. I mean, don't get me wrong, Lex is a good-looking dude, but I know some guys in the math department who'd give their right testicle to be with you." Louis inclined his head toward me. "How do I know this, you might ask? Because they told me so themselves and even specified which testicle."

I laughed at the absurdity of it. "I don't require testicular sacrifices for first dates anymore."

He threw his head back in laughter. "How did this even happen?"

"Her car broke down. Lex was waiting outside. It's a long story. One that I'm still bitter about," Stuart responded. "I'm usually the one waiting outside for him most days."

"Yeah, it was first come, first served," I said, and the room burst into laughter again.

"Anyway, it doesn't matter," Stuart said, waving me off. "Can we get back to the game?"

I heard Louis mumble, "Hadley freaking Olivier" once more under his breath before they went back to their cards.

"Do you want to sit?" Lex offered me his chair.

"No, I'll stand. I'd like to watch."

He sat down, and I stood at his side, draping my arm over his shoulder, and looked down at his cards, trying to decipher the game.

"So how does it work?" I asked, not familiar with the game at all.

"It's a partner's game, which is why I'm glad you're here, Betty, because now maybe my *partner*," Stuart said the word accusingly, "will actually concentrate instead of glancing at the door every thirty friggin' seconds."

Lex didn't even deny it. He just chuckled, placing his free hand on my hip and rubbing gently.

Louis was staring holes in the hand Lex had on my hip with his mouth gaping. Neurobiologists, in my limited experience, could really be so dramatic. I decided to mess with him a little more.

"Hey, do you guys have any coffee? I could really use some. Someone kept me up all night last night." I winked at Lex and bumped his shoulder with my hip.

"Kitchen," Stuart said without looking up from his cards.

"You want any?" I asked, looking down at Lex.

He smiled up at me. "No, I'm good. Thanks."

I bent down to kiss him and got the satisfaction of seeing Louis's jaw nearly hit the table, which had me biting my lip to keep from laughing. *Too easy*, I thought as I went through the swinging door to their kitchen.

"You're my hero, dude!" I heard Louis say. "Maybe you could set me up with one of her other friends from the blind community."

That was the last thing I heard before, "Ouch! Hey! C'mon, I was just kidding!"

Lex must have thrown something at him, and I started to chuckle. I found the coffee pot and made myself a cup because I really was dragging. Lex had told me he always had trouble sleeping, but I was starting to see just how easily he managed it. It seemed he could function on little to no sleep at all. His tolerance must have built up over the years of late nights in the lab.

When I came back to the card table, they looked like they were on their best behavior now. I leaned against Lex, settling in to watch them play. I came to see the game was mostly about trying to outmaneuver the other team. You kept separate scores and ultimately played for yourself, but the partnership made it possible. They would often play out the possibilities in their heads before the losing team threw in their cards for the round, making it more difficult for me to understand what was happening, but I was enjoying myself.

I eventually found myself sitting in Lex's lap, holding the cards while he whispered instructions in my ear, trying to explain the game and telling me what moves to make.

More and more people had started showing up, including Nicky, who had been throwing daggers at me with her eyes ever since she'd walked in and spotted me sitting in Lex's lap.

Stuart groaned. "Great, the ice queen's here."

"Fuck you, Stuart," was her favorite response.

"I'd rather play checkers on a cheetah's ass, Nicky."

"Why'd you invite me if you're just going to be an asshole?" she snapped.

"Isn't it obvious? Lex made me."

That turned her attitude around. She shot me a smug smile, and I felt a knot twist in my stomach. Lex had already explained to me that he did it so that she wouldn't be ostracized by her coworkers, but it still stung, and she knew it.

"Just do me a favor and go outside if you have to shed your skin," Stuart said to her. "I'm still cleaning the rug from the last time you were here."

Stuart's latest insult wasn't enough to elicit a further response as she continued grinning at me.

I shifted uncomfortably in Lex's lap. He pulled me close to his chest, ignoring both of them as he casually planted kisses along my neck and shoulder. That essentially shut her up as she walked off into the kitchen.

"Hey, where's Jace tonight?" Peter asked.

Stuart nodded towards me. "Ask Hadley," he said bitterly.

"He's on a date with my friend Sarah," I announced cheerfully. I had convinced her to take a chance and told her she wouldn't regret it. She'd reluctantly agreed. I'd been checking my phone every so often, hoping she wouldn't send me an SOS text to come and rescue her.

"What?" Peter asked incredulously. "You're setting Jace up with your friends and not me?"

"Get in line," Stuart said. "We've already had this discussion."

"Jace is a lucky man," Louis interjected.

"How would you know?" I said, chuckling. "You've never even met Sarah."

"It's a known fact that hot girls travel in packs," he answered.

"Exactly what I said!" Stuart exclaimed, and I started to laugh even harder. Lex smiled, his eyes fixed on me, looking like he was really enjoying himself. I was glad we had agreed to come.

They settled into a discussion about work as they continued playing, and I couldn't even begin to keep up. I listened closely, fascinated by how their minds worked. They were on a different level of thinking that really humbled me.

"Okay, but every time we put it through the electron microscope, we're getting low throughput. The flow cytometric EV isn't stable enough for those particles," Peter was arguing.

"The smaller refractive index is what's leaving the cells intact, dumbass," Stuart fired back. "We need better fluorescent markers."

I had listened to them arguing about the best way for these particles to pass through this microscope for ten minutes now, and the words slipped out without thinking.

"Sounds like it might be better as a waveform," I said. "Kinda like musical notes."

Silence followed as everyone in the immediate vicinity froze, and I felt my cheeks redden.

I looked around at them. "What? Was that really stupid?"

"No... that... might... actually... work," Stuart said slowly, pausing between words. He had a glazed look in his eyes, his mind obviously somewhere else.

"Do you think?" Peter asked Lex.

"If we run the variables through the PMT-based flow cytometry then I think... maybe," Lex said, his eyes narrowing a fraction.

"It's worth a shot," Stuart said excitedly, abandoning his cards. "Come on, we could still get into the lab. The security guard probably hasn't left yet."

The rest of the guys stood up, but Lex stayed rooted to the spot.

"I guess I'll see you later," I told him, smiling, even though I was a little disappointed our evening together was over so soon. I went to stand, but he held me in place with a torn expression.

"What's wrong?" I asked, but he didn't answer me.

"Hadley, please come with us," Stuart said, rolling his eyes and guessing what was wrong with Lex. "I can already see Lex is going to be insufferable if you don't."

I didn't realize that was an option, and I grinned broadly. "Could I? I'd love to see you work."

His eyes brightened. "You'd really want to come?"

"Of course. It's not often someone like me gets the chance to see the greatest neuroscientist of our time at work."

Stuart made gagging noises from behind me. "Please don't make his ego any bigger, Betty."

Lex grinned at me. "Apparently, you're the smart one."

I laughed as we stood to follow the guys out to their cars.

"I can't believe I'm going to have to share my Nobel Prize with a liberal arts major," Stuart grumbled as we walked along the sidewalk.

The whole team—including Nicky, who was still shooting me dirty looks—got down to work as soon as we got into the lab. There was a buzz of excitement in the air as they each went to their respective stations and started pulling different equipment and textbooks out. I got a front-row seat to their animated discussion of the problem and why waveforms might actually be the solution.

Lex sat next to me, scribbling furiously on the sheets of paper in front of him. I tried not to bother him as he worked since he seemed to be fully engrossed in it. The tiny furrow in his brow was so endearing to me as I watched him concentrate. He had put his glasses on, which made it even harder for me not to jump his bones. I sat on my hands to keep myself from reaching out to touch him like I wanted to do so badly.

Peter came over and peered over Lex's shoulder, watching him work out the variables on paper. When Lex was done, he paused to let Peter read it fully.

"Incredible." Peter smiled as he looked it over. "This is some of your best work, Lex. You solved it in no time."

"What did I say about his ego?" Stuart shouted from across the room. "Keep it up and he's going to turn into a real-life Russian doll—completely full of himself."

Lex smiled at me proudly. "It was all Hadley's idea."

"We're definitely keeping Hadley around from now on," Louis said, also looking over Lex's work. "Every great artist has his muse."

I started to laugh, and Lex leaned over to kiss my temple sweetly. "Let's get started," he said to the other guys.

I observed for a while, totally lost, but still fascinated. Lex tried to explain different points to me, but I knew he was wasting time when he could be working so much quicker, so I told him to just let me observe so he could get focused.

Once they seemed fully immersed in the experiment, I slipped out to get them some food. I brought back pizza, drinks, and snacks, knowing it was going to be a late one for them.

"You're my hero, Hadley!" Dan said, running over to the pizza.

"Inspiration and pizza? Seriously, your girl's amazing," Louis said, digging in as the rest of them swarmed on the food.

"Calm down. It's pizza, not the discovery of penicillin," Nicky said, refusing to eat a thing.

"We already know how grateful you are for penicillin's discovery, Nicky," Stuart interjected. "Its ability to cure most venereal diseases is a matter close to your heart."

She flipped him the bird before walking away.

Lex came over with a look of amazement, shaking his head. He leaned over and whispered, "I don't deserve you," close to my ear, sending shivers down my spine.

I said under my breath to him, "Keep whispering in my ear, and I'll drag you out of this room and you won't ever finish this experiment."

His eyes flared as he looked down at my mouth. I bit my lip, trying hard not to think of every way I wanted that mouth of his on me again. Stuart discreetly cleared his throat, breaking us out of our little trance.

"Alright," Lex said, his throat bobbing. "Let's get back to it."

They worked well into the night, and I ended up falling asleep across one of the tables. I felt warm hands picking me up, and I barely registered that Lex was carrying me back to their car. I fell back asleep immediately once we were in the car with my head in his lap, only coming to again once I felt him laying me down on his bed. I curled up next to him, totally exhausted, and drifted off to sleep in his arms.

Chapter 26

The first thing I did when I woke up the next morning was check my phone to see if Sarah had ever called or texted. She hadn't, so I was hoping that was a good sign. Lex was still sleeping, his arm draped over my midsection. He seemed thoroughly asleep, so I crawled out of bed slowly, trying not to wake him. Once I got in the hallway, I called Sarah.

"Hello?" she answered quietly, but not sleepily. I knew immediately from her tone of voice that she wasn't alone.

"You dirty whore!" I said, giggling.

"Shhhh! Keep your voice down," she whispered. "He's still sleeping."

"So what?" I teased. "Wake him up. Take care of his morning wood for him."

"No, asshat. I'm not ready to face him just yet," she said, still whispering. "Come meet me outside and take me to breakfast. I'm starving."

"Having sex all night long will do that to a girl."

"Just come get me," she said before abruptly hanging up.

I went back into Lex's room and left him a note to tell him where I was going before slipping out to meet Sarah.

She was running down the walkway from Jace's house with her heels in hand, wearing a dress that was clearly meant for nightlife and not breakfast with a friend.

I laughed at her disheveled appearance as she ran up to me saying, "Shutupshutupshutupshutup."

We drove to a breakfast spot downtown, and I grinned at her suggestively as she gulped down her coffee.

"You're going to make me say it, aren't you?" she said.

"Yep," I said, still grinning.

"Fine. You were right."

I cupped a hand around my ear. "A little louder, please."

She rolled her eyes. "While I may have been the *teensiest* bit resistant to having your leftovers, I'll admit I was wrong."

"I'm so happy for you, you filthy slut."

"So am I," she said. "I forgot what sex with an actual man felt like. I thought I was going to have to buy stock in a battery company at one point."

I laughed, feeling ecstatic with my matchmaking skills. "So, you like him then."

She sipped her coffee and shrugged noncommittally, refusing to meet my eye.

"Oh, you *really* like him." I knew she'd be more than happy to tell me if she didn't.

She smiled into her mug. "Shit. I think I do."

"Sarah, that's great!"

"He's just so fucking cute." She began to blush, and I almost spit out my coffee. Sarah wasn't the blushing kind. "And smart," she continued. "Too smart. It makes me feel like a dumbass."

I nodded. "Tell me about it."

"He told me nothing happened between you guys." I had already told her this, but I guess she wanted more reassurance.

"Very true," I confirmed. "He asked me out once, but you know..." I smiled, knowing she knew I had always been into Lex.

"Speaking of… Jace mentioned he's never seen Lex like this." She smirked. "Said it's the happiest he's ever seen him."

I shrugged. "Well, sex with me will do that to a guy."

"I knew it!" She drummed on the table. "I knew you slept with him! And you call me the dirty slut."

I laughed. "You missed a lot these last few days. Garrett showed up on my doorstep Friday night wanting to work things out."

Her eyes widened. "You're kidding me."

"Nope. Lex made him sleep at his place with Stuart, and he stayed at my house. That's when… you know."

"Bow-chicka-wow-wow," she sang, and I giggled. She leaned forward. "So how was it?"

I smiled over the top of my mug. "Which time?"

"You dirtyyyy frigginnn' whoreee. The nerve of you calling me out for sleeping with Jace."

I laughed even harder. "So, are you going to see him again?"

"He asked me to go out again tonight." She tried hiding how happy that made her.

"Bring a change of clothes this time," I said before dodging a piece of egg she flicked at me.

I was tuning the strings of my guitar with my notebook splayed out in front of me, trying to think through the verse I'd been grappling with over the past few weeks. The song was intended to have a visceral image of the narrator feeling duplicitous in their existence and trying to make a hard decision—not a clue where the inspiration came from. However, the verse was feeling more like rambling prose with no end in sight, and I'd been attempting to fix it day after day with absolutely no luck.

My phone started ringing with a FaceTime call from Lex, and I was happy for the distraction from my muddled thoughts. He had left for a conference in San Diego yesterday and would be gone the whole weekend. He had to give a big presentation Saturday morning about their project, and I could tell he was nervous.

I answered the call to see his hair still wet from his shower, and he was naked from the waist up. Worst of all, he was wearing those damn glasses.

I frowned. "Oh Lex, I don't think I'm ready for this."

"Ready for what?" he asked, confused.

"Phone sex," I replied.

He paused before throwing his head back, laughing. "Your mind is always in the gutter," he said, still chuckling.

"That's because you look like sex on a stick lying there with no shirt on and those damn, freaking glasses."

"I didn't realize they were such a turn-on." He smiled, adjusting them on his face.

"Can you tilt the screen lower? Your chest went out of frame."

"Pervert," he teased but tilted the screen anyway.

"Hey, you were the one who called trying to have phone sex with me."

He sighed. "This was supposed to be a regular goodnight phone call."

"You think I believe that?" I narrowed my eyes. "You're trying to seduce me again."

"You caught me. I put my glasses on, knowing you couldn't resist."

"At least you're finally admitting it."

He shook his head, chuckling.

"Are you ready for tomorrow?" I asked.

"I think so. I've been practicing for the last hour. There are a lot of big companies that will be there who could potentially sponsor us in the future. I don't want to mess it up."

"You won't," I told him. "Just keep your glasses on. They're your superpower."

He laughed. "I might just do that."

The phone shifted, and I got a glimpse of something truly frightening behind his head.

I gasped. "What is that?!"

His brows pinched together. "What is what?"

"That abomination on your headboard!" I cried.

He looked back and started to choke on his laughter. There were pictures of large, ornate birds carved into the wooden frame of the headboard.

"I don't know how you're going to sleep! I've still got nightmares from my close call."

His mouth pulled into a half grin. "I think I'll be alright."

"If you say so." I made a face of disgust. "Where is everyone else tonight?"

"They all went out to the bars downtown."

"You didn't feel like joining them?"

He shrugged. "Not my thing."

"A drink might help to calm those nerves."

"No, I just need a good night of sleep. I told them I was heading in early and not to bother me, because I was going to take a sleeping pill to get some rest. I want to be ready for tomorrow."

"Do those work for you?"

"Yeah, they usually knock me out. But I try not to take them too often unless I really need it, like tonight."

"Well, I'll let you go so you can get some rest," I said. "Although, I don't know how you will with that atrocity hanging over you all night."

He chuckled. "I'll call you after the presentation tomorrow."

"Okay. I'm off to spend a little me time before bed," I said with a wink.

His eyes darkened. "What does that mean?"

"Just that I've got a great visual to use now, and I don't want to waste it." I raked my eyes over his chest one more time.

"That is definitely not helping me calm down before bed."

I laughed. "Good luck tomorrow."

He let out a heavy sigh. "Goodnight, Hadley."

"Night, Lex."

I stayed up for a few more hours working on the song, but still wasn't able to get very far. I started thinking about Lex, hoping he wasn't too nervous for this presentation. I wished I could be there with him. He had invited me to come along, but I didn't feel comfortable leaving my mom for that long. Once she was better, though, I thought I might have more freedom to travel with him. I knew we were in that frenzied stage of dating, but I never seemed to be able to get enough of him. I'd always heard absence made the heart grow fonder, but in my case, absence made the heart grow hornier.

I had my morning routine nailed down now. After waking up, I'd head downstairs and grab a tennis racket from the hallway closet before slowly opening the door to the kitchen to make a sweep for any feathered intruders. Once the perimeter was secured, I would make a cup of coffee before getting ready for the day.

Today was no exception.

Tennis racket in hand, I crept into the kitchen, ready to swing at the first thing that moved. I never left the windows open anymore, because once you have a brush with death, you're just never the same. After a quick sweep of the perimeter, I determined that the home was avian-free, so I lived to fight another day.

Heart rate under control and coffee in hand, I grabbed my phone to wish Lex good luck when I saw a message from a blocked number. I opened it and had to look twice at what I was seeing. It was a picture of Lex lying in bed sleeping with pink hair draped across his chest, his arm around her. She was topless as well, and I felt my stomach clench painfully.

My heart was racing, and I tried to calm down, hoping this was just an old photo someone had sent to mess with me. Then my eyes zeroed in on the headboard. *The fucking birds.* I ran to the bathroom, thinking I was going to be sick.

My hands started to shake, and I fought to get control as my thoughts began colliding in a downward spiral of unbridled chaos. How could he do this? He told me he was done with Nicky. That he was just going to sleep early that night. He'd just neglected to mention that he wouldn't be sleeping alone. I pictured his wet hair, fresh from the shower, when he had called me. Had she been there in the shower with him? Bile rose to my throat.

Is that why he always fought to have her around? Maybe that was why he hadn't stood up for me outside the bathroom that night. Was it some kind of sick game the two of them were playing? If so, it was definitely not one I wanted to be a part of. The image of the two of them lying there together felt forever branded in my brain.

I dropped to my knees on the bathroom floor clutching my phone, the image still taunting me. Someone had obviously wanted me to see this. The possibilities raced through my mind. Was it Stuart? Did he want me to know what was happening without Lex knowing he was the one who ratted him out? That didn't seem likely. It was probably Nicky herself who had taken the picture just to antagonize me, but why was she in his room in the first place? Why was his arm around her? None of this made sense.

Sobs wracked violently through my chest with a pain I'd never experienced before. I stayed frozen on the bathroom floor for hours, staring at nothing but seeing entirely too much.

When I finally managed some semblance of calm, I drove to my mom's house and knocked on her door.

"Hey baby girl," she said, opening the door. "What's wrong?" Her tone changed instantly when she looked at my face. She grabbed me, pulling me into her arms as the tears came out in another fierce wave. We went to the living room, and she held me until I could finally tell her what happened.

She stayed quiet for a while, just listening before she said, "This doesn't make any sense. He's crazy about you. Why would he have waited for you all this time just to sleep with his ex-girlfriend the first weekend he went away?"

"I don't know. They're together all the time. They wouldn't need to go away if they really wanted to be together," I said as the horrible possibility sank in. I tried to push the thought out of my mind, but the seed had already been planted. All those late nights in the lab together... it was how they had gotten together in the first place. I had no way to know how long this had been going on, but I knew one thing for certain—he and I were done.

Lex tried calling me after his presentation, but I didn't answer. I was too busy getting shitfaced with Sarah and Lionel because that was the only solution we could come up with for my problem. He had texted me that everything went well and that he would try calling again later.

"Hadley, just so you're aware," Lionel slurred after we'd had far too much wine. "I'm an avid true crime fan and dedicated podcast listener. I know the perfect way to get rid of this douchenugget, and we'd never leave a trace."

"Here we go," Sarah said, just as drunk. "Everyone knows you'd use the old icicle trick."

I hiccupped. "What's the icicle trick?"

"See? Not everyone knows," Lionel said, giving her the side eye before turning to me. "All you have to do is freeze a giant icicle and use it as a spike to drive into your enemy's heart. And then there's no murder weapon to be found because it melts! Easy peasy."

"Ohhh." To my booze-addled brain, that sounded like a brilliant plan. "Although, I don't think your plan would work in this case."

"And why is that?" Lionel said, sounding offended.

"Because you'd have to have a heart to drive the spike into," I explained. "And that assface definitely doesn't!"

I knew that wasn't true, but with the picture fresh in my mind and my inability to come up with another explanation for what I saw, I let the hurt spill out.

Lionel cackled. "I see we've moved on to the trash-talking phase of the evening, and I am here for it!" he said, lifting his glass in the air.

"It just doesn't make any sense," Sarah said, unknowingly echoing my mom's words from earlier.

"He fucked someone else. What about it doesn't make sense to you?" Lionel asked, and I flinched at the image his words conjured up.

Sarah swirled the wine around in her glass. "No, I get that, but I swear, if you had seen him around her, you would have sworn her pussy was made of pure gold."

"If you say so." Lionel shrugged before turning to me. "Hadley, maybe this was all some big misunderstanding. What rules did you guys come up with?"

My brows knitted. "Rules?"

"Yeah. Did you guys ever talk about what you could and could not do?" he asked. "Like, I once dated this guy who came up with the hundred-mile rule. We could sleep with other people as long as they lived outside a hundred-mile radius. Is San Diego more than a hundred miles away?"

"We didn't have any rules like that," I told him. "We never even talked about it."

"What do you mean you never talked about it?" Sarah asked, confused.

"I mean I just assumed we were on the same page. I haven't been seeing anyone else. He acts like we're together. He basically threw my ex out of my house a few weeks ago when he showed up on my doorstep. Not to mention, we've been sleeping together practically every night for the past month. I didn't think I'd have to spell it out that I didn't want him screwing other people."

They exchanged looks between each other.

"What?" I asked. "Spit it out."

Lionel put his drink down. "If you guys never said you were exclusive then maybe he didn't think he was doing anything wrong."

I scoffed. "He's told me a million times he's not interested in her anymore, and yet for some reason, she made it inside his room and into his arms last night, long enough for someone to capture a photo of the encounter," I said, my voice shaking. "How is that not a betrayal?"

Sarah was looking at me sympathetically. "Just say it," I huffed at her.

"Lionel might be right. If you never talked about it, then maybe he didn't consider it cheating," she said in a gentle voice, trying not to upset me further.

But I just shook my head. Were they right? Was I an idiot to have assumed that we were together and not seeing other people? This was too much for my drunken brain to consider, so I grabbed the bottle of wine and tried to drown out any more thoughts about Lex and what else he could possibly be doing right now... or *who*.

My head was pounding the next morning as I stepped over Sarah and Lionel, who had passed out on the floor next to me last night. I chugged a bottle of water and rifled through her cabinet looking for aspirin. I had several missed calls from Lex as well as Stuart, along with numerous texts from them asking if I was okay.

I wasn't ready to talk to Lex or face this situation yet, so I texted him back that I was fine and that I had gotten drunk at Sarah's, which was completely true.

He texted back almost immediately asking if he could come over tonight once he got back. I made up some excuse, saying I was staying at my mom's. I didn't know how long I could put him off, but I needed a little more time to think about things.

Lucky for me, this week was fall break at the university, which meant we didn't have classes. It gave me the opportunity to stay with my mom and avoid Lex for the time being. I went home and packed a bag to stay with her for at least the next few days.

The more I thought about it, the more I thought Sarah and Lionel might be right. I was an idiot for never talking to Lex about the expectations I had for us. The thought of him with another woman clearly made me sick, but it felt like a complete and utter betrayal that it was Nicky. I still believed he owed me an explanation even if he didn't consider it cheating, but I didn't know how we were going to move forward from here. I couldn't stomach the thought of them working together side by side, day after day, knowing they had just slept together. I had to tell him we were through, but even thinking about saying those words out loud made me want to crawl into a hole and disappear.

I started running out of excuses as to why I couldn't see him over the next few days, and it was clear he knew something was wrong. He kept asking to see me, begging even, but I wasn't ready. By Wednesday, I stopped answering him completely. I shut my phone off and just spent time with my mom and Carl. She was sympathetic but still pushed me to go home and talk to him. She figured there must be some explanation, but I couldn't think of any that would explain what I saw.

After dinner one night, I was checking my emails to see I had an obnoxious amount from my old producer friend, Logan Shipley. I smiled at the colorful language he was using to tell me he found out from Jimmy that I'd been in California all this time and that no self-respecting New Yorker would ever stoop so low. I decided it might be time to finally give him a call.

"Hadley Olivier," Logan answered. "As I live and breathe." Logan was in his late thirties, impatient beyond measure, and brutally honest—a New Yorker through and through, so we'd always gotten along really well. We'd worked together a handful of times over the years and our collaborations were always successful.

"Hey Ship," I said, calling him by his nickname.

"No one's been able to get a hold of you in months, including me, and now I have to hear from Jimmy fucking Blackmore that you're doing some weird teacher cosplay out in California."

"Jimmy's got a big mouth," I retorted.

"Seriously, Olivier. What could you possibly be doing in the land of the gluten-hating, tree-hugging, lip-plumping hipsters?" He was biased against pretty much any state that wasn't New York, but California was at the top of his shit list.

"I just needed a change," I told him, not wanting to get into it.

"Alright. Whatever you say," he said, dropping it. That was the great thing about Logan. He never prodded, probably because he really didn't care. He was all business, all the time.

"Well listen, I haven't been calling you for shits and giggles. I've got this new girl, Fiona Lockwood... I'm telling you, Hadley, she's really got something. Her record company hired me to produce her debut album, and we've got some great stuff so far. But we need your ear for the ballads. Feedback from the label is that she still sounds a little too bubblegum. It's a pop album, but they want a single that sounds a little more sentimental that will really showcase her pipes, and you know I can't do that kind of shit. There's only one person for the job, so spare me the bullshit and just agree to it."

I laughed. "If I did agree to it, I couldn't stay long."

"I don't need long," he said. "Besides, if I know you, you've already got about twenty songs ready to go."

He was right. My mind was already going through my catalog, thinking of which ones in particular would fit a young pop solo artist.

"When does the record company want it finished?" I asked.

"They want to release it in early March."

"Alright, I'll see what I can do." Hopefully, my mom would get to a point where she was well enough to fend for herself for a few days, but we weren't there yet, or at least I wasn't.

"I need an answer, Olivier," he pushed.

"I said I'd let you know," I countered. I learned a long time ago you can't let these guys push you around or they'd walk all over you, especially if you're a woman in the biz.

"Fine," he huffed. "But next time, answer your fucking phone."

I didn't take his advice. I shut my phone off as soon as we hung up, not ready to face what was waiting for me.

On Thursday morning, I had no choice but to go home. I was out of clean clothes, and I couldn't stay holed up at my mom's forever. I went home early that morning, still hoping to avoid my problems, but it seemed my problems were waiting for me on my doorstep... literally.

Lex was sitting on my porch, eyes closed, with his head leaned back against my front door. He looked terrible. He had deep, dark circles under his eyes, and the angles of his face seemed sharper, like he'd lost weight.

"Lex," I breathed. His eyes snapped open, and my heart picked up speed as we stared at one another. *God, I'd missed him.* I couldn't help it. There was still a huge part of me that was elated to see him, despite what had happened.

"What are you doing here?" I asked as he stood up, slowly taking me in. I probably looked just as shitty as he did.

"Seriously?" His tone was full of disbelief. "You won't return any of my calls or texts, and you've been making up crazy excuses not to see me. You're avoiding me and I want to know why." His voice was thick with despair. "Just tell me what I did wrong, Hadley. I'm going fucking crazy here."

I sighed. I guess it was time to face the music. I opened the door as he followed in behind me.

"You didn't do anything wrong." I decided I wasn't going to blame or accuse him, but I was going to ask for an explanation before I told him it was over.

"Then what is it?" he demanded. "We go from seeing each other every single day to now not having heard from you in a week."

"A week's not that long," I said pathetically.

"That's bullshit and you know it. Tell me the truth." He closed in on me. "Are you done with me?" he asked miserably, just inches from my face. "Is that it? If it is, then just say it. I can't stand not knowing."

"It's my fault, really," I mumbled. "I just thought—"

"You just thought what?" He put his hands on my shoulders, and I hated that my body responded so easily to his touch.

"I don't know. I guess I thought we were on the same page."

His eyebrows pinched together. "What do you mean?"

I took a deep breath. "I'm falling for you, Lex," I admitted in a small voice, eyes lowered to the ground. "I've *been* falling for you. I know we've only been seeing each other for a month, but I haven't dated anyone else since we got together. I guess it just hurt to find out you were seeing other people, and I had no idea."

He was breathing heavily. "What the hell are you talking about? I haven't been seeing anyone else."

Hot, burning anger rolled through me, and I couldn't take it anymore. I pulled out of his grasp.

"God, I'm such an idiot!" I said angrily, trying to keep the tears from spilling over. "Even now you seem so earnest. I can't believe I fell for this. I never thought you were capable of it, but here you are, lying straight to my face."

"I don't understand," he said helplessly. "What makes you think I've been seeing other people?"

"This!" I said, pulling out my phone and showing him the picture.

A thousand emotions flashed across his eyes in the span of a single second. His face contorted with rage. He snatched the phone out of my hand before turning and racing out the door.

"Where are you going?" I called after him.

"Nicky's," he said without looking back at me.

Well, that's just great. I didn't know why he needed my phone to do that, but I ran after him, intending to take it back. He ran up the steps of her porch, taking two at a time, and started pounding on the door.

She opened it, and her face split into a sultry grin that made me sick when she saw it was Lex standing there.

"You bitch," he said so harshly that I almost stumbled back from the intensity. "Stuart was right about you all along. I defended you even after you said the shittiest things about Hadley, about me, about my relationship, but I let all of that go because you were never even important enough for me to care about. But I still never thought you could do something like this."

Nicky stood frozen, her face a portrait of shock that quickly melted into practiced composure. "What the hell are you talking about?"

He smiled bitterly. "I have to hand it to you, Nicky. It was really fucking clever. Coming to my room in the middle of the night saying your shower broke. How long did you wait for me to fall back asleep before you staged this?"

"Staged what?" she demanded, though the attempt at looking innocent didn't quite land.

He pulled out my phone, shoving the picture in her face.

She paused to look at it before rolling her eyes and brushing the photo aside with a dismissive wave. "So there's a picture of us sleeping together. Big deal. I don't know if you remember, but we used to do that all the time together."

Lex's face twisted into a cruel smile. "You might have gotten away with that excuse if you hadn't caught the headboard in the photo," he said. "Notice anything unique about it, Nicky?"

She looked at the photo again, and I saw the exact moment she realized the same thing I had. *The fucking birds.* Her eyes widened, and the color drained from her face, a brief flash of panic crossing her features.

"That's what I thought." He handed me back the phone. "Listen to me now and listen closely... After today, do not ever speak to me again. If you have something to say when we're at work, you email me or send someone else to tell me. Do not say hello when we pass each other in the hallway. Don't even look at me. I don't want to see you outside of work ever. Never show up where I'm at, and if you're already out somewhere and I show up, then leave. The same goes for Hadley. I don't want to hear Hadley's name out of your mouth *ever* again. I let you get away with this kind of shit for way too long, but that's over now. If you even breathe in a way I don't like, I promise to have you fired, and I will make it my life's mission to see to it that you never work in this field again."

"Lex, it was just a joke—" Nicky tried saying, but he cut her off.

"We're done." His face was full of disgust. "And let me be clear about one last thing—I never loved you... not even close."

He stormed out, grabbing my hand and pulling me back to my home.

When we reached my house, his chest was still heaving with anger as he stood outside my doorway. I was too shell-shocked by this revelation to be angry with Nicky. I knew it would come, but all I felt in this moment was complete and utter relief. *He hadn't slept with her.* As I let that sink in, a new feeling started to fill every square inch of me.

I was elated.

I waited another minute for him to calm down before asking, "Do you want to come in?"

His gaze lifted to meet mine. He simply nodded before following me inside.

"I didn't sleep with her," he said as soon as we were inside. "She was banging on my door in the middle of the night, spouting some bullshit about her shower being broken. I let her use mine, but I fell back asleep the second I laid back down. I'm sorry I didn't tell you, but I barely remembered her coming in. She knows how those sleeping pills affect me."

"I know." I believed every word he said. "I'm sorry. I know it hurts that she betrayed you like that."

He scoffed. "I couldn't care less about that. I meant what I said. She was never important enough for me to care about. I only ever put up with her bullshit because I didn't want her to be excluded purely because we broke up. My feelings and loyalty ended there. I only care about the fact that she upset you and made you believe I slept with her."

"That's what I think we should talk about," I said. "This isn't working for me."

He looked crushed. "Hadley, just give me another chance. I can make this right—"

"No. Lex, listen to me," I said, cutting him off. "I didn't confront you about this whole thing because I felt foolish for making assumptions. I realized we'd never talked about what this is, but I'd like to do that now."

"Okay," he said warily.

I took a breath. "I don't want to see anyone else. I've never felt this way about anyone, and I want to hear you say it here and now... That you're mine and I'm yours."

He gazed into my eyes like he couldn't believe what he was hearing. His throat dipped as he swallowed. "I'm afraid I'd scare you if I confessed the true depth of my feelings for you. So, I'll just say this... I'm yours. There is no one else for me."

"Good," I whispered, the emotions rising up in my throat. "Now kiss me and don't be gentle."

His eyes locked with mine and a split second later his hands were in my hair and his mouth was covering mine. I groaned at the contact and the relief I felt at coming together again. And he wasn't gentle. On the contrary, it was like each of us was barely able to hold back. Our tongues clashed, our mouths moving together in a rapid frenzy.

He kissed me until I knew my lips would swell as he held my head securely to him, turning it exactly how he wanted it to deepen the kiss. I pulled at his shirt, trying to tug it over his head as he did the same to mine. Our hands were everywhere, pulling each other closer as we tore our clothes off in no time.

We didn't make it to the bedroom. He bent me over the couch, and I heard a condom wrapper tearing moments before he pushed into me. I cried out, gripping the edge of the sofa. I felt his chest leaning over me as his tongue trailed across my back and along my neck before he slammed into me again. He reached around to grab my breast as he picked up the pace and pounded into me. I matched his thrusts, and I could hear his heavy breathing as he whispered things in Russian above me. One hand held my waist, while the other gripped my shoulder as he steered my body onto his. The pleasure was mounting, and I desperately wanted to see his face when I came apart for him, so I turned and pulled him in for another searing kiss before dragging him down to the floor with me.

I pushed at his chest to lie back, his eyes never leaving my face. I straddled his hips, lining him up at my entrance before I slowly sank down. He groaned loudly, gripping my waist as his head fell backward. I started to move, and his hands tightened around my hips, rocking my body back and forth over his. He was staring up at me with a raw hunger in his eyes that bordered on primal as his hands rose to caress the swells of my breasts. The air was thick with the sound of our ragged breathing. I leaned forward to place my hands on his pecs, giving myself better leverage to move faster as sweat began beading at the base of my neck.

He lifted his hips while simultaneously pulling me over him, hitting the exact spot I needed until I came so hard my vision started to blur. He continued pushing and pulling at my hips as I convulsed around him until he found his release moments later. It came out as an agonized moan at the same time my body had collapsed on top of his.

Our breathing was harsh as we lay there together, his hands stroking gently over my back. We lay that way for a while until I dragged my eyes up to meet his, and the frenzy began all over again.

Chapter 28

I felt warm hands slipping around my waist while I worked at the stove making breakfast.

"Did I wake you?" I asked, smiling. "I was hoping you would sleep in a little later."

His hands were caressing my waist as he kissed softly along my neck. I closed my eyes and tilted my head, giving him better access, before I eventually turned down the fire on one of the burners and twisted in his arms.

"No, the bed was suddenly freezing cold," he said with a lazy grin. "I needed someone to warm me up."

I wrapped my arms around his neck and stood on my tiptoes to press a kiss to his lips. It started off sweetly, but the reunion over the last day seemed to be too much. Our hands started to move as the kiss deepened until I found myself pinned against the kitchen counter with his erection pressing into me. There was a hissing sound from the stove next to me, bringing me back to reality as I pulled away, laughing.

"You're going to make me set the house on fire." I grabbed the pan off the burner and tried to unstick the contents.

He chuckled but still stood behind me, stroking his hands along my sides. "What are you making, anyway?" he asked with his chin tucked into my neck.

"French toast."

"Smells amazing." He inhaled deeply. "My mom used to make the best French toast. It's called grenki in Russia."

"Is it different than American French toast?"

"Not really. The only difference is we use baguettes instead of sliced bread. But my mom used to make it every Sunday along with all the other mountains of food we could never finish."

"You miss her." Not a question.

"Yes," he answered with a gentle smile. "And the rest of my family too. I haven't seen them in almost three years."

"You're going back to see them over the Christmas break though, right?" I remembered he had told me not long after we met that he would be visiting his family over Christmas.

"Yes, for about a week." He paused like he was contemplating something.

I turned to look at him. "What is it?"

"Come with me," he said, tucking my hair behind my ear.

I chewed on my lip. That was so tempting, but I just couldn't leave my mom for that long. Our own Christmas plans to go back to New York had gotten cancelled since my mom was in no state to travel.

"My mom—" I started. He nodded like he already knew the answer but had to ask anyway.

He kissed my forehead and said, "I know. I just don't know how I'm going to leave you for that long."

The thought of it was painful, especially after the week apart we'd just had, but I tried not to let that show on my face as I made our plates.

Instead of sitting across from me at the dining room table, Lex sat down in the chair next to me, pulling my legs into his lap, and we ate breakfast that way.

"Do you have any plans this weekend?" he asked.

"Oh, yes. Big plans, actually. There's an I Love Lucy marathon playing Saturday night and all day Sunday," I said excitedly.

"You're a big I Love Lucy fan I take it?"

"That's all I was allowed to watch growing up. My parents loved classic movies and TV, so on Saturday mornings, we weren't watching cartoons. We were watching The Brady Bunch, Gilligan's Island, MASH, and best of all—I Love Lucy!" I said cheerfully. "That's really the only one that stuck."

"My mom was the same way," he said. "No TV with the exception of old westerns, for some reason."

"Really?"

"Yes, a lot of foreigners really love American Westerns and cowboy culture. It's how I learned most of my English when we first moved here. I found out the hard way though that no one in Chicago said the words 'howdy' or 'tarnation.'"

I laughed and started singing, "Where is my John Wayne? Where is my prairie sun? Where is my happy ending? Where have all the cowboys gone?"

He smiled before pulling me completely into his lap and pressing his lips to my ear. "Is this marathon something you do solo or is company allowed?"

"Of course. Any marathon is much better with company. You know, they throw the word 'genius' around about you a lot, Lex." I tapped my finger to the tip of his nose. "But now you'll get to see a real genius at work—a *comedic* genius."

He chuckled. "I can't wait."

We cleaned up the kitchen together before Lex went upstairs to take a shower. He was going in to work today, which meant I'd finally have a chance to tend to my garden that I'd been neglecting. Maybe Professor Dunbar would help me whip it back into shape.

Just as I was about to head upstairs, there was a knock at my door. I answered it to find Stuart standing there without his usual look of mischief.

"Hey, you're back," he said. He must have noticed my car was back in the parking lot after being gone for almost a whole week.

"Yeah, I was at my mom's," I told him.

He nodded. "Listen, I know it's none of my business, but I'm worried about Lex. I know something happened between you guys, but he won't talk to me about it. He's in bad shape, Hadley. He didn't even come home last night."

"Stuart, he—" I started to say, but he interrupted.

"Look, whatever it is, I know you guys can work it out," he said determinedly. "And I know I give him a lot of shit, but he's the best person I know. And he's crazy about you. I've never seen him like this. Just give him another chance."

I didn't get the chance to explain myself, because Lex walked down the stairs at that exact moment in nothing but a towel wrapped around his waist.

The look of shock on Stuart's face was almost comical before his face split into a wide grin, and he shook his head.

"Hey. What are you doing here?" Lex asked.

"Hey, buddy. I was just telling Hadley that you didn't come home last night, but I guess I didn't need to worry after all."

"Yeah, there was a misunderstanding," Lex said darkly. Stuart's eyebrows raised when he heard Lex's tone.

"Why don't you come in, Stuart?" I offered. "I still have some French toast left over if you want some.

Stuart pretended to twist his French mustache. "Merci, mademoiselle."

I went to the kitchen to make Stuart's breakfast when I heard Lex say to him, "You were right about Nicky."

"What do you mean?" Stuart asked.

Lex proceeded to tell him the whole story, and Stuart seemed truly appalled.

"What did I tell you?" Stuart said, but his tone wasn't gloating. It was sympathetic.

"I know," Lex answered.

Stuart sighed loudly. "I always knew she was a waste of space." He paused before adding, "I'm sorry, man."

I came back in and gave Stuart his breakfast. He thanked me as I sat down next to Lex, whose hand automatically found my legs.

Stuart dug in. "Work should be really fun today."

A knot twisted in my stomach. I hated the thought of what this falling out with Nicky would mean for all of them at work. Lex started stroking my knee with his thumb when he noticed me shifting around uncomfortably.

"So, did you ask her about tomorrow?" Stuart said, perking up.

"What's tomorrow?" I asked.

"Nothing important," Lex said. "Our team got invited to Lookout Mountain this weekend. The guys from the astronomy department are hosting an event to observe some cosmologic occurrence."

Stuart rolled his eyes. "Oh yeah, just some silly star show," he said, voice dripping with sarcasm. "Are you insane?" He shot Lex a look of annoyance. "Hadley, this is a once-in-a-thousand-year meteorological event that Lex has decided he won't attend unless you're there."

I turned to Lex. "Why didn't you tell me?"

"We were busy," he said with a roguish grin. "Besides, you already had plans."

"Whatever they are, cancel them," Stuart cut in. "Alpha Mono-cerotids is going to be visible to us here in California for the first time in over a thousand years. It's a cosmological phenomenon, Hadley. You'll get to see streams of cosmic debris entering Earth's atmosphere on parallel trajectories at speeds of up to sixty kilometers per second!"

That did actually sound pretty cool. "Do you want to go, Lex?"

"Not without you," he said, still lazily stroking my knee.

Stuart groaned impatiently.

"Would I be the only one there who isn't part of the astronomy department or Lex's team?" I asked Stuart.

"No, we were told we could bring guests. I just happen to have no one to ask, thanks to you," he said, and I stuck my tongue out at him.

"Jace told me yesterday he was asking Sarah to go," Stuart added. He said it like he was dangling a carrot in front of my face, but it was working. If she was going, I'd definitely feel more comfortable.

"You want to go?" Lex asked.

"If you do," I answered.

"What about Lucy?" he asked, smiling.

"We'll save that for another time. They play the reruns more than once in a thousand years."

"So you'll come then?" Stuart asked impatiently.

"He hasn't told you everything," Lex said. "The show doesn't start until well after midnight."

"I'll be fine."

"And there's camping involved. We'd have to share a tent."

"Could we share a sleeping bag too?" I said, wiggling my eyebrows.

His answering smile had my heart picking up speed as he leaned over, pressing his lips to mine.

"Okayyyyy," Stuart said uncomfortably. "It's settled then. You're both coming?"

"Yes," Lex said, his mouth still pressed to mine. "Now get out, Stuart."

"See you at work, buddy," Stuart said, making his exit as Lex carried me back up to the bedroom.

"I'm sexy and I grow it" was the tune I was humming to myself as I spent the morning working in my garden with a few tips from Professor Dunbar. Per his instruction, I started the day by digging out fistfuls of clay from the cold ground, trying to make room for my new larkspur plants. The tall, spiked petals were a deep shade of indigo that mixed beautifully with the pink and white rhododendrons Professor Dunbar had already planted.

The morning was cool, but California was living up to its name as the sun was shining brightly above without a cloud in the sky. I spread the loamy soil around each plant with my bare hands, loving the feel of the damp earth beneath my fingertips. The crisp smell of fresh mulch filled my nostrils as I grabbed handfuls of it from the bag to start covering the roots.

The me of six months ago would have laughed in your face if you'd told her she'd one day be planting a garden in her spare time when she wasn't in the classroom teaching. How quickly things could change. That was the wildness of life though, holding the beauty with the chaos.

As I scattered handfuls of the warm mulch around my new shrub- bery, my mind drifted to Lex, wondering how his day was going having to work with Nicky for the first time since this all happened. He hadn't wanted to talk much more about it last night besides telling me he didn't know how he was going to keep working with her. I told him he did the right thing. She owed him so much more than an apology, but she had been with their team for so long. It didn't seem fair that she lose everything over this.

Lionel and Sarah had called to check on me, and I let them know everything that had happened yesterday. They both said they were sharpening their icicles. I ended up telling my mom what happened too, and she had a similar reaction. Despite what Nicky had done, my feelings were still mixed. Maybe it made me a complete idiot, but I think there would always be some small part of me that felt sorry for her.

I stood over my newly planted garden, dusting my hands off on my pants as I took it all in... It was perfect. Granted, it would never find its way onto the cover of *Better Homes and Gardens*, but I was still proud of the work I'd done. As I watched the tall stalks and delicate, airy petals of the larkspur fluttering and dancing in the breeze, an idea suddenly came to me.

I pulled out my phone and did some research for a few minutes before I went next door and asked Professor Dunbar if he had the number for the only other Russian professor I knew besides Lex—Professor Anna Sokolov. Luckily, he had access to the directory, and I was able to get in touch with her.

Lex got home earlier than I thought he would, but thankfully, I'd finished just in time. I answered the door to see him holding a very large box as he walked inside.

"What do you have there?" I asked.

"It's an air mattress," he explained. "I stopped on my way home to pick it up so you don't have to sleep on the ground tomorrow."

I shook my head. "You're too good to me," I said, closing the door behind him.

He smiled and kissed me lightly on the lips before putting the box down.

"What's that?" he asked, noticing the smell coming from the kitchen.

"I made something for you," I said excitedly. "Sit here. It's a surprise." I pointed to the chair at the dining room table. He smiled curiously and sat down like I'd asked.

I went into the kitchen and made us both a bowl before coming back to the dining room and placing it in front of him.

He looked down, and his eyes went wide with surprise.

"You made borscht?" His tone was incredulous.

"Yes," I answered, praying it turned out okay. I didn't have a chance to try it. "I mean, I had help. Professor Sokolov gave me some pointers." I was so nervous he wouldn't like it, so I continued to ramble. "I know it's probably nowhere near as good as your mom's, but I know how much you've been missing her and home and well... I hope it's okay."

Most of the reviews of borscht recipes I'd found online said they weren't authentic, which is why I called Professor Sokolov. I wanted to get it as close to a traditional Russian borscht as possible.

"Hadley, I..." His expression was unreadable.

Anxiety filled me. "What is it? Does it not look right? I did exactly what she said."

He stood, taking my face in his hands, and started kissing me until I felt like putty in his arms. I fought to think rationally.

"Wait!" I said, finally coming to my senses. I backed out of his arms. "I worked on this for three hours. You have to at least try it before it gets cold or turns to crap."

"I don't want to wait," he said, reaching for me. "And I don't care if it tastes like shit either. It would still be one of the nicest things anyone's ever done for me, and all I can think about is being inside you right now."

He stalked toward me, his eyes bright with humor. I yelped and ran around the kitchen table, trying to give myself space to think, because his words sent heat waves straight through me.

"There will be time for that after." I giggled as he continued stalking me around the table. I put a chair in his path to stop him. "And it won't taste like shit. Sit down and try it."

"Fine, fine." He put his hands up in mock surrender.

"And no funny business, mister," I chastised. "I'm easily distracted when it comes to you and those hands, so keep them to yourself until we're done."

He laughed, but finally complied and sat down. I watched his perfect lips close around that first bite as I stared at him like a dog in a window watching cars go by.

His eyes closed for a brief moment before he looked up. "Tastes exactly like home," he hummed. "It's amazing, Hadley. Truly."

I tried it for myself and decided he wasn't lying. It really was good. I mentally patted myself on the back for pulling it off.

"This is the most thoughtful thing anyone's ever done for me," he said, voice raw, eyes shining with sincerity. "I don't know what I've done to deserve your kindness, but I'm grateful, nonetheless."

I smiled. "A little education and a great amount of kindness is what is required if we are to secure harmony in this life and the lives of those who will come after us..."

His eyes widened. "You remembered my speech." He appeared touched.

"I thought it was incredible. I thought *you* were incredible. I could have listened to you speak all night."

His eyes flared. "I have something better we can do all night."

Chapter 29

I peered through the window with a wondrous look in my eye as we traveled up the winding road to the campsite. It was a view unlike anything I'd ever seen before. The granite cliffs of the mountain stood tall and proud against the dusky sky. The soft mist nestled around the towering hemlocks, and the furrowed bark of the pine trees made my yearning for urban life feel like a distant memory. I could feel Lex's eyes on me, but he said nothing, letting me take it all in.

Once we reached the campsite, I took the time to stretch and look around at the bustle of people pitching tents, setting up telescopes, and cooking around campfires. As soon as the tents were set up, Stuart ran off to talk to a few people from the astronomy department about their telescopes, while Lex and I went to look for the rest of his team.

As we started making our way through the crowd, Lex was immediately approached by several strangers asking about his work or just generally gushing over him. He made several attempts to try and politely steer us away, but it was no use. It was still a shock to me just how many people were familiar with Lex and his work. If science had a celebrity, he was definitely it, as far as I could tell.

Lex's admirers were still peppering him with questions, so I excused myself to go look for Sarah. I walked around until I spotted some of the guys from Lex's team gathered around a BBQ pit grilling burgers,

Sarah and Jace included.

"Hey! You finally made it," Sarah called out when she saw me walking toward them. She and Jace came over to greet me.

"This is pretty amazing, don't you think?" I told her, looking around.

"You're definitely not going to see this in New York," she answered. That was true. The only stars we ever saw in New York were the movie kind.

"Looks like most of the team is here," I said, noticing all the guys gathered around. "Except for..." I trailed off, realizing who was missing.

"And she better not show up, or I'll rip the pink right out of her fucking head," Sarah said viciously.

Jace chuckled. "Easy there, babe."

"She's a fucking monster. If it were me, I would have smashed her teeth in for pulling a stunt like that."

"Does everyone know?" I asked Jace.

Jace shook his head. "No. I mean, it's pretty obvious something happened. They didn't speak the entire day yesterday or today, and Stuart seemed extra happy, so we knew she fucked up. But no one would ever ask him, and I won't say anything. I promise."

Relief came over me. "Thanks," I told him. I really didn't want the rest of the guys to know what Nicky had done and cause even more problems for Lex.

We chatted for a while, and Lex found us not long after.

"I'm sorry about that," he said as soon as he reached me.

"It's okay. I'm pretty used to it now, big shot," I said with a wink.

His hands found my waist. "I'm not."

"Well, you're kind of a big deal," I said, looping my arms around his neck. "I just hope they know that *I'm* actually your number one fan."

He grinned. "How did you earn that title?"

"Because, unlike the rest of them, I've seen your *entire* body of work," I said, letting my eyes slowly slide down the length of him.

Lex let out a laugh from deep within his chest, and I reveled in the sound.

"Food's ready!" Peter announced.

"Finally," Stuart groaned. I hadn't noticed him come back.

The night was getting chillier, so I snuggled between Lex's legs with my plate of food in my lap as we ate by the campfire. The rest of the guys had gathered around the campfire as well, chatting animatedly about different topics, most of which were way over my head. They were currently in a heated debate about Star Wars, however.

"In principle, lightsabers are one-hundred percent possible," Stuart was arguing.

"No, they're fucking not, Benowitz," Louis fired back.

"What about the fact that particle accelerators have conclusively proven that photons have the capability of colliding?" Peter chimed in. Sarah and I were looking at each other like we'd just stepped into an alternate universe.

"Irrelevant!" Louis shouted. "How is light going to travel out three feet and then stop? It makes no sense!"

"All I'm saying is the physics of it is completely plausible," Stuart said.

Louis set his plate down angrily. "That's the problem. You're completely disregarding the engineering aspect."

Stuart turned to face us. "Lex? You want to chime in here?"

"No, thanks," Lex answered. "I'd rather not let my girlfriend know exactly how nerdy I am."

A thrill shot through me at hearing him call me his girlfriend.

"She already knows," Stuart remarked. "We need you to settle this or it's just going to keep going."

Lex sighed. "You're both right. Photons can collide at very high energies, but you would need a mirror or some other object for the light to bounce off of or it would just keep going."

Stuart grinned smugly. "I told you."

"He *just* said we were both right, dipshit," Louis shot back.

"Can we talk about something else?" Dan interjected. "You guys are boring me."

"Actually, Hadley, I wanted to ask you something," Jace said, changing the subject.

"Sure," I said through a mouthful of food.

"I wanted to see if you might be interested in giving me a few guitar lessons," he said, surprising me. "I'd really like to learn, and Sarah said you were an amazing guitarist."

I made an "aww" face at her, and she flipped me the bird.

"I didn't know you played the guitar," Lex said, surprise coloring his tone.

"Do you guys ever actually talk or do you just spend all your time fucking?" Sarah asked while the other guys started to laugh. I shot her the bird back, and she smirked at me.

"No seriously, she's incredible," Sarah said. "She's a musical mimic. She can hear any song and play it right back to you."

Louis scoffed incredulously. "Bullshit."

Sarah shot him a look like she was ready to throw down. "You want to put money on it?"

"What did you have in mind?" Louis asked, grinning.

"Hundred bucks says you can't give Hadley a song that she doesn't already know," Sarah said, narrowing her eyes at him. "And if she doesn't, then she only gets a minute of hearing it before she plays it back perfectly to you."

Louis extended his hand. "You're on."

She shook his hand, staring him down, and said to Jace, "Go get your guitar, baby."

The other guys started laughing and saying "oooooo" like a fight was about to break out. When Jace came back, he handed me his guitar.

"This is really beautiful," I told him, tuning the strings.

"Thank you. It was my grandfather's," Jace said fondly. "That's why I wanted to learn."

"Okay boys, do your worst," Sarah said confidently. "I already know what I want to do with my hundred bucks."

She winked at Louis, and he laughed before saying, "I've got to see this."

"Stevie Ray Vaughn, Pride and Joy," Peter said, throwing out the first song.

Sarah rolled her eyes. "Too easy."

I smiled before I started to play. I did have quite a catalog of music in my brain. Notes and chords had always come easily to me. Sarah knew I was a safe bet. They all started whistling and cheering as I played the song through the first chorus.

"Bring It on Home." Louis narrowed his eyes. "Led Zeppelin."

Sarah made a scoffing noise. I skipped the intro and started to play the section Jimmy Page comes in on the song because I knew that's what he wanted to hear. I heard more whistling and cheering as I played. They started to throw more songs out at me in rapid succession. Most of them I knew until Dan gave me an obscure Creedence Clearwater Revival song that he had to play for me off his phone. I was able to play it back for him after about thirty seconds of listening.

"Pay up." Sarah stuck her hand out. Louis shook his head, grinning, before he pulled out his wallet and slapped the money into her hand.

"Unbelievable." Louis looked dumbfounded, and I just laughed. Lex was watching me the entire time with an expression that could only be described as awe.

"You can sing too, right, Hadley?" Peter asked.

"So can Sarah," I said, nodding at her sitting in Jace's lap, looking happier than I'd ever seen her.

"What?" Jace looked up at her. "I didn't know that."

"That's because we spend all our time fucking, baby," she answered with a sweet smile.

Jace grinned wickedly. "That mouth," he said staring down at her lips hungrily. They looked like they were seconds away from tearing each other's clothes off.

"That's actually a good idea. Why don't you sing for us, Betty?" Stuart said. "We don't have anything else to do. The show doesn't start for a few more hours."

"I'll sing if Sarah will." I tilted my head toward her.

She tore her eyes away from Jace and sighed. "Fine, but I'm just doing backup. I have nowhere near her vocal range."

She came to sit beside me on the small stump I had found myself on while the guys were peppering me with songs earlier. I chose a Journey song I knew would be a crowd-pleaser.

I started to play "Lovin', Touchin', Squeezin'" and sang along this time as I strummed while Sarah harmonized with me.

"You're such a lucky motherfucker," I heard Louis tell Lex, who was watching me with a mixture of lust and adoration in his eyes.

"I know," he said, his eyes never leaving mine.

After that, it turned into karaoke hour as I played songs that I knew most people were familiar with and everyone jumped in on the choruses, singing loudly. We had started to draw a crowd as more people had filed in to watch. The sound of laughter and off-key voices filled me with happiness. It was an amazing feeling not to take music so seriously for a change and just enjoy the company of my friends.

"I'm running out of ideas," I said after finishing what felt like the hundredth song of the night.

"Why don't you play a song for Lex?" Sarah said coyly. "He's been awfully quiet. Play something that you know he'd like."

"Hmmmm." I looked at him and grinned.

He grinned back at me. "Don't do it."

I started to play the intro to "If I Could Turn Back Time," and the guys started howling with laughter.

"No!" Sarah shouted. "I can't stand that song," she said, plugging her ears. "No offense, Lex. Choose another one."

He shook his head, smiling at me. I tilted my head and studied him for a few seconds before a song popped into my mind.

As I started to play the intro chords, those in the crowd who recognized the song started to whistle and cat-call. I began singing the first lines of "Sex on Fire" by Kings of Leon, giving Lex a sultry smile and winking as I reached the chorus. A smile played across his lips as I sang, but his heated stare was making me feel flushed even in the freezing night air. As the song wrapped, I was about to tell everyone I was done playing so I could drag Lex back to the tent, but my eyes went wide with shock when I saw the one person I never expected to be here walking over to us.

Chapter 30

"Yοu've got to be fucking kidding me," Sarah said as she shot up to her feet with a look of murder in her eyes. Nicky was standing near the edge of the crowd, looking around uncomfortably until her eyes found me.

Lex turned and saw what we were staring at. His entire demeanor changed, and I barely recognized the man standing in front of me as his face held an expression of pure loathing.

"I guess I didn't make myself clear enough." His voice was unnervingly calm, but his tone was lethal.

She put her hands up. "Wait! Please, I just came to talk to Hadley."

Everyone turned to stare at me.

Lex glared at her. "You're done."

"Please, I'm begging you. I know I fucked up, but just let me talk to Hadley. It will only take five minutes. I swear, after that, I'll leave. Just... please."

As I looked at her, practically in tears, I made my decision. I got up and put my hand on Lex's shoulder. "It's okay. I'll talk to her."

"Hadley..." he said.

"I'm just going to hear her out," I told him. "After that, you can make your decision."

He looked into my eyes for a few moments, searching. For what, I didn't know. I guess whatever he found was enough to convince him that I was okay because he finally nodded at me.

I followed her out to a quieter area near the lake, where there wasn't as much foot traffic. Once we stopped, I looked at her expectantly, waiting for whatever it was she had to say. She seemed to be struggling for words as she glanced over at me a few times, kicking the ground with the toe of her boot.

"I don't know where to start..." she said.

"Let's start with the fact that you took your clothes off and laid on top of my boyfriend naked, knowing he was knocked out on sleeping pills."

She at least had the decency to appear mortified. "I know," she said, her eyes downcast. "I know what I did was beyond fucked up."

"Then why did you do it?" I demanded.

"I don't know!" she shouted as tears started pouring down her face. "I don't know what I was thinking. I'm not this person. I'm not a cruel, heartless bitch, despite what Stuart has told you. I knew what I was doing was wrong, but it's like I couldn't contain this overwhelming hatred I felt for you."

I was taken aback by her admission, but I didn't say anything as she continued, "I know you did nothing to deserve it. I just felt like you were taking everything away from me." She sighed heavily, looking out toward the lake. "I didn't have the easiest childhood. I never felt like I fit in anywhere, but then I found this job, and well... It was the first place I ever really felt accepted. I love my job. I just happened to have the shitty fucking luck of falling in love with my boss too," she said before meeting my eyes again.

"I loved him, Hadley. I was so fucking in love with him. But when I told him, he said he didn't feel the same way and broke things off with me. I was devastated. I thought about quitting then and there. But I went back. And things were okay, for the most part. Mostly because he was so obsessed with his work. It made me feel better that he was never interested in dating anyone. He ate, drank, and slept neuroscience. It seemed to be his only passion in life… until he met you."

She smiled, but it didn't touch her eyes. "I knew something was different right away. I could see it. We all could. And it was like every insecurity I'd ever had was being shoved right in front of my face." Her eyes lowered. "He's never looked at me the way he looks at you. It was clear from the start just how taken he was by you, and I couldn't see past my own pathetic jealousy."

She frowned, shaking her head. "But that doesn't excuse what I did, and I came here to tell you how truly sorry I am. What I did was… it was disgusting. I haven't been able to live with myself. I understand if he wants to fire me. In fact, he told me the only reason he hasn't is because you didn't want him to."

"I don't," I told her honestly.

She nodded. "You're a good person, Hadley. Even I can see that. This whole thing has been a wake-up call for me. I'm getting in therapy to try to work through some shit. I just hope one day you can forgive me."

I looked at this woman baring her soul to me, and it was like I was seeing the person I always knew was there. Underneath all of Nicky's cattiness was just an unhappy person who was hurting badly.

"You crossed a very big line, Nicky," I said. "I appreciate you coming and telling me all of this, but I'm not the person you need to make things right with."

"He won't talk to me. I've tried." Her tone was desperate. "I know I have no right to ask you for anything, but could you just see if he'd be willing to hear me out? I promise I'll leave as soon as I'm done."

"Sure," I agreed. "I'll ask. But don't be surprised if he refuses."

"He won't refuse if you're the one asking," she said with the ghost of a smile on her lips. "He won't refuse you anything."

I didn't think that was completely true, but I would try anyway. I started to leave, but I realized there was something else I needed to say. I turned and looked her squarely in the eye. "I told him you made a mistake and you didn't deserve to lose everything over it because I really do believe that everyone deserves a second chance. If he gives it to you, don't fuck it up this time."

"I won't," she said solemnly.

I nodded. "One last thing." I took a step toward her. "He's not yours anymore, Nicky… Are we clear?"

Her lips thinned as she gave a sharp nod. I shot her one last warning glance before walking away.

Only a few of the guys were still at the campfire when I got back. Sarah and Jace were gone and so was Lex. I walked back to the tent to find Lex checking to make sure the poles on the tent were secured, even though he'd done that a million times already.

He looked up at me as I approached. "Everything okay?" His tone was edgy like he was ready to unleash at any moment.

"Yes, everything's fine," I assured him. "But she wants to talk to you."

He scoffed. "I have nothing to say to her."

"I know. But she has some things to say to you, and I think you should hear her out."

"Why?" he asked with a puzzled expression.

"I think it might be good for both of you."

He looked into my eyes for a few moments before he said, "You really want me to go talk to her?"

I nodded. "She knows she fucked up. She just wants the chance to tell you that herself. It might make things better for you at work if you hear her out."

He sighed before taking my face in his hands and pressing a kiss to my forehead.

"Fine," he said. "Let me go get this over with then."

Just as he started to walk away, I cried out, "Wait one sec!"

I took two giant steps and jumped onto his back, wrapping my legs around his waist and my arms around his neck. He took a stumbling step forward before he recovered. I started to make the sound of the letter "h," like when you're trying to make condensation with your breath. I blew the steam coming from my warm breath on the wintry night air all over his head and neck as he stood there with me clinging to his back.

"Um, Hadley?" he said, sounding bewildered

"Yes, Lex?" I asked, still holding on.

"What exactly are you doing?"

"I'm putting my pheromones all over you," I said as if it were obvious. "Just in case she gets any funny ideas with you guys all alone out there. Maybe my scent will throw her off, and she'll think twice." She might be on a redemption tour but that didn't mean I trusted her.

He started to shake with quiet laughter. "You know there's no scientific basis for what you're doing, right?"

"Better safe than sorry." I gave him a final huff and jumped down off his back.

He turned to look at me. "Good?" he asked with amusement in his voice.

I scrutinized him. "I think so."

"You're the one who wants me to do this. I'm more than happy to stay here with you."

I waved him off. "No, no. You should go."

He gave me one last fleeting look before turning to leave. But I just couldn't help myself. I grabbed his arm to pull him back to me before jumping up and wrapping myself around his front side this time.

"I think I missed a spot," I said, huffing down the side of his neck and planting kisses in its wake.

He shook his head, chuckling. "I know what you're doing."

"What am I doing?" I asked innocently, still kissing along his cheek and neck.

"I promise I'm not going to bite her head off. I told you I'd hear her out."

"That's good," I said, pressing my lips to his before he set me down.

I thought he did seem more even-tempered, so I relented. He kissed me one more time and patted my hip before walking off to meet with Nicky. This time, I let him go.

The temperature outside was really starting to drop, so I went inside the tent, kicking off my shoes, and snuggled into the extra-large sleeping bag Lex had brought for us. I pulled out one of my books to read before Lex came back about ten minutes later. He unzipped the tent and walked in, his expression unreadable.

"Well?" I asked. "What did she say?"

He took off his shoes and sat down next to me on the air mattress before slipping his legs inside the sleeping bag. "Same bullshit she told you, I'm sure."

I put my book down and started to make room for him. "I take it you're not planning on forgiving her anytime soon?"

He zipped the sleeping bag around us and pulled me into his arms. "I'll never forgive her for taking you from me for an entire week."

I stroked his hair, looking into his beautiful eyes, trying to figure out if he was upset or not. "Are you going to fire her?" I asked.

He seemed to think about it for a second. "No," he finally said. "She told me you said everyone deserves a second chance, so I'm going to give it to her. But I don't think I can ever forgive her for what she did."

I ran my thumb across his cheek. "You're doing the right thing."

He pulled me in even closer. "I don't want to talk about it anymore. I just want to enjoy the rest of this night with you. Can we do that?"

I grinned at him. "What did you have in mind?"

He started moving his hands lower, caressing my hip before moving to my backside.

"I've been wanting to get my hands on you all night," he crooned.

"Oh yeah?" I said, looking down at his mouth. "What exactly were you planning on doing with those hands?"

He rolled me onto my back and leaned over me, stopping when our lips were barely skimming against one another. Our breath began to mingle as he slid his hand inside my pants, my core already slick with need for him. His fingers moved over my wetness before he slipped one finger inside and I gasped, leaning up to try to kiss him, but he pulled back teasingly. He was sliding his finger in and out slowly, watching me, watching my every breath.

"When everyone was watching you by the campfire earlier, I knew what every guy was thinking... how badly they all wanted you," he said, stroking. "And all I could think was... she's mine."

I laughed breathlessly. "So dramatic. I'm starting to think it's a prerequisite for all scientists," I said, closing my eyes as he leaned over and began running his tongue along my neck.

"It's just been my luck that you have no idea how incredibly beautiful you are... how endearing," he murmured against my skin. "It makes everyone drawn to you. I don't know how I tricked you into being with me, but I really must be a genius of some sort."

He slipped a second finger in, and I groaned against his neck. "Definitely a genius," I agreed, and he chuckled, still working me over.

I let my hand trail down his stomach, slipping under his waistband as I began stroking his already hard length. His breath hitched, and he finally leaned down to capture my lips. Our tongues immediately tangled, and I whimpered slightly at the feel of him in my mouth and in my hand.

His tongue worked in tandem with his fingers until I started feeling like I was close. I wasn't sure how quiet I could be if I came.

"Do you think anyone can hear us?" I panted.

"Maybe," he whispered with a wolfish grin, still working his fingers in and out.

"I'm close, Lex," I said breathlessly. "I don't want anyone to hear me."

"I want to watch you come, Hadley," he whispered back. He was staring down at me, eyes blazing. My name on his lips, the look in his eyes, the way his skillful fingers moved over me—that was all it took.

His free hand clamped down over my mouth as I came hard. My body writhed underneath him as he held me tight, watching me heatedly. I was breathing heavily as I came down from the orgasm, little aftershocks still pulsing through me.

As I stared into those beautiful eyes, all I could see was desire rippling through their depths. He pressed a soft kiss to my lips before he turned me onto my side with my back facing him and pulled me close to his chest. I could hear the sound of the condom wrapper before he slipped his pants down.

When he was done, he tugged mine down as well, and I helped push them the rest of the way until we were both naked from the waist down. He gathered me up, positioning himself at my entrance, before sliding into me slowly, groaning into my ear and stopping when he reached the hilt.

I turned my face up toward him, and he pressed his lips to mine once again. I deepened the kiss immediately. He slid his arm underneath me until both arms were wrapped around my torso, holding me close.

He made love to me slowly at first, each stroke causing our breathing to become more strained. I felt his hand trailing down my body, caressing my thigh before he hiked my leg up and buried himself in even deeper. I could hear voices outside not far from our tent, so I had to remain focused on not crying out as the pleasure continued to build.

He stifled any moans that escaped my lips by covering my mouth with his, but he had worked me back up in no time. One hand held my breast while the other slid down, stroking that bundle of nerves as he continued to push inside me with those long, teasing strokes.

"Lex," I whimpered. "I'm going to come again."

"Good," he said roughly. "The only thing better than watching you come is feeling it happen when I'm buried inside you."

I groaned at his words. He ran his tongue along my neck while his fingers worked against my clit until it was all too much. I turned to bury my face in the pillow as I started to come undone. He held me even tighter, his breathing becoming louder as he picked up speed. I whispered to him how good he felt, how much I loved having his cock inside me, and he gripped my hips to the point of pain as he slammed into me with his final thrusts, burying a groan in my hair.

When our breathing finally slowed, he took my chin and tilted it up toward him before leaning down to kiss me.

"It never feels like enough," I murmured against his lips. "I already want more of you."

His thumb caressed my cheek. "You can have all of me... always."

I smiled. "Is that a promise?"

"It is," he answered, and I shivered with pleasure.

We heard the others outside starting to gather, so we knew it was time. I hurried to put on all my extra layers of clothes before we made our way out into the freezing night air, leaving the warmth of our tent behind.

We found everyone gathered in the open field where they had set up an array of telescopes, and the head of the astronomy department was giving a lecture on what we were about to see.

"And where have you two been?" Sarah said suggestively when we walked up. Jace's arms were wrapped around her, holding her close to him.

I shrugged and said, "Guitar lessons."

She made a sarcastic face at me. "Okay, well I'd appreciate it if you didn't give my boyfriend the same kind of guitar lessons."

My eyes widened at hearing her call him her boyfriend. Jace's did as well but then he smiled, looking down at her. "Your boyfriend, huh?"

"Oh, didn't I mention?" she said playfully. "I don't want you fucking anyone but me."

He laughed, leaning close to her ear, and said, "I wouldn't dream of it."

Sarah was always so private about the people she dated, even in college. Hearing her blatantly call him her boyfriend in front of all of us made me realize just how much she really liked him. Her happiness was contagious as I smiled up at Lex. He pulled me into his arms, and we all looked up toward the night sky.

Ten minutes later, the sky lit up as the meteor shower began. Everyone gasped as hundreds of shooting stars shot across the sky, and I thought I'd never seen anything so beautiful in all my life. As I looked on in wonderment, a sudden realization hit me—I was making the kind of memories here that I could never have in New York. It was in that moment that I made my decision.

I wasn't leaving California.

Chapter 31

The rhythmic sound of my foot tapping anxiously on the floor of the exam room was the only sound that could be heard as we sat waiting for Dr. Gremillion. The office had called for my mom to come in to discuss her latest bloodwork and scans. I held her hand as different scenarios played through my mind. I started to formulate a plan to convince her to go to MD Anderson if he told us the news wasn't good. Maybe I could get Lex to talk some sense into her. It might mean more coming from him.

"Hello, ladies," Dr. Gremillion greeted as he entered. I could barely hear him over the sound of my pulse hammering in my ears. "I'll get right to it," he said, sitting down on the rolling chair. I held my breath, waiting.

His face broke into a smile. "You're officially cancer-free, Ms. Olivier."

My heart stopped, falling into my stomach before it restarted again, beating with a renewed vigor.

"Are you serious?" My mom's eyes were wide as saucers.

"Completely," he said. "Your scans and bloodwork show you have no cancer cells left in your body."

My mom and I turned to look at one another. The tears began to fall heavily from our eyes as we exhaled shakily. We threw our arms around each other, sobbing and laughing all at the same time.

"So-so what now?" I stuttered, wiping the tears from my eyes.

He smiled at my mom. "You'll still need to do the chemotherapy treatments for a few more months to prevent any recurrence, but all signs point to you being in remission. Congratulations. I know this has been a long road."

We had waited so long to hear those words, and I still couldn't quite believe what he was saying. She'd done it. She'd beaten this.

Dr. Gremillion spoke with us about remaining cautious about my mom's health, because the chemo had taken such a toll on her immune system, and that it might be a while before she was able to interact normally with the outside world. She still looked so fragile, but I knew every day she would only get stronger now that she knew she was cancer free.

We were giddy on the car ride home, laughing together and making plans for the future that we'd been hesitant to make when it felt like her condition was balancing on the edge of a knife.

"I think I'd like to go to Greece first," she said, pulling off her hot pink wig and tossing it in the back seat. "Find a topless beach to take the girls out and dip my toes in the Aegean."

I laughed. "Not sure Greece needs to see that much of you."

"You think Lex would want to come to Greece with us?" she asked.

"Maybe," I said. "But he's definitely not going to that topless beach with you."

"Carl has already volunteered."

"Gross," I said, but couldn't manage to do anything but smile.

She became serious all of a sudden. "Hadley, how can I ever thank him?"

"Lex?" I asked even though I knew who she meant.

"This is all because of him. I'm alive because of him."

I let the steady stream of tears fall down my face at her words. I'd thanked him so many times already, but he never wanted to hear it.

He would always change the subject, seeming uncomfortable with my gratitude. Hearing my mom say those words, however... it was almost too overwhelming to think about just how big a role he'd played in my happiness.

I sniffled. "I don't think he wants you to, Mom."

She nodded but I could tell by the look on her face that she was still planning on telling him. She wouldn't be able to live with herself without saying it.

"He's going to be so happy to hear you're in remission." I dabbed at my eyes. "Even if he doesn't want any of the credit."

She smiled. "You really found a good one."

I nodded fervently. "I did."

She looked over at me, her smile widening. "We're staying in California, aren't we?"

I looked back at her for a few moments before my face split into a huge grin.

After I dropped my mom off at her house, I immediately called Lex.

"Hey," he answered. "What did Dr. Gremillion say?"

"Do you have a second?" I asked. He'd been invited to do a pretty famous podcast that discussed different topics in the scientific community, and he was their special guest for the day, which meant I wasn't seeing him until tonight. But I couldn't wait that long to tell him the news.

"Yeah, we haven't started yet."

"How do you feel about Greece?" I asked.

"Greece?" he asked. "What about it?"

"It's the first place my mom wants to go now that she's cancer-free."

I could hear him exhaling roughly before he said, "Baby, that's amazing." His voice was thick with emotion.

"I know," I said, becoming emotional all over again. "And I know you don't want to hear it, but my mom insisted that I thank you again. She's alive because of you, Lex. We owe you everything, and it still wouldn't be enough for what you've done for us."

"You don't owe me anything," he said quietly. "And it's got nothing to do with me. Your mom did this. She fought this fight, not me."

I could hear someone calling for him in the background. "You've got to go."

"I'll see you tonight?" he asked.

"Yes," I told him, even though it was a given. There were very few nights we ever spent apart anymore.

I drove back to my house, feeling like I could float away with happiness. I tidied up around my house, but with nothing left to do, I started searching for the podcast Lex was on. I probably wouldn't understand a word of it, but I wanted to hear his voice anyway.

The show broadcasted live, so I got to hear him speaking as soon as I found it. He was talking about the project they were working on at Stanford, and how close they were to being able to go to the trial phase of their device. He dumbed it down, so even someone like me could understand what their project was about, but he eventually got to the more complicated processes, and I was left to just enjoy the sound of his voice. When they finally wrapped up the science discussion, the hosts started to ask him a few personal questions about his childhood and his family, but he only gave vague details.

The female host pushed a little harder. "Well, when we announced that you were coming on the show, a lot of our female listeners wanted us to inquire about your relationship status." She giggled after saying it, making me want to reach through the phone and strangle her. "So can you tell us if you're seeing anyone?"

"I am," he said. I could hear the smile in his voice.

"What a shame," she said wistfully. "I know we'll have a lot of disappointed fans."

I really did not like this woman.

"So go on," she encouraged. "Tell us about the lucky lady who's won your heart."

"She's incredible." He still sounded like he was smiling. "She's a professor in the music department at Stanford, but she's also a composer and really beautiful singer. She's really just the most amazing person I've ever met. I'm incredibly lucky."

"Wow, sounds like Dr. Alexsander Strovinski is in love," she commented.

"I am," he confirmed.

I stopped breathing completely. Did he really just say that he was in love with me? I knew I was in love with him, but I never expected any kind of declaration from him this early in our relationship, especially not one that was being broadcast to thousands of people.

My heart began hammering in my chest. A part of me was thrilled to hear him say it, but the other part was disappointed that I was hearing it for the first time over my phone with that annoying woman's giggle coming through the speaker. I shut off the podcast, my mind reeling.

I set my phone on the counter and took a deep breath, trying to gather my thoughts. I stared at my phone for a moment, the silence in the room feeling heavier now that the podcast was off. My heart was still pounding, a mix of emotions swirling inside me—excitement, disbelief, and just a little frustration.

The rest of the day passed in a haze. I drifted from task to task, barely aware of what I was doing. I found myself staring out the window at nothing, replaying the moment over and over. Part of me felt giddy, wanting to relive the way he talked about me—the pride, the affection, the admiration. But another part of me couldn't stop feeling a twinge of disappointment that this wasn't how I imagined hearing those words for the first time.

When he got home later that evening, we didn't have much time to talk, because we headed straight to my mom's to have dinner with her and Carl. It probably wasn't the best idea to have multiple people in her home, but she insisted that we come over to celebrate. We took extra precautions to make sure we didn't give her anything.

The mood was light as we popped champagne, laughing together and making plans to go to Greece next year, but in the back of my mind was the constant replaying of Lex saying he loved me.

My mom pulled Lex aside toward the end of the night, and I knew she was telling him how grateful she was again for everything he'd done. I gave them some space, knowing I would start bawling if I overheard them talking about it.

As we drove home together in mellow silence, the memory of what Lex had said on the podcast seemed to be all I could think about. I couldn't help but be a little bothered by the way it went down. It felt like a moment that was supposed to be just for us was taken from me, and I wanted it back. More than anything, I wanted to hear him say those words to me and only me.

When we got back to the house, I was so preoccupied, overthinking everything, that I barely registered Lex standing by the door watching me. I was taking off my makeup in the bathroom when he walked up behind me, wrapping his arms around my waist.

"What is it?" he asked quietly.

"Nothing," I said a little too quickly to be believable.

He turned me around so he could look me in the eyes.

"You've been distant with me all night." He brushed the hair from my face. "Tell me what's wrong."

"It's nothing," I said, but he held me in place, waiting for me to answer. I let out a sigh. "It's just something you said on the podcast."

He looked genuinely surprised by that answer. "The podcast?" His head tilted. "What did I say?"

I couldn't look him in the eye as I said in a quiet voice, "You said you loved me."

He froze. His expression was unreadable. "I see," he said. "And it bothers you that I feel that way?"

"Of course not," I said quickly. "It's just that you've never said it to me. I would have liked to have heard it straight from you and not over my phone's speaker."

His brows knitted together. "I've never said it to you?"

I shook my head, and he really looked shocked by that news. He smiled though, pulling me into his arms. "Forgive me," he said into my hair. "Surely, you must have known though. I think it every time I look at you. I'm not sure how I've managed to go this long without actually saying it out loud."

He brought me to sit down on the edge of the bed before he took my hand in his, bringing it up to his mouth. "There isn't anything I don't love," he said, taking my index finger and wrapping his lips around the tip of it. "I love your smile," he murmured before moving on to give my middle finger the same treatment. "I love the sound of your voice. I could listen to you sing the ABCs and be absolutely enthralled." My ring finger was next. "I love your kindness. It makes me want to be a better person." He moved on to wrap his lips around my pinky finger. "I love every sound you make when I'm inside you." He moved to my thumb, running his tongue over the tip of it. "I love the way you say my name—like a prayer." I stopped breathing completely as he pressed his lips softly to the center of my palm.

"I love you, Hadley," he said, looking me squarely in the eyes. "Nothing I've waited for in life has ever been quite as worth it as you."

I inhaled sharply, my heart hammering in my chest. I brought his hand up to place it over my heart so that he could feel how his words affected me because my own words were failing me at the moment. He looked at his hand placed over my wildly beating heart before his eyes moved to stare at my lips hungrily.

I leaned in instinctively, pressing my mouth to his before wrapping myself around him completely. He kissed me hard, his tongue sweeping the length of my mouth, making my core pool with wetness. We frantically tore at each other's clothes until we were completely naked, and I pulled him on top of me.

"Wait," he whispered. "Let me grab my wallet."

"No," I said. "I've been on the pill for months now. I had a full screening done when I came to Stanford. I'm clean, and I haven't slept with anyone else."

He was staring down at me. I could see his chest rising and falling heavily. "I did too. I'm clean, and I haven't slept with anyone else either."

"Good." I reached down to position him at my entrance.

His lips were parted, and he was breathing raggedly as he said, "Are you sure?"

"Yes. I don't want anything between us anymore. I love you, Lex."

He closed his eyes and a slight shudder went through him. When he opened them again, they were so bright, they looked as if they were shining even in the darkness of the room.

"You were right to be upset with me," he said. "I wouldn't have wanted to hear that from anywhere but your beautiful lips."

I smiled before pulling him down to kiss me. Our tongues danced slowly across one another before Lex pulled back, pressing his forehead to mine, and pushed into me fully in one swift movement. We both gasped at the pleasure of not having anything between us. He held still for a few moments, closing his eyes, and muttered, "Fuck, you're so wet." His voice was raspy with need. "I won't last long. It feels too good."

I ran my hands across the muscles of his chest, feeling my way across his beautiful body. He rocked into me again, and my head fell back. I whispered his name, and he grabbed the headboard to use as leverage to push into me deeper. Once he really began to move, I held onto him, feeling his muscles flexing and rolling underneath my hands.

I groaned loudly at the intense pleasure I felt. I didn't know if it was because we weren't using a condom or because he had said he loved me, but this time felt different. An orgasm came upon me quickly as he pounded into me, but another one followed right behind it. I'd never had multiple orgasms like this. I had started to doubt that it was even possible. But here he was, drawing every last inch of pleasure from me.

Lex came to an abrupt stop, holding himself still inside me as my body continued to furl and unfurl around him. I felt sure that he hadn't finished, so I peered up at him questioningly. "What's wrong? Why'd you stop?" I panted.

It took him a moment to answer and when he did, his voice was strained. "You can't imagine how this feels."

I skimmed my lips across his jaw, the salty taste of his sweat lingering on my tongue. "Tell me," I whispered.

His head dropped to my shoulder as he let out a long exhale. "It's the way you fit me so perfectly... body and soul," he said. "I'll never be able to make sense of it... It feels like you were made just for me."

My heart twisted in my chest. "Things that are meant to be are always like this."

His lips brushed slowly across my shoulder, sending shiver down my spine. "Like what?" he murmured.

"Easy," I replied softly. "As effortless as breathing."

His eyes lifted as he pinned me with one of his raw, heart-stopping looks. "Falling in love with you was the easiest thing I've ever done."

I could never keep it together when he was this way with me. A tear trickled its way out the corner of my eye, and Lex quickly kissed it away. He knew me well enough now to know these weren't tears of sadness as a smile spread slowly across his face.

"What hasn't been easy is having to constantly hold it together," he said, his hips beginning to move again. "It takes everything in me not come apart the second I'm inside you."

I grinned back at him. "Don't hold back on my account. I'm more than ready to know exactly how it feels to have you come inside me."

I felt him grow harder as he suddenly pushed in deeper. "Then I'd hate to make you wait any longer," he said before his lips claimed mine again.

He threaded his fingers through mine and brought them over my head. His movements were deliberate and unhurried, each stroke blending our bodies together in a seamless rhythm. I wanted so badly to touch him, to feel his taut muscles beneath my fingertips, but Lex held my hands pinned above me. So instead, I did everything I could to draw closer to him, squeezing my thighs tightly around his hips. It took an embarrassingly short amount of time for him to work me back up again. The sweat beaded across his forehead as I watched his brows furrow in concentration. I could tell he was still holding back, waiting for me to finish (again). I tilted my hips to change the angle, causing his cock to brush deliciously across my most sensitive area.

As Lex picked up speed, my grip tightened around the fingers he still had threaded through mine, my insides suddenly tensing as I exploded, shattering into a million pieces. Lex groaned loudly in what sounded like relief more than anything as he found his release, thrusting into me one final time. I was surprised by how much I liked feeling his warmth spreading inside me as he rolled his hips slowly, drawing out his pleasure.

I lay back completely spent as Lex rolled on his back next to me, trying to catch his breath.

I turned my head to look at him, already missing the feel of his weight pressing onto me. "I've never done that with anyone before," I told him. "Without protection, I mean."

His eyes met mine. "Neither have I."

I smiled. I liked that we were each other's firsts in that way. "Was it a lot different for you?" I always imagined the contrast would be more pronounced for the guy.

"Yes, but it's always felt different with you."

I heaved a sigh. "Stop doing that."

"What?" he asked with a puzzled expression.

"Stop saying the most romantic shit anyone's ever heard. I can't cry anymore today."

He chuckled lightly before turning onto his side to face me. His hand lifted to caress my face while his fingertips slowly began tracing my lips. Even without saying anything, he still managed to bring tears to my eyes with his quiet tenderness. *Romantic bastard.*

His hand suddenly came to a halt as he stared at me for a few moments before letting it drop from my face completely. A serious look came over his expression as he propped himself up on his elbow. "There's something I need to say to you."

His tone had me worried. "What is it?"

"I know it's selfish, but I'm going to say it anyway." He took a breath. "I want you to stay... I know how much you love New York and how much you miss your dad, but I want you to stay here with me. Stanford wants to renew our contract for next semester, but I didn't want to give them an answer until I talked to you. I want to be wherever you are. So if that's in New York, then we'll go, but I think we could be happy here. So I'm asking you to stay."

I looked at him, really looked at him. Every line of his face was beautiful to me. I was so completely in love, and I wasn't going anywhere.

"There's just one problem," I said.

His face fell. "What is it?"

"I don't know if Stuart's going to be willing to switch houses with me."

Crinkles formed at the edges of his eyes as a smile spread across his face. I didn't know if I'd ever seen him look so happy.

California might not feel like home yet, but this certainly did.

Chapter 32

The nervousness showed on my face as I stared at the live image of Lex and I huddled together on the screen of his phone.

"She's lost a lot of her English," he said as the FaceTime call was ringing. "I'm going to have to translate for her."

"Okay," I said, smoothing down the front of my shirt.

He ran his thumb across my hip. "She's going to love you."

The call picked up, and a woman's face appeared on the screen. The resemblance to Lex was uncanny. They had the same Slavic slope to their eyes and the same full mouth. The slight difference came with the eye color. Hers were a deep shade of brown while Lex's were a lighter, more amber shade.

Lex greeted his mother warmly, and I heard my name being spoken through the Russian dialogue.

"Hello, Hadley," she said with a slight accent.

"Schastlivogo Rozhdestva," I said to her. I'd been practicing how to say Merry Christmas in Russian for the last hour.

I could see the surprise on both their faces as they smiled at me. His mom replied in Russian, and he answered her before they both started to laugh.

"What is it?" I asked, wondering if my pronunciation had been terrible.

"She said you are way too beautiful for me," he said, grinning. "I told her I agree."

I smiled at her. "You've raised an amazing son. I'm very lucky."

Lex translated that for me, and she said, "Spasibo," which I knew meant "thank you."

She said something else to him. "She wants to know if you'd come to Russia with me. She'd love to meet you in person."

"When my mom gets better, I'd love to."

"Your mom is sick?" Lex said, asking as his mom.

"She had cancer. But your son helped her get the treatment she needed, and now she's in remission."

He translated for me.

"I'm very happy to hear that," Lex said for her. "Alexsander would do anything for the people he loves."

I nodded, and of course, tears started to fill my eyes. Her eyebrows pinched together as she said something to Lex. The expression on her face was so similar to the way Lex looked when he was concerned, it was almost unnerving.

He turned to me and said, "She wants to know why you're crying."

I smiled, dabbing away the tears.

"I'm happy," I told her before looking up at Lex. "I like hearing that I'm someone you love."

There was a fierce tenderness in his eyes as he murmured, "You have no idea."

She was watching our exchange with a smile on her face. She may not know English very well, but love was a language everyone understood.

Lex translated what she said next. "I've always wanted this for my son. He works too much. I've tried telling him that *this*," she said, pointing between us, "is what is most important in life. Not work."

I smiled at her, and Lex pressed a kiss to my temple. She asked me a few more questions about my family and my writing career. I was surprised by how much she knew about composing music. Lex explained that his grandmother had been an opera singer and was always passionate about music, but that gene skipped over him completely.

His mom was exactly what I imagined—warm, funny, and tough as nails. She reminded me so much of my own mother, who we were planning on seeing tonight so we could exchange gifts before Lex left for Russia. I thought of how Christmas this year looked nothing like the Christmases of years past. My mom and I wouldn't be in New York to do any of the things we normally did this time of year, like driving to a Christmas tree farm in upstate New York to pick out our tree, or ice skating at Rockefeller Center. While I missed the nostalgia of Christmas in the city, I couldn't feel anything but happiness, since Christmas would have meant nothing at all without her here with me. And there wasn't a better gift I could have asked for.

"So you're actually going to stick this thing out with that Russian fellow, huh?" Stuart asked as we browsed the local music shop. I had more guitars than I had fingers, but one more couldn't hurt, right? I had my eye on an old Gibson J-180, and I dragged Stuart along to come look at it with me for about the hundredth time.

"I think I am," I told him as I ran my fingers along its mahogany neck.

Lex had left for Russia three days ago, so I decided to treat my loneliness with a little retail therapy.

"What do we really know about the guy though? Claims he moved here from Russia at ten years old, but where's the accent? Explain that to me."

"Pretty suspicious," I agreed absently. I could barely hear Stuart over the sound of the rosewood fretboard on this gorgeous guitar calling my name.

"All I'm saying is you should have really thought this thing through before jumping into a relationship with someone who, to this day, is still confused by Groundhog Day."

"That one confuses me too, to be honest."

"What's confusing about it?" he asked. "Every year an overgrown rodent emerges from hibernation, and we base our winter forecast on whether or not it can see its shadow... makes perfect sense to me."

"Okay, but why is it always named Phil?"

"You have something against the name Phil?"

"No, but groundhogs live for like five years max. Yet somehow, every year we have the same groundhog named Phil telling us how much longer winter will be."

"You know Hadley, the more you question these great American traditions, the more I'm beginning to suspect you've been in cahoots with the Lex character all along."

"Busted," I said, strumming the six strings of this angelic device. The sound was heavenly.

"Should've known," he said. "But you can still get out of this, Betty. It's not too late!"

I gave it another strum. "I think I'm good."

He shrugged. "Can't say I didn't try... So, you getting this guitar or are you just going to keep drooling on it?"

"Her name's Trixie, and yes," I said excitedly. "She's definitely coming home with me."

"Do you have some weird disorder that makes you name every inanimate object in your life? First the car, now the guitar."

"Something I picked up from Boris back in the Gulag," I said before bringing my hand to my lips. "Oops! Have I said too much?"

He snorted. "Trixie's a dumb name for a guitar."

"Well, what do you suggest?"

"Something manly," he said, puffing his chest. "The kind of name that makes women want to put their hands all over it. Oh, I know! How about Stuart?"

I smiled. "Trixie it is."

With a small chunk of my savings depleted, we walked out of the music shop with Trixie in hand. It was just the remedy I needed to treat my lonesome heart. Once we made it back home, I scurried up the walkway, excited to break her in. Before we could make it there, however, we encountered an uncomfortable-looking Nicky. She was casting furtive glances around, as though unsure of how to proceed.

"Hey," I said awkwardly. We would never be friends, but I wasn't going to pretend like she didn't exist.

"Hey," she said in a somewhat friendly tone as we crossed paths on the sidewalk.

"Well, I *was* having a good day," Stuart mumbled, but she ignored him.

"We were just heading in." I pointed to my house, which she was currently blocking the path to.

She nodded but remained rooted in place. Her body language suggested that she had something more to say but was holding back. I lingered for a few seconds longer as the awkward silence stretched on. I was wishing this sidewalk had a trapdoor so I could make a quick exit. Eventually, I cleared my throat before side-stepping around her to make my way home.

Just as we started to walk away, Nicky blurted, "Did Lex tell you about the offer we got from Empros Pharma?"

Stuart let out a heavy sigh. "You really don't know when to shut the fuck up, do you?"

"No, he didn't." I looked questioningly at Stuart. Why was it a secret?

"They were at the conference Lex spoke at," Nicky said, not meeting my eye. The same conference where she had taken that photo in his hotel room.

"Anyway." She cleared her throat. "They were very impressed with our work and have offered us more money than we could have ever dreamed of to finish the project with them. It would cut our time in half if we had access to all their equipment. They're an advanced institute, and they've had a lot of successful collaborations with the teams they've funded in the past."

"Lex is definitely going to fire you," Stuart interjected. "That is, if he doesn't kill you first. You know what? Never mind. Keep talking."

"This affects all of us, Stuart," she shot back. "Hadley might be able to talk some sense into him."

"Quick question. What kind of flowers would you prefer at your funeral?" he asked her.

"I don't understand," I said, looking between the two of them.

"Lex doesn't want to take the job," she explained. "And he probably *will* kill me for telling you, but I don't care. He's making a huge mistake."

I was still confused as to why she was telling me all of this. Why wouldn't Lex want to take this job? What did any of this have to do with me? Then it hit me.

"Where is Empros Pharma located?" I asked her.

I could tell from the look on her face that I'd identified the problem. "It's in Sweden."

My palms suddenly felt clammy. "Sweden?" I repeated. My thoughts were racing, and the anxiety started to build as I considered what that would mean for us. But... hadn't she just said Lex didn't want to take it?

"I know what you guys have, and I'm not trying to ruin it, I swear," she said.

"Sure you're not," Stuart grumbled.

"I know that's why he doesn't want to go, but you have to under‐
stand what this would mean for the whole team. This would be the
best shot we'd have at a Nobel Prize for our work. The rest of the guys
have been trying to talk some sense into him, to tell him that this
is exactly what we've been working for all these years, but he won't
listen."

"What do you want me to do?" I asked in a small voice.

"If you could just talk to him," she suggested. "I know this doesn't
mean much coming from me, but I know you guys can make it work.
We're only talking about a year... maybe not even that long."

"A year?!" I choked out. The current ten day separation was already
killing me, and we were only a few days in. How was I supposed to
handle a year?

"Maybe if you came with us..." she started, but I shook my head.

"I can't leave," I told her. I couldn't leave my mom right now. Not
when she was still in such a fragile state.

Stuart put his hand on my shoulder and gave Nicky a scathing look.

"Let me think about it," I told her, already starting to walk away. I
needed some space to think.

"I had to say something," she said desperately. "You understand,
right?"

I nodded, unable to speak at the moment.

"This decision doesn't just affect Lex. It affects all of us. The
company only wants to take on the project if Lex is involved," she
said. "This would change all of our lives. It would make Lex's entire
career. Everything he's ever worked for will finally be at his fingertips.
I don't know that we'll ever get this kind of opportunity again."

"I'll talk to him," was all I could manage to say as I reached the
steps of my porch.

Stuart turned on her. "Hey Nicky, in your next life, try and come
back as someone actually pleasant."

I didn't listen to the rest of their bickering as I walked up the steps of my porch. There were too many thoughts warring in my mind. If what she was saying was true, I didn't want to be the reason Lex wasn't taking this opportunity. I couldn't stomach the thought of us being apart, but would he eventually grow to resent me for being the reason he didn't take it?

I heard Stuart walking up behind me as I unlocked the door. He followed me inside, and we sat down on the couch together.

"Was she telling the truth?" I asked.

He sighed. "Yes. It's the biggest deal anyone in our industry's ever been offered."

"Do you think he should take it?"

"It's the best opportunity we're ever going to get," he replied. "Lex's career would be set... All of our careers would."

I tried to fight back the tears as I nodded.

"But I don't think he should take it," he added. "And I told him as much."

"What?" I asked, surprised. "Why?"

He shook his head. "None of the other guys understand. They didn't see the way he was that week the two of you weren't speaking. It would ruin him," he answered. "He needs you, Hadley. I care about my friend more than I care about the money. I don't want him to take it."

I leaned my head against Stuart's shoulder, feeling defeated. Lex couldn't ask for a better friend than Stuart, and neither could I, for that matter.

"You want to come over? I could make us something for dinner," he offered.

"No," I said, letting out a small sigh. "I think I want to be alone."

He nodded, and I knew he understood why.

After Stuart left, I spent the evening stewing over everything they had told me. I didn't want to be the reason he didn't take this job. I knew he would regret it. His team had given him so much, followed him across the country, even. They deserved this just as much as he did. Our relationship shouldn't be the reason he was holding everyone, including himself, back. I would have to talk to him about it. I just wasn't sure if he was going to listen.

"Did Jace tell you what's going on?" I asked Sarah the next day when we met for coffee at Peet's.

"He just told me this morning," she answered. "He said they got an offer to work in Sweden, but he doesn't want to go."

Surprise flickered through me. "Really?"

"He said he and Lex are the only ones who don't want to take the job," she said. "And then he told me that even if Lex changes his mind, he still doesn't think he's going to go."

"This is all so fucked up," I said, bringing my hands to my hair. "I don't want Lex to go either, but this is such a huge opportunity for them. I don't want to be the reason he doesn't take it."

"I know." She nodded. "I told Jace the same thing. I said we could make it work and that phone sex is a personal favorite of mine."

I laughed at her method of trying to convince him. It was especially funny since Sarah had worked as a phone sex operator on the weekends back in college to make extra cash. "Audio erotic performer" is what she'd called it. Funny as it was, she was actually really good at it. She would walk around our dorm doing dishes or folding laundry, all while spewing absolute filth. She could have written a dissertation on dirty talk. I teased her endlessly about it, but unlike me, she walked away from college debt-free.

"I don't know," I said. "It's been a while since you've had to use your 'special skills'."

"It's not a skill you lose, Hadley," she said matter-of-factly. "Don't worry. If they do end up taking this job, I'll write some things down for you that'll have Lex on his knees."

I chuckled. "I don't even know how to bring this up to him. He clearly didn't want me to know about it."

"I think that's why Jace didn't seem too worried. He said there was no way in hell Lex was ever going to leave you."

I sighed. "What have we gotten ourselves into?"

"I blame you," she retorted. "You set me up with the only guy I've actually cared about in almost ten years, and now he might be going away to help your boyfriend save mankind, or whatever the hell they're doing."

I paused to look at her before I said, "My bad."

She stared at me deadpan for a few seconds before we both erupted in laughter. We laughed until tears streamed down our faces. If we were going to be miserable, at least we'd be facing it together.

Chapter 33

When Lex got home a week and a half later, he came straight to my house from the airport, sweeping me up in his arms as soon as he walked through the door.

"I missed you," he said into my hair before kissing me in a way that sent waves of desire straight through me. I was so happy to see him. I didn't want to ruin our moment together, so I tried to put everything I'd heard on the back burner.

"Are you hungry?" I pressed my lips to his again. "I made some dinner for you."

"Yes, starving. Thank you," he said, smiling. "I just have to send a few emails really quick."

"Okay, I'll go heat your food." I was trying to act normally, but I couldn't stop thinking about what Nicky had told me.

I knew what the right thing to do was, but I also knew I was going to have a hell of a time convincing him of it. I just needed to reason with him that this wasn't just about us.

I walked back into the dining room and brought him his plate of lasagna. He thanked me and started telling me all about his trip back home. "...and my mom was crazy about you. All she talked about the whole time was how I better bring you next time I come or don't bother coming at all."

"That's so nice," I said, chuckling. "I would really love to meet her in person."

"Well, maybe we can go after the next semester is over. During summer break, if your mom is doing better," he suggested. "What do you think?"

Crap. I didn't know if this was the right moment, but I figured it was now or never.

My stomach tightened. "I think we need to talk."

His eyebrows furrowed, and I could see the worry on his face. "About what?"

I figured being direct was the only way to handle it, so I took a deep breath. "Did you get a job offer from Empros Pharma?"

He seemed stunned for a moment before his face twisted with anger. "Who told you that?" His voice was calmer than he looked.

"Does it matter?" I asked gently.

"No, it doesn't," he answered sharply. "Because I'm not taking it."

He grabbed his plate and started to stand when I reached out to stop him. "We need to talk about this."

He brushed me off. "No, we don't."

He was being stubborn, but I wasn't going to give up that easily. "Is it true that this is the biggest deal anyone in your field has ever been offered?"

His eyes narrowed. "So?"

"So, if it's going to make such a huge difference in the careers of your entire team, not to mention all the lives you could impact with your work, how could you not consider it?"

"I have considered it!" He stood up abruptly, the chair scraping loudly across the floor. He stood there seething for a moment before he shook his head and said more calmly, "I can't do it, Hadley." He brought his hands up to cup my face. "I won't leave you. And I know you can't leave your mom."

"It would just be for a year," I said, trying to sound confident but my voice broke on the last word.

"No," he said softly but resolutely.

"Lex." I covered the hands he had on my face with my own. "This is everything you've been working for. You could change so many lives."

"It would change me completely not to be with you."

"They don't just offer this sort of thing to anyone. You've worked so hard," I whispered. "You have to take it."

He shook his head. "You don't know what you're asking."

"I know it would be hard, but we can make this work. We'll do long distance."

He recoiled from me like I'd slapped him. "You can't be serious," he said, his eyes widening in disbelief. "You wouldn't even try long distance with your ex when you lived in the same country. How do you think it's going to be when we're an entire ocean apart?"

"That's not fair, Lex," I protested. "I love you. You know it's not the same."

"It doesn't change the fact that you've said multiple times that you don't believe long distance ever works for anyone."

I shook my head. "It's different with us," I reiterated. "Besides, what's the alternative?"

"I stay here," he answered simply. "Just like we talked about. I continue to do my research *here*... with you."

"You aren't thinking about the big picture. This job could cut your time in half if you have access to their equipment."

He narrowed his eyes, clearly unhappy that I had these sorts of details. "You don't understand."

"Explain it to me then."

He raked his hand through his hair. "The job I have now already pulls me away from you, and it's nowhere near as demanding as the one at Empros will be."

I moved to stand directly in front of him, so he'd have to face me.

"I get it will be hard, but this is the opportunity of a lifetime for you. You can't refuse it just because we don't want to be apart. It isn't fair to anyone."

His expression shifted, eyes wide and searching. "Are you saying you'll be okay with it? With us being separated indefinitely?"

"Of course not, but you have to consider what it would mean if you don't accept this offer—It would mean delaying your life's work, your ambitions, everything you and your team have worked so hard for all these years," I said, my voice steady but filled with quiet urgency. "And I can't be the reason you turn your back on all of it."

I watched him, waiting for him to understand, the silence hanging heavy between us. His eyes worked over my face. "And if I say I won't go? What happens then?"

"You have to," I said, trying to make him understand there wasn't another way. "I can't let you stay here, only to have you look back in five years and resent me for standing in the way of all the amazing things I know you're destined to achieve."

Lex straightened, his features hardening. "It sounds like you've already made up your mind."

I placed my hands on his chest. "I'm just trying to make you see that what you and your team are doing is bigger than the two of us."

His hands remained at his sides as he peered down at me. "Is that the only reason you want me to go?"

My brow creased. "What else would there be?"

"You haven't been thinking about going back to New York?"

"What?" My cheeks burned from the accusation. "Why would you say that?"

"I saw the paperwork. I know you renewed the lease on your apartment in New York."

My pulse quickened. "It's not what you think," I rushed to explain. "I've been subleasing the apartment to a friend."

He didn't say anything, but I could see the thoughts racing through his mind, the doubt plainly on his features.

"I'm not leaving. I renewed my contract with Stanford last week. I'm all in this with you," I said emphatically. "You have to believe me."

Lex's expression softened, but only slightly, as he stepped back, running a hand over his face. His anger had simmered, but there was still a shadow in his eyes. "I don't know what to believe anymore."

"What does that mean?"

"I just need some time to think," he said, fisting his hand in his hair. "You've obviously had time to think about all of this, and I need to do the same."

He grabbed his coat off the chair and started making his way towards the door.

"You're leaving?" I asked, my voice breaking.

He nodded. "I have to," he said as I followed behind him. "You've asked me to think about this pragmatically, but I can't do that when it comes to you... I never could. But especially not with you right in front of me, making everything else seem insignificant."

I choked back the tears. "But you'll come back tonight?"

"I don't know," he whispered. "I just need some time... Is that okay?"

I nodded, a lump forming in my throat. "Just... try not to take too long."

He leaned in, his lips brushing softly against my forehead, a moment of warmth that lingered just long enough to feel like forever, but before I could blink, he was gone.

Chapter 34

"So put your first finger at the fifth fret of the second string and your middle finger directly underneath it. That will leave an anchor finger between the G and E minor," I said to Jace as we sat on the floor of my living room.

It was Tuesday night, so even though I was in a shitty mood, I still honored the commitment I'd made to give him weekly guitar lessons. I chose E and A minor to go over this week because those chords matched the sullen emotional state I currently found myself in.

"Like this?" He positioned his hand and gave his guitar a strum.

"Yes, good," I said. "But keep your fingers at more of an angle to the frets, especially when you have to change to the C chord. It will be a more comfortable grip for you."

He did exactly as I said. "Perfect," I told him.

Jace was a natural. He picked up on the chords so effortlessly. I never had to give him the same instruction twice, which always made the lessons so easy and enjoyable. *I* was the killjoy on this particular evening.

Jace's phone started to ring, so he excused himself to take the call. After he walked away, I peeked at my phone for what felt like the thousandth time today to find I still had no calls or texts from Lex.

I sighed. It had been two days since I'd heard from him. He asked me to give him some time to think, so I was trying to respect that, but I was growing more fearful with every passing minute that he was pulling away, and soon he'd be gone from my life for good.

Every time I closed my eyes, all I could see was the horrified look on his face when I had said we could try long distance. And I guess I knew why. It was no secret that Garrett and I broke up because I didn't believe we could make long distance work. But this was different. *We* were different, and I thought he knew that.

I massaged my temples, feeling completely exhausted. I couldn't sleep at all last night, just imagining Lex telling me that things were over when I saw him again. I lay awake, staring at the ceiling, unable to quiet the storm of thoughts swirling inside me. The more I replayed our conversation, the tighter the grip of fear became, until it felt like I was drowning in it.

"Sorry about that," Jace said, interrupting my melancholic trance as he came back in.

"No worries," I said, trying to keep it together, but failing miserably as I felt the sadness settle on my shoulders.

Jace easily picked up on where my mind was at. "He's just as miserable as you are, you know," he said, taking a seat next to me.

I shrugged. "I wouldn't know," I said. "He left Sunday night after I told him I thought he should take the job, and he hasn't spoken to me since."

He looked taken aback. "Jesus, so you don't know."

I was immediately struck with anxiety. "Don't know what?"

He sighed. "I shouldn't have opened my big mouth. I'm sure he was going to tell you eventually."

"What is it?" I asked apprehensively.

"He took the job," he answered reluctantly.

A pang of sadness sliced through me. It was what I wanted for him but hearing it from someone other than Lex made the hurt feel bone-deep.

"Are you going with them?" I asked quietly, fighting back the tears. Sarah had made it seem like he was still unsure.

"Yes. I need to do this. I didn't want to but... Sarah convinced me," he said with a smile. "She said she knew what we had was real, and a year apart wasn't going to change that."

"I wish other people felt the same way," I said glumly.

Jace stared at me for a brief moment. "Did Lex ever tell you how he and I met?"

I shook my head. "I assumed it was through work."

"We became a lot closer through work, but we actually met in our first semester at MIT."

"I didn't know that," I said. "I always thought Stuart was his oldest friend out of everyone in the group."

"No, you were right," he responded. "Stuart is his oldest friend in the group."

I titled my head, giving him a questioning look.

"I've known him longer than Stuart, but let's just say he and I weren't exactly friends back then," he explained, a smile playing across his lips. "Rivals might be a better way to describe our relationship in college."

"You and Lex?" I couldn't have chosen two more unlikely people to have a rivalry. "Were you guys like the modern-day Tesla vs. Edison? Was there backstabbing and pistols at dawn?"

Jace started to laugh. "Hardly," he answered. "It wasn't much of a competition. It was pretty clear from day one just how much smarter he was than everyone else, and I'm ashamed to admit how much that bothered me."

I gazed at him curiously. "What do you mean?"

"Just that it was the first time in my life that I had met anyone who was better than me at anything academic. I had to work twice as hard to keep up with him, but no matter how hard I tried, he still always outshined me."

"What a know-it-all," I teased.

He chuckled. "That's the thing. He really wasn't. Lex never seemed to care or even notice how hard I was working to try and beat him. The jealousy was all one-sided."

Surprise flickered through me. "I can't even picture it," I mused. "You're always so easy-going about everything. The first time I met you, all I could think was that this guy doesn't have an insecure bone in his body."

He gave me a half grin. "A lot has changed. I'm not that person anymore, and I have Lex to thank for that."

"How so?"

His eyebrows knitted together. "He never told you what I did to him?"

"No," I answered. He only ever told me what a great asset to his team Jace was.

Jace shook his head, chuckling. "Figures."

I was curious to hear what happened between them, but I didn't want to push. "You don't have to tell me. It's none of my business. We've all done things we aren't proud of."

"I will tell you only because I want you to understand something about Lex."

"Okay," I said, waiting for him to explain.

He paused for a beat, seeming lost in his memories before he finally spoke. "Every year, MIT has this competition where teams try to come up with the most innovative research proposal to win funding for a community-based project. You get the prestige and a ton of money, and I was desperate to win. I wanted so badly to beat the great Alexsander Strovinski just once..." he said, lowering his eyes. "So I stooped really low and convinced his partner to switch to my team in the last few weeks of the competition. He wasn't exactly Lex's biggest fan either." He smiled wryly. "I told myself that my ideas were better, but I'd essentially copied Lex's ideas that his partner stole, and we built our proposal around it. Lex had to finish the proposal on his own, and there just wasn't enough time for him to complete all of the work... although he still came pretty damn close."

That didn't sound anything like the Jace I knew. "Did you win?"

Shame tugged at his expression as he nodded. "Yeah, we won," he said. "I thought Lex would be furious. I thought he would report us for what we did, but he did something even worse... When they called our names as the winners, Lex was the first one to stand up in front of all our classmates and start clapping for us. He even came to congratulate me and his old partner after the ceremony. I thought I would be on top of the world when I finally beat him, but I felt like an absolute piece of shit and a complete fraud."

His shoulders sagged as he finished the story, and I could tell how badly he still felt about it.

"That's not you anymore, though," I said, letting him off the hook.

"No. I wasn't the same after that. I realized how much time I wasted trying to be the best when the opportunity to learn from the best was right there in front of me. I apologized to him so many times for what I did, and Lex, being the person he is, forgave me like it was nothing. Years later, even after all of that, he still gave me a job on his team and a life doing something I love. It's crazy to think how much I owe that man."

I smiled, becoming teary-eyed listening to him talk about Lex this way. "Same."

He smiled back at me in understanding. Jace had become a close part of my circle through Sarah, so he knew what Lex had done for my mom.

"My point to this very long, rambling story is to tell you that Lex has never been jealous of anyone or anything, ever. He didn't care in the slightest that I won that award with ideas that were stolen from him… But that same man didn't talk to me for almost a month after he found out that I asked you out. Asked. You hadn't even accepted!" Jace started laughing so hard, and I couldn't help but smile. "Sometimes I still catch him giving me the side eye when your name comes up."

He continued to laugh, and I shook my head, thinking of how I was standing by my statement that these men of science could really be so dramatic.

"I guess all I'm trying to say is to cut him some slack," he said. "It may not be as obvious to the rest of the guys why he didn't want to take this job offer when he's been completely focused on our work for so long. But I know exactly why… He's never wanted anything as badly as he wants you. Not even this project."

I sniffled. "I feel the same way about him," I said, the emotion getting caught in my throat. "But I can't be the reason you guys don't finish this project. It's too important."

He nodded. "I know… Just don't give up on him, Hadley. He really is the best person I've ever known."

I pulled Jace in for a hug and thanked him. There was no shortage of wonderful people in my life.

Jace and I called it a night not long after that, and I walked him to the door.

"Thanks again, Hadley," he said with a wave as he walked out the door, but almost ran straight into an irritated-looking Lex. I saw Jace's face break into a grin.

"Just here for my guitar lessons, man." He held up his guitar like it was exonerating evidence. He turned his head back to wink at me before running down the steps.

Once Jace was gone, Lex and I stood in the doorway staring at one another, so many unspoken things moving between us. It had only been a few days, but I had missed him like we'd been separated for twenty lifetimes.

"Can I come in?" he asked quietly. The tone in his voice made my chest instantly tighten with worry.

I cleared my throat. "Of course," I said, gesturing for him to follow me inside.

We went to sit down on the couch together, the stillness pressing in around us, and I waited, heart pounding, for him to say the words I'd been dreading.

"I'm sorry I took so long," he said, his gaze finally lifting to meet mine. "This is the hardest decision I've ever had to make in my life."

"You took the job," I said, acknowledging it out loud for the both of us.

He nodded, his hands twisting together like he was trying to wring the guilt from them. "I thought a lot about what you said, and I realized you were right—I was being selfish by not considering what this would mean for my team. They've all worked so hard. They deserve this chance."

"You deserve it, too," I said, placing my hand over his to still them. "I'm so proud of you, Lex."

He forced a tight smile, but his eyes seemed lost somewhere beyond the room.

"There's more, isn't there?" I said, seeing the conflict etched in his expression.

He nodded again. Anxiety curled in my stomach as my mind became fixated on the worst-case scenario. "There was something else you said that helped me come to a decision."

"What was it?"

He began interlacing his fingers and pulling them apart repeatedly. "You told me it wasn't fair that I was making this decision without considering what it would mean for everyone... But that also includes you."

I tilted my head, trying to piece together the meaning behind his words. "What do you mean?"

"I know they told you that this job would just be for a year, but that isn't a guarantee. Our contract doesn't specify a timeline. It could take an entire decade to figure this thing out for all any of us knows."

My pulse was pounding in my neck, making me feel lightheaded as I started to sense where this was heading. "What are you saying?"

His gaze drifted downward. "I can't ask you to put your life on hold for me, Hadley. It isn't fair."

My breath came quicker, the air between us felt thick, suffocating.

"Are you... Are you breaking up with me?" My voice barely came out above a whisper.

He swallowed hard before letting out a shaky breath. "I never want to be without you, but you were right—the work we're doing is important, and I can't walk away from something I believe in so deeply... But your work and your life are just as important," he said, taking my hand in his. "This job won't leave room for anything else in my life, and for you, that would mean having to live your life around me and my strict schedule."

"S-so, you don't even want to try?"

He looked up towards the ceiling, blinking rapidly. "Trust me, I've tried looking at this from every possible angle, trying to find a solution that makes sense for everyone, but I always came to the same conclusion—I can't have both. I can't chase my dreams while also making you stand in the shadow of them."

My chest ached as the reality of what he was saying slowly sank in. "But you're not even giving us a chance."

His gaze lowered to me again. "You said you didn't want me to resent you if I stayed, but I can't bear the thought of you resenting me for trying to make you mold your life around a schedule that's not yours, just waiting for scraps of my time. There's no way for me to win here."

"So, you've decided we lose instead."

He shook his head. "This isn't a loss. Not to me. You'll always be the best thing that's ever happened to me."

"Then why does it feel like you're throwing it away?"

He looked up, his expression devastated but resolute. "Because if I ask you to wait for me, if I ask you to put your life on hold for something I can't promise, I'll ruin the very person I love most."

I choked back a sob. "Please... Let's just try," I begged.

He took both my hands in his, bringing them to his lips to brush across my knuckles. "You're the most selfless person I've ever met. It would be foolish of me not to try and emulate something I admire so much about you."

"What does that mean?"

"I love you, Hadley. I love you so fucking much," he said, his voice breaking. "This is absolutely destroying me, but I can't keep only thinking about myself... You need to focus on your mom and her recovery, not waiting around for those few hours a day I would be available to you on the other side of the world... That's not a relationship. And I'd be a completely selfish bastard to even ask that of you."

The tears were pouring down my face. "Is this it then? You and me... It's just over?"

His head hung low. "I'm sorry," he whispered. "I wish things were different. I wish I could give you everything you deserve."

A sharp pressure clamped down on my chest. The words I had feared were now hanging in the air, unbearable and suffocating. His apology only deepened the space between us, making everything feel more absolute. My hands shook as I wiped at the tears spilling down my face.

"When do you leave?" I asked, wondering how much time, if any, we had left together.

The expression on his face told me everything I needed to know—the answer he was about to give was going to be another blow to my already breaking heart.

"In a week."

I inhaled a sharp breath, feeling my heart fracture with a wound that felt too deep to ever heal.

"I don't know how I'm going to say goodbye to you knowing it might be forever," I said, my voice trembling.

He stared at me for a long time, his face a battlefield of emotions. Finally, he whispered, "I'll never stop loving you, Hadley. What we have... it's everything I never knew I needed. And I hope like hell that someday, somehow, our paths cross again."

Before I could respond, before I could beg him to stay one more time, he kissed me. It was slow and aching, filled with everything we couldn't put into words. When he pulled away, his eyes were red, his face etched with pain.

He turned and walked toward the door, each step feeling like a nail in the coffin of us. When the door finally clicked shut behind him, a dark realization came over me—Not even the deepest, truest kind of love is enough to keep two people together.

Chapter 35

I leaned my head against the window of the airplane watching as thousands of shimmering lights came into view. There it was... New York City.

It had been almost a year since I'd seen her last. The concrete giants that shaped the city's skyline looked pencil-thin beneath me. The sun had set, but the city that never sleeps had light blazing from every vantage point, illuminating the night sky, beckoning me home.

I couldn't believe I was back. The emotions stirring inside me felt both hollow and deep. Memories flooded my mind as the roaring sound of the plane landing on the runway of JFK filled the cabin. The first time I'd ever flown had been with my dad, and it was just a quick flight to the Jersey Shore for summer vacation. Nothing like the cross-country journey I'd just taken from San Francisco to get here.

As I walked the city's streets, I pulled my coat tighter around my body, the wind whipping across my face. It was drizzling and about thirty degrees out. *Welcome to New York!*

I finally made it back to my old neighborhood in Greenwich Village, and the soundscape that had been a constant in my life for so long surrounded me once again—bustling crowds, the continual murmur of traffic, the hum of distant sirens, all blending together to sing New York's distinctive melody. I realized how much I'd missed it.

I took the elevator up to my old apartment before setting my things down and knocking on the door. I'd been subleasing the apartment to Garrett's sister, Sophie, and she said I could stay with her for the duration of my time here.

I tried knocking again, but no answer. After waiting a few minutes longer, I tried calling Sophie, but it went straight to voicemail. I didn't want to barge in, but I also didn't want to wait out here forever. I fished the keys out from my purse before letting myself in.

"Soph?" I called out. "It's me." Still no answer. I heard a rustling sound coming from the bedroom, so I went to investigate.

"Sophie?" I said, pushing the door open slowly and nearly jumping out of my skin when I spotted a man hunched over next to my bed.

I let out a horrified scream, startling the man as he cried out in response.

"Shit, Hadley!" I heard Garrett shout. "You scared me half to death! What are you doing here?"

"Me?!" I said, clutching my chest, waiting for my heart to slow. "What are *you* doing here?"

He stood up, resting his hands on his hips as if trying to catch his breath.

"Sophie called me freaking out," he explained. "Said she saw a mouse run under the bed and was refusing to go back inside the apartment until it had been apprehended, so I came over to help."

I let out a long breath. On the upside, at least it wasn't a bird.

"I'm surprised she didn't set the house on fire," I said, remembering the time she nearly fainted during rehearsals when a lizard had crawled onstage.

"Don't worry. I'm taking the matches with me just in case," he said, and I smirked.

"So did you catch it?" I asked.

"Not yet. I was putting a few traps out when you came in," he answered. "Sorry I scared you. Sophie didn't tell me you were coming."

I wasn't surprised. It was a sore subject, and we usually avoided talking about her brother anytime we spoke.

"Yeah, I'm just here for the weekend. Logan's been hounding me to work on a new album with him," I said, and he nodded.

My mom had finished her cancer treatments close to a month ago and was doing better than ever. It seemed like every week she was getting closer to looking like her old self again. She'd put a little bit of weight back on, and I was happy to see the color returning to her face. I finally felt comfortable enough to leave her for longer than a day, so with Logan's relentless harassment, I took the opportunity to get away and get my mind off... things.

"Well, I'll get out of your hair," he said. "If you hear a snapping sound from under your bed, it means the criminal's been detained."

I made a face. "Welcome home," I said sarcastically.

He chuckled before grabbing his coat and heading toward the door.

"I'll text Sophie to let her know the traps have been set for the intruder if she wants to come back," I told him.

"She probably won't come within a mile of this place with Chuck E. Cheese still on the loose."

I laughed. "Yeah, you're probably right," I agreed. "Thanks for the pest control services."

He gave me a warm smile. "It was good to see you again."

"Yeah, you too."

Just as he reached the door, he turned to me and said, "Did you mean what you said before?"

I looked at him, confused. "What did I say?"

"Before I left California... You said we could try being friends again once you got back."

I was apprehensive about where he was going with this. "I'm not back. I'm just here for the weekend."

He gave me a half-grin. "Could we try to be friends for the weekend then?"

I studied him for a moment, wondering if this was a terrible idea. "What did you have in mind?"

"I was thinking we could go grab dinner at O'Hara's," he suggested. "Just as friends of course," he added quickly.

Nope, nuh-uh, definitely not. "Okay," I heard myself say. Internal facepalm. Damn my pathological people-pleasing ways.

Minutes later, I found myself walking side by side with my ex-boyfriend, heading around the corner to the restaurant bar that had once been a favorite of ours. They had these coconut shrimp I still sometimes dreamt about. A strong feeling of déjà vu came over me as we sat at the same high-top table near the window that had once been "our" spot.

After we removed our jackets and got settled, all that was left to do was stare at one another awkwardly. Garrett gave me a tight smile that I returned.

"We're going to need drinks, aren't we?" he asked.

"Yup," I agreed quickly.

He grinned before going over to the bar and ordering for us. He hadn't asked, but clearly, he remembered my drink order as he walked back with a Manhattan in hand. I didn't know how to feel about it.

The irony of the situation wasn't lost on me—the fact that I was back in New York having a casual dinner with the man I might have still been in a relationship with had I never left.

"So, how's your mom?" Garrett asked, taking a sip of his beer.

"She's doing great actually." It felt so good to say that. I knew in my bones that if I'd never met Lex, my mom and I would be planning our return home to NYC now that she was on the mend... But maybe that wasn't true at all. The harrowing thought crossed my mind that I'd probably be returning home alone had I never met him.

I took a large swallow of my drink.

"And um... how's the scientist?" he asked.

Pain gnawed at the open wound I still carried at the mention of Lex.

"He's fine," I said quickly, hoping to move on.

It had been nearly three months since Lex left for Sweden.

I don't know what I expected. He made it clear he didn't want to try and continue a relationship with me, but I still never could have imagined it would play out the way that it did. For the first month, we talked almost every single day, and a glimmer of hope took root inside me—that maybe he'd changed his mind, maybe he did want to try after all. But it wasn't long before our conversations began to grow less frequent, and each day that passed without a message felt heavier, until the hope I'd clung to eventually began to fade.

Our conversations now were few and far between, and they were mostly centered around checking in on my mom. He started blaming it on the time difference as to why he was never available to speak, and after so many unreturned calls, I eventually gave up trying... And it seemed he did as well.

"So, what is it then?" Garrett asked.

"What do you mean?"

"You look so different from the last time I saw you."

I smiled. "Not this again."

He chuckled lightly. "No, I just mean that the last time we saw each other you seemed so happy. It stung that I wasn't the one making you look that way, but it actually helped me move on knowing that at least you were happy. But now..."

"Now what?"

"Now you just look miserable," he said plainly. "Is it me? We don't have to do this."

Misery was my constant companion these days, though I tried to hide it. I didn't want my mom to have to worry about me on top of everything she had going on, but if Garrett picked up on it within ten minutes of us being together, then I knew there was no way my mom hadn't noticed.

I was practically living with her at this point. I would go to work, bring her to her appointments, we'd have dinner together, and I'd fall asleep on her couch. Rinse and Repeat. I couldn't stomach being at my house. It felt like torture to be in the same bed Lex had slept in with me night after night, his scent still lingering on the sheets. The only outlier to my routine was when I'd meet up with Sarah, and we'd commiserate over how much we hated Sweden. Jace, as it turns out, was much more of a willing participant in trying to make long distance work. Sarah said he'd call every single night, which meant he was getting up early every morning just so they could talk. The time difference didn't seem to matter so much to them.

"No." I shook my head. "No, it's not you."

"Then..."

I sighed. "I'm still trying to figure things out with..." I couldn't even say his name without feeling my chest tighten.

"Are you guys not together anymore?"

Tears filled my eyes, but I fought them back down. I wasn't going to cry about this in front of Garrett.

"No," I admitted in a small voice. "He took a job in Sweden and... things just didn't work out."

I waited for Garrett to gloat or make mention of the fact that this was yet another relationship I'd failed because of distance. But he didn't. He was looking at me with concern in his eyes.

"Listen, I've been wanting to apologize for the way I acted when I came to California," he said. "I shouldn't have done it. I knew things were over, but I didn't want to accept it."

I nodded and muttered, "Thanks."

He looked at me pointedly and said, "Letting someone you love go isn't as easy as everyone makes it seem."

I don't know why that struck me so hard. It felt like the wind had been knocked out of me. Were Garrett and I two sides of the same coin? Was I refusing to see the signs that things were over between Lex and I?

I don't know how long I was caught up in my own reverie, but the sound of Garrett's thumbs drumming on the table as he clutched his beer brought me back to reality. It was always his tell when he was anxious.

"Sorry," I said, eyeing his hands. "I didn't mean to space out."

"No worries," he said but his thumbs continued tapping on the table.

"Am I making you uncomfortable?" I asked.

He shook his head. "No, why?"

"Because it sounds like you're trying to recreate the drum solo to In the Air Tonight on our table."

His fingers immediately froze before his mouth curled into a grin. "I didn't realize I was doing that."

"It's your nervous tick," I reminded him.

He smiled. "Remember when we saw Phil Collins in the elevator at the Skylark?"

"How could I forget?" I said, grinning. "You broke out into a cold sweat and ended up challenging him to a thumb war."

"It was all I could think to say!"

I laughed. "You couldn't come up with anything better than trying to declare a thumb war?"

"He had abnormally small thumbs. It was a no-brainer," he stated. "I think he was about to accept the challenge if his security wouldn't have body-checked me into the wall."

"I'm not so sure about that," I said, chuckling. "But I appreciate your commitment to your own idea of reality."

He burst into laughter, and I couldn't help but join in. A frenzy of emotions came rushing back to me at the sound of our combined laughter. I remembered how easy this was... how much he made me laugh... how good he was to me. I took another large sip of my Manhattan, the sweetness of the bourbon lingering on my tongue.

After that icebreaker, both the conversation and drinks flowed easily for the rest of the evening. The more we reminisced, the more I lost count of the number of drinks I'd had. We ended up at a karaoke bar in Midtown, where I surprised myself by jumping on stage to sing a medley of Britney hits as the crowd cheered and sang along. I handed the mic back to the MC once my time was up, and Garrett helped me down from the stage.

"Next up we have Garrett Lawson coming to the stage," the MC announced, and I looked over at Garrett wide-eyed. We both knew he couldn't carry a tune. He winked at me before he ran onto the stage.

"Looks like he'll be singing In the Air Tonight by Phil Collins," the MC said. "A classic!"

I started choking with laughter as Garrett took the mic and began his off-key performance. The drinks had made him a little too confident as each "Oh Lord" began sounding more like shrieking than singing. Booing started up from the crowd, and I motioned for him that it was time to wrap it up, but he continued on. The MC came up and tried to wrestle the microphone away from him, but he held it up out of his reach.

"Has anyone else ever noticed Phil Collins' thumbs?" Garrett said, still holding the mic out of reach. "Anyone?"

That's when I noticed security coming.

"Let's go!" I called out to Garrett between fits of laughter. He downed the rest of his drink before tossing the mic over, and we ran out of the club.

"That was awful," I told him as we stumbled onto the subway, drawing annoyed looks from everyone around us as we continued giggling like idiots.

"What do you mean?" he asked, leaning against the handrail. "The crowd was going wild!"

"I think they were looking for one of those long hooks to pull you off stage."

"I beg your biggest pardon." He put his hand on his chest. "The MC told me I was really going places."

"I think he meant jail for holding his mic hostage," I said, making Garrett throw his head back in laughter.

I leaned my head against the handrail, looking over at him. His bright blue eyes were shining with amusement as we gazed at one another. I couldn't tell if what I was feeling was true happiness. I could barely remember what that felt like these days, but it seemed close.

After he insisted on walking me the rest of the way home—if you could call it walking, since it more closely resembled stumbling—I stood outside my doorway, suddenly overcome with exhaustion.

"Thanks for tonight, Garrett," I said to him. "I'm glad we did this."

And I meant it. Maybe we could pull off being friends after all. It was the most fun I'd had since...

He leaned against my doorway and nodded.

I began to sway as the jetlag and alcohol really started catching up to me, and I knew it was time to call it a night.

"Well, goodnight," I said as I made my way inside.

Before I could shut the door, I heard Garrett say, "I lied to you, Hadley."

I turned to look at him. "About?"

"I said I moved on," he said with a serious look on his face. "But I haven't. I still love you just as much as I did before you left... Maybe more."

I looked into his pale blue eyes and saw nothing but adoration shining through them. My heart throbbed painfully at how much I missed that look, even if the color was all wrong.

The drinks clouded my mind as I started to wonder if I'd made a mistake writing Garrett off so quickly. I knew I'd never feel the same fierce, all-consuming type of love I'd had with Lex, but I deserved to at least *try* to find happiness, didn't I? Hearing Garrett say he loved me felt like a lifeline was being thrown to me as I was drowning in grief.

I couldn't make sense of what I was feeling. The rational part of my brain was fighting against the sad, messy part of my heart that just wanted to feel loved again. That part was telling me that maybe we hadn't had enough time before... maybe if I just gave this another chance...

He took a step closer to me, and I froze. His hand reached out to cup my neck, and I watched in slow motion as his lips came closer to finally press against mine.

I knew at once that I'd made a huge mistake. I pulled back instantly, feeling my shoulders beginning to shake. Guilt started to rise up within me until I became sick with it. It felt like I'd been doused in cold water, and I sobered up quickly as the realization of what I'd done came crashing over me.

He stared at me for a long while. I couldn't seem to find the words to say as my thoughts were spinning out of control.

Garrett finally broke the silence. "You're not ready to let him go."

I shook my head as the tears I'd been holding back slowly slid down the sides of my face. I was kicking myself for sinking so low. Garrett didn't deserve this.

"I'm sorry," I whispered. "I'm such a piece of shit." Never in my life had I felt so small.

"No, you're not," Garrett said softly. "I wish that you were... It would make it a hell of a lot easier to hate you."

"I'd deserve it."

Garrett exhaled a long breath through his nose. "Take care of yourself, Hadley," he said before walking out of the door and out of my life.

I headed straight to the studio in the West Village the next morning to meet with Logan. With the alcohol out of my system and sound judgement fully restored, I decided the rest of this trip would be all business. I buried what happened last night deep inside, not ready to perform the autopsy on what I let happen just yet.

"Glad you could finally make it," Logan said as I walked through the door of Sonic Music Studio. He was sitting at the soundboard and continued adjusting the aux knobs before he finally looked my way.

"Hey, Ship," I said.

He eyed me from head to toe. "You look tanner."

"Thanks?"

"It wasn't a compliment," he replied. "You look like California threw up on you."

I smiled. "It's good to see you too, Ship."

"Spare me the pleasantries, Olivier," he said, and I laughed.

"With this kind of warm reception, it's crazy I didn't rush out here sooner," I told him.

His face reluctantly broke out into a smile. "Fine. Have it your way." He leaned back in his chair. "Tell me all about life out in Kaleifornia. Are you able to make Pilates classes in between sampling different avocado toasts and pursuing the perfect Instagram sunset? Let's really get into it."

I shook my head, smiling. "I'd rather not."

"Great, me either." He turned back to the soundboard. He made a few more adjustments before he pushed his chair back and said,

"Come on, I want you to meet somebody."

I followed him over to the sound booth, where I spotted a petite blonde girl taking off her headphones as we approached.

"Hadley, I'd like you to meet Fiona Lockwood."

She came out of the booth beaming. She couldn't have been older than eighteen, but she was dressed and made up to look about twenty-five. I was willing to bet my life that Fiona Lockwood wasn't even her real name.

"It's so nice to meet you," she said nervously. "I'm such a huge fan. I can't believe you're working on this project with us."

She seemed sweet, innocent even. I knew the industry would beat that out of her in no time.

I smiled back at her. "Ship told me a lot of great things about you. He said you're destined to be one of the biggest stars there is. I couldn't pass up an opportunity like that."

He gave me a disparaging look, and I had to bite my lip to keep from laughing. I guess that was a bit of an exaggeration. What he actually said was that he thought she really had something. But for Logan, that was basically saying she was a superstar in the making.

Her cheeks turned bright red as she looked over at Logan, smiling shyly. I was grateful the record company had paired her with him. He could be tough to work with, but he was one of the few producers in the city who wasn't an absolute creep.

"What kind of song are you looking to compose?" I asked her.

"Well, I've released a few singles that had some moderate success on the charts. But the label is asking for something a bit edgier, something more dramatic, and Logan said you were the best."

"He's right," I told her before I glanced over at him. "For once."

He rolled his eyes. "Alright, enough chit-chat. Time is money."

After that, we got right down to business. We worked all through the night and into the next morning, coming up with different mixes and samples of a really melancholy song about a couple who drifted apart, and the singer was left wondering if any of it was real. I wouldn't look too deep into where that inspiration came from.

Fiona was an incredible singer and had a great ear for rhyme schemes. She came up with many of the lines herself, and by the end, I was just as convinced as Logan that she would be a star.

We laid down the track the following evening. Fiona and Logan thought it was perfect, but something was nagging me as I listened to it back. I couldn't put my finger on why the song seemed so familiar. I kept racking my brain, trying to figure out if I'd heard it before or if I was copying someone else's composition, which sometimes was easy to do when it came to songwriting, since we all used the same twelve notes and intervals. Logan suggested it might be the pitch she was using, so he made her go back and try it in a different key.

As I watched Fiona in the booth pouring her heart out into the song, it hit me like a ton of bricks as to why it seemed so familiar. I realized I'd inadvertently written the female perspective to "The Scientist." In Coldplay's version, we hear him trying to win her back after letting their relationship fall apart because of his work. In this version, we were hearing her side of the story—every heartache, every moment of doubt that they were ever going to make it.

I stand alone in the pouring rain
One last attempt to wash away the pain
Lost in thoughts I can't explain
Searching for any reason to remain

I stand alone in a crowded room
Echoes of laughter fade into silent gloom
You thought it would be easy, just like our song
I thought it would be easy, now we're both wrong

Help me rewind the time
Help me get back what's mine
Help me rewrite our song
Before this feeling's too far gone

You said you're sorry, didn't want the fight
Now every breath just feels too tight
I claw my way back to the start
Do you know how to mend a broken heart

I look down at all the shattered pieces
You pulled it apart, now tell me your thesis
Did you think it through to the end
Or did you believe it would always mend

Help me rewind the time
Help me get back what's mine
Help me rewrite our song
Before this feeling's too far gone

Caught in a world where truth often lies
Searching for answers in your whispered sighs
Tell me it's not too late to try
I never wanted your silent goodbye

Nobody said it would be easy
To mend a heart that's been torn apart
Nobody said it would be easy
To find a way back to the start

I felt my hands starting to shake. I needed to step away before I went to pieces right there in the control room.

I hurried to excuse myself and ran outside for a breath of fresh air before I fell apart completely. It was a typical New York evening in the dead of winter—bitterly cold, but I welcomed the sharp bite of the freezing air on my skin. Its icy touch helped soothe my frayed nerves. Even when I was trying to escape thinking about Lex, it was no use. Here he was, popping back up in the music I was writing. The floor of my room back home was littered with attempts I'd made at writing in these last few months. I just couldn't do it. I was completely devoid of the emotions needed to compose music, so I eventually gave up trying. And just like us, the songs were all left unfinished.

When I finally regained my composure, I went back inside, and they had finished the song. Logan played it back for me, and I knew in my gut that it was a hit. The song felt like a breakthrough for me, both personally and professionally. I'd broken free from my musical catatonia and managed to create something exceptional. I wanted nothing more than to do it again and again.

"You know, we could make this a permanent gig between the two of us, Olivier," Logan said to me once we'd wrapped and were heading out for dinner. "The record label is always asking how we can keep you in the studio. They're really going to flip when they hear this. It's some of your best work ever. And it only took you two days to write... Unbelievable."

I scrunched my nose at him. "I'm uncomfortable with you giving me compliments."

"I have ulterior motives, if that makes you feel better," he said, smirking. "All jokes aside, they told me to offer you whatever you wanted."

What I wanted, they couldn't give me.

"Think about it, Olivier," he continued. "You could be a full-time composer making millions instead of whatever the hell you're doing out in Crunchy Valley."

I chuckled. "Alright Ship, I'll think about it."

I was trying to placate him, but the thought crossed my mind that maybe I should actually consider it. This weekend had been amazing. Having the opportunity to be collaborative and make something this special had been incredibly fulfilling. It gave me a rush like I hadn't felt in a long time.

Despite how the weekend started, being in New York allowed me to feel something other than complete misery for the first time in months, and I didn't want to let it go. It was like the vibrant chaos of the city was breathing life back into me. It might be time to consider returning to my roots, because even with my mom there, California barely felt like home any longer.

Home was over five-thousand miles away on another continent, blatantly ignoring me.

Chapter 36

"Hadley, you have to stop this," my mom said as I sat at her dining room table one evening.

"What?" I asked. I hadn't been paying attention. "I'm sorry. What did you say?"

She sighed. "You can't keep going like this. You barely sleep. You hardly eat more than a few bites at any meal. You aren't even really living anymore."

"I'm fine," I lied.

Life had gone right back to the way it had been before I left for New York—work, doctor's appointments, hanging out at my mom's, and most notably, no word from Lex. I considered talking to my mom about me possibly moving back to New York, but I wanted to wait until she was further along in her recovery. Until then, my plan was just to keep going through the motions of living, hoping like hell she didn't notice how unhappy I'd been.

"Hadley, look at me."

I put down my fork and turned to look at her.

"I know you think you have to be here to take care of me, but I'm fine. Better than fine, actually. My appetite's returning, and I'm starting to have more energy. I'm really beginning to feel like my old self again. The only thing that isn't doing well in my life is you."

"Gee, thanks," I mumbled.

"You know what I mean," she said.

"No, I don't," I stated plainly. "What are you trying to say?"

"That you don't have to stay here for me," she answered. "I finished my last chemo treatment months ago. You don't have to be here to babysit me anymore."

"You're far from being ready to start running marathons, Mom."

"I'm not saying that," she replied. "But if you haven't noticed, I've got a really great partner now. Carl is more than willing to pick up any slack. We've actually been talking about moving in together."

"What?" This was the first time in weeks I actually felt like smiling. "Really?"

"It just makes sense. We're always together. It's just not practical to keep up two mortgages."

"Practical... right," I said, feeling that unfamiliar sensation of my face breaking into a smile.

"I want you to be happy, my sweet girl. You *deserve* to be happy," she said. "You need to go there and make this right with him."

My face fell. "I don't think he wants to make this right. He won't even talk to me."

"That man is in love with you. Living in a different country didn't change anything except for making the two of you miserable."

I kept my eyes lowered. "I don't know."

"Think about this for one second. If the situation were reversed and god forbid, you were the one who was sick," she said. "Once you started to get better, would you want me watching over you day after day, wasting away with unhappiness, especially if you had Lex by your side to take care of you?"

When she put it that way... No, I wouldn't want that. I could see exactly the point she was trying to make, but it still didn't sit right with me.

"If the situation were reversed, you wouldn't want to leave my side either."

"That's true," she confirmed. "But I'm the mom, so you have to do what I say."

We both started to laugh. Our relationship had never been that way. We'd always made decisions together and this wasn't any different.

"Go to him, Hadley," she encouraged. "Don't let it bend so far that it breaks."

I choked on the words that were threatening to spill out. I didn't want to confess to her that I was afraid it may already be broken.

A few days later, I got a call from Stuart. I hadn't heard from him in weeks, and I hurried to pick it up.

"Hadley, hey," he said with an urgent tone. "I'm sorry to call you like this, but I didn't know what else to do."

"What's wrong?" I asked anxiously.

"It's Lex..."

My heart slammed in my chest. "Is he okay?"

"No, he's not okay. He hasn't been okay since we got here." Concern was unmistakable in his tone. "He's killing himself, Hadley. He works non-stop. He never sleeps. He goes to the lab first thing in the morning, and if he bothers to come home at all, he'll only sleep for a few hours before he goes right back to it. It's like he's singularly obsessed with finishing this work, and nothing else matters. I think he's determined to get this done, so he can get back to you as soon as humanly possible."

"Why didn't you say anything sooner?" I demanded as the anger and worry crashed over me. If I'd have known, maybe I could have done something.

"He asked me not to say anything to you," he replied. "But I can't watch him do this to himself anymore. He's going to end up in the hospital when he collapses from exhaustion."

Hearing Stuart say those words had my stomach in knots. "Where is he? Let me talk to him." He and I both couldn't keep going like this. We had to get this figured out once and for all.

He remained silent for a few moments, probably trying to decide if it was a good idea or not. "Stuart, please," I pressed.

"I don't know where he is," he admitted in a quiet voice. "He left yesterday morning, and I haven't heard from him since."

Panic surged through me. "What do you mean you don't know where he is? Have you tried calling him? What if he's hurt?"

"I don't think he's hurt," he said calmly.

"You don't know that. Something could have happened," I nearly shouted. "How can you be so calm about this?"

"Because he told me he was going to Empros this morning to discuss our contract," he said hesitantly. "I'm pretty sure he was going to try and terminate it."

I froze, replaying what he just said over in my head. Betrayal and frustration collided, forming a knot of rage in my chest that was almost suffocating.

"*No.*" Not after everything we'd been through.

I said the words that threatened to shatter the last bit of hope I'd been holding onto for us, "This can't have all been for nothing."

"I'm sorry, Hadley," Stuart said, his voice soft with regret. "I told him that was only going to make things worse, but he wouldn't listen."

"Find him, Stuart," was the last thing I said before I hung up and started dialing Lex's number.

I was planning on calling his phone so relentlessly that even telemarketers would start to envy my determination. And if that didn't work, I would call every police department in Sweden to find him and tie him up, so he'd have to listen to me.

I paced back and forth across the living room as the phone continued to ring and ring. *Fine by me.* My phone's battery was fully charged and my refrigerator fully stocked. *I'll be here all night, folks.*

I didn't have the slightest clue how long I walked around my home obstinately making one call after another, but the sound of the phone ringing in my ear felt like it might be permanently embedded on my acoustic nerve.

Eventually, I began questioning my own sanity as the ringing in my ear started to sound like it was echoing from a distance. I hung up and dialed again. The ringing seemed even louder like it was just outside my front door. I hung up again, my finger hovering over the number to dial it once more when suddenly there was a knock at the door.

There was a surreal sense of detachment as I watched my body making its way towards the door. I observed my footsteps falling into place with perfect clarity. It was like being on autopilot as my consciousness began hovering just above me, watching the scene unfold—arm outstretched... hand lifting... knob turning.

It was both exhilarating and disorienting to watch everything happening right before my eyes, but reality itself became blurred as the door was pulled open.

My perception shifted unexpectedly. A gentle pull and my senses came flooding back to me with a vivid intensity as I found the most beautiful pair of whiskey-colored eyes staring back at me. They had always been the most beautiful thing about him to me, a window to an extraordinary soul. I'd missed them more than I could ever have imagined. At the moment, those eyes were wide with disbelief, his lips popping open slightly as he gazed back at me.

Stuart had been right. He looked utterly exhausted. The deep, purplish color under his eyes was alarming. The angles of his face were sharp and his complexion pallid as if it had been months since he'd seen daylight. I pushed all that aside though, and really looked at him, taking in every inch of him, and I started to cry at the sight of him. I cried for every moment we'd been apart. I cried for those days we would never get back. But mostly, I cried from happiness at finally seeing him again.

I started to shake, and my knees buckled where I stood. He caught me just as I was about to hit the floor. I inhaled deeply, closing my eyes, and let his scent wash over me. I tucked my face into his neck and really began to sob. He pulled me into the living room, and I could feel his body trembling against mine as he sat us down on the couch. He said nothing as he held me close, running his hands up and down my spine, trying to soothe me. It took a full five minutes before I regained some semblance of composure.

I drew back and looked at his face. It was a sanctuary to me, bringing with it a sense of calm I hadn't felt since the day he left. He was looking back at me as if he were seeing a ghost. His hands traced over my entire body, touching me everywhere—running his hands down my arms and across my back, waist, hips, thighs, and back up again, before they moved to cup my face.

"You're here," I choked out.

"I am," he confirmed with a gentle smile that didn't quite touch his eyes. His hands moved to the nape of my neck. "Is that okay?"

Was that okay? I turned the question over in my mind. My heart sang out with yes, of course! But my mind couldn't answer the question so easily. I pulled out of his arms feeling like a ship being pulled from its anchor.

"Tell me you didn't quit," I said, letting the accusation hang in the air between us. He stared at me with a look I instantly recognized as his eyes roamed over my face. He was trying to figure me out, trying to decide what I wanted to hear.

"I didn't quit," he said, and my shoulders sagged in relief. Then he added, "Not yet, at least."

I stiffened. "What does that mean?"

"I told them I couldn't do it anymore. I asked them to terminate our contract, or at least release me from it and let the others continue," he explained. "They told me to take a leave of absence for a few weeks before I made a final decision."

"You can't quit," I said, my voice sharp as I rose to a standing position. "Not after all of this. Not after everything we've been through."

He was quiet for a few moments before he shook his head and said, "I don't know how to make myself want it anymore. It feels like my soul is slowly being torn apart the longer I'm away from you."

I closed my eyes, trying to block out the anguish I saw plainly on his face. "It didn't have to be like this. I begged you to try. You were the one who stopped taking my calls. You were the one who gave up on us. And now you're telling me it's all been for nothing?"

He shot to his feet to stand before me, my heart thumping unevenly at our renewed closeness. "No. I'm telling you that I've been fighting like hell to make it through even a single minute without thinking about you, Hadley... but it was useless," he said, frustration lacing every word. "You've occupied every corner of my mind since the day I met you."

I wanted to turn away from him. I didn't want his words to affect me like this, distracting me from the anger I still felt at him for not only giving up on this work but giving up on us as well. But I couldn't make myself turn away, bound by a force stronger than my will as if my heart was anchored to the sight of him.

"Then why did you do this to us?" I asked, my voice barely above a whisper.

His sigh was long and heavy. "I was convinced that if I threw myself into my work then I could forget about how much it was killing me not to be with you," he said, stepping closer. His voice lowered an octave. "But it didn't work. Every time I would break down and call, I couldn't stand it—hearing the sound of your voice but not being able to see you or hold you in my arms..." He trailed off, his hand lifting towards me almost absently. "I've never known this kind of pain—this raw, unrelenting ache that just sits in my chest." I watched as he placed his hand over the center of his chest, pressing it against his heart, like he was trying to soothe the ache within.

I blinked away the tears rising up. "The pain isn't any less for me... But you can't do this to me. You want me to tell you it's okay, but it's not. I haven't even heard from you in almost a month."

His head lowered, shame painting his features. "I thought I was doing the right thing."

"For who?" I demanded.

"For you!" he said, anguished. "You deserved so much more than what I was able to give you there."

I shook my head in frustration. "I know what I wanted. I know what I deserved... But you took that away from me. And you being here now... it's like it was all for nothing!"

He was breathing slowly through his nose, his gaze penetrating as he said, "Do you want me to leave?"

Absolutely not, my heart rang out fervently. But the answer wasn't that simple.

"I want you to go back and finish what you started," I said, choosing my words carefully. "You have a chance to do something great, something bigger than you and me, but you're throwing it all away."

"I can't do it anymore. Being there made me realize that I would sacrifice anything for you... anything *but* you."

"Lex..." His name felt so natural on my lips, but I was at a loss for words. He always could shatter my heart in the best and worst ways. It was an unnerving realization to discover that one person held the potential to evoke my greatest joys while also igniting my most profound sorrows. A beautiful paradox.

"I realize what I've done, how badly I've hurt you. The weight of my mistakes feels unbearable, but I need you to tell me." His hands reached for me, settling around my shoulders, and this simple contact brought the depth of my feelings into sharp, undeniable focus. I had to remind myself to breathe as he drew in even closer. "Tell me if this is over, Hadley. Nothing has changed for me. I still love you in a way that will never make sense to anyone but me," he said, his eyes boring down into mine. "There's a certainty to it that feels fundamental to my life. Time and distance have done nothing to change that... Has it changed things for you?"

Time and distance kills even the best relationships. At one point in my life, I believed that to be true. But here I was staring at the one person who was capable of unraveling all my tightly held beliefs. As I looked up at him, I was struck by the undeniable truth that nothing could ever change the way I felt about this man.

"No," I whispered back. "Nothing has changed. You're still the man who gave a woman he didn't know a ride to work when her car broke down. You're still the man who showed me how real my father's addiction was. You're still the man who saved my mother's life when we thought all hope was lost. You're still the man who would give up everything for the people he cares about. And you're still the man I love... deeply."

He exhaled roughly before his lips came crashing into mine, and I didn't even try to fight it. Resisting seemed impossible. One hand cradled my head while the other fisted at the base of my skull.

I couldn't describe the feeling that was coursing through me. All this time apart made it feel like the first time again, and yet I knew those lips better than my own. We kissed until I thought our lips would bruise from our unwillingness to part, never wanting to come up for air. Breathing was overrated anyway.

I pulled back from him a fraction and whispered, "I need you." I meant it in every sense of the word, but in this particular moment, I meant it in the way of needing our bodies pressed together.

Lex knew exactly what I meant, as he always had.

He lifted me effortlessly into his arms and carried me to the bedroom, laying me flat on the bed. I sat up as his fingers found the hem of my shirt, and he pulled it up over my head. I reached around to unhook my bra, tossing it aside before I lay back down. My breathing felt tight, aching.

He pulled off his own shirt, staring down at my naked torso for a few moments before he reached down and pulled me to the edge of the bed. I was surprised by how nervous I felt. My stomach dipped as he dropped to his knees in front of me, popping open the button of my jeans and unzipping them slowly. He pressed a kiss to my stomach, running his tongue along my abdomen, dipping into my belly button before moving lower.

"Just a warning," he said roughly as he looked up at me through thick lashes. "I plan to take my time."

Chills. The good kind.

I nodded, the anticipation bordering on the edge of painful with how badly I needed him.

He tugged my jeans down the rest of the way, his hands caressing each leg as he pulled them off slowly. I felt my pulse beating everywhere—pounding in my chest, hammering loudly in my ears, throbbing even lower. His eyes never left my face as he began kissing along the inside of my thigh and didn't stop kissing as he reached my panties. I could feel the warmth of his mouth as he sucked at my apex through the fabric, and I let out a long moan. He teased me that way for a while before he finally slipped his fingers through the elastic. I placed the tips of my feet onto his sturdy shoulders, lifting my hips so he could pull them off completely.

I felt the tip of his nose grazing against my heated skin before his tongue suddenly slid down the center of me in one long, teasing stroke. I groaned loudly, dropping my head back onto the bed. His mouth pressed over my core as he began licking and sucking along my slick heat. I'd never had anyone who was as good at this as he was. Instead of just flicking his tongue around and hoping something would happen, he pressed his whole mouth against my sensitive flesh, working me over like a man starving. His hands drifted up toward my breasts as he caressed them in both hands, pinching lightly at my nipples. I propped myself up on my elbows to see he was watching me. It took everything I had to keep my eyes from rolling back in my head, wanting to continue the intimacy of our eye contact. I watched each and every thrust of his tongue against me and that hedonistic look in his eyes was something I never wanted to forget.

"I'm close," I whimpered, and he wrapped his hands more firmly around my thighs.

"Watch me, Lex," I said breathlessly. "I want your eyes on me when I come apart for you." He growled a noise of approval as I pushed myself harder against his mouth. With a final few flicks of his tongue down the center of my core, my body surrendered. I cried out as the orgasm ripped through me, my body convulsing under the soft pressure of his mouth. His iron grip held me firmly in place as my hips began to buck, not allowing me to move an inch.

His tongue never slowed until the final waves of pleasure gradually dissipated. I felt exhausted from the intensity of it, but I needed more, and it appeared he did as well.

He stood up, dropping his pants to the ground as his erection sprang free. He stroked himself a few times, looking down at my naked body.

"I've thought about this so many times," he said roughly.

"So have I," I admitted.

"Tell me what you thought about," he said, still stroking.

I swallowed. "I thought about you running your tongue along my breasts." I let my fingers drift across them. "I thought about your hands squeezing my hips as you thrust into me." I slid my hands down to my hips. "I thought about how good it would feel to have you come inside me again and again." My hand drifted down even further, and I slid my fingers through my wetness.

He groaned at my words as his hand moved faster across his shaft. His eyes were transfixed on the spot where my fingers were moving, and I could tell he was no longer interested in taking his time.

He rushed to gather my legs, the air thick with anticipation as he held them at his sides. Our heavy breathing became synchronized as time seemed to stretch and contract with each heartbeat.

Eyes locked with mine, he eased into me slowly. The stretching sensation and fullness were almost too much. We both groaned, and I watched his eyes squeeze shut. His head fell back as the Russian started flowing from his lips. He once told me that he had no idea that he slipped in and out of speaking Russian when we made love, so when he did, I knew that he was completely lost in the moment.

Lips parted, he withdrew inch by inch, a tantalizing retreat, before he slammed into me, eliciting a strangled moan from deep within. He repeated the motion several more times, focus drawn to the sight of himself thrusting into me over and over. I dug my feet into the mattress, anchoring myself so that I could take everything he wanted to give me.

His eyes were frenzied as he climbed onto the bed, hovering just above me before leaning down to capture my lips. Our lips and tongues moved in harmony, and I reached up to thread my fingers in his hair. It was as soft as I remembered. He lowered his head, pressing his lips against the curve of my neck and running his tongue all along my heated skin. I wrapped my arms around him, drawing him closer until his weight settled on top of me.

He began moving inside me again, his hips pressing firmly into mine.

There was a desperation to the way we were clinging to each other so tightly, our faces tucked into one another's necks. No words were exchanged between us. They weren't needed. The way our bodies communicated was a language in itself, one we both instinctively understood.

Our hips rolled in unison as he slid deeper inside me, groaning softly in my ear with each thrust. The cords of his neck were strained, and I realized he needed to move faster. I let go as he lifted, placing his hands on either side of my head. I held onto his forearms as he really began driving into me with purpose.

The only sounds in the room were those of our heavy breathing mixed with the steady pounding of his body into mine. The sweat started to bead across his body until we were both slick with it. I whispered how good his cock felt and how badly I wanted him to come inside me until eventually, his movements became more erratic.

He lifted himself higher up, wrapping his hands firmly around my hips, which I'd come to know as a sign that he was close. He guided my hips down onto his cock as he thrust into me a few more times until his breathing grew ragged. A raw, guttural sound rose from deep within his chest as he finally came apart with my name on his lips.

I could feel him pulsating inside me as he finished, but he continued to push in and out of me, gazing down at our joined pelvises. I remained still as his hands caressed my waist, gently stroking up and down my body.

He looked utterly spent as he collapsed on top of me, and we lay there for a while afterward, just trying to catch our breaths. I ran my nails lightly across his back, wondering how I ever went so long without this feeling. Everything felt right as long as we were together. He finally lifted his head to kiss me softly on the lips.

"Ty sogrevayesh' moyu dushu," he murmured against my mouth.

"That's beautiful," I whispered. "What does it mean?"

He withdrew slightly so he could meet my gaze as he said, "You warm my soul."

I didn't even try to stop the tears that welled in my eyes. He pressed his forehead to mine as his hands wandered over my body, worshipping it. I committed every line of his face to memory, and he looked to be doing the same. His eyelids were starting to grow heavy, however, so I tried sliding away from him.

"You need to get some rest," I said, because he looked completely drained.

"No," he said, firmly holding me in place. "I want to look at you a while longer."

I was apprehensive, but I stayed where I was as he ran a fingertip along my arm, leaving goosebumps in its wake. His eyes were locked with mine as he moved his hand up to cup my cheek.

"God, I've missed this face," he whispered.

I took the hand he had on my face and kissed the center of his palm. "I love you, Lex."

His eyes sparked to life, his irises shining brightly as he started tracing my lips with his fingertips. "I think I fell in love with you the moment I saw you," he murmured. "But I knew it with every fiber of my being that day at the well when you were singing that Coldplay song."

I smiled. "It's called The Scientist."

"Is it really?"

"Yes. It's about a man who's consumed by his work, and he's trying to find a way back to his love."

He smiled back at me. "A perfect choice."

"I agree completely," I said. "Especially now that I know it was my siren's song that made you fall madly in love with me."

A deep rumbling laughter escaped his lips, and I almost burst into tears at the sound of it. It had been so long since I'd heard his laughter.

I placed my hand over the center of his chest, and he covered it with his, holding it there.

"I hope this never goes away," he said, looking down at our joined hands. "This feeling I get when you touch me... It's like an intense craving that never fades no matter how much I have you."

"Sounds uncomfortable," I teased, wrinkling my nose.

"It's the best and worst feeling," he said. "But I don't even remember who I was without it. It feels like it defines me now... how badly I need you."

"You have me." I said it like a promise. "But we've got to figure this out, Lex. You have to go back and finish what you started."

"I know," he murmured. "But I don't want to think about that right now. Just let me have tonight. We'll figure out the rest tomorrow. I promise."

"Okay," I whispered.

He pulled me in, and I closed the distance between us, pressing my lips to his. His tongue swept across the seam of my lips, beckoning me to open for him. I hesitated. He was so tired, and I knew what would follow if I let it go further, but I felt helpless to resist.

Our tongues met in a gentle caress, and I started to feel my way down his chest and abdomen. I took his already hard length in my palm and began to stroke him gently. He groaned into my mouth. I knew he was exhausted, so I swung my legs over his hips, positioning his erection against my entrance. I made sure he was looking me in the eyes before I slid down, taking him completely inside me. His lips parted, and he placed his hands lightly around my hips, urging me on. I rocked back and forth, enjoying every sound he was making and every look he was giving me.

After a few minutes of riding his cock, he sat up and continued pushing and pulling at my hips as he captured one of my breasts in his mouth. I moaned, tilting my head back, tangling my fingers in his hair, and holding him to me. Every swish of his tongue along my breasts and every press of his cock against me had me dangling on the edge until his hips met mine in the perfect spot. Pleasure shot up my spine. I tucked my face into his neck, crying out as I convulsed around him. He squeezed my hips even tighter as he thrust into me one final time, finding his own release, and we came apart together.

Chapter 37

The light of the morning was barely peeking through the window when I peeled my eyes open to see Lex sitting in a chair at the side of the bed, watching me. He smiled, and the sight of it made my breath catch. I thought of how long I'd been wanting to see that smile, the kind that reached all the way to those whiskey eyes.

The dark circles under his eyes were much lighter now, and the tension around them had dissolved completely.

"Hey," I said softly, reaching my hand out so he would come to me. "What are you—"

"Marry me," he said, cutting me short.

My eyebrows knitted together. Did I just hear what I think I heard? I shot up to a sitting position, wondering if I'd just imagined that. I was about to ask him to repeat himself, but he got up out of the chair and knelt beside the bed, one knee on the ground, the other pulled forward.

"Marry me, Hadley," he said again. This time I knew I'd heard him correctly as my heart began pounding in my chest. "I called your mom this morning and asked for her blessing. She asked what took me so long."

I choked out a laugh as the tears started rolling down my face.

"I don't have a ring for you yet, but I couldn't wait a single second longer. As soon as you're ready, we'll go out today and I'll get you the biggest one in the whole damn country, if that's what you want."

He pulled me to the edge of the bed and took my hands in his. "I realized a long time ago that I only need two things in this life—I need you, and I need us. I know we still have so much to figure out, but I also know that I'm incapable of doing life without you. So I'm asking you to say yes. Say that we'll spend our lives together."

I slid out of bed and dropped down on my knees in front of him. There were so many emotions coursing through me, so many thoughts going through my mind, so many things I wanted to say, but I didn't.

I pulled his hand to cover my wildly beating heart and said, "Yes."

His smile was breathtaking as he pulled me in for a kiss that seemed a lifetime in the making. There was still so much we needed to talk about, but I gave myself to this moment, savoring that perfect feeling of belonging to each other.

I drew back to look up at him, my fiancé. My heart turned over in my chest at just the thought of that word.

"I need you to do something for me," I said, threading my fingers through his.

"Anything," he responded solemnly.

"I need you to take me to my mom's."

Surprise flickered across his face, but he nodded in agreement. In less than ten minutes, we were driving up to her house. Before I could even knock on the door, my mom had swung it open and had me wrapped in a tight embrace.

"You said yes!" she squealed in my ear as she bounced up and down on the balls of her feet.

I chuckled. "How do you know that?"

"One look at Lex and it was perfectly clear," she replied before pulling him in for a hug.

I glanced over to see him wearing a proud smile as he wrapped an arm around her. His other hand had never left my waist throughout any of my mom's exuberant displays of affection.

"Congratulations," she whispered to him as tears started to well in her eyes. I had to turn away before I became a sobbing mess right here on her doorstep.

As excited as I was to share this moment with her, there was something serious she and I needed to discuss. "If it's okay, I'd like to talk to you and Carl about something, Mom."

She released Lex and gave me a disconcerted look. "Okay."

We followed behind her into the house. "Carl, honey," she called out. "Can you come here for a moment?"

There was a loud, rustling noise before Carl came rushing down the hallway. "What is it? Are you okay?" His face was full of worry until he spotted me standing there. "Oh, Hadley's here! Hi, dear," he said, relieved. "And Lex..." He said his name with a hint of uncertainty, as if unsure if his presence was welcome, but then his eyes slid to our intertwined hands.

"Yes. Keep up, honey," my mom said in faux exasperation. "I swear you miss everything with all the tinkering you do in that room back there."

"You mean the same room you ask about every morning to check if I finished building the bookcase you wanted?" he said, smiling.

"Oh, is that what you've been doing back there all this time?" she replied with a wink.

"Why don't we all go sit at the table?" I suggested, feeling the nerves gnawing at my insides. She gave me another concerned look as her eyes searched my face.

I started heading towards the table when my mom leaned over to Lex and asked, "Any idea what Serious Sally wants to talk about?"

He shook his head, grinning. "Not a clue."

We sat down at the table, and I looked around at the most important people in my life.

"Well, don't leave me in suspense, Hadley," my mom said. "I already know you're engaged so what else do we need to talk about?"

"Wait. They're engaged?" Carl said, wide-eyed. "Since when? And how long have you known?"

My mom rolled her eyes. "Honestly, Carl, if you weren't so obsessed with that bookcase, you might be more informed with the happenings of the world."

I sighed. "Mom..."

"Okay, I'm sorry," she said, putting her hands up in surrender. "What is it, sweetheart?"

I glanced over at Lex. His face held nothing but curiosity as he leaned closer to my side. I took a deep breath and said, "Lex is going back to Sweden."

I felt him go stiff as a board next to me as his grip on me tightened. I turned to look him in the eye. "And I'm going with him."

His eyes went wide with shock.

"Really?" my mom said, sounding absolutely giddy.

"Really?" Lex repeated, a hopeful gleam in his eye.

I nodded. "You have to go back," I said. "You have to finish this."

He turned his body completely to face me. "But you're coming with me?" he asked, a hint of unease in his tone.

I smiled. "I can't let my fiancé go to Europe without me."

He took me by surprise by leaning over suddenly and pressing his lips to mine. "If I hadn't done it already, I'd drop to my knees right here and beg you to marry me."

I kissed him once more before turning to look at my mom who was beaming with happiness.

"But I can't leave without knowing you'll be okay," I said to her.

She opened her mouth to answer but it was Carl who spoke. "She will be," he said, more like a promise than a statement, as he placed his hand over the one she had resting on the table. "You don't have to worry, Hadley. I'll care for her life as if it were my own." The sincerity in his voice left no room for doubt.

I nodded, my shoulders relaxing a bit. "It's settled then," I said, looking to my mom. I was ashamed to admit that I had been so absorbed in my own world over the past few weeks that I hadn't realized until now just how much her face had changed. Her cheeks were rounder, and the color was completely restored to its natural, vibrant glow. Her face was now the picture of resilience, each line a testament to what she had endured. I smiled at her, and she gave me a nod in return.

"I guess I better get packing," I said, turning to Lex, who appeared flushed with happiness. He leaned over, pressing a kiss to my temple.

"Wait!" my mom cried out suddenly. "There's something I want to give you before you go."

She practically tripped running over to her bedroom, and I heard her start pulling open drawers and rustling through them. She finally came back with a small black pouch and handed it to Lex before sitting back in her chair wearing the biggest smile on her face. My curiosity was piqued as I watched Lex pull open the pouch.

His eyes shot to my mom. "Are you sure?"

She nodded. "Absolutely."

"What is it?" I asked, barely able to contain my curiosity.

Lex turned to me with a serious look on his face. "I know you've already answered this question, but I wouldn't mind hearing the answer just once more," he said, taking my left hand in his and dropping to one knee in front of me. "Hadley Marie Olivier, the day I met you was the day my life started to make sense. You are my best friend, my greatest love, and my soul's completion. Will you—for a second time—say that you'll marry me?"

I was too stunned to speak as my eyes landed on the mystery object he held between his thumb and index finger. My heart began to race as my mind registered what I was seeing.

"Well?" he asked with a playful smile. It was only now that I realized I had never actually given an answer, though I'm certain he already knew what it would be.

"I'll say it as many times as you want," I said, choked with emotion. "Yes. Always yes."

His answering smile became blurred beneath the steady stream of tears rolling down my face as he slid the ring my father gave to my mother on their wedding day onto my fourth finger.

A perfect fit.

We had been running in circles, chasing our tails, only to come back as we are.

Epilogue

en years later

I was sitting next to Stuart in the front row of the Stockholm Concert Hall. The chairman of the Nobel Committee was on stage giving a summation of the work Lex and his team had accomplished over the years. They had successfully created a device that was now being used to treat Alzheimer's and a vast array of other conditions in which neuronal death occurs. The speaker was commenting on the innovative and revolutionary methods the team had used in the creation of the device.

Stuart held my hand as they called Lex's name as the winner of this year's Nobel Prize in Physiology or Medicine. I watched as my husband took the stage, barely able to see through the tears that were pouring down my face. Not much had changed in that department. If anything, it was actually much worse now that I was pregnant with our second child.

"Your Royal Highnesses, Esteemed Nobel Prize Laureates, Ladies and Gentlemen... good evening," Lex said, casting his gaze across the assembled crowd. The velvety timbre of his voice still managed to send shivers down my spine even after all these years.

"I have the deepest gratitude for this honored distinction that the Academy of Science has bestowed on myself and my team. Any man of science will attest that the true reward lies in having the opportunity to work amongst the brilliant fellowship of men and women who seek to discover scientific truths. It is impossible for one individual alone to render any meaningful progress in the advancement of science, and I have had the great fortune over the past two decades to be at the helm of this joint pursuit. I wish that I could pay tribute to each of my team members individually for this prodigious achievement because I am undeserving of this recognition as the sole recipient for a project that was entirely a group endeavor."

Lex's eyes moved to Stuart first and then over to the rest of his team who were seated behind us. I held Stuart's hand even tighter. This moment was just as meaningful for him even though he wasn't the one on stage accepting an award for their work.

"I must confess to you all that the first time I set foot in this great city, I was not the happy, gratified man you see before you today," Lex continued as his gaze settled on me.

We smiled knowingly at each other.

So much had happened to us over these past ten years that led up to this moment. We lived in Sweden for sixteen months in total after my arrival as the team worked tirelessly to finish the project. Lex and I were married two months after that. We had two ceremonies, one in California and one in Russia. Both were the happiest days of my life until the day we had our baby girl, Mila James Strovinski. The middle name we chose in honor of my father. It was a full circle moment, knowing I'd achieved what he'd always wanted for me—a happy life.

"I am ecstatic to return under different circumstances as a man whose heart has known nothing but the rarest and deepest kind of love since the day I met my beautiful wife," he said, his eyes locked with mine. "Hadley, my every happiness is owed entirely to you, and to the beautiful child you've given me."

Great. Now I was ugly crying at a Nobel Prize Ceremony. I could still remember perfectly the day I told Lex I was pregnant. It was only the second time I'd ever seen him cry. Lex was an amazing husband, but he was an even better father. He was so loving and doting with her, and she had him wrapped around her tiny finger from day one. I didn't think it was possible, but the first time he held her in his arms, I fell even that much more in love with him.

"It is self-evident that the researchers of today can no longer make progress in the pursuit of scientific advancement without material aid. I know I speak for my colleagues as well as myself when I say that this research endeavor would have never been possible without the generous help and resources we received from Empros Pharma Laboratory here in Sweden as well as those at Stanford University."

I don't think Lex or I had any idea just how big a role Stanford would play in our lives when we first moved there. California officially became our home not long after we got married. Luckily, Stanford was willing to take us both back, because we quickly realized that's where we wanted to make a life together. While California was now the place we called home, we still spent every summer and our Christmases together in New York, so I was able to keep that piece of myself alive.

The money I'd earned off of my collaboration with Fiona and Logan was more than enough to support our family for many years to come, especially after I'd won a Grammy for songwriting the year it was released. After that happened, I pretty much had my pick of songwriting jobs and allowed me the flexibility of choosing who I wanted to work with. But as time had gone on, the fulfillment I found in teaching gradually ushered in the next phase of my life. I continued to write, but my time was now mostly spent in the classroom and with my family.

Most of Lex's team had moved on with the exception of Stuart and Jace, who had become like family to us. Stuart was now head of the chemistry department at Stanford, and I'd managed to do something I thought was impossible—I successfully set him up on a date with one of the women I worked with in the music department, Jane Cohen. She had the perfect blend of unassuming naivety and unwavering patience to withstand all of Stuart's many quirks. They had been married for just under five years now. Stuart had always been like family to me, but it was even more official when he became the godfather to baby Mila.

Jace and Sarah had survived the year-long separation and got married the year after Lex and I. Sarah stood by my side at both of my weddings as I walked arm in arm with my mom down the aisle. Sarah was still at Stanford and became the head of the music department after Captain Creeper retired. Jace had moved on to start his own successful tech company, but we all lived on the same street and raised our kids together.

"I am confident that our understanding of the human mind and its vast capabilities will continue to confound our species for generations to come, but it has brought me the greatest of satisfactions to have unearthed even this one demonstrable answer to what was once an incurable suffering for so many. But my work does not end here. I will continue to relentlessly pursue answers to the critical problems that plague mankind..."

He was talking about cancer. As if he hadn't done enough for me, Lex had shifted his area of focus from Alzheimer's to cancer research. He had partnered with Dr. Gremillion to conduct large-scale testing and research into the treatment and cure of many types of cancer, all in honor of my best friend.

My mom had survived and remained cancer-free to this day.

She and Carl had also gotten married and remained in the Stanford area. I got my wish of seeing her become the most amazing grandmother. I owed every bit of my happiness to the man currently accepting his Nobel Prize.

Lex ended his speech in the same way he did on that very first night I met him, stating that a little education and a great amount of kindness is the only way to secure harmony in this life and the lives of those to come. He said the last part looking down at my rounded stomach before his eyes finally lifted to meet mine.

Bonus Content

The story doesn't end here...

If you want to read more about Hadley and Lex's story, visit the author's website www.kristenbcole.com for an exclusive bonus chapter.

A simple favor...

Since you've made it to the end of "The Scientist", that means we're officially best friends... right? You've now read my inner most thoughts and feelings, so it's time to share yours! It's only fair.

Seriously, reviews are so important for indie authors, so if you loved this book (or were even mildly amused), please share a quick review on my Amazon page or Goodreads. Or like a true bestie would do, share some love on both! Thank you again, and if you need me, I'll be off trying to dream up more fabulous nonsense.

Acknowledgments

Writing this book has been an exhausting, albeit self-inflicted, exercise in perseverance, and I'm both relieved and grateful that it's finally complete. To be honest, it's a small miracle that this book even exists, and I have a lot of people to thank for making it happen.

Firstly, a very special thanks to my editor, Margo Lipschultz, who did her best to salvage my disjointed draft and managed to turn it into something coherent. I was so eager to work with you, and you did not disappoint. You not only helped shape this story I wanted to tell, but also helped shape me as a writer. I am so incredibly grateful for your time and investment in this book and for taking a chance on me.

To my line editor, Alexandra McLaughlin—I can't thank you enough for the many hours you spent polishing my prose to perfection and for your endless words of encouragement.

I want to also acknowledge my amazing aunt, Aimee Blankenship, who graciously took the time to read my very rough draft and gave nothing but her love and support in my very vulnerable state. The teacher you are helped inspire the teacher I found in my MC.

A huge shoutout goes to my very first beta reader, content editor, number one fan, and best friend in the world, Sarah Samaha. I can still remember that day at work (so many lifetimes ago) when I first told you I was trying to write a book. Your face lit up and your excitement was contagious. You've read every word I've ever written, met characters no one else will, gave suggestions about pet turtles that made absolutely no sense, but most importantly, you believed in me. And for that, I'll be forever grateful. Your namesake in my book is the supportive best friend to my main character as you have always been to me.

The biggest thanks goes to my husband, Blake. When I first told you I wanted to write a book, you didn't laugh. You looked me dead in the eye and said, "Do it." Within a week, I had three journals to map out ideas and five books on writing delivered in the mail. That's how much you believed in me. Your support has meant everything to me. I've always known the "naughty scenes" were what you were most interested in, always wanting to be the inspiration ;). But your heart is what has inspired me. Your love and kindness are splashed all over the pages of this clumsy attempt at a debut novel.

And lastly, to you, the reader: You've made it to the acknowledgments page, which means you've taken a chance on a unknown, hopeful writer, who simply had a crazy idea before bed one night. I'll never be able to thank you enough for taking this journey with me. My only hope is that you found something in these pages that made the journey worthwhile.

About the Author

Kristen B. Cole is a debut author, who leverages her experience as a nurse to create authentic, relatable characters while adding her own brand of humor to their romantic adventures. Her passion (*cough* addiction) for romance novels coupled with the unwavering support of her husband led to the pipe dream turned reality of writing her very first novel, "The Scientist." Before embarking on a journey of writing happily ever after's, Kristen earned her nursing degree from Nicholls State University in Thibodaux, Louisiana, where she and her family currently reside. Kristen loves to hear from her readers. Visit her website at www.kristenbcole.com to sign up for her newsletter to receive updates about upcoming books and exclusive bonus content. You can also find her on Facebook (Author Kristen B. Cole), Instagram (@authorkristenbcole) or Goodreads (Kristen B. Cole).